TOO CLOSE TO CALL

TOO CLOSE TO CALL

A Novel of President Election Politics

LEIGHTON L. SMITH

ARPress
45 Dan Road Suite 5
Canton MA 02021

Hotline: 1(888) 821-0229
Fax: 1(508) 545-7580

Ordering Information:

Quantity sales. Special discounts are available on quantity purchases by corporations, associations, and others. For details, contact the publisher at the address above.

Printed in the United States of America.

ISBN-13:   Softcover   979-8-89330-618-7
                eBook   979-8-89330-619-4
                Hardcover   979-8-89330-620-0

Library of Congress Control Number: 2024900788

CONTENTS

Chapter 1

William Buford Collins, VI sat in his spacious Alexandria, Virginia office and looked out at the summertime Potomac River vista. He wasn't really seeing the river in the misty haze. His body was facing that way, but his eyes weren't seeing anything. Without turning away, he idly tapped a thick packet of papers on his desk with his hand. Then, he quickly turned his head to look at it almost as if he thought that it wasn't there anymore.

He turned his head back to face the window as he'd done uncountable times before. The gesture was genuine but still he wasn't really looking out the window at the sailboats on the river like he'd done so enjoyably before. It was a reflex—he was seeking out a pattern of behavior that he was accustomed to, one that had a history of simplicity and comfort.

He looked up, as there was a tap at his door. In the open doorway, there stood a striking woman of indeterminable age. The only thing one could ascertain about her was that she was no longer in her early twenties. Her bearing was regal, and her clothing, pocketbook, shoes, and jewelry radiated excessive wealth.

"Lucy, my Dear," he said and got up and stepped over to a wet bar. "Would you like something to drink? Some sparkling water or perhaps something stronger?" He wanted to make her comfortable but was in no way solicitous. It was a graciousness exemplary of a long and close friendship.

"Mmmm. Yes," she replied, "I think that the occasion calls for something stronger than water. Perhaps a glass of wine?"

"Of course, my dear," he said softly and quickly poured a glass of Merlot for them both.

Once they were settled Collins spread out his hands and mimed an "are you ready?" expression with his face.

Lucy nodded her head solemnly and took a hearty draught of her wine. "Yes, all right, Buf," she said firmly, steeling herself for the report on what was in the packet on his desk. "But first, I'd like to review where we are. All right? You can do that for me, can't you?"

"Okay, we can do a review, if you like," Collins replied.

"Good," she said sipping at her wine. "Go ahead."

"All right," he said. "The whole thing started when your husband Roland was found dead in the bathtub of his hotel room in Washington, dee-cee about a year-and-a-half ago. The cause of death was determined to be either suicide or possibly accidental drowning. You were suspicious and knew of no reason why Roland might've killed himself. He was in good spirits when you saw him last and had given you no indication that he was despondent. Then, you went down to Washington and saw his body at the mortuary. You were shocked to find that it was covered with cuts and scrapes, and it looked like there were burns in some places—places where people shouldn't have burns."

"Mmmm," Lucy murmured. "So, I thought that maybe the District of Columbia police had missed something. I told them that the terrible condition of my husband's body didn't look like he just was taking a bath and then, somehow, accidentally slipped or something and then drowned. I told them that it was obvious that it didn't happen the way they said. I also told them that Roland could not have possibly committed suicide. I said most emphatically that there is no way that he could have ended up in the bathtub with his body injured in the way that it was found, if he had done those things to himself and such that it ended his life. I accused them, I am unashamed to admit, that they were making a big mistake."

"Okay," Collins said softly and paused a bit to allow Lucy to calm down and then continued to say, "It seemed to you like a perfectly normal thing to do—go to the police and tell them that you thought that it wasn't an accident and that maybe there had been foul play. In fact, you believed that you were helping them by showing that they might have a homicide on their hands instead of an accident. Well, you found out that the police in the District weren't interested in your opinion, didn't you?"

"Uh huh," she agreed. "Their reaction made me even more convinced that Roland's death was suspicious. I couldn't put my finger on it, but I sensed that the police weren't acting properly. This upset me greatly. I was sure Ro was murdered and no one in authority wanted to hear anything about it."

Collins arose to go refill their glasses.

"To say that you were frustrated and highly distressed," Collins observed, talking over his shoulder, "barely describes how you felt. But you didn't leave it alone. You couldn't let your honor and respect for your husband be sullied by not doing anything about this."

"So, I hired a private investigation firm to look into Ro's death," she continued. "The best firm in New York City where Roland and I lived. I gave them carte blanche to put together as much as they could for me to take to the police and give them the crime and, if possible, the criminals as well, all on a silver platter as it were. I was willing to pay as much money as was necessary, in effect, to do the job the police should be doing."

Collins brought the refilled glasses back, handing Lucy hers and nodded. "Then you began to get the reports from the private investigators. They were impressive, weren't they? Your money was being well spent and your spirits began to rise. You were sure that there was no way that the police would be able to ignore the evidence that you were going to take to them. And it was evidence that was based on official sources that was the most compelling and suggestive."

"For example," Lucy offered, "there was the autopsy report. It provided an explicit description of every cut and contusion and burn on Roland's body, none of which, by the way, was severe enough to have caused his death. Then, there was the result of the examination of his lungs that indicated they contained only a small amount of water."

"And there were other facts that your investigators found," Collins said picking up the narrative, "such as that Roland didn't check into his hotel until about four in the morning after arriving at the airport about two in the afternoon the day before. And there was the odd situation of Roland's clothing. His body was naked when found in the bathtub, of course. So, it's natural that whatever he was wearing would be nearby. But the only things found in the hotel room besides his body were his unopened overnight bag, a pair of trousers, and a dress shirt. No shoes or socks."

Lucy nodded in agreement. "I told the investigators that when Roland left our apartment for the airport, he was wearing a suit and a tie. He had shoes and socks and a belt, of course and also, a matching pen and pencil set that he always carried with him. He had an overnight bag and his briefcase."

"That confirmed there was a discrepancy," Collins said. "The inventory of Roland's effects that you received from the police included only the overnight bag, the shirt and pants, and his wallet. What was missing were his suit jacket, his shoes and socks, his belt, his tie, his briefcase, the pen and pencil set, his gold wristwatch, and the stuff he typically carried in his pockets besides his wallet like a set of keys, a handkerchief, and a money clip with some folding money.

"The only things that you lacked were evidence and information about how Roland died and who killed him and why. What was clear however, was that unquestionably Roland didn't drown at all, let alone in that bathtub, that his death wasn't an accident, and that he probably didn't die in his hotel room meaning that his body was brought there from somewhere else—by person or persons unknown."

"That's right, Buf," Lucy said. "So, I took the report from my investigators to the police in Washington. What happened was that the Captain of the homicide division made no attempt to do anything. He said that even if there wasn't compelling evidence that Roland drowned, it was still likely to have been some sort of accident, perhaps suffocation. He suggested that maybe Roland choked on something while in the tub. He told me he had to stand on the coroner's determination of the cause of death and since there was no overt indication of an external agent that contributed to Roland's death, he didn't see that there was anything that he could do. He said he was very busy with more real homicides than he had staff or resources to deal with and then he curtly saw me out of his office.

"Mmmm," she mused. "All this has me reliving it all over again and it doesn't feel any better now than it did the first time." She sat up and her face flushed pink with emotion. She arose and went to get the half-empty wine bottle and brought it back refilling her and Collins' glasses. "I mean, can you believe it? The gall of that man to sit there and smugly ignore the evidence that I had. Telling me that he had real homicides to deal with!

"But what about Roland? That's what I wanted to know. His death was a real homicide too, wasn't it? Why couldn't he see that? Why wouldn't he acknowledge it? Why?" She stared at Collins with a look that could bore holes in steel.

"And it's that indignation that brought you to me, wasn't it?" Collins asked.

"You told me the whole story," he continued, "that the police weren't going to do anything about it. In turn, I too became outraged. I was shocked that the police would blatantly refuse to open an investigation in light of the large amount of information that your private investigators compiled. I agreed with you that Roland's death was suspicious. I told you that it must be some sort of mix-up with the police in the District and that I'd go talk to them. I was sure that they would see our point and an investigation into Roland's death would be opened. It was a simple situation of changing the messenger, not the message."

He looked at her, meeting her eyes with his. "I thought that it'd be child's play, you know? I'm a lawyer. I understand these things. Never in my wildest dreams would I'd have said that a public official would openly ignore not only evidence that suggests a serious crime had been committed but also to calmly tell a criminal trial lawyer that he's wasting his time.

"I have to tell you, Lucy, that I was blown away by it. I came back to my office that day feeling like a whipped dog. I'd failed to accomplish what was an elementary mission and worst of all, I had to tell you that, at that point, there didn't seem to be anything that could be done about it."

He stopped again but this time he arose and strode over to his desk and picked up the packet of papers that had been a prominent fixture in each of their minds the whole time. He brought it over and sat back down.

"And so, my Dear, that day, like the mythological Phoenix, we raised ourselves up out of utter dejection. You, in spite of the brick wall that we had run up against, refused to give up. Rather than let it go as too hard to do or as something beyond our capacity, we decided to do something about it, and we did. It is what's represented in this." He patted the packet of papers that he held in his lap.

"Yes, that was a remarkable day," she said. "We sat here while you told me about it. Afterwards, we were about as low as one can get. But we persevered. We talked it through, put our heads together, and came up with a plan that we thought would work. We surmised that what happened with me about Ro's death might've happened with other deaths and with other families. That was our plan, to see if there've been other deaths that had suspicious circumstances but still were treated as accidents or suicides by the authorities."

"We wanted to see if there was a pattern," Collins said.

Lucy looked down at the packet of papers that he was holding on his lap and nodded her head slightly.

"Before you tell me about it Buf, there's something else that I want to say." She stopped to take a sip from her wine. "Our conversation so far today has been therapeutic for me. It's given me the chance to take another look at things. A more objective look. And I must admit that I can see now what I couldn't see then. I think that I know why that homicide detective wouldn't give either of us the time of day.

"It wasn't until today that the truth crystallized in my mind. The police did what they did by choice: They could investigate Roland's death to find out whether it was or wasn't suspicious; or they could use only the information that allowed them to say that Roland's death didn't need to be investigated and ignore the rest.

"That was it, wasn't it Buf? What they did was deliberate. They knew what they were doing. There was a choice that they could make, and they took the option that made their jobs easier."

"That's what it looks like, Lucy," Collins replied.

"And that's what that policeman meant when he was talking about real homicides, wasn't it?" she asked.

"Excuse me?" Collins asked, raising his eyebrows.

"He said he had too many real homicides to work on and didn't have time to spend on deaths like Roland's. Right? I see now what he meant, using the word real. It was so innocuous and subtle back then and of course I was pretty upset too. I didn't pick up on it. Not until now."

"Pick up on what?" Collins asked.

"His attitude, Buf," she continued. "He was inadvertently telling me that he was doing his job on an elective basis. He was focusing only on real homicides and that he'd determined what the rule was for a death to be a murder or not."

"And the rule was?" Collins prompted.

"Ah, well I'm not so sure about what it was exactly but my guess is that whenever there turns up a dead body and it either has a bullet wound or a knife sticking out of it, then it's a real homicide in their book and hence all other deaths aren't."

"Ah," beamed Collins. "You're saying that the police have a set standard for whether they'll open murder investigations or not. This standard is one of their own choosing—one that allows them to control their workload."

"Yes, I suppose that's it," she said.

"Fascinating." Collins paused a moment, thinking it over.

"Mmmm," Lucy agreed, cautiously. She looked at Collins. "It makes me cringe to think that this is how they approach their jobs. It's wrong for them to do this, isn't it?"

"Yes." Collins nodded. "It's clearly wrong. The police shouldn't be making up their own rules that govern how they do their jobs—particularly when such decisions are in their own interest, meaning that the end result is that the workload is lightened, not to mention the fact that they claim after the fact that the resulting drop in homicides is due to their own meritorious service." He stopped for a moment and scrunched up his face as if he'd just taken a bite of something unpleasant. "And it's a terrible, terrible shame."

Lucy looked sharply at him running her eyes up and down as if she were trying to use his body language to help her understand these last words.

"But wrong that it is, am I to understand from you that it's not illegal?" she inquired, her tone solemn.

Collins looked at Lucy and hesitated before answering. This was a paradox of unfathomable dimension. "Well, technically it is illegal. The rub is that the legalities are very subtle. What we're talking about is the use or misuse of the authority that public officials have been empowered with. The legal terms that apply here are malfeasance, misfeasance, and nonfeasance."

"I think that it's horrendous, Buf," Lucy said, trembling with emotion and raising her voice a decibel or two. "Someone killed my poor Roland and they've gotten off scot-free and then when I think about all the other poor people and families that have lost a loved one, I start to get . . ." she paused to dab at her nose with a lacy handkerchief that seemed to have materialized out of nowhere, ". . . uh, I start to get teary-eyed but before I start to cry, I realize that it has been our own public servants who've done this! And then I start to get really angry!" She stopped to catch her breath and realized that she'd almost been shouting, her intensity was so great.

"Yes, I know," Collins said holding up his hand indicating that she needn't go on. "I know. This is why we've been doing the investigation." He nodded his head towards the packet in his lap. "Why you've engaged me as your lawyer and why it's cost you a lot of money."

"And I gather from your reluctance to get to the point," Lucy said, tilting her head towards the packet, "that even after this much expense, you're about to tell me that we don't have anything. Is that it?"

Collins looked up sharply at the stately woman and stared into her eyes. Although he knew her well, her perception surprised him. He nodded his head in acknowledgment, trying to suppress an expression of awe. Inadvertently, his mind drifted back to how all this got started.

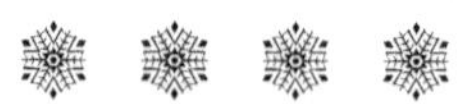

About eighteen months ago, when Collins noticed that his secretary had made an appointment for him with a Mrs. L. Doering Walton at his office, he hadn't picked up on the name. The noted reason for the meeting was merely "a personal matter" and hence provided him with no useful information.

When his secretary showed Mrs. Walton in that day, he was engrossed in a legal brief for a court case that was scheduled to begin the following week. She sat down in one the three nut-brown leather club chairs that sat in a rounded array in front of his antique Italian rococo mahogany desk that served as client chairs and waited patiently for a couple of minutes while he read on, oblivious to her presence. Ever so slowly he began to get an eerie feeling. It is believed that our olfactory sense is centered in the hypothalamus or the base of the brain, which many scientists agree is the most direct link to our distant antecedents. It's for this reason that it is commonly felt our sense of smell is the most instinctual of the senses.

The eerie feeling that Collins felt that afternoon was that he'd begun to sense his visitor's perfume and although he had not fully sensed that he was not still alone in his office, he was imbued with a powerful sensation of familiarity. He felt an embracing warmth as if he were being intimately clasped in the adoring arms of a lover. He had a sense that the source of this pleasurable feeling was a familiar scent. He wasn't sure whether it was a memory of some smell or something that he was experiencing in the present, but the notion that his euphoria was scent-based was growing on him rapidly. In fact, it was more than just something that he had previously experienced. It was crystallizing in his mind. He had a very strong feeling that it was a scent that held a special significance to him personally.

All this came over Collins while he was still desperately trying to concentrate on the legal notes on the desk's blotter in front of him. Finally, he became so totally distracted that he took off his reading glasses and leaned back and closed his eyes trying to dredge up a distant, yet pleasurable and definitely tangible memory. He hadn't made the connection that his urgency to bring forward the desired remembrance from the depths of his mind was being stimulated by the aroma that was slowly pervading his office.

Then he had it! He remembered. It was on his fifth wedding anniversary that he and his wife, Jane, had decided to take a second honeymoon and since they had vacationed in Hawaii a couple of times, they chose to stay on the Atlantic side of the continent for this trip. They therefore chose to go to St. Thomas in the U. S. Virgin Islands. Collins had always joshed about how visiting Hawaii was just like going to a foreign country, except that you could drink the water, speak your own language, and you could even use your own money there. It seemed to him that St. Thomas was a win-win situation: It had all that was good about Hawaii, and you could get there from Virginia in about eight fewer hours of travel.

It didn't take much convincing for him to instruct his secretary to make the travel arrangements for St. Thomas. She'd been proud to secure lodging at the old estate home.

The home was owned by a descendent, a great-great-great-great granddaughter apparently, of the original state family of the island. She called herself the "Seigneurie of the Estate" and her name was Lucy Doering. She was about twenty-three years old then, which made her nearly ten years his junior. She was very athletic and had a spectacularly trim physique. She was also smart as a whip and her pulchritude would have put a young Elizabeth Taylor to shame.

He fell in love with her.

During the brief episodes when he and Jane crossed paths with Lady Doering during the two weeks that they were on the island, Collins couldn't take his eyes off the alluring woman. At night when he made love to his wife, he fantasized that it was the Seigneurie whom he was pleasuring.

And Collins felt deeply ashamed of his reprehensible conduct and inwardly chastised himself for being so disrespectful to his young wife who, he openly admitted, he worshipped as if she were a goddess.

He never spoke to Lucy Doering about his feelings for her and as far as he knew she never suspected. He simply couldn't face this dilemma by putting it into words. He also vowed to make no mention of this to Jane. While on the island, he struggled heroically with not letting Jane sense that his attentions were not all directed towards her—it was their second honeymoon, for God's sake. Afterwards, he agonized over whether to tell Jane, mostly so that he could solicit her forgiveness, but also to assuage his guilt about not telling her everything which was something that he usually did. Needless to say, he was a total wreck for about a month after they got back.

He never told anyone about this emotional nadir. He was intensely relieved when it was finally time to return to the mainland, but it was more than a year before he stopped thinking about the lovely Seigneurie.

This was the time and event that he'd been searching for. In a flash the image of Lucy Doering flooded his consciousness, and he began to break out in a cold sweat with the magnitude of the emotion that this recollection brought him.

The eeriness of the moment continued to nag at him. He tried to fathom why he had suddenly wanted to bring back his feelings about his vacation to the Caribbean Island, but he was unable to make any sense of it. In the course of this emotional roller coaster ride, he had assumed a sprawled posture in his high-backed executive office chair. Had he known that he was being closely watched by someone, he would have been instantly self-conscious and embarrassed.

Then, his visitor cleared her throat and Buf Collins jerked upright, abruptly snapping back into consciousness out of his reverie. His last mental image was that of Lucy's remarkably beautiful physiognomy at the point when the muted "ahem" caused him to open his eyes.

The shock of seeing the very same face looking back at him in the stark reality of his office made him reel back in his chair to the point that he nearly overturned it. He caught his balance just in time and leaned back forward blushing bright pink and laughing nervously, making a very lame attempt to make light of this excruciatingly embarrassing moment.

But it was the woman sitting quietly before him, a woman with a beauty of stunning proportions, a woman that Collins had once been infatuated with, that the Seigneurie was physically present, a mere three feet from him, that brought him to his feet in a sudden bolt of his muscles.

"My God! Lucy! Why didn't you say something to my secretary that it was you!" he spluttered. The old feeling surged back into his breast as if it had been less than an hour since he'd last seen her and the pain of the absence was acute. He quickly stepped out from behind his massive mahogany desk and moved around to the front to stand next to the sitting woman.

He took her hand and looked into her sparkling sapphire-blue eyes as they rose up to meet his while she slowly stood up. She placed her hands flat on both of his cheeks and kissed him lightly on the lips and then sat back down.

"Still got it bad, I see, Buf," she said coyly.

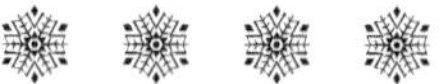

Collins blinked his eyes as they came back into focus. He realized that Lucy was staring at him, waiting expectantly for him to continue.

"Yes, Lucy my Dear, you're right. I've been reluctant to get to the point of this meeting. As you've astutely observed, what I have to report isn't altogether good news. Oh, don't get me wrong, we've found out a great deal; more than enough in fact to conclude that this sort of thing has been going on in several large cities for more than twenty years. Sad but true. This part of the report is the good news in that it confirms our supposition that we made several months ago: Was there a pattern of this kind of action on the part of public officials?

"But the bad news part of my report, Lucy, is that unfortunately I don't think that there's anything that we can do about it. In other words, I don't think that there are any legal remedies that we can pursue. The wrongdoing that's been committed is criminal in nature and as private citizens, there's nothing that you nor I can do."

Lucy stared at him with a wild look in her eyes and opened up her mouth wide but didn't begin to say anything as Collins held up his hand, stopping her.

"Hold on now!" he exclaimed. "I know what you're about to say. Let me finish and then you can tell me what you think. Okay?" He looked at his old friend, and she closed her mouth and nodded her head in silent acknowledgment.

"What's important, Lucy, is that in spite of a considerable amount of effort, my investigation into Roland's death hasn't discovered either who did it, why it happened, nor how he died."

"So, we don't have anything to go to the police with that can make them open a murder investigation?" Lucy asked her look betraying her disappointment.

"No, we don't," was Collins' solemn reply.

She turned to look up at Collins, her eyes beaming out a bluish light ray that seemed to bore right through him. "All right, Buf. If we can't solve Roland's murder and if we can't make the police do their job, then I want to expose them and all the other officials for this. I don't care if you say we don't have enough evidence to do something legal. We can still make what we have available to the public can't we? And if I keep paying for it, we can continue to collect information about other suspicious deaths that were treated improperly by the authorities, can't we? We can put the stuff on the Internet or something, can't we?" Her voice was firm, but there was also a sense of urgency that was creeping in. It was clear that she was keeping herself under control but only just barely.

She looked at him pleadingly. "We can do those kinds of things, can't we Buf? You're not going to tell me that after all this, we're going to stop and not do anything, are you? Please tell me Buf, that there still are some things that can be done. Things that we can do. Please, Buf."

"No Lucy, I'm not going to say that we're stopping," Collins said softly. "And many of these ideas about what we can do in lieu of solving Roland's murder are good ones and I fully support your desire to do them."

"But?" Lucy asked, sensing his hesitation.

"But there's something else that I've been thinking about—some other option that we might pursue." He paused as if he was contemplating his own thought.

"What's that, Buf?" she asked.

"Well, I've been wondering whether we've been doing the right thing but for the wrong reasons."

"What do you mean, wrong reasons?" Lucy inquired.

"I mean that we did what anyone would normally do. We were angry and frustrated and we wanted to prove that the police officials were acting improperly. We wanted to find out how and why your Roland died, and we wanted the make the police investigate it. I'm saying that this was the wrong motivator to go out and try to find a pattern."

"What should've motivated us, Buf?" she asked.

"We should've wanted to find a pattern of this kind of behavior so that we could show that public officials were doing this on purpose—as a normal part of their jobs."

"Huh?" Lucy was now confused. "I don't get you. Don't we already know this?"

"Ah!" Collins beamed. "Yes, you're absolutely right. We already know this but without facts and evidence, we can't prove it. Now that we've done the homework, our original thought was that we could, you know, jolt the police into starting to see things in the right light and open up a homicide investigation into Roland's death.

"But now in retrospect I see that such a purpose was folly. There's no way that we could've expected to be able to do that. In fact, by being able to show that there's been a long-standing pattern of this type of behavior, we were really doing more to defeat our main purpose than otherwise."

"Mmmm." Lucy was thinking this over. "Yes, I guess you've got a valid point, Buf. It does look like if we show someone that the police have been doing this over and over and that no one before has ever objected to it like we are, we're only likely to make people think that we're the crackpots not the police."

"Exactly," confirmed Collins.

"You're not helping me feel any better with this line of conversation, Buf," Lucy said disparagingly. "I hope that your idea about a different motivator is a good one. I need some good news here."

Collins nodded his head encouragingly as if he, in fact, did have the necessary good news. "What struck me about this was that a pattern of doing one's publicly authorized job in a consistently improper manner, such as what we have here, is a strong indication of widespread corruption."

"Corruption?" Lucy was trying to make sure that she heard him correctly.

"Right," Collins continued, "a consistent set of actions all resulting in the same, out-of-the-ordinary outcome, usually is what's needed to prove that someone is deliberately doing it. And when you put this into the perspective of malfeasance, misfeasance, and nonfeasance, it's a short step to full-blown corruption."

"Really?" Lucy asked. "Do you think that we can show that the police and other public officials have been doing this on purpose?"

"Yes, I do, Lucy," Collins responded.

Lucy straightened herself up in her chair. "Before I start to let myself get excited about this, tell me one thing, William Buford Collins, the sixth. Do you think that this is something that we can prove? I mean, do you think that we can get the bastards on this? Really get them?"

Collins squirmed a little in his seat. "The fact that it's true, of this I am completely confident. That I can prove it in a court of law, is something that I'm not so sure of, but I think it's worth a try." He tried to sound confident.

"This is what I think, Lucy. This is what all the information, data, and in many cases, the evidence, that I have accumulated leads me to believe." He looked carefully at Lucy sitting across from him to assure himself that she was both listening and, in his opinion, ready to hear what he was about to say.

"You see, the strange facts about how Roland's hotel room was found really bothered me. I'm speaking of the lack of a complete set of what we would normally expect someone on travel, like Roland was, to have with him. I kept asking myself why wasn't there more there? Why was there such a curiously incomplete set of his personal effects? And more pertinently why wasn't this something that the police should have been very curious about as well. Why?" Collins shook his head as if doing so would clear the fuzziness this information was clouding his mind about. "Then, it hit me."

Lucy looked sharply at him. It seemed that she was paying apt attention to what Collins was telling her. "What hit you?" she asked a bit breathlessly.

"It was that it could only be explained, at least to my satisfaction, that the police had not been surprised about the lack of a normal compliment of personal effects."

"They weren't?" Lucy prompted.

"No, Lucy. I am sure that they weren't surprised about it. In fact, I am pretty sure that they almost expected it."

Lucy leaned forward on the edge of her seat, seemingly eager to learn more about this. "Expected it? How so?" she prompted again.

"They expected it, Lucy, because I think that they had seen this sort of situation before. In fact, many times before" he answered.

"What?" Lucy spluttered, incredulously.

"Yup," Collins acknowledged, nodding.

"What could that possibly mean, Buf?" Lucy asked, her intense desire to know more hanging heavily in her tone.

"It means, my good friend," Collins replied slowly, "that I think that the criminals in these cities where the coroner-declared homicides have been declining but the total death count has continued to rise and the law enforcement agencies there are in this thing together."

"In it together?" Lucy blurted. "How could that be possible, Buf?" she said glaring at Collins like he had just told her that the Earth was actually flat and not round after all.

"It seems to me that it is the only acceptable explanation, regardless of how implausible it might seem, as Sir Arthur Conan Doyle's' famous detective, Sherlock Holmes was wont to say." Collins abruptly held up his hand squelching another excited response from Lucy. "Hold on, dear. Let me finish. I deduced that the only way that the police in all the big cities that we have been investigating have been regularly and systematically ignoring gross anomalies in the situations surrounding huge numbers of deaths has been to permit them to declare that the deaths have not been occurring under suspicious circumstances to ease their workload just as the police in the District of Columbia ignored obvious anomalies surrounding the circumstances of Roland's death.

"And I am also saying that the law enforcement people are not operating independently on their own. Rather, they are doing what they are doing, more aptly not doing what they should be doing because they are being guided by the politicians in their cities."

"What?" Lucy said, almost at a shout. "The politicians?"

"Yes, my dear. The politicians," Collins answered almost meekly.

Lucy was taken completely aback, hearing this revelation. "But what does that mean, Buf?" she queried.

"It means, at least I am pretty sure that it does, that there is collusion between the politicians and the law enforcement officials in these cities, and I also am pretty sure that there is some sort of tacit collusion between the politicians and the local criminal elements in these cities, too."

Lucy opened her mouth, but no sound came out. She was speechless.

Collins nodded knowingly. "Incredible, isn't it? The information, data and relevant evidence that I have uncovered and accumulated, when looked at as a whole and from the ten-thousand-foot level, as it were, says that what our investigation has revealed is the unworldly combination of corruption, collusion, conspiracy and cover-up," he declared quietly, almost reverently. "It is perhaps the only time that these four 'cees' have occurred at the same time in the same places in American, if not world, history, Lucy. And it's not a coincidence."

"What do you mean, it's not a coincidence, Buf?" she asked and then added, "And what did you mean by saying that the collusion between the politicians and the criminals is 'tacit'?"

Collins turned to look out his window overlooking the beautiful scene of the famous Potomac River and the spectacular Woodrow Wilson Bridge in the distance off to the South and paused a moment before turning back to face Lucy and answer her questions.

"It's a matter of perspective, I'm thinking. Because of the way that I went into this situation, you know, from the point of investigating what happened to your poor Roland, my dear, that gave me a perspective that no one else has had the whole time this is happening has had. Nearly everyone else has only been in a position to hear about the statistics of the homicide and violent crime rates going down, which they universally viewed as good news.

"No one individual can single-handedly do anything about the kinds of numbers and information that are reported 'officially,' of course. They can't do their own analyses and assessments. They don't have the resources nor the time. And also, look at it this way, the only people in the big cities who are close enough to the deaths and their possible causes are the inner-city types and we generally can surmise that they don't care. The people who would care and do care and who comprise the majority of the people who vote for public officials rarely set foot in the inner cities and are content in accepting what the politicians they vote for, or against, are telling them as reasonably acceptable truths. It is what many say is the big lie, hrumph, heh, heh—not a truth at all.

"But I digress. The answers to your two questions, Lucy dear, are that I don't feel that what my investigation has found is going on in the big cities today is a coincidence because it is a result of an active act on the part of the politicians to basically look the other way. Twenty, maybe even thirty years ago, the politicians were confronted with alarmingly high rates of crime in their cities and rates that were increasing measurably every year. They campaigned for more funding to hire more law enforcement personnel and were regularly turned down. So, what could they do? How could they help their chances of re-election in such dire circumstances, you might ponder? The answer is that they had to subtly suggest that the police focus on crimes that they had some level of confidence that they could solve and do so rather quickly. The attention span of the normal voter is very short, you see. So, without saying it in so many words, the politicians sent out guidance or hints or suggestions that the law enforcement folks use their limited resources to investigate homicides that were obvious murders, i.e., crimes that they thought they could easily and quickly solve, and to let the others go."

"Aha!" Lucy exclaimed exultantly. "They suggested that the police look into deaths that were obviously homicides, real homicides. Is that it?"

"It is Lucy," Collins affirmed. "And then more than probably very, very slowly the criminal elements in the cities began to pick up on this and realized that they no longer had to worry about trying to avoid having the people they killed on a regular basis being found and investigated by disposing of the bodies and all sorts of other sneaky things. Nope. All they needed to do is just stop shooting or stabbing their victims and just leave the bodies lying in plain sight. Because the new attitude growing in the city law enforcement offices was that they were only going to investigate so-called real homicides, simply made the criminals' worries about getting caught disappear almost instantly. It saved them time. It saved them unnecessary effort. And it saved them a lot of money. In a single word, they liked it. And then over time the criminals got lazy about the situations surrounding their regular and ongoing killings and made little effort to clean up the resulting crime scenes because they knew the police investigators were going to ignore any sort of anomalies—as long as the dead bodies didn't qualify as real homicides in their minds.

So, when I say that the criminals and the politicians were in tacit collusion with each other, I am simply observing that what the politicians were doing to save them time and money and also make them look good in the public eye was very synergistic with what the criminals started to do by no longer killing their victims with gunshots or knife stabbings. It meant that the criminals could proceed with their regular killings without any worries of getting caught and not having to tidy up their crime scenes resulted in them saving a lot of time and money.

"The classic win-win situation," Colling concluded smugly.

Lucy frowned and nodded slowly. She was dumfounded. Then, she looked back at Collins and saw the moué he was making with his face.

"What's the matter, Buf?" she asked pointedly. "What is it?"

"The matter, Lucy, is that now knowing, or at the very least suspecting, what has been going on, is that I am not sure what to do about it."

Lucy frowned at him. "What's the trouble with it, Buf?" she asked. "Is it that we don't have enough evidence?"

"No, it's not that," Collins replied. "The problem is that even though corruption, collusion, conspiracy and cover-up are all criminal acts, there's nothing that I, as a private-practice lawyer, can do about it."

"You mean that it's supposed to be the public officials who deal with the crimes?" Lucy asked quietly, already knowing the answer.

"Exactly," Collins confirmed. "And therein lies the dilemma."

Chapter 2

Gardner James sat in his plush executive office chair and stared out the ogee window that arced around behind his massive desk. He drummed his fingers on the buttery oxblood-colored leather on the armrest and tried hard to think about what he'd just been told.

Robert Finch stared at the back of his superior's chair as he stood uncomfortably in front of the huge desk. He felt that the report that he had just presented had somehow been received as bad news and he was afraid that as the messenger, he was about to be shot.

He cleared his throat, hoping that the reminder that he was still there would trigger the man into turning back around. He had been the bearer of bad news many times before in various forms and venues. If he were going to be blamed for this, he wanted to get it over with and move on.

After another few moments, Finch saw no other option but to speak. "Mr. President? Is there something wrong?"

This did it. James slowly rotated his chair so that he was again facing his attorney general. He smiled unctuously at the head of the Department of Justice of the United States. It was one of his best ploys and it always put the recipients off their guard.

"No, no, Bobby," the president said in a casual tone, "there's nothing wrong. What you told me about the Grand Jury investigation just got me to thinking about my old days as a district attorney in Los Angeles. It was what got me started in this business, you know."

"Yes, Mr. President, I know," Finch said dutifully, his apprehension dissipating like a snake sloughs off an old skin.

James looked sharply at his cabinet member. "But back to business, Bobby. I'm late for another appointment and I'm sorry to seem brusque, but I am glad that you brought this to my attention. What I suggest is that you continue to support the Grand Jury as much as you can, with all the power of your office, and so on. And when it comes time for them to decide what to do with it and my intuition tells me that they're going to want to hand down some indictments, I want you right there with a solid game plan for how to handle a trial."

"Game plan?" Finch asked unsure of James' meaning.

"Yes, Bobby. The Grand Jury has lots of power but make no mistake, they never lower themselves to actually see any of their recommendations through, you see? When they say that there's enough evidence to arrest some people and try them for egregious criminal acts, that's where they stop. It will then be left up to you to take it from there.

"Sooo, I'm telling you that you are a lead-time away from having to do this which should be more than enough time for you to come up with a good game plan for how you're going to keep a trial out of the public light and also, how you're going to keep it short. Right?" He arose out of his chair and began to stride purposefully to one of the alcove doors that was hidden into the curved walls of the ovate room.

"Don't forget that we have an election coming up, Bobby. And any press about wrongdoing and such like while it's on my watch is by definition bad press." He patted the older man on the shoulder supportingly. "I have confidence that you'll come up with an excellent approach to deal with this, Bobby. I have to go now. Keep me informed."

Robert Finch suddenly found himself standing all alone in the most famous room in the country, still feeling the sensation of the president's brotherly pat on his shoulder, wondering how in the world he had accidentally opened up Pandora's Box.

There was a message waiting for Finch when he got back to his cavernous office in the Justice Department building. It was an ominous message, he was certain, if the dour look on the messenger who was sitting on one of the richly upholstered brocade chairs outside his office and whom he suspected was entrusted by the Grand Jury to bring it to him was any indication.

It was the clerk to the Grand Jury that he'd just been telling the president was investigating what was emerging to be a far-reaching probe into alleged obstruction of justice on the part of several state and municipal officials. It'd been he, the attorney general, who had first become aware of the problem as information that was obtained from several independent Federal Bureau of Investigation cases and then pieced together by a clever special agent trainee at the F.B.I. academy as part of a special study project.

He had been brought a "bootleg" copy of the study report by the head of the academy, a man whom he'd known for more than twenty years.

"I wanted you to look at this before it goes out for review and comment with the academy faculty, Bob," his old colleague had said one evening a few months previously at Finch's home. "Ordinarily, as you well know," he continued, "these special studies are pretty innocuous and really are only to help certain trainees focus on their designated specialty areas. I can't remember the last time there was one that had any purport in the real world, as it were.

"But this one, well Bob, I have to tell you that when I read it the night before last, it sent a chill up my spine. To think that there is any possibility that something like this is happening is this country makes my blood boil. Anyway, I thought that I should get your cut on it before we went any further and let anyone else see this report—even if they would only be insiders."

Finch was not a man to belittle people simply because he had the power and position to do so, and he certainly never reacted before he had all the facts before him. It was a mode of conduct that served him well over the years and one which postured him for becoming the Attorney General of the United States long before the event occurred. So, rather than complain to his old friend that he was too busy to read reports of insignificant studies by students, and rather than chastise the poor fellow for breaking the chain of command and going around the Director of the F.B.I., and also rather than simply taking the report to humor his paranoid friend and then relegate it to the ever-growing mountain of reading material that he might get to some day when he didn't have mail placarded with "Top Priority," "Most Urgent,"

"Congressional Inquiry," "Eyes Only," or "To Be Opened by the Addressee Only from the President" in his in-box, he took the report upstairs to his private study and sat down to read it right then.

It took only about ten minutes to scan it and then about twenty more to read it carefully all the way through. At first, the allegations and the facts described to support them struck him as nothing more than coincidences as he read through the thirty-five-page précis that preceded the citation of data. But when he found himself still in his study and still thinking about it afterwards more than three hours later, he realized that there was an insidious sense about the assertions the author was making. It was at the same time both facilely believable that such a thing could be happening all over the country as well as unnerving that, if true, the culprits were being rewarded for doing their jobs well. He continued to ponder the conundrum until his wife sleepily looked in on him wondering why he hadn't been to bed. Did he know that it was after two in the morning? she wanted to know.

But his instincts were on target. He was relieved that he took his old friend's concerns at face value and read the report that night. The next morning, groggy from very little restful sleep, he discreetly called down to the academy and asked for his friend to hold off on the review and comment process for a while. He then asked for the Director of the F.B.I. to come to his office as soon as possible.

Even though the man didn't technically report to Finch, the bureau's director was nonetheless at the complete disposal of the attorney general's office and hence he was seated before Finch's desk inside of fifteen minutes. What he'd been doing and where he'd been were completely transparent and the director sat in one of the several heavy club chairs in the attorney general's office, breathing comfortably and looking sharp in his dark blue suit. He calmly looked directly at the man who had summoned him there and who stood behind his desk, too wound up to sit.

"What do you have, sir?" the bureau director asked politely.

"Dean," the attorney general began, "I want you to look into something. It's official, of course, and make sure that you document the hell out of your actions and involvement but at the same time, it absolutely has to be kept deeply under wraps. I want your assurance that there will be no breaches of security on this. All right?

"Absolutely sir," the director replied. "It goes without saying."

"Okay, then," Finch continued, "In that envelope there is a draft study report that provides a good bit of specifics that you can use as a starting point. Based on that analysis, I've good reason to believe that there's something rotten going on in some of our major cities and maybe in the state capitals as well. What I want to know is whether the information that's in that envelope is accurate and whether there is any possible, plausible explanation for the data other than what is being alleged in the report.

"I want it done with top priority and I want it done fast, Dean. You know the drill. Sooner or later, someone'll leak this information, no matter how hard we try to keep it internal. So, the faster you can do your work the sooner I'll know which way it falls and hopefully we can put the thing to rest before anyone's the wiser. Got it?"

"Yup." The bureau director reached for the envelope and as he did the attorney general stepped around his desk and grasped his arm firmly.

"Read it first, Dean, in the car as you go back. All right? As you will see, this is very sensitive and likely involves many people we know and work with. I want you to be very careful about who you pick to run the investigation. There are conflict of interest issues all over this thing. Okay?"

It'd not been long before the director was back in his office to report that as far as could be found out, there was no other plausible explanation for the allegations that were made in the report Finch had given him. Moreover, he said, the evidence was so compelling that it'd be impossible to prove without any doubt that what was being done was random or coincidental. Finch had nodded morosely at this "news" and soon after called for a Grand Jury to look into the matter formally.

The attorney general was brought out of his reverie by the sharp clicks of a briefcase being snapped open. He focused his eyes on the source of the noise and saw the Grand Jury's clerk sitting before him in the same club chair that the director of the F.B.I. had sat in back when this whole mess got started. He sighed and waggled his hand in a feeble attempt to waive off any insult that his lapse in attention may have wrought on the clerk.

"Yes, David," he asked, "how may I help you?"

The clerk was rummaging around in his briefcase and for a moment his head was behind the lid of the case. Then he apparently succeeded in finding what he was looking for and pulled out a sheaf of papers and closed up his case.

"Sir, the gee-jay is beginning to wind down and the chairman has asked me to bring you this draft executive summary. This is a professional courtesy, and it is for your eyes only, if you understand. I mean that this isn't an official record and essentially, in actual fact, doesn't exist." He paused and pursed his lips presumably reflecting on his redundant syntax. He ran his hand over the pack of paper, almost caressingly. "After reviewing it," he went on, "the chairman has instructed me to urge you to return it or destroy it. Under no circumstances are any copies to be made nor is any portion of this to be made available to anyone but you alone. And" he fumbled through the top few sheets of papers and brought out a single page, "I need for you to sign this receipt, if you would be so kind." He handed it over, carefully retaining the rest of the papers in his possession.

Finch frowned. He was unaccustomed to being treated like a normal person. He was, after all, at the top of his game. He was the one who made all the rules, wasn't he? He was the one who in the first place formed the "gee-jay" as the clerk had so affectionately called the Grand Jury, wasn't he? But again, Finch's innate pragmatism prevailed, and he reached out and took the receipt from the clerk and signed it with a flourish without so much as giving the wording above the signature line a glance.

The clerk happily took back the signed receipt and put it into his briefcase. He then put the rest of the papers on the lip of the attorney general's desk. "There's a copy of the receipt there on the top." He snapped shut his case and arose to leave. "Don't forget to call me to come pick this up when you've read it or to inform me that you have destroyed it."

Finch began to glare at the lowly clerk but then checked himself. He might be willing to take the brunt of being a culpable messenger as he was just a little while ago in the Oval Office, but he was loath to practice the fine art of messenger shooting himself.

"Of course, David," he said evenly. "I'll look it over right away. Why don't you go get a cup of coffee or something and come back in about half-an-hour to take it back? Would that be convenient?"

The clerk was standing halfway to the door of Finch's office and nodded his head, approving of this plan. "Okay," he glanced at his wristwatch, "I'll stop back by at about eleven. Will that give you enough time?"

Finch nodded his head. "More than enough, David. See you then."

He looked down at the papers that the clerk had given him and had a quick flash of déjà vu. The size and weight of this packet was remarkably similar to that of the draft special study report the head of the F.B.I. training academy had brought him. He quickly looked at his schedule for the rest of the morning on his computer terminal, told his special aide to hold his calls, and settled down in his chair to read the Grand Jury's executive summary.

Shortly after eleven in the morning after David, the clerk, had returned to collect the document, Finch sat in his office reflecting on what the president had said to him earlier that morning about having a good game plan. After reading the report, he now knew where the Grand Jury was going with this, and he foresaw that it was inevitable that there would be indictments and a subsequent trial. Of course, the president was right about this, as it seemed he was in just about all things. He as the attorney general would run the show from the point when the Grand Jury announced their recommendations for the indictments. There was no question that this was a federal case since it would be implicating city and state officials in more than one state.

So, it was going to be his call, subject to guidance from Gardner James of course, as to how this played out. He stretched out and put his feet up on his credenza and made a steepled gesture with his hands on his chest, musing about the possibilities. The magnitude and scope of the trial could easily get way out of control; he knew that already. And it was intuitively obvious that as inevitably more people were indicted, as more charges were made, and as the length of the trial increased, there would result in more publicity which as James so astutely observed in an election year, no matter what kind of publicity there was, such was always bad for a presidential campaign. Always, always, always.

He began to wax philosophical and pondered the imponderable nature of public service at the top of the political heap. He sensed that this trial could easily be seen as a microcosm of the larger political landscape and that if the implicated parties were found guilty then by association all other officials would likely be viewed with suspicion by the public. He was suddenly convulsed with a shudder. This thing was like a Chinese puzzle: the more he got himself involved in it the more difficult it became for him to pull back.

He closed his eyes and slowly rotated his head from side-to-side miming the woeful lament of the doomed, "Noooooooo." The noise of the moan brought him back and he pulled down his feet and sat upright. He quickly looked around reaffirming that he was alone. He was slightly embarrassed that he had inadvertently uttered this sobriquet aloud.

He drummed his fingers on the hard surface of his desk and realized that there was no gain in complaining about being on the downside of a slippery slope. That was not his nature. He started this whole thing with his eyes open. All of the barn doors that had become open during this process were ones that he knew about beforehand. As his mother always said, there's no use in crying over spilled milk—the satisfaction is in doing a good job in cleaning up the mess.

He turned to his computer and fiddled with the mouse and clicked a few keys locating a particular "page" in his digital address book. He picked up the phone and opened up his private line and punched in a ten-digit number with the Northern Virginia seven-oh-three area code.

A thick gravelly voice growled, "Yes?" into the line after two rings.

"Tom?" the attorney general asked softly, "This is Bob Finch. I wonder if I could drop by and see you this afternoon. It's a matter of some urgency and I need to have your cut on it before I proceed."

The voice on the other end didn't speak for a moment and Finch imagined that he was mentally considering this request in conjunction with an afternoon full of other commitments. Then the voice said, "Two o'clock. Thirty minutes. I've got a tee time at three." And the line went dead.

Finch replaced the handset and smiled to himself.

That old dog, Tom Laughlin. For all he knows this is something that is tantamount to a national crisis, and it just might be that, and he's not about to miss his afternoon golf game with the old boys.

Finch was not being critical in thinking this; rather he was showing respect for the man. Tom Laughlin, a former attorney general himself, was the top legal and political guru in the country. Add in the fact that the old man was arguably one of the wealthiest men in the country if not the world, Finch acknowledged that for Laughlin, national crises are a dime a dozen and certainly nothing important enough to miss a tee time for. Not at all.

Finch was at Laughlin's home promptly at two p.m., knocking at the deeply varnished oak door that must've weighed at least a ton and was caught sneaking a look at the size of the hinges when the old man answered the ring of the bells himself.

"Bobby Finch!" he exclaimed in mock surprise exhibiting a sensation that he was happy to find the attorney general of the United States standing on his doorstep that afternoon. Even though Finch well knew that he was expected, he still felt flattered at this show of exuberance. It was one of Laughlin's innate traits to always make people around him feel lucky in some way. It was how he almost always got his way.

"Come in!" Laughlin continued, his enthusiasm radiating to the point of almost glowing. "Come in Bobby, come in. It's so good of you to come." He gave the big door a nudge and it easily swung shut without so much as making an audible click of the latch. He then turned to stride down a long dark hallway. "Let's talk in the study, all right with you Bobby?"

"Of course, Tom," Finch replied and followed the old man like a puppy would follow its master.

They debouched into the bowels of the mansion in a paneled study that could have entertained nearly fifty people, it was so big. All along one wall were floor-to-ceiling bookshelves full of books neatly arranged on the burnished mahogany wood. All along the facing wall were windows that looked out over what appeared to be the eighteenth green of a spectacularly landscaped golf course.

Although Finch had been in this room before, he took in the view with renewed awe. Somehow the memory of it paled to the reality of the breathtaking vista that it afforded its occupants. His awe was also fueled by the sudden notion that this was certainly the course on which Laughlin was scheduled to play later on and he slyly glanced over at the old man as he rattled around at a wet bar set in the far corner of the study.

The old dog probably owns the course lock stock and barrel, he thought, and could have any tee time he wants.

He sat on a chocolate brown leather sofa and took in the view.

"I'm having a gin and tonic without the gin, Bobby," Laughlin said with his back to Finch. "Something for you?"

"I'll have the same, thanks Tom," Finch replied.

The former attorney general sat in a luxurious wing back chair that half faced the windows and half faced the sofa on which Finch sat. He turned his head to regard the sylvan panorama that seemed to engulf the study, the house, and beyond. He looked like he was seeing it for the first time.

"It never gets old, Bobby. Never. Quite a remarkable phenomenon, I have to say, and many years ago I realized that by trying to understand why it is the way it is, I was missing the entire point of the lesson. Ever since, I've basked in its glow with total abandon."

He rotated his torso about a quarter-turn away from the windows and completed the maneuver of turning to face Finch by turning his head in the same direction another few degrees. It was as if he couldn't bring himself to put his back entirely to the windows.

"So, what is it, Bobby?" he asked casually.

Finch told the old man everything, all that he knew about the study report, the F.B.I. investigation that he'd ordered, the Grand Jury that he'd called, everything. There was no reason to hold anything back from his host as he knew that first of all it was highly likely that the old man already knew about it and if so, already knew more than he did. And second of all, Finch knew that if not, Laughlin would know it all by the end of the day. His resources and sources were that extensive.

So, Finch told it all to him merely for economy of time purposes. He even told Laughlin about his visit with the president that morning and that his advice was to put together a good game plan. Finch didn't relate this to Laughlin verbatim, however. He was a man after all and as the teller of the story he was unable to avoid recasting himself as its hero.

Laughlin was silent throughout and only nodded every so often to indicate that he understood what was being said. When Finch was done, he didn't respond for a couple of minutes as if he were sorting it all out. Then he looked down at his glass and noticed that it was empty, and he arose from his chair and reached over and took Finch's half-empty glass from him. He moved with a grace that belied his age which had to be in the late seventies by the most patronizing estimate. While refreshing the drinks, he began to speak more or less to the room at large.

"Yes Bobby, I agree that a good game plan is the right thing to do. Good advice that; even if you discount the source, ha ha. But the crux of the matter is just exactly what is the criterion of good in this situation, given what the Grand Jury is going to do."

He turned away from the bar and returned to his chair while dropping off Finch's freshened drink. As he sat, he cocked his head harking the chiming of an ornate grandfather's clock in the corner of the study behind the doorway. It was three o'clock and he gave no indication of concern that he was missing his tee time nor for that matter even had something planned that day or that week. He was giving Finch his undivided attention and it made Finch feel especially important in spite of himself.

"Mmmm," the old man murmured, "I suppose that's why you're here, eh Bobby? The good in the game plan, mmm?

"Yes," Finch answered meekly.

"Well, it's a puzzler, I give you that, Bobby. You really know how to pick 'em.

"But" he continued and smiled cryptically, "in my view, there's really a simple solution to it."

"You think so, Tom?" Finch asked unable to keep the eagerness out of his voice. "How would you do it?"

"Well, I could tell you what I would do if I were in your shoes if that's what you really want, Bobby. But I don't think that's the right approach. What would be more effective would be for me to make a suggestion about what you should consider doing. All right?"

"Of course," Finch said obsequiously. "A much better approach, I agree. So, what do you suggest that I consider doing?"

Laughlin put down his drink and stood up. "Why don't we go for a walk outside while we talk about this?" Although it was phrased as a question, Finch followed the man just as if it'd been a command from a high priest and he was the sacrificial lamb being innocently led to slaughter.

But it was salvation that he sought and that is what Laughlin gave him.

"It seems to me that your problem as it was so artfully characterized to you by Gardie James this morning, Bob," Laughlin said in a pedagogical tone as they meandered through the garden that fringed upon the golf course, "is quite simple. You are to continue to support the furtherance of this criminal investigation being handed down by the Grand Jury but do it as quickly and as quietly as possible."

"Yes, but . . ." Finch began.

"Yes, but that's a whole lot easier to say than to do is my guess as to what you were about to say. Exactly, my boy. Exactly. Hence, your sudden desire to seek out my suggestions for your consideration, I gather, eh?

"Yes, well I reiterate that it strikes me as the way out of these treacherous, politically speaking of course, waters is a straight and short path."

Finch realized that he was concentrating so intensely on the old man's words that he was not taking in much of the scenery and suddenly felt a pang of regret. Man has always seemed to be infatuated with things of his own creation and habitually overlooked nature's gifts. He forced his focus back on his host's words.

"And so, my thinking is that the best solution to your dilemma is to get the right person to prosecute the case. I'm thinking that it would need to be someone who knows his business, certainly, but also someone who can get the job done quickly and without any fanfare—someone who cares not a whit about the publicity nor for that matter about the so-called fifteen minutes of fame that I understand we are all due to have in our lives.

"And having said that, Bobby, it should go without saying that the right person for this job is someone who is outside of the system."

Finch looked at Laughlin. "You're saying, uh, suggesting, that I get a lawyer to prosecute the case who isn't a United States attorney?"

"I'm suggesting exactly that, but before you start to suspect that I've lost my marbles, which Bobby Dear I haven't—not yet anyway—you should remember that there are many lawyers in private practice who still have their yew-ess attorney chevrons. Once you're on the books, you don't come off just because you go into private practice, you know."

The light went on in Finch's head. "I get it! You're suggesting that I get a former United States attorney to prosecute the case. Someone who's known for his aggressiveness and also someone who has no political aspirations meaning that he, or she, would eschew any or all publicity."

"That's it," said the old man beaming. Then he turned to face his younger colleague and put his hand on the man's shoulder as if he were a favorite brother. "And I think that I'll help you along just a bit further, if I might Bobby. I know just the right man for the job."

CHAPTER 3

That evening Tom and Ellen Laughlin had dinner with their daughter Jane and her husband at the spacious country estate home in Alexandria, Virginia that she'd meticulously remodeled and redecorated over the years to the point where the hobby had become an avocation, if not an obsession.

After the sumptuous, meal the ladies retired to Jane's sitting room to talk about the grandchildren and so on and the gentlemen took their coffee in Jane's husband's private study.

Laughlin's only daughter had been happily married to her husband for close to thirty years and for just about the same length of time the two men had been close associates, friends, and confidants. Laughlin knew just about everything about his son-in-law and the younger man knew a great deal about his father-in-law, but certainly not everything, he'd be the first to point out. But what he knew was enough to know that Tom Laughlin had uncountable wealth and unmeasurable power and as such was the single most influential individual in America's political sphere.

In a word he was honored to know the man and he was humbled by the intimacy that he enjoyed by virtue of being the man's only son-in-law. Since he, William Buford Collins, VI, was a highly successful lawyer, it often seemed that Laughlin was as proud of him as if he were his own son and many times the connection that the two men had was this strong. The only blemish in the idyllic bond between them was that Collins hated politics and was apolitical by preference and choice. For this, Laughlin graciously forgave him and Collins, for love of Jane, magnanimously tolerated his father-in-law's political predilections.

"So, it looks like Stanton's going to have trouble getting the nomination, I guess," Collins said after they were settled into the soft leather of the study's sofa. He knew more than this of course but was merely attempting to open up a line of conversation that was not overtly accusatory. The point was that first of all, it was now a foregone conclusion even amongst elementary school children that Lloyd Stanton, the leading candidate for the presidential nomination after the primaries were in, was now yesterday's news. And secondly, Stanton was the carefully chosen, groomed, and prepped wind-up doll of the highly secret, immensely influential group of power brokers that only a very few people knew about. They called themselves the Panel. And also, Collins knew what perhaps less than twenty people on Earth knew: His father-in-law was the chairman of the Panel.

The Panel was formed shortly after the end of the Civil War by a small group of industrialists with the intent of making sure that the people elected to Congress and hence became lawmakers were sympathetic to their business objectives and also, their personal agendas. The idea was simple: pick the people in advance and then use money and power to ensure that they are elected. It worked like a charm, and it was not long before the Panel was controlling enough members of Congress to influence almost every outcome. But that was when Congress was much smaller than it is today. Almost as soon as the Panel achieved a controlling critical mass, it began to lose ground as more states were added and it found that it simply couldn't keep up—particularly in the Western states where they had little influence. That was when the Panel changed its focus to the executive office—the presidency of the United States.

From that moment, for all elections, the Panel carefully screened potential presidential candidates during the first year of the presidential term that preceded the term where they wanted to install their man, in other words, candidates for the successor. During the course of this screening, they selected two or three who showed the most potential and then proceeded to secretly interview each one, inquiring about aspirations and making sure of positions on key policies and issues. Most important of all in this process, which sometimes took several months to complete, was the securing of unwavering loyalty to the Panel and its concerns.

By the end of this first "planning" year, the Panel usually had their man. More often than not, they also had targeted the candidate's running mate as well. The selection process for the vice-presidential candidate was primarily focused on geographic compatibility (for vote-getting purposes) with the Panel's main man. Yes, they did consider how the number two would fit the suit of the chief executive, but this was only a passing concern. There hadn't been any assassination attempts in more than twenty years and the Panel always made sure that their top pick was in salubrious good health—and not too old. They remembered the Reagan years only too well.

The second year (i.e., two years before the next election year) was dedicated to what the Panel called posturing. This was a carefully choreographed process that got the chosen man just the right amount of exposure and visibility in just the right places at just the right times. Sometimes the posturing took more than a year due to various scheduling glitches and other factors that the Panel had difficulty controlling. For example, there were the two San Francisco earthquakes—in 1906 and 1989—and the great drought in the 1930's. Each of these events had unpredictable impacts on the presidential elections that followed those years. (If the Panel had known that the drought was going happen, they would have probably postponed the Great Crash which was something they did have control over.)

The posturing process had been refined over the years by the Panel and its successive members to an exact science. They knew just how to present their chosen candidate to the government and the people, in order to establish a subliminal feeling of liking and usually of endorsement in most rational and normal individuals. The Panel was clearly aware that there were millions of people in the United States who were not very rational nor normal, but who did cast their votes in presidential elections. So, although the process was well understood by the Panel and invariably executed with acute precision, their chosen candidates did not always win. But by anyone's standards in the more than a century of its existence, the Panel's batting average was more than respectable, in fact their candidates had won more than seventy-five per cent of the time. As a result, with the level of control the Panel was able to exert over their protégés, the Panel had a secret offshore bank account balance of more than eight trillion dollars and each member of the Panel was a multi-billionaire in his own right.

On balance, the Panel's win record, all in all, was something that the Panel was more than happy with. They figured that they really were only sixty-five per cent successful due to their own efforts. The other ten per cent or so, they attributed to the vagaries of the American voting public, who in their irrational and capricious way had over the years inadvertently elected the Panel's choice in spite of their "best" judgment.

The third year in the planning cycle was dedicated to carefully "outing" their candidate from obscurity into public view as a presidential hopeful. Ideas were carefully placed in various minds and allowed to germinate. After a bit of cultivation, there were soon voices from many different fronts suggesting the possibility of the Panel's man being a good presidential candidate.

The Panel's infiltration techniques were so subtle that not one of these soothsayers and forecasters would ever believe that they hadn't come up with the ideas on their own.

At the right time, the Panel's man publicly expresses a willingness to run for president stating that he senses that there is a lot of public interest in seeing him run, there seems to be a growing public mandate for his candidacy, and/or that there is a powerful necessity to stop the atrocities being perpetrated by the current president—even though that man may also be one of the Panel's men. (It's always good politics for the aspiring presidents to not talk favorably of the sitting presidents, at least not publicly.) The Panel designated its man to put forward one of these reasons (or some other variant) on the basis of specific political climate conditions, world and national economies, strife, and threats, et cetera. Note that as it was not unusual for the sitting president to be a Panel man, in those election years, the Panel had a field day with choreographing the banter between the two jousters. They felt that they were able to take some liberties in these years because it didn't really matter to the Panel who won—they owned both of the candidates.

The Panel basically was non-partisan and had in its time put up presidential candidates in several (remember, there once was a time when there were more than two) political parties in about equal numbers. Sometimes it got a little confusing.

"Mmmm," Laughlin acknowledged his son-in-law's observation about the bleak outlook for the Panel's choice this year, "it doesn't look too good for poor Lloyd."

What Laughlin was referring to was that in June, the Panel's man, Lloyd Stanton, who had been campaigning relentlessly, futilely trying to keep the presidential approval rating from going through the roof, ran into an insidious bit of bad press. This man had been selected by the Panel as their choice for the next president almost three years ago. They had checked his background thoroughly and they had complete confidence that he had no skeletons in his closet. They had also checked his extended family and that of his wife for druggies, pederasts, pedophiles, fetishists, transvestites, cross-dressers, coprophiliacs, necrophiliacs, murderers, tax evaders, illegal aliens, crackpots, fugitives from justice, et cetera. You name it.

All had checked out. The Panel's investigators had discretely looked into the man's business associates, former clients, fraternity brothers, professional colleagues, members of his church's congregation, neighbors, even his superiors and subordinates during his stint in the military service. They checked out his veterinarians, manicurists, barbers, masseuses, mail carriers, travel agents—even the parents of his children's friends. Everything and everybody they could think of. Nothing. Zip. Nada.

What they had failed to check—or more particularly failed to note and then check out—was that their chosen man had gone to a private boarding school, the same one from pre-school Montessori through twelfth grade. His father had been in the foreign service and was posted in Iran, Afghanistan, Bangladesh, and the like. Hence, it was understandable that the parents had felt that it was best for their son to go to school in the United States. It was a difficult trade-off but in the end Stanton's mother and father had bit their lip and decided that it was best for their son to be free from the inherent risks American children face in those countries versus being absent from his parents for such long periods of time. All in all, the Panel's investigators had thought that there was nothing suspicious about this. The sleeper was that he'd roomed with the same boy the entire time. The investigators hadn't checked on this roommate. If they had known that there had been only one, they would have looked him up just for grins.

If they had looked up their man's old roomie, they would have found that he was no longer living in the United States. If they had looked further, they would have learned that the fellow was living in the South China Sea on an independent island called Margollin—actually the loon had declared himself king of Margollin. His name was Arthur Beecher.

No matter that the Panel's investigators had missed this curious part of their man's past. These things were found out in due time by an enterprising young journalist during the lull after the presidential primaries. He was just trying to get some deep background on the man most likely to become the presidential nominee. He was also looking to get some recognition for himself in a cutthroat business. It took some time for the story to develop, and it was not until mid-June that the reporter's editor began to take an interest in it.

There were three things particularly bad about the story about Beecher: First, Margollin had been highly visible in recent years since it'd been bought and taken over by Beecher. This visibility was because he'd began to publicly practice a pagan religion that he called "Motherearthism." The premise of Motherearthism is that everything on Earth springs from the soil and thus must return to the soil at its designated time. It was "King Arthur of Margollin" as the high priest of Motherearthism who was the sole decider of whose time had come and when it was. His favorite selection was a young Margollin native boy or girl, usually around thirteen to fifteen years of age. His means of returning these poor children to Mother Earth was by eviscerating and exsanguinating them on a marble slab in the courtyard of his stone palace in front of a large gathering of Motherearthists. He also had been broadcasting these grisly human sacrifices worldwide on satellite television. Anyone with a direct-t.v. hookup or satellite dish could watch the king slice up his victims in living color close-ups, virtually as if they were the first attendant to his majesty.

This inhumanity had been regarded by the public media pretty much as non-news, as unbelievable as this might seem. But during a presidential election year and with a budding bonhomie bursting forth in all corners of the globe, the Margollin stuff had appeared to be just a little too bizarre. No one wanted to be first. But this didn't stop the channel surfers from finding it and from watching it and taping it. Once this happened, it was a very short step to the Internet and before long there were virginal sacrifice home pages all over cyberspace. So, even though the respectable media and the sensible fourth estate were trying to ignore it, by the Spring of the current election year there was not an American over the age of twelve who didn't know who King Arthur of Margollin was and what he liked to do for recreation. Lloyd Stanton, Arthur Beecher's old roommate, was aware of King Arthur of Margollin and his macabre affairs, but only felt a deep compassion for the dementia that his school chum was suffering.

The second bad thing about the Margollin story was that by June the outcry was enormous and universal. King Arthur was an animal. The tenor of everyone who brought up the subject was that he was an international atrocity of Adolph Hitler proportions and they wanted him stopped. The Motherearthism "religion" was too pagan for modern times and should be eradicated. Various aspects of the thing were lambasted from the pulpits every Sunday, disdained on all the talk shows daily (television as well as radio), and the talk of the idle at every juncture: supermarket, bus stop, carpool, water cooler, and hallway.

The third bad thing about the story was not the obvious connection between the president's likely opponent for the next term in office. That they had been roommates in school was in itself not something to commit political hara-kiri over. With King Arthur's vile public image, it would have cost him votes for sure, but it was still a form of damage that clever politicians or more appropriately those with powerful backing could control and suppress. The real problem was that the young journalist's editor had insisted that King Arthur be interviewed in person before the article went to press and that was when the unbelievable, the shock of the decade, was revealed.

There is no way that anyone could have anticipated this—let alone the Panel. It was just too crazy.

The young journalist had to get to Margollin by boat from the nearest "civilized" island where the plane he'd chartered in Hong Kong put into. Even though he was not invited, he was received warmly by Beecher. Apparently the Motherearthists didn't have any quarrel with foreigners. Once in audience with the heinous monarch, the reporter took to his work and asked a host of unrelated questions. He didn't know what he'd find out, but he was certainly not going to go home without something printable. What he got was literally out of this world.

That King Arthur was totally insane was evident from the outset. But as with many deranged individuals, the King was often lucid and generally rational, in his own way, of course. When the interview got to where Arthur Beecher went to school, the subject of the leading candidate for the presidential nomination who happened to be his old roommate came up, as if it'd been scripted.

It was what King Arthur had to say about his old roommate that had the young reporter falling off his chair. It was lucky that he was tape-recording the interview, or his editor would not have believed it.

"You know buddy, Lloyd Stanton and I were roommates the entire time we were in school there," Beecher told the reporter glibly. Then his tone changed to one of confidentiality. "The entire time. We were the best of pals. We used to do all kinds of stuff together. We got into trouble more often than not. Oh, most of it was just kid stuff, you know. Playing hooky. Pranks on the other kids. Innocent stuff." The king stopped talking and his attention seemed to drift away, and his eyes got a far off look in them as if he was recalling a distant memory.

Then he came back in a flash and when he looked at the young reporter his eyes were blazing as if they were on fire—the unmistakable eyes of a maniac. "You know where the Motherearthism religion came from? It was Lloyd's idea. Yup. All his. We must've been in third grade, and he told me that he'd dreamed it up when we had been studying the aborigines in history class. We decided that we would become the first Motherearthists and we used to perform sacrifices on anything that we could find, mice, rabbits, birds, even a mangy old cat once."

The bald truth of it was that all people did things when they were kids. Most of it didn't amount to anything and invariably as adults most people never mention these things. They were various forms of experimentation and exploration but usually were so inconsequential that they rarely withstood the test of talking about them to any other adults.

The problem with Lloyd Stanton and Arthur Beecher was that one kid grew up normally and one didn't. The former was slated to be nominated for the presidency of the United States, arguably the most publicly exposed thing a person can do, and the latter had based his adult worldview on some outlandish childish illusions who as a result was perhaps the most publicly hated person on the planet.

When the story hit and instantly was picked up by the wire services and the media, Lloyd Stanton's goose was cooked to a blackened charred hulk. There was virtually no one who would sup at his table ever again.

It did not matter that Stanton had long forgotten the imaginary games that he played in elementary school. It did not matter that who Arthur Beecher turned out to be was not in any way Lloyd Stanton's fault.

What mattered was that Lloyd Stanton was postured to become his party's nominee for the presidency of the United States. The simple fact that it was Lloyd Stanton, who, however innocently, gave the idea to Arthur Beecher that he was using to justify savagely and bloodily sacrificing young children and was evilly trying to propagate these vile notions by broadcasting his acts on worldwide television, was more than enough to turn off even the most loyal partisan voter. Thus, it was clear to every delegate planning to attend the upcoming convention that if they nominated Stanton, they were most assuredly guaranteeing a second term for the current president.

Who would you vote for? The man who has been president for four years and appears on all accounts to be rational and normal or an unproven commodity whose best claim to fame is that he invented Motherearthism?

Add to this misery was the fact that earlier in the year the Panel had begun to lose interest in its chosen man. The reasons were varied and mostly inconsistent, but it was generally thought that it was due to the combination of a number of unrelated and extremely unlikely events that had all occurred in rapid succession in the past few months.

First, in April during the last of the four big "Super Tuesday" presidential primaries, the Panel's chosen man had unexpectedly come in second in a number of them. Given his strong showing in the previous primaries, he still was on a path to have enough delegate votes for nomination at the convention. This assumed that he would do well on the remaining primaries and as they came and went, his lead at the end of the primary season was very slim. The certainty of Lloyd being nominated on the first ballot was problematic because not all states required that their delegates vote for the winner of their primaries. This eventuality put fear into the hearts of the Panel members. It was highly regrettable that their careful planning and execution of the proven formula might go wrong.

Then, in May the Secretary of State disclosed the signing of an omnibus worldwide peace treaty by every recognized nation on Earth. Apparently, all the recent trips abroad by the president hadn't been all that had been advertised at the time. The Secretary of State, at the press conference, attributed the historical coup solely to remarkable statesmanship on the part of his boss, the president.

The Panel had greeted this news with despair. Of course, the members were pleased with the event itself—who wouldn't be? But they also foresaw that the president was a shoo-in for the next Nobel Peace prize and untold other accolades and honors. The dolt didn't deserve it, they were certain. Nevertheless, the Panel's opinion aside, at that moment the president's second term was virtually a done deal. In May, no less!

Needless to say, the Panel was not overly pleased with the prospects of unseating the president in the upcoming election. Its candidate, if nominated, would be lucky not to be laughed out of the campaign by September first. The week after the announcement of the peace treaty, the presidential approval rating was over eighty per cent and climbing. This kind of support for a president in the modern era was unheard of, inexplicable, and the talk of the nation.

The only problem, and it was a stretch to find any sort of shortcoming in the president's re-election campaign, was that this tide of good favor and support came a bit early. In other words, since there were still more than five months to the election, a lot could happen in that amount of time. For one, the American public was as skittish as a butterfly and was highly likely to forget about this stunning event in the vast expanse of five months' time.

Then there was the summer laying directly ahead and with it could come droughts, floods, tornadoes, hurricanes, riots, and economic collapses. Plus, most people would go on vacation during the summer in order to forget about their humdrum existences in the real world. In the past, many combinations of these things had happened and when they did so in election years, the presidential approval rating always suffered. It didn't matter whether any of it was the president's fault or whether he'd handled the particular affair or mess well. It was just that when people suffered, the man at the top usually took the heat for it. It didn't matter whether it was an act of God or something else; the voters always seemed to blame the White House for all their ills.

There were innumerable other fiascoes that could happen. They had happened before. Look what happened to Bill Clinton in 1998. At the first of the year, his approval rating was excellent. There were few conflicts worldwide and none that directly threatened the United States. The economy was strong with a very low unemployment rate. The stock market was setting new highs almost weekly. Inflation was at a twenty-year low and interest rates were below seven per cent. You can't get a better situation than that. But then the bubble popped and the public discovered Monica Lewinsky. Clinton's currency went to near zero at the speed of light. The truly cynical observer would say that Americans can't stand too much of a good thing. They get bored. When there isn't something bad happening for too long, they will make up a disaster or simply overly inflate a small incident of some sort just to keep things interesting.

But having said all that, Gardner James, who was seeking re-election, was in the catbird seat. He was far, far ahead of the competition. The way things were going for the president in May, it'd probably have to be all of these things happening at once to keep him from being re-elected.

CHAPTER 4

Collins sat and looked thoughtfully at his father-in-law. "But you're going forward with Stanton at the convention anyway," he stated more than asked, looking over at Laughlin sitting beside him on his study's sofa.

"Well, yes we are, Buf," the old man said shamelessly. "It's part of the game, as of course you know. We picked Lloyd and set him up for this and even though it's been a rocky road here of late, we still think he's right for the job." He stopped and stared into his coffee cup for a moment. "We have to do it this way because it's too late to change ships in the middle of the storm or the middle of the river or whatever the old saw is."

He looked up at his son-in-law and peered into his eyes. "I mean, do you really think we have any choice? You do know that we don't have a fallback position on this—a, uh, Plan B, as it might be called. Right? If you were me Buf, what would you do?"

Collins stared back at the old man who he respected more than anyone and loved as one might a brother or father. He was surprised at this sudden expression of fallibility. If anything, Tom Laughlin was not a man who made many mistakes and when he did so, they were small ones, rare and far apart, and certainly anomalies in the grand scheme of things; quirks of fate that he never openly admitted any culpability for.

"Me?" he asked, feigning surprise, when in fact he was mentally formulating a response. "Well, of course I am not you and there's not much chance that I ever will be, and also of course, I'm not much of a player in your chosen game of politics as you well know. But since you've posed the question, I guess that if it were up to me, I'd use my power and influence to accentuate the positives about Stanton and there are many or you wouldn't have picked him. And then, I'd make sure that when the convention comes, the delegates, even if they're not strongly inclined to nominate him, are made aware that they have no alternative to do so because there's no other suitable candidate. And this is something that I, as you, could use my influence and resources to assure. So, even though it might take a few ballots, reason will prevail—after all Stanton has no real connection with this King Arthur character—and your, uh, my man will get nominated."

Laughlin cast an admiring look at his daughter's husband. "Ah Buf," he appraised, "you've got more political juices flowing in you than I'm sure you're willing to admit. That's a pretty good strategy that you, as me, have outlined. Even better than the one that I was currently favoring. I really like that part about working on the unsuitability of the other candidates going into the convention—just to make sure, as you say, that the delegates don't have any real alternatives to Stanton. Thanks. I'll use it as if it were my idea. With your permission, of course."

Collins tilted his head towards the old man in mock deference. "Of course, Tom. Feel free. All that's mine is yours." It was a moment of intimacy that the two men rarely shared but one that was a keystone to the unshakable bond between these them.

Laughlin arose and refreshed his coffee from the carafe on Collins' desk. He turned to look at his son-in-law. "Changing the subject now, all right?" he asked in a low tone.

"Okay," Collins said, pricking up his ears. He wondered what could have more interest in the old man's mind than the upcoming convention.

"There's something I'd like to talk to you about, something that came up earlier today that I think will interest you. You've been working on an extended investigation into Lucy Doering Walton's husband's death. Right?"

"Yes, I've mentioned it to you a few times, Tom," Collins confirmed. "What about it?"

"The gist is that Walton's death was determined to be accidental, but Lucy believes he was murdered. And even with strong evidence, the police won't budge off the accidental determination. So, you've been looking into other quote-unquote accidental deaths in the District where Walton died and other cities to see if there's something that you can use to get an investigation into Walton's death opened. Right?"

"Yes," Collins replied, impressed with Laughlin's depth of knowledge on this.

"How're you coming on that?" Laughlin asked.

"Well, coincidentally Lucy and I had a meeting on this just today and even though the investigation has uncovered an alarming number of deaths that were suspicious, but no actions were taken by the police to investigate them, we haven't really come up with anything that helps.

"What I mean is that with Lucy as my client I'm bound to serve her purpose which is, as I'm sure you know, to try to find out who killed her husband and hopefully why. And of course, I'm not a private eye, and so, there's only so much that I can do in this direction, but so far, what we've found doesn't help the specific goal that Lucy has set for the investigation.

"When we talked about it today, I suggested to her that the information that we've gathered might be contributive to a different goal."

"Different?" Laughlin asked. "In what way?"

"Well, since it doesn't appear that we'll be able to solve Walton's murder for the police and deliver the culprit to them bound and gagged, my thoughts were that perhaps it'd help Lucy deal with her frustration and grief if it could be shown somehow that the police have done something wrong."

"Done something wrong?" Laughlin queried. "What?"

"Well, at first I was thinking that we could show some kind of abuse of authority, or misuse of it," Collins said.

"You mean malfeasance?" Laughlin asked. "Or the other two, um, misfeasance and nonfeasance? Buf, surely you know that stuff is mighty difficult to prove in a court of law."

"Yes, of course, I know this," Collins agreed without any animosity, "but it was my thinking along those lines—that it was a tough road to prove malfeasance, et cetera without catching them red-handed—that opened up my eyes to what I ultimately brought before Lucy today."

"And that was?" the old man prompted.

"Widespread corruption," Collins replied in a low voice, almost as if he thought they might be overheard.

"Oho," Laughlin exclaimed. "Slightly more than a quantum leap above malfeasance, et cetera."

"Indeed," Collins agreed.

"And Lucy's reaction to this?" Laughlin asked.

"Well, she's no lightweight, as you know, and before we could really discuss her predilections, she zeroed in on the legalities."

"That corruption of public officials is a criminal charge and not something that's brought before the civil courts?" Laughlin asked.

"Exactly," Collins answered.

"So, let me guess," Laughlin offered, somewhat tongue-in-cheek. "You ended up with Lucy like the dog who chased the streetcar and then caught it. You've gathered together evidence that might be enough to prove that the police in the District of Columbia, and perhaps other cities as well, have on their own decided to classify suspicious deaths as something other than homicides. Then, once done, you realize that all of this is outside your bailiwick as a private practice attorney and that this should be something that a district attorney, someone on the other side in other words, should be doing. And then it hits you. How can this happen? How can the people who are doing the crime be the ones to expose it? Now, of course it's possible that not every public official is in the practice of regularly doing this, but the rub is who's who?

"How am I doing so far?" he asked.

"On the money, Tom," Collins answered. "You're not so old after all," he added playfully.

"So, what's the bottom line?" Laughlin asked, too focused to be amused.

"Well, Tom, when explaining what my investigation and research has found to Lucy today, I presented to her more than mere corruption," Collins replied.

"Oho!" Laughlin exclaimed, his eyes shining brightly. "And that was?" he prompted, his face exuding excited anticipation.

"And that was, Tom," Collins continued, "that my findings can show, yea even prove, that in addition to corruption in the big cities, there has been collusion, conspiracy, and more than probably cover-up," he added with a straight poker face.

It only took a few seconds for Laughlin to absorb this additional information, in spite of its obvious legal implications. He was no novice in the game of political legalities, having, at least up to this point, been more than willing to say that he had seen it all, more than once. His eyes twinkled with amusement as he digested what Collins had just told him.

"Ah, the four cees, eh?" he said with a sly smirk. "I guess you've been thinking now for a while what I am now thinking, right Buf?"

Collins nodded in agreement and said, "Yes, Tom. The four cees. It is more than likely that this has happened many times before in history, but this, in these instances here based on my investigation that the murder of Lucy's husband and her money has motivated and enabled, is arguably the only time that this has happened where there is enough culpable evidence to prove it.

"But as I told Lucy earlier this afternoon, at the moment, as we left it today," Collins said, "we're at a standstill. We really can't go forward with the corruption, let alone a case with the other three cees of collusion, conspiracy and cover-up simply because there's no one to take it to and we don't know any more about how and why Lucy's husband died. So, in a word, our meeting ended on a low note.

"I mean, look at Lucy's situation. She's got all the money in the world—probably more than anyone except maybe you, Tom—and she's willing to spend it all. But she can't seem to get there from here." Collins grabbed his coffee cup and arose and began to fidget with the carafe and accoutrements on the Sterling silver samovar.

"She must mean a great deal to you for you to be this wrought up about the death of her husband, Buf," Laughlin said in a level tone.

"Well, of course you know how far back we go, Tom. But it's really much more than that."

"Ah!" Laughlin said. "It's the body politic, isn't it?"

Collins shot a glance at his father-in-law. "Yes. It really bothers me that those people can violate our trust that we've placed in them and do it openly and defiantly and blatantly and . . . and smugly get away with it!" He came back to the sofa without any more coffee and plumped down into the soft cushions exhaling loudly in an expression of defeat.

"I think that I have something for you, Buf," Laughlin said softly. "A genie's been let out of a bottle, and you've been granted a wish."

Collins looked inquisitively over at the old man. "What? A genie? What are you talking about, Tom?"

"I'm talking about what happened today that I said you might find interesting," Laughlin answered. "I had a visit from Bob Finch. He called this morning and said he needed to meet with me on an urgent matter."

"Finch!" Collins exclaimed incredulously. "The ay-gee? I didn't think that you knew him, Tom—certainly not well enough for him to pop over to the house on short notice."

"Buf, I thought you knew that I know nearly everyone and the rest think that they know me."

"Yes, yes, but James' head of Justice?" Collins posed. "That's a bit high up in the enemy's camp, isn't it?"

"Perhaps according to one viewpoint, I suppose you're right, Buf," Laughlin answered. "But you have to understand that at my level there really isn't any need to make good-guy, bad-guy distinctions and thus, I don't consider the current administration to be the enemy. As a matter of fact, we have a number of our people highly placed in Gardie James' organization and so we don't regard his administration as hostile."

"Finch is one of your, the Panel's, people?" Collins asked.

"Let's say that I know him, and he knows he can call and come over to the house on short notice," Laughlin replied tersely.

Collins mouthed a 'wow' and nodded silently to himself as if he were reaffirming something that he should've already known but somehow had forgotten. "So, what did Finch want to see you about?" he asked trying to stifle his eagerness to know.

"Well, it seems that he's gotten himself into a fix that under most circumstances would be almost impossible to get out of," the old man responded with a wry smile.

"Uh huh," Collins said, interested. "Go on."

"He apparently got wind of some far-reaching corruption in the larger cities and had the eff-bee-eye do an investigation and based on those results he ordered a Grand Jury to look into it.

"And now it looks like there are going to be indictments and a recommendation for a trial. As appropriate, he brought the president up to speed on the matter this morning and was curtly reminded by the president that there's an election coming up and since he, Finch, is already well down the slippery slope, meaning he can't undo what the Grand Jury will find, he had thus better make sure that the trial is short and as low a profile as possible."

"Which then compelled him to come and ask you how to do it," Collins surmised.

"Mmmm," Laughlin acknowledged.

"What did you tell Finch?" Collins asked.

"I told him, rather I suggested that he consider having you be the lead prosecutor in the trial," answered the old man.

"Me?" Collins spluttered with exasperation. "What! Why on Earth would you tell the attorney general of the United States that I could do his trial for him?" He was about to voice more objections and do so more loudly, but Laughlin stopped him with a sharp look and a held-up hand.

"You haven't heard what the trial will be about," he said.

"Tom!" Collins was not yet mollified. "I don't have to hear about the trial! Don't you see that I don't have the time to commit to a major criminal trial in federal court—and as the prosecutor! My God, Tom! I'm a defense lawyer."

Laughlin patted his distraught son-in-law on the shoulder, much like a father consoling a young boy who has lost his yo-yo. "No, no, Buf. You're a lawyer and I don't think that I have to remind you that you once were a United States attorney and so you are qualified to do the prosecution. But of course, that's not why I suggested to Finch today that he get you to do it. It just makes it possible. That's all."

"Well then, why did you tell Finch to get me, Tom?" Collins asked more calmly, genuinely curious about this now.

"You shouldn't be asking me this question," Laughlin said. "You should be wanting to know what's Finch's trial is about."

Collins scrunched up his face in a rebellious expression. "All right. We'll do it your way. Tell me what the trial is about. . . . Please."

"In a nutshell, the Grand Jury will be indicting several current and former city and state officials for wide-spread corruption, namely obstruction of justice and abuse of authority."

"For what?" Collins prompted.

"For deliberately classifying as many deaths as possible as accidents or suicides and then claiming that with the homicide rates in steep decline they have done the impossible and made our cities safer."

Collins stared at Laughlin. "What did you say?" He'd heard it but he couldn't believe it.

"You heard me," Laughlin responded.

"But Tom!" Collins exclaimed, all excited again. "That's impossible! That's the same case that I've been investigating for Lucy!"

"It certainly looks that way to me," Laughlin said through a broad cheek-to-cheek smile. "And I might add with one essential difference."

"And that would be?" Collins queried.

"And that would be that you can try Finch's case when as you just told me a few minutes ago that you can't try yours." The old man sat back and smiled smugly.

Collins leaned back into the cushions of the plush brocaded sofa in the study that his wife had meticulously decorated and nodded his head in agreement. "Of course. An essential difference if there ever was one. And this is naturally why you thought of me when Finch gave you the details of what was going on with the Grand Jury that he called."

"Bingo," Laughlin said, smiling brilliantly. "You win the teddy bear. I should also say that I of course didn't tell Bob Finch about your case and the investigation into Lucy's husband's death and so on. That, of course, would not have been my place to share that little factoid with Finch."

"I see," Collins said slowly. "But if the perfect solution to Finch's problem was apparent only to you, then how did you convince him that you suggesting that he consider me was a good idea."

Laughlin continued to grin. "That's the best part," he said. "I told him that the best way for him to handle this like the president wanted was to use the best defense lawyer in the country who was also a former United States attorney and also someone who was completely outside of politics. Who else is there who fits that suit but you, Buf? I ask you, who?

"Really that's the best reason for Finch to use you. The fact that you're already briefed on the facts of the case, and then some, as you have just shared with me, is really only a lucky break for both of you.

"And Finch bought it. All of it. He was quite enamored with my suggestion, and I suspect that he'll visit you sometime tomorrow morning, certainly no later than right after lunch. It'll be a personal visit, too, you can be sure. He won't be comfortable talking about this in a phone call. There are too many ways people can tap into phone calls these days.

"Anyway, since he's afraid that you won't have enough time to prepare and get the trial done and out of the way before the election, my guess is that he's not going to waste any time trying to second guess my suggestion. He has no alternative but to go forward with it." The old man stopped and chuckled gleefully. "Won't he be surprised to find out that you've been working for him—meaning on this very case—unbeknownst to him for several months?"

"Mmmm," Collins agreed. "There's just one thing, Tom."

"Yes, and what might that be?" asked the old man.

"Did Finch say anything about collusion or conspiracy?" Collins asked. "Is the Grand Jury looking into whether the corruption suggests that the public officials have colluded or conspired together?"

"As a matter of fact, he didn't, Buf," Laughlin said. "Such is a more visceral difference between where he is and where you are. I'd think that a clever fellow such as yourself will be able to lead the horse to water on this."

Collins nodded again. His mind was beginning to whirl with the possibilities. Maybe Lucy was going to get what she wanted after all. And the idea of being a prosecutor again titillated his senses. A case to die for—from a lawyer's perspective, of course.

CHAPTER 5

The next morning on his way into the office, Collins got a call on his mobile phone. It was Finch.

"Hello, is this Buf Collins?"

"Yes," Collins replied, knowing instantly who it was.

"Great, this is Robert Finch. I hope you don't mind me calling you like this, but I got your number from your wife. Apparently, I just missed you at home. She's a wonderful woman. Very helpful."

"Yes, Jane is a true dear," Collins said glibly. "She's also Tom Laughlin's only daughter, as I am sure you know. The Laughlin's were over for dinner last night and Tom and I had a chance to talk privately afterwards."

"Ah," Finch said, sounding relieved. "That saves me the trouble of trying to explain over the phone why I'm calling. I hate talking business on phones. Um, would it be possible to see you first thing this morning?"

Collins hesitated, trying to recall what his morning schedule was. As senior partner in his own firm, he usually didn't have early morning appointments. "I think that that would be fine, Mr. Finch. What time would be good for you?"

Finch laughed lightly, the noise tripping over the connection sounding like rippling water. "Well, as soon as you can get here," he said, "I'm in my car out in front of your offices as we speak."

Collins got Finch settled in with a cup of fresh coffee and a slice of Danish pastry and closed the door to his office less than twenty minutes later.

"Why don't you go first, Mr. Finch," Collins suggested.

"All right, but first, please call me Bob. I'm much more comfortable working with my close associates when it's on a first name basis."

"Are we going to be close associates? uh, . . . Bob?" Collins asked.

"Oh!" Finch seemed surprised. He was momentarily knocked off his train of thought and fidgeted with this cup. "I'm sorry that I may be rushing the cadence as it were. When you said that you and Tom Laughlin spoke privately last night, in my eagerness to resolve my problem, I was inclined to think that your father-in-law had generously acted upon my behalf and secured a commitment from you to help me.

"I see now that of course such didn't happen and without question it really shouldn't have. It's my mistake, Mr. Collins, one predicated by the vagaries and stresses of my job. Again, I apologize. I'm sincerely sorry for being so presumptuous—I mean look at me: here I am camped out in front of your offices, for all you know all night, waiting to pounce on you the moment you show up," he added meekly. "Of all things the Attorney General of the United States might do." He looked as morose as the cat that slipped and fell into the lake.

Collins smiled a toothless smile but one designed to put the top lawyer in the country a little more at ease. "I understand completely, Bob. Apology accepted. And please call me Buf. Why don't we start again, but this time perhaps I should start. Okay with you?"

"Of course, Buf," Finch said contritely. "Go ahead."

"Tom told me only a little bit about your conversation with him yesterday at his house and also gave me just the barest sketch of the Grand Jury investigation. He told me that he recommended that you appoint me as the special prosecutor for the trial that will result from the grand jury's indictments. He also told me what he told you that justified me as your best choice, and I agree with the rationale.

"But what Tom didn't tell you yesterday was the real reason why he feels that I'm your best choice. He couldn't tell you because it wasn't his business to do so—it's mine. The real reason why I'm the right lawyer for you is that I've been investigating the same crimes in virtually all of the same venues for more than six months."

"What?" Finch was aghast. "You know about this? How could you have found out?" He put down his coffee cup in disgust and sprang to his feet and began striding around Collins' office. "I tell you what," he said pointing his finger for emphasis. "When I find out where the leak in my security is, I'm going to . . . I'm going . . ."

"Hold on now!" Collins interrupted. "Hold on. There was no breach of your security, Bob. Come back here and sit down. There's no need for you to get all riled up. Let me explain."

Finch stared at Collins and silently returned to his chair and sat. Collins then gave him a précis of his investigation into the death of Roland Walton and his subsequent investigation into and analysis of the phenomenon of classifying seemingly suspicious deaths as accidental or suicidal in several major cities across the country.

When he was finished, Finch looked at him admiringly much like a philatelist might dote on a newly found long-elusive stamp needed to complete a favorite set.

"Would you say that based upon what you've found out, there is foundation to believe that there's been widespread corruption in several major cities over many years?" Finch asked.

"Without question," Collins replied emphatically.

"Provable?"

Collins hesitated. At first, he felt that Finch wanted to know if he felt that there was enough evidence to be able to convict those who would be accused of these crimes but before he could answer he got an eerie feeling that maybe Finch was up to something. Just exactly what this was, he couldn't put his finger on. He took a sip from his coffee, hoping that Finch wouldn't interpret his hesitation as a lack of confidence.

"In a criminal court, yes, I think so," he said. "In a civil court however, probably not."

Finch leaned back and nodded his head as if Collins had just confirmed something that he suspected.

"So. The sudden emergence of my case, from your perspective is like an answered prayer. Yes?" Finch was still nodding his head.

"You could say that" Collins replied exhibiting a toothless smile. "As my father-in-law put it last night: A genie's been let out of the bottle, and I've just been given my first wish."

"Then, it's not really a question that you'll do it?" he asked.

"None," Collins said nodding his head slowly. "It gives me the chance to do what I've been striving to do for months and couldn't do in any other way. For me, regardless of your motivations Bob, you are my genie and you've just granted me my wish."

"All right then," Finch said decisively and stood up. "I'll get out of your way and go back to my other distractions. I'll make an office in my executive suite available for you and I'll also send over a set of the pertinent documentation by courier this afternoon."

"Excellent," Collins replied. The two men shook hands and then Finch made his departure.

Collins went to sit down at his desk for the first time that day and leaned back in the expensive Morrocco-leatherbound chair. "Well, now the fun is really going to begin," he said in a half-whisper to himself and reached for the phone. He was halfway through dialing Lucy Walton's number when he realized that he was now more than just her lawyer: he was now working for the United States government and with this came an incumbent responsibility of privilege and privacy. He slowly replaced the handset in its cradle and clasped his hands together on the top of his desk suggesting that he was trying to restrain himself from succumbing to the urge to call and tell someone about this. He shook his head seemingly denying him of his right to make a call.

He thought about it and realized that he hadn't mentioned Lucy to Finch. In fact, he hadn't made any reference to having a client when he was telling the attorney general about the investigation, he'd been conducting, and Finch hadn't seen the need to inquire. So, now that he had a new "client," namely the citizens of the United States, it presumably was just as prudent to be discrete when he next talked to Lucy. In any event, he thought that it wouldn't be wise to talk about this over the phone to anyone. After all, the president was in the loop on this as well as the Director of the F.B.I. Who knows how long it'd be before all of his communication lines were monitored? Maybe it had already happened, he bemused to himself ruefully.

He spent the rest of the morning making arrangements with his secretary and other members of his firm to take over his caseload and other commitments for the next few months. He didn't have to give any reason for this, but to keep the rumors and idle speculation under reasonable control he told them the truth—or at least part of the truth anyway: He was going to be a special prosecutor in a federal trial that was soon to start and that he'd been selected by the attorney general. How was he to refuse?

The couriered package arrived from Finch right after lunch and Collins spent the rest of the day going through it.

That evening he drove home in his Buick Park Avenue four-door sedan. It was fully loaded with every luxury, cost just under sixty thousand dollars, and was paid for with a flourish by personal check earlier in the year. Although he was wealthy enough to own a Mercedes, a BMW, or a Lexus, he chose to buy American, on the one hand, and usually opted for a loaded top-of-the-line model of a second-tier brand versus a Lincoln or a Cadillac because ostentatiousness was not "his style," on the other hand.

At age fifty-four, Collins was at the peak of his game. He was senior partner of Collins, Peat, and Worth, the most prestigious law firm in Alexandria, Virginia and easily the most successful and respected attorney in the state—if not the entire Washington, D. C. to Boston, Massachusetts corridor. There were some who in fact would say he was the best East of the Mississippi River.

There was hardly a person in the legal profession who hadn't heard of William "Buf" (short for Buford) Collins, VI. Those who'd encountered his hard-hitting and uncannily precise legal maneuverings, were predominantly in awe of him—and several openly admitted they actually feared him. He was highly respected, comfortably rich, and shamelessly confident in his ability. A product that only the United States could produce and one that it could laud with as much enthusiasm as it could in envy of him.

He adroitly maneuvered the Buick up the narrow, winding lane that led to the sprawling colonial estate in southern Fairfax County that he and Jane had bought from a descendant of a Virginia founding father nearly twenty years previously. He reached up and fingered the security system and garage-door opener controls that were mounted where the roof of the car met the windshield, nestled neatly between the sun visors. As he rounded the last turn and the four-story red brick and white trim columned home came into view through the birch and beech trees, a series of external and internal lights began to sequentially illuminate.

Collins was an inveterate gadgeteer and he had personally designed the security system for the house and grounds. It wasn't as if he and Jane had anything particularly valuable to protect—neither was into jewelry or art—and it wasn't as if they lived in a crime-ridden neighborhood or anything. It was, however, de rigueur for the moderately wealthy to believe that there were criminals behind every tree. Thus, it was a forgone assumption that when he and Jane bought the place and began to renovate it, they would include a sophisticated security system in their plans. The system that they ended up with, after Collins had put his typically thorough and inventive spin on it, would have put many of the world's most well-known art museums to shame.

That evening, over dinner, Collins told Jane about Finch's visit. He was careful to talk in broad generalities and didn't mention any particular person by name or any specific dates or places. This was his typical way of "talking business" with his wife—giving her the gist of the cases but not any of the details.

"Don't you think that it's rather remarkable that the government's looking into the same stuff that I've been investigating?" he asked her when he was finished.

Jane looked carefully at her husband while she chewed on a piece of chicken à la Jane. On the surface it appeared as if she were contemplating her answer to this question but instead, she was taking the opportunity to give her husband a good hard look and take stock of the man. She smiled to herself thinking that he was more handsome today than when she'd met him more than thirty years ago. He didn't look his age and she reflected on how men seemed to become more distinguished as they aged, while women were loath to accept, or even acknowledge the effects of senescence. He had a full head of hair and most of it was still jet black—some graying was just beginning to show at the temples (and on the thick thatch of his chest hair, as well). He kept his face clean-shaven, and his hair cut short and somehow for all that, it made him look incongruously even younger! His teeth were straight and white, with hardly any cavities. "It's in the metabolism," he was wont to say. "Either you've got it, or you don't." His nose was aquiline, but not too big. His ears were just the right size and laid flat against his skull. He didn't need glasses, except for reading when the light was low. All in all, her husband, Jane reflected, was a truly remarkable man— arguably a perfect man. There was really almost nothing to slight him on. Everyone who knew him respected him and most genuinely liked him. He was, as they say, a straight shooter. She smiled again. He was also very good to her and their children. She really didn't have anything to complain about. In fact, she rarely complained about anything.

"Something amusing you, my Dear?" Collins asked, noting her smile.

She shook her head as she swallowed her mouthful of food. "Nothing to do with what you were saying, Dear." She put down her fork and took a sip of the chilled Chablis that they were sharing. "As a matter of fact, I was thinking that your thought about what a remarkable coincidence it is that the Department of Justice and you are working on the same problem is perhaps due to you being so focused on your involvement."

Collins stopped chewing on his food, so as to be able to hear her without interference. "How do you mean?" he inquired.

"Well, it strikes me that it's Mr. Finch who should be much more surprised that you were looking into what he has been doing than the other way around." She picked up her fork and speared another morsel.

"Huh!" Collins exclaimed. "In fact, he was surprised and actually thought that there had been some kind of security leak in his organization that got me onto it."

"There, you see?" Jane said through a mouth full of food.

"But why do you think it's more understandable for Finch to be surprised by the coincidence than me?" he asked.

"Because you're working at the problem from the bottom and he's been working on it from the top," she answered cryptically.

"And how would that make a difference?" he asked.

"The difference is that since you've been working at the problem from the point of view of the victims and as you've told me since there are so many of them in so many places and that it's been going on for so many years, you of all people shouldn't be surprised to find out that someone else has been looking into the same thing. You see? It's something that I think you should be expecting to find—not the other way around."

"Ah!" Collins said, understanding. "I see now. Once you take a look at just a couple of the deaths it's not rocket science to see that there's something rotten in the barrel and thus it's something that's likely to have been noticed by others. Therefore, you're saying that it stands to reason that there would be other investigations like mine and other people trying to figure out how to get the public officials to start doing their jobs right."

"Yes," Jane confirmed. "And then I'm also saying that Mr. Finch by the fact that he's working on this problem from the top—meaning that his investigation has been looking into wrongdoing on the part of the public officials at the inception—it's understandable to see that he'd never suspect that anyone else would be looking into the same thing. It's just not possible by the simple fact that corruption investigations are a big part of his job—one could say the primary reason why he's there.

"So, to find out that a private practice lawyer is looking into the same crimes and at almost the same breadth and scope, should've been truly shocking to him, it'd seem to me."

"Well, you're right about that, Jane my Dear," Collins said. "Bob Finch was definitely surprised."

This was Friday night June twenty-ninth, one hundred and forty days before the election.

On Monday, July 2, the Grand Jury handed down its indictments and delivered its files to Finch's office by the end of the day.

On Tuesday, Collins began his commute to his new office in the Department of Justice. His first order of business was to review the body of data, information, and inferences that Finch and the Grand Jury had. Next, he wanted to incorporate into this what he'd compiled on his own in the six months that he'd been working on the death of Roland Walton. Then, he needed to formulate a trial strategy which would dictate subpoenas and then when the trial date was set (which Finch promised would be soon—very soon) the final stage was to get on with it.

The task was daunting considering that his charter didn't allow for him to proceed at a pace that was set by the job—rather he was to get the trial finished and out of the way as soon as practicable—as much before the election on November Sixth as possible. The burden of this responsibility was such that the only way Collins could concentrate was to force time out of his mind. It wasn't long before he questioned the wisdom of his eagerness to take Finch's offer and it was at this point that he realized that he needed some help.

Finch had anted up an ample team of analysts, paralegals, and young U. S. attorney aspirants which allowed him to get organized in the first several days. But he was uncomfortable being the ringmaster of this small army of justice department staffers. He was not the business manager of this project. On the contrary, he was the special prosecutor and thus, he shouldn't be expending valuable time and cluttering up his mental capacity keeping the team humming at optimum efficiency.

So, he went back to the well. He asked Finch to authorize a deputy prosecutor—what is called in trial jargon a "second chair."

"All right, Buf," Finch said. "For this case, you are the Aladdin, and I am the genie, an analogy that I believe you originated to describe our relationship, and, if I'm not mistaken, you have a wish or two still due to you. Do you have anyone in mind?"

"Yes, I do Bob," Collins replied, having already thought this through before going to Finch. "Shawna Wells. She's . . ."

"Excellent," Finch blurted out, cutting Collins off. "I know her, and I think that she'd complement the team admirably." He reached for his phone. "I'll call her right now."

"Hold on Bob," Collins said quickly, taking his turn to be abrupt. "Why don't you let me talk to her first. I've known her for years and we've worked on opposite sides in court many times. Then, after I've sounded her out on this and she's amenable, you can make your call to make it official. All right?"

"Sure. No problem, Buf," Finch said guilelessly. "Keep me informed."

Collins returned to his office and called Wells' office and learned that she was currently not in court but in conference, due to be out in about thirty minutes. He told her administrative assistant to try to pin her down at that time as he was on his way over to talk to her about an important matter.

Shawna Wells was the United States Attorney for the Alexandria, Virginia federal district and had worked hard to keep a clean house and also, unusually, to keep out of the limelight. This aspersion to publicity and thus the political aspects of her job was one of the primary reasons why Collins liked her so much. It also was why he wasn't surprised that Finch knew about her, as attorneys in the federal system with absolutely no political aspirations were noteworthy in today's world. But it also is the reason why Shawna Wells isn't a household name even in her own backyard. She and Collins had been colleagues (and friends) for many years, although they had bitterly argued many a legal point in and out of the courtroom.

Chapter 6

Collins was waiting in her office when Shawna returned from her conference. She looked up in surprise as apparently her assistant hadn't had a chance to tell her about his call nor his presence.

"Why, hello there Buf, old boy," she said with a smile, accepting his presence much as if he were a box of long-stem roses from an unknown admirer. "What brings you here today? And by the way, where have you been? I haven't seen you in court in months."

He told her about Lucy's husband's death and what happened with Lucy and the authorities in the District. Then he told her about how he got rebuffed and the investigation he conducted after that. She listened carefully without speaking, undoubtedly mentally noting questions that she'd like to ask when he gave her a turn to speak.

Then he told her about the F.B.I. investigation ordered by Finch and how that predicated forming the Grand Jury. At this point her eyes lit up as she was certainly aware of the indictments that had just been handed down. Then he told her that Finch had appointed him as the special prosecutor for the upcoming trial.

"What the fondue are you doing, Buf?" she blurted out loudly, not realizing that her strong reaction to this was being telegraphed by the intensity of her tone.

Shawna had her own special form of mock profanity. In a profession that was still mostly dominated by men, she'd heard said about every "four-letter word" in the book in about every conceivable context and although many women, to hold their own, had slowly begun to give as good as they got, Shawna had taken a different route. She spoke in the vernacular like the others, with the same vehemence and the same inflection but with one minor exception: she used her own substitute words for the typical swear words. These pseudo swear words usually sounded like their correlatives, started with the same letter, and had the same number of syllables. She was wont to say such things as "Bill shirt," "frigging," and "Dad-gum it." Everyone knew what she meant when she said these things and only rarely did anyone complain or point out that she was not saying them right. It seems that, at least from the point of view of the hearers, Shawna was able to make her points just as well with her made-up curse words as the more forthright swearers did.

Wells was not interested in Collins' answer to her question. She was just getting warmed up. "Don't you realize what this looks like?" She spluttered a bit, searching for the right words to express her incredulity at Collins' seemingly asinine decision. "Gol-dang it, Buf! There are people out there who are going to be convinced that you've gone off your flipping rocker. This is going to come back to haunt you. I know it. And there's not a single flocking thing that you can do about it." She paused and wiped a bit of spittle that was leaking out of the corner of her mouth without any sign of embarrassment.

Collins looked at her with an amused expression, as if he'd heard something comical, but was not allowed to laugh out loud at it. After a few moments, he responded by saying "Don't you see? It's like a story from Grimm's Fairy Tales. I'd gotten to a point with Lucy's case where I knew what needed to be done but there was no way that I could do it. Then, out of the clear blue sky comes Finch and the Grand Jury. Like on a platter. Spinning straw into gold. I had to jump at it. Don't you see?"

"Mmmm," Shawna thought this over. "I suppose you have a point, Buf," she acknowledged. She nodded her head, deciding. "Okay, I've got it now. You're a lucky man and I hope you knock them on their keisters." Then, she looked at him slyly. "But I'm guessing that wanting to tell me all this isn't why you just popped over to see me this morning, right?"

"No, Shawna, you're correct; it isn't," Collins replied. "I came because I need your help. I want you to second chair for me. This job is . . ."

"Hold on! Hold your frigging horses, Buf," she said, blustering. "Don't give me your rationale until I've digested the dad-gum premise. All right?"

He nodded his head and stopped talking while he watched her knit her brows and purse her lips in an exaggerated expression of pensiveness. He'd seen her do this many times before and even though at first it appears that she's merely putting you on, it turns out that in spite of how ludicrous it looks, she's actually thinking hard about something.

After a moment, she looked up at Collins and smiled. "You've come to see me because you need me. It's always nice to feel that one's needed. You say that you want me to second chair. Given what you've told me so far, it seems like you're going to need a whole lot more than that to get through this trial, but I'll be honored to second for you, Buf."

He stared into her pale blue eyes and immediately felt relieved. He'd been fretting internally about the difficulties of overseeing a massive prosecution as well as an elaborate investigation involving many people all needing guidance and direction without being able to have some capable help. It was help from someone like Shawna Wells, who he admired greatly but also trusted completely that he hoped would be the answer to his second wish.

"Excellent, Shawna my Dear," he said, unable to hide showing his relief. "Excellent. Welcome aboard. Bob Finch will call you later today to make it official. I want you to start working on the strategy of the prosecution. You're one of the best prosecutors in the country and I'll defer to your advice. I'll confer with you regularly but the reason why I wanted you to help me is because I have a nearly full-time burden supervising the army of analysts and staffers that Finch has put on the job for me. Once I get them organized, I want you to cross over and start overseeing their efforts while I concentrate on the prosecution and the strategy that you're going to develop for us."

"Okay," she said cheerfully as if he'd just told her she was going on an all-expenses-paid two-week cruise. "I'll clear the decks on my calendar right away and I'll get started working on the trial strategy first thing tomorrow morning."

Things moved very quickly after that. Collins' team of investigators was uncovering case after case of potential wrongdoing and nearly all of them had clear evidence of corruption and many had indications of collusion and conspiracy. As Collins' own investigation had suggested, it went back more than twenty years, and it was happening in every medium-to-large city in the country.

Among other things, Collins had some statistical analyses done on the data and found that on the average during the years in question, the total death rates continued to rise, in some cases at alarmingly high rates. This was happening in all the cities that were reporting drops in homicides and violent crime. What was most interesting was that when the total death toll was used, it appeared that the cities were actually getting more dangerous not less. Collins had a mathematician do some graphics of the data. When partitioned into "before" and "after" segments, the rates "after" for deaths due to natural causes were more than triple the "before" rate, suicides were more than double, and accidental deaths were nearly quadruple what they had been "before." All the while the homicide rate was dropping slowly but steadily. It was incredible.

What was more insidious was that at the same time, the city officials were taking credit for the big drops in violent crime rates, claiming that their policies and measures were having a positive effect. The voters liked what they heard, and these officials were getting reelected and were moving up the ladder, like from mayor to state senator or to governor, from governor to congressman or senator, from district attorney to federal judge, and so on.

It was like a dam bursting or a massive avalanche. Collins felt that he was losing control, drowning in the volume of the data that his team was unearthing and discovering. But he knuckled under and did his best to keep abreast of it. They were making progress and Collins was bolstered by the reports that he was receiving daily from his "department" chiefs, as he called them, that he was doing the right thing and that he was on the right track.

Although he'd been very specific with each person that was brought on board about what he wanted him or her to do, he told no one what he or she was doing it for—what the master plan was. This was important until he and Shawna decided what they were going to do about this. He didn't want the media to get wind of any details of the trial too early.

It wasn't that he thought that any of the bad guys would run away if they thought he was on to them. It wasn't that he thought that any of these people would take any action against him. It wasn't that he felt that they would suddenly rush to their shredders and destroy evidence. It wasn't that he feared that the media would make a big splash about it once they got hold of it. It was not even that he thought that he might be at some risk if the bad guys found out what he was doing. No, Buf's sensitivity about discretion and secrecy didn't seem to be traceable to any of these factors. He and Shawna had discussed it at length and even though he couldn't quite put his finger on it, he knew the feeling was there and that it was strong. He knew deep down that secrecy was quintessential—he felt it in his bones, and he went with his gut on this one. So, he saw no reason but to support it until it either went away or he had further information that suggested a different course of action.

That was how it went for the entire month of July and well into August. The political convention that was nominating Gardner James' opponent this year was in Atlanta during the week of August Thirteenth. The trial was set to begin the following Monday, on August Twentieth. It was outrageously early, but Collins sensed the president's influence on this and reasoned that as soon as the opposing party had a nominee and the official campaign for the presidency began, it seemed like a good time to start a trial when you want it to get as little media coverage as possible.

It was during the week of August Sixth that things began to gel, and Collins and Shawna began feel comfortable with the strategy and the quality and quantity of evidence they had to present. They both agreed that they believed they would be ready. It was an elusive feeling however, and it didn't last very long.

On Thursday, August Eighth Finch called them into his office asking for a progress report. Collins gave the attorney general a quick overview and ended by saying that he and Shawna felt good about the case and were cautiously optimistic that they would be able to get some convictions and do so quickly.

Finch received this last with a frown. He drummed his fingers on his desk and looked at a spot on the carpet.

Collins shot a glance at Shawna, and she raised her eyebrows back at him indicating that she didn't know what was going on.

"Bob?" Collins prompted. "Is there something wrong? This is good news, isn't it?"

Finch snapped out of his reverie and focused his eyes back on Collins. He smiled benignly, like a Buddha. "No, Buf," he began, "there isn't anything wrong exactly, but I'm afraid that there's been a complicating development."

"What kind of complicating development, Bob?" Collins asked, trying to keep his voice level. It was far too late to be running into new bumps in the road. He and Shawna had the case finally on an even keel and he, as its "captain," didn't want to hear about trouble that might lie ahead.

"Hmmm," Finch mused. "Well, it's just as much a surprise to me as it will be to you guys, I'm sure."

"What will be a surprise?" Shawna asked.

"Well, you see, I've just been with the president," Finch said, "on regular business, you understand, and before I could leave, he asked for a private audience with me alone. He wanted to know how the case was going. He, of course, knows that we have a trial date and wanted a report. When I told him pretty much what you've just told me, he got angry with me."

"Angry?" Collins said. "Why would he be angry? Isn't he the one who wanted us to hurry? And haven't we been hurrying?"

"Yes," Finch acknowledged, "we have. But I guess in the meantime, the president has been thinking and now he wants more than just for us to hurry."

"More?" Shawna asked. "What kind of more does he want?"

Finch didn't answer and started to drum his fingers on the desk again.

"Bob?" Collins prompted. "What more could James want from this?"

Finch stopped stalling and blurted it out. "He wants the trial to acquit—not convict—the defendants."

Collins shot to his feet. "What!" he exclaimed. "He wants what?"

"The president said that perhaps it was going to be too murky politically for the trial to proceed along a path that would end up convicting any of the defendants. He thinks that the best approach is for the trial to end up with acquittals and do so about a month before the election in order to get the best leverage for his reelection." Finch looked like he had a stomachache.

"Well, it's a little too late for that now, Mr. Finch," Shawna said. "We've already got enough to convict and there's no way that we're going to soft-pedal this thing. You have to know that."

"Yes, I know that Shawna," Finch said looking at her coldly. "And so does the president. That's why he's decided to up the ante."

"What does that mean?" Collins asked, alarmed at how little control he seemed to have on this as the "lead prosecutor."

"It means, that as of today, the trial will no longer be about corruption in the cities. Shortly, I'll escalate the charges to collusion to obstruct justice."

"What the funk?" Shawna muttered.

"Collusion? Collusion with whom?" Collins spluttered, doing his best to feign surprise and even a little outrage. He had known, of course, almost from the start that the president might do something like this and had been secretly preparing his case to be ready to take it on, once an escalation of the charges like this arose. "Bob, that's impossible! We can't possibly put together a case against the defendants on collusion that will stick—not in the nonexistent amount of time we have left to prepare. We would, of course, have to identify who the city officials have been colluding with and add them to the indictments."

"That's exactly the president's point, I think," Finch answered morosely.

Collins and Shawna were silent as they walked back to his office. Just before they got there, Collins turned to her and jerked his head toward the elevators. "Let's get some air," he said and continued walking past the door to his office.

Outside the Justice building, they meandered in the summer afternoon heat out onto the Mall, where Collins bought them both an ice cream cone. They found a bench in the shade and sat down to eat their treats.

"Keep the cone in front of your mouth when you talk. All right?" Collins whispered secretively. "Try to keep your voice as low as you can."

"Okay," she said in a whisper. "What's this all about?"

"The president is pulling all the strings on this, and he's been manipulating Finch by short-leashing him. This stuff about upgrading the charges to collusion is a crock. He is trying to make it impossible for us to get convictions because he wants the good press he would get if the trial ends up in acquittals."

"You've got that right, Buf," Shawna said out loud and then realized that they were trying not to be overheard or show their moving lips. She hunched down below her cone. "James or Finch or maybe both are deliberately doing this to make it impossible for us to get any convictions by hamstringing us at this late date to add new defendants to the case—people we don't even know who they are." She made a spitting gesture off to her side in indication that she found this to be highly distasteful. "It stinks to high heaven of politics."

"You've got it exactly, Shawna," Collins said under his breath. "But I've something to tell you."

She looked at him and then remembered to move the cone back in front of her mouth. "What?" she asked.

"I already have the evidence that we need to prove collusion," he said so lowly that she had to stare at him and work it through her brain syllable by syllable.

"You do?" she asked incredulously.

He nodded his head. "It's all part of the investigation that I was doing into the Roland Walton death. I didn't start looking for evidence of collusion, you understand. I was only trying to find a lever that I could use to force the police in the District to open a murder investigation. But then after I started reviewing the mountain of data and information, collusion started to creep into my consciousness.

"The problem was, of course, that there was nothing that I could do about it civilly, as Lucy's lawyer."

"Huh, and then Finch showed up," Shawna said, "like a miracle."

"Yup," Collins agreed. "Just like manna from Heaven."

"But Finch's case, at least up until just now, was only corruption. There was no collusion in it when he brought it to you. Right?"

"Right," Collins confirmed.

"So, why didn't you tell him that you had more—that you had enough to show collusion?" she asked, keeping her voice a low whisper.

"I thought that I'd see it in the evidence that he had and then would point it out," he answered. "I thought that there would be a good time to bring it up."

"And just now in his office, that wasn't a good time?" she asked.

"No."

"Why not?"

"Because, just now in his office, I realized that the whole thing was political and that because we're both devout non-politicians, the politicians think they can dupe us and get their way."

"So, you're going to try to dupe the dupers?" she asked. "Beat them at their own game?"

"Uh huh," he said. "As of now, we acknowledge that we're in a knife fight and remember that there are no rules in a knife fight."

"I hope you know what you're doing, Buf," she said.

"I hope so, too," he said, finishing his cone. "I hope so, too."

Collins and Shawna worked furiously over the weekend revamping their trial strategy to include the new collusion charges. Shawna was impressed with the depth and scope of the evidence that Collins had that could prove collusion and to name names.

By Monday morning, the day the convention started, they felt that they had recovered from the setback they incurred four days previously in Finch's office. Collins went to give Finch a status report and then took Shawna out for another ice cream cone when he returned. Outside while walking, he told Shawna that he'd complained the whole time with Finch about how difficult this trial was going to be and that he needed more time.

"So, you're scamming him," Shawna said smiling.

"We can't trust him anymore. He's not our friend."

"He's going to find out once the trial begins, isn't he?" she asked.

"Certainly," Collins agreed. "But then it'll be too late at the very least extremely difficult to change."

"Do you think that it's wise?" Shawna asked.

"I don't know, but if we want justice, and I guess that's a concept that is only understood by apolitical people such as us, then I fear that we have no alternative but to keep information from Finch."

"But he's the ay-gee, Buf!" Shawna exclaimed. "It's not nice to fool Mother Nature."

"I know, I know," Collins soothed. "But I'm thinking that they're not finished with us, you see. This is like a chess game. We've got to keep our guard up on the one hand and also think as far ahead as we can on the other."

"You think that they're going to pull something else?" she asked.

"As soon as they sense that the trial isn't going as they want, I'm sure of it." He continued to eat his cone while they walked.

"Hmmm," she murmured, thinking it over. "Buf, maybe we shouldn't wait for the next time."

"What do you mean?" he asked.

"I'm not sure it's in our best interest to think defensively," she said. "Maybe we should try go on the offensive. You can do it, you know. You're the special prosecutor and with that title comes a lot of power."

"I know now why I like you so much, Shawna," he said, smiling at her. "You're the best lawyer I know. Take the offensive is a wonderful idea and I know exactly what we should do."

She looked at him inquiringly.

"There's more about my investigation that I haven't told you," he said cryptically. "In addition to collusion, I think that I can prove that there's been conspiracy and also, I am pretty sure a cover-up."

Shawna stopped dead in her tracks and stared at him. "No sheet!" she exclaimed and then cringed, realizing that she was talking out in the open. Then, in a much more discreet voice she said, "Both conspiracy and cover-up? On top of corruption and collusion to obstruct justice?"

Collins nodded, smiling satisfactorily. "Both on top of those two," he said.

Shawna shook her head in awe. "Holy wow," she said. "That's an offensive ploy that will go down in the history books, if I've ever heard one."

"There's just one problem," Collins said.

"Yes?" she prompted.

"I really think I should talk to Tom Laughlin about this, but he's down at the convention busy as all get out."

"Mmmm," she agreed. "Maybe it'll wait until next week."

Chapter 7

It was on Wednesday, August Fifteenth, five days before the start of the trial and also the day when that evening the convention was going to start balloting for a nominee, when Collins discovered something important. He'd run into to some information that suggested that the corruption might be more extensive than what was covered by the Grand Jury's indictments. He already knew that his information clearly indicated that the wrongdoings extended to collusion, as the president has now escalated the charges to, but also to corruption and cover-up. What his further analysis was now starting to indicate that the involvement of law enforcement and elected public officials was much more widespread than previously understood. He needed to know how to deal with this information as soon as possible. The ramifications were galactic: Would the Grand Jury need to reconvene, thus delaying the trial? The consequences of this outcome would be highly undesirable to the attorney general and presumably, in turn, to his "boss" the president. And there was another problem: This new information opened up the possibility that the corruption (and the other 'cees,' collusion, conspiracy, and cover-up) might reach as high as the attorney general's office, more specifically Bob Finch. This was a scary thought at best. This meant that there was almost no one that he could trust implicitly. No one that is, except Jane, Shawna, and Tom Laughlin. He knew that he had to keep this from Finch until he knew more and could decide what to do. The problem was whether the charges needed to be expanded. This was a worrisome thought. There just did not seem to be any easy way around it. And time was becoming very, very tight.

He reached out for the phone on his Justice Department desk and was halfway through punching in Tom Laughlin's private home number when he remembered that his father-in-law was not at home, nor for that matter currently in town. He replaced the receiver and scrunched up his face in frustration.

Tom Laughlin had been out of town for more than three weeks: the first two were spent in Fort Lauderdale with the Panel strategizing about what to do about Stanton's failed candidacy and probably wringing their hands in helplessness and then all last week they were in Atlanta getting everything ready for the convention that began there on August Thirteenth. Jane had said that her mother had joined Laughlin in Atlanta. Usually, convention weeks were full of various social and fund-raising events and Tom and Ellen Laughlin were regular attendees at these galas.

Collins looked at his watch and wondered what Laughlin might be doing on nomination day at eleven o'clock in the morning. He knew that he could call his father-in-law on his mobile number which nowadays worked virtually anywhere but since the old man was undoubtedly up to his neck in alligators by this time, he also wondered whether there was any way that he could get Laughlin to help him with this problem.

It was a difficult decision. On the one hand, Collins thought that perhaps he was being too conservative in thinking that he had a problem that required outside help in the first place. On the other hand, he continued following this train of thought, couldn't there be someone else besides Laughlin who could help? Maybe Shawna might know of someone, for example, or even help him think this through herself. And on another hand, maybe he was just being paranoid and if he just waited a bit, the problem might go away or not pose any difficulty. *Good luck with that hope* he thought unhappily to himself.

He drummed his fingers on the top of the desk. But he thought, frowning, on the last hand, if he could just have ten minutes with the old man, he'd sure feel a lot better about this.

He reached over and got his mobile phone out of his briefcase and this time he punched in Shawna's personal number.

"Yup," she said answering on the first ring. "What's up?"

"I need to talk to you," Collins said in a low tone, knowing that she knew it was him from the caller-identification feature on her phone. "Where are you?"

She said she was in her car on the way over to see him in the Justice building.

"No, don't come here—at least not for this," he warned carefully keeping his tone even. "Have you crossed the bridge yet?"

"Memorial?" she asked. "Um, I'm getting close, but no, not yet."

"Okay, stay on the gee-double-you parkway and go into Rosslyn. All right?" He said and then forged ahead without waiting for her to confirm this. "I'll meet you at Tom Sarris' in ten minutes. We can discuss this over lunch."

"All right," she said over the crystal-clear connection. "The Orleans House. Ten minutes. Lunch." And she was gone.

Collins closed the connection on his phone, put it into his pants pocket, and grabbed his coat.

He strode into the foyer of the amazing reimagination of Arlington, Virginia's oldest structure in Rosslyn's new high-rise hybrid residential-slash-office complex that rose up over the original site of the restaurant, only twelve minutes later. He found Shawna at the salad bar, and she pointed out their table to him and joined him a few seconds later with what looked like a serving platter containing a small mountain of rabbit food.

After they ordered and he did a run at the elaborate salad bar himself, Shawna peered at him over a poised fork with which she'd speared a ripe olive.

"Something's come up, Buf?" she asked, seemingly ready for anything.

Collins paused before responding taking a moment to remind himself how much he liked this woman and her style. Nothing seemed to faze her, and nothing seemed to be beyond her ability to deal with. He was glad that he'd elected to discuss this matter with her first.

"I told you over the phone that I needed to talk to you. It's because we've got a new problem," he began, "and I'm worrying whether I was too explicit about it over the phone. I hope no one overheard me there in Justice. This is something that we need to keep extra close to our chests and let's, um, give it a nickname, you know, a code word."

Shawna picked up on this immediately and her eyes lit up like it was going to be fun. "Okay!" she said cheerfully. "Let me pick it, Buf. Okay?"

"Sure," he said agreeably, "you pick it." He smiled pleasurably in spite of the weight that was on his mind and that had caused this impromptu meeting. He was amused at how Shawna seemed to be more interested in the mechanics of this intrigue than in the substance of it.

She looked up at the ceiling while she munched on her salad. "Let's see. We could use the *affair*. No, that would set off a different set of bells if someone overheard us. Hmmm. What about the *matter*? No, I guess that still sounds sinister. Mmmm. Maybe it's the use of the article *the* before the noun that gives the reference too much distinction." She frowned, as if this was turning out to be harder than she'd thought.

"How about a name?" Collins suggested.

"A name?" she queried. "Oh, of course, a name! That's a super idea. Okay, let's think of a name. Hmmm. I guess it should be something different because otherwise there really might be someone with that name who's around us and then we'd have to explain ourselves. Umm. Let's see. What about . . . *Jefferson*?"

"Jefferson?" Collins asked curiously. "Why Jefferson?"

"Well, it just came to me," she said. "It's for Thomas Jefferson the champion of our republic, of course, and the one single person who would be the most offended by the crimes we are investigating."

"Right, old tee-jay," Collins mused. "Okay, I like it. Good choice, Shawna. Jefferson it is."

"Okay, then," Shawna said starting back on her salad, "so tell me about Jefferson."

"Well, I was going over some of the latest reports in from the eff-bee-eye and comparing them to my own information this morning and I started to get a sense that there was more there than what seems to be."

"More?" Shawna asked. "More in what way?"

"Well, there's an indication that there are more people involved and more deaths that go farther back than what is covered in the Grand Jury's indictments."

Shawna sat back and considered this. She even stopped eating. "Oh, that kind of more. Uh huh. I see."

"Well, I'm not sure that you really do see, Shawna. Not yet anyway," Collins said with concern.

"There's more?" she asked.

"Yes," he replied.

"Jefferson is bigger?" she asked.

"Well, not exactly bigger," he said. "We've already talked about that part. What concerns me, Shawna, is that Jefferson looks like it goes higher."

Shawna looked at him and cocked her head much like a dog who has heard something but isn't sure what it is. "Jefferson goes higher?" she asked.

"Yes, higher as in that it may involve other, more important people than those currently indicted."

"Holy shoot," she said and started eating again, this time with a vengeance as if it were going to be her last meal for a long time. "If it does go higher, do you think that we're talking corruption, collusion, conspiracy and cover-up all the way?"

"Yes, Shawna," Collins replied in a flat tone. "All of those," he said. "The higher it goes the more it stinks of those. Absolutely."

Their entrées arrived at this point and Collins fell into eating himself. They munched along silently for several minutes, each lost in his and her own thoughts. They looked at each other every so often as they ate but neither indicated to the other that he or she was ready to break the silence. It was as if they both knew that once they started talking about Jefferson again it might go on for a very long time and thus it was prudent to stock up on as much nutrition as possible before going forward.

After they were done and the plates were cleared away, dessert and coffee having been refused by both, Shawna looked over at Collins and then cast her eyes down onto her place mat. She doodled with the flimsy paper with her forefinger. "I guess the best thing to do is for you to call your father-in-law, Buf," she said in a low tone.

Collins looked at her and wondered if her reluctance to make eye contact with him was indicative that she felt she was failing him in some sort of way by suggesting he seek out other counsel. She was, of course, right that talking to Laughlin was the next step but also at the same time there was no reason she should feel bad about this.

He reached out and caught her doodling hand and squeezed it. This caused her to look up and he held her gaze with his eyes. "That's the best idea I've heard in a long time, Shawna, my friend. I'm so glad that I brought this prob- . . . uh, brought Jefferson to you. I knew that you would know what we should do." He released her hand and leaned back.

Shawna continued to look into Collins' eyes. She knew he was dissembling with her. She was one hundred percent certain that he'd already thought of calling Laughlin. In fact, she'd have bet a large sum of money that he'd already tried and that having somehow failed to make contact with the old man was what had precipitated this sudden lunch meeting. But he was patronizing her a little and she had to admit that she liked it. It showed that he knew how much of a difference the little things made and she found this comforting. She realized how much she liked this man and how much she was enjoying working with him on this case.

She brought down her eyelids a fraction instantly transforming her expression into a look of cunning. "So, where is he?" she asked smiling coyly. "I don't believe for a second that you haven't been trying to reach him ever since you found out about this . . . found out about Jefferson."

Collins slumped his shoulders slightly in a mock posture of having been caught with his hand in the cookie jar. "He's down in Atlanta at the convention and probably busy as all get out. Politics is his milieu, you know."

"Well, so what?" Shawna blurted out in exasperation. "Jefferson is important, isn't it? What's a bunch of political convention fluff compared to Jefferson? I ask you! You've got your phone with you, don't you? Let's call him right now."

Collins stared at her, amazed at her forcefulness but also aware that she was unaware of Laughlin's real purpose in being down at the convention. He shrugged his shoulders. It was inevitable that he'd call the old man on this Jefferson thing. It might as well be now as at any other time. After all, he needed as much lead time as possible—just in case.

He nodded his head. "You are of course, right, Shawna Dear," he said agreeing with her. "I was thinking that this thing mightn't be as big as it seems and that it might blow over, you know? I was thinking that as Tom was down at the convention doing his thing, maybe I shouldn't bother him and so on.

"But now having mulled it over with you some, I guess we might as well call him and get his sense about it. What harm could there be? How long could it take? Right?" He reached into his pocket and pulled out his phone and started to punch in Laughlin's personal number. He put it up to his ear and could hear the trilling sound as the connection was made.

After two rings, the connection opened and he heard Laughlin growl into his handset, "What?"

Collins momentarily felt rebuked, wondering if he had caught him at a bad moment, knowing full well that such was highly likely, this being nomination day and all. But before he could speak, Laughlin continued.

"No, wait," he said more evenly. "Let me get my glasses on." There was a short pause on the line while Laughlin presumably donned his glasses and looked at the display screen on his phone. Then he came back, "Oh, it's you Buf. How are things up in dee-cee? Is Janie all right?" He was sorting out his thoughts trying to anticipate why Collins was calling. "No, Ellen talked to her just a little while ago, I think. Hmmm. Oh, it must be the case, then. Is that it?" he asked perceptively.

"Yes, Tom," Collins confirmed, "it's the case."

"Oh," Laughlin said without much surprise. "I see. Well, you wouldn't be calling me about this on today of all days unless it was important. So, we probably shouldn't talk about it over the phone. Hold on a second," he said, and the connection went silent as he more than likely pushed a mute button on his phone.

Then he was back. "Buf? You still there?" he asked. The septuagenarian in him was always doubtful of modern technology.

"I'm here, Tom," Collins answered.

"I guess you'd better come down here so we can talk about this face-to-face. It's not a good time, but so what? You're working on something just as important as what I'm doing. Ha! Probably more important, now that I think about it. Okay, it's about one o'clock now. I'm due in a meeting right now that will last most of the afternoon—and nothing ever starts on time nor ends on time these days. So, let's say that I'll be free from about seven to nine this evening. Why don't you take my Gulfstream down here? I can have it pick you up at National Airport at, let's say six—make it five-thirty. That should give us plenty of time. All right?"

Collins was awed by the old man's ability to juggle so many odd objects in the air at once. "Sounds good, Tom," he said. "I'll be bringing Shawna Wells with me."

"Excellent," Laughlin said, "I've always liked her. She's much better looking than you, too. See you tonight," and he disconnected.

Collins closed the connection on his phone and put it back in his pocket and looked over at Shawna. "We're flying down there to meet with him this evening," he said matter-of-factly.

"When? Where? What flight? Which airport? How can we be sure we can get a seat?" she said, all in a bluster.

"We'll be taking his private jet. He's having it pick us up at National at five-thirty."

"Your father-in-law has a private jet?" Shawna asked, her voice trembling a little as if she realized she was moving up into a higher plateau of life and was unsure she was ready.

"Umm, he has two, actually," Collins said. "It gives him more flexibility and reliability and it makes the maintenance costs more manageable, I think."

"Two private jets!" Shawna was aghast. "Who is he? A sultan or an oil baron or something?"

"Yes," Collins said levelly. "Tom Laughlin is in the or something category. You can be sure of that." He started to stand. "Let's get going. There's a lot to do before we have to go to the airport."

It turned out that Laughlin continued to do his juggling act even while in his meeting. Collins received a call about four from one of the old man's personal staff, a man he'd known for many years.

"We're going to have a car pick you and Ms. Wells up and take you to the airport, Mr. Buf," he said. "Where will you be?"

"Oh, Johnnie that's not necessary," Collins objected. "We can drive over to the airport or take a cab or something."

"No, no, Mr. Buf," Johnnie said. "Mr. Tom was very clear about this. He said that you were very busy and that you shouldn't have to worry about driving and parking and such. Besides, you need a special pass to get on the ramp at the airport where Mr. Tom's plane's going to be."

Collins thought about it and decided to let his father-in-law run the show. After all, it was the old man that got him involved in this case in the first place. So, why not let him continue to steer the ship as he saw fit, right? "Okay, Johnnie. We'll be at my office in Alexandria."

"Okay, got it," Johnnie said. "In that case, I'll have the driver collect you at five. Okay, with you?"

"That will be fine, Johnnie," Collins said. "Thank you."

Collins and Shawna worked at his offices for the rest of the afternoon. He showed her the information that he'd discovered that got him to start thinking about Jefferson and she agreed with him that there definitely was substance to his suspicions.

The chauffeur-driven limousine was out front a few minutes before five and they sat together in the back seat on the short drive to the airport. They barely spoke trying to be cautious about the security and heavy purport of Jefferson that had begun to burden them throughout the afternoon.

They were passed through airport security without a hitch and arrived at the foot of the steps onto one of Tom Laughlin's two private jets promptly at five-thirty. The plane was painted a spectacular shade of French blue with brilliantly artistic flourishes of gold and silver on the fuselage and tail. They were greeted at the door by the steward who identified himself as Rolf.

"Welcome aboard the Lady Jane," he said formally. "The Captain will speak to you in a moment. In the meantime, please get settled. I put out something for you to munch on. Can I get you anything to drink?"

Shawna asked if he had any beer and in response to Rolf rattling off an impressive list of brewed beverages, decided to have a bottle of Heineken. Collins asked for a bottle of sparkling mineral water. They sat down in facing captain's chairs that swiveled completely around. Between them was a small table heaped with cold cuts, sliced cheeses, and a cornucopia of crudités and slices of fruit.

Shawna gawked at the food which looked more like a smorgasbord big enough to feed fifty hungry lumberjacks than a snack for two passengers. She took her beer from Rolf which he served in a tall pilsner glass and had a large swallow.

"Lady Jane as in . . .?" Shawna mused as she started to nibble on some prosciutto ham and Havarti cheese nicely stacked on a Carr's water biscuit.

"Yes, one and the same," replied Collins. "Jane's his and Ellen's only child."

"Lucky girl," Shawna commented guilelessly. "And lucky you."

"It has its perks," Collins said dryly.

They were interrupted by the opening of the door to the cockpit. A tallish, grayish man in crisp dark blue trousers and light blue military shirt with shoulder-board insignia stepped into the cabin.

"Mr. Collins, Ms. Wells," he said in a deep, lazy voice, "welcome aboard the Lady Jane. I'm Captain James Bridges and you can call me

Jim. We're happy to be at your service on this trip to Atlanta. If there is anything we can do to make your trip more comfortable, please do not hesitate to ask Rolf here or you can buzz me at any time on the intercom phone there." He pointed to a sleek handset that fitted into a console on one wall of the cabin.

"There has arisen a small problem which I fear will not be regarded as favorable news but I'm sorry to say is outside of our control," Bridges said, slowly.

"What's that, Jim?" inquired Collins.

"The weather report for down South of here isn't the best. It's never good in the Southeast in August, you know. There's a long line of thunderstorms that's moving up from the gulf across Alabama and Georgia. So, the eff-ay-ay is metering the flow of traffic and in order to control the volume of flights in the air, they've put all yet-to-take off aircraft on hold."

"So, you're saying that we can't take off?" Shawna asked.

"That's right, Miss," Bridges replied, with a sadness in his voice that seemed to be an art form amongst airline pilots. "We have to wait until the Air-Route Traffic Control, or ay-tee-cee, gives us a departure time. Right now, they are estimating that we will be on hold for about an hour. Really, it's the best thing," he continued, "to stay on the ground. This way we have much more flexibility and from what I hear some of the flights that were already in the air southbound and eastbound have been in holding patterns for more than hour already and now some of them are having to divert to alternate locations because of low fuel."

Collins took a sip from his drink and glanced at his watch. He looked over at Shawna and held up his glass in a mock toast. "Well, it's out of our hands. I say we eat something and relax and let Jim take care of the rest for us."

Shawna nodded her head in agreement as her mouth was already full of another bite of "snack." Captain Bridges bowed his head slightly in deference to his charges and returned to the cockpit and closed the door.

The ATC clearance came through but more like an hour and half later. Captain Bridges made the announcement to the passengers via the public address speakers mounted in the ceiling of the cabin and Rolf quickly closed the outside door and went about securing the cabin for take-off.

As they took off, they were treated with a spectacular view of the nation's capital in the evening sunlight. It was not long however, before all view of the ground was obscured by a thick layer of clouds. Looking out the window, they could see in the remaining daylight huge bulges of white cottony clouds towering up over the darkening gray layer. Inside these towers could be seen bright flashes of white-yellow light going on and off several seconds apart. These presumably were the thunderstorms and it was more entertaining than an in-flight movie to watch Mother Nature do her work.

The flight was scheduled to be about an hour and forty minutes down to Atlanta's Hartsfield Airport. At about the time they should've begun descending, Captain Bridges's voice crackled over the speakers. "Folks, this is Jim on the flight deck. The weather hasn't gotten any better and we're now being told by ay-tee-cee to begin holding. We're at twenty-five thousand feet. They say that we're in a queue based on our available fuel levels. Since we've got enough fuel to last us another several hours, I'm sorry, but that that puts us rather down the list. Up here, I have to tell you, we're all treated the same: public, private, whatever. So, anyway, I'm told that we're number ten in the holding pattern and that we might have to wait over an hour to get down. They're calling them in with ten-minute spacing.

"So, since it's out of our control, I advise you to lean back and relax. Have another drink or some more to eat. Take a nap. Your choice. Once I know something, I'll be back. Over and out."

CHAPTER 8

There was a car waiting for them outside the plane when they finally got their clearance to land and taxied to the parking ramp. They climbed aboard feeling numbed by the long wait above the Earth and it was several minutes past ten o'clock by the time they got past security at the convention center and rode up the private elevator to the executive suite.

Tom Laughlin greeted them nervously. "I was beginning to wonder whether you were going to make it at all. Now that you're here, I can relax but you're going to have to wait a little while before I'll have a chance to talk to you. All right?"

Collins looked out the picture window at the writhing mass of humanity down on the convention floor. "What's going on?" he asked.

"It seems that the hyenas are attacking the elephant before it has had a chance to die with dignity," Laughlin replied. "We've been working on the counterattack approach that you and I discussed a short while back—you know, point out the undesirability of the other candidates, but it quite clearly is not having its desired effect, I'm sorry to say." Collins turned to look at his father-in-law. He noticed that the old man seemed to look even older and also physically drained.

"Well, all evening, the lectern has been occupied by nominee hopefuls trying to get the delegates to swing their way after the first ballot is over." Laughlin looked apologetically at Lloyd Stanton who was sitting across the room against the wall. "And I must say that they've been liberal with their venom trying to poison every other possible challenger in each and every way."

Laughlin smiled ruefully. "I must admit that it's been rather lively down there. Undoubtedly the most spirit at a convention that I've seen in many years. And it's gotten the delegates worked up something awful. At the start of the evening's agenda, the floor was pretty deserted. I guess many of the delegates were back in their hotels cooling their heels until ballot time and watching the doings on television. When they saw what was going on, they all seemed to decide to come over here at the same time. Traffic's been snarled outside for over an hour."

Shawna called from over at the window. "They're starting to cast the first ballot." Everyone forgot the conversation and moved over to join Shawna.

Casting ballots at a political convention isn't an orderly nor a speedy affair. The first ballot is the only one that is somewhat predictable in that most state delegations are required to cast their votes according to how the registered voters in their districts voted during the primary. There are several states and territories that don't require this commitment for its delegates but collectively, their numbers don't amount to much. The most important thing is that the commitment to vote as the voters voted is universally only required on the first ballot. After that, if further ballots are needed, each delegate can vote at his or her discretion.

That night by ten-forty-five, what virtually everyone in the United States down to fourth graders already knew, became mathematically certain. Lloyd Stanton was not going to get the nomination on this ballot.

The convention's general chairman wasted no time in regrouping the delegates into beginning a second ballot. The votes as they were cast which was now by electronic means (the first ballot was cast the old-fashioned way—by polling the delegation chairs and recording what they shouted out over the din). Hence, now with this and any other ballots the pace of tallying up the votes would move along much more briskly.

By shortly after eleven, there were two things that were clear: Lloyd Stanton was completely out of it and there didn't seem to be any other candidate that was emerging as a front runner. At eleven-thirty, the general chairman instructed the delegations to caucus internally for thirty minutes and that polling on ballot number three would begin at midnight sharp.

This instruction was interpreted by most delegates as a potty break.

No single candidate got even close to a lead on the third ballot, nor on the fourth, either.

Upstairs in the skybox Laughlin led the Panel members into a side room and closed the door. Stanton had made his excuses after the second ballot and quietly went back to his hotel. That left only Collins, Shawna, and Ellen Laughlin.

These last three were talking idly about what they thought might happen next when Tom Laughlin opened the door and came out to join them. He had a concerned look on his face, and he sat down next to his wife without speaking. He looked up and watched the other members of the Panel slowly file out of the anteroom and come back and sit down. All looked solemn and did not speak.

"What's the matter?" Collins asked casually.

"Buf, we need your help," he said. He looked at Collins with worried eyes.

Collins couldn't tell whether the old man was worried about whether he'd be willing to help or about bigger, more important things. He looked at the others. They looked worried, too. Collins sensed an electricity of tension in the room.

"Sure, Tom," he said smiling trying to keep his demeanor relaxed. "What can I do?"

"The convention is falling apart down there, Buf." Tom Laughlin waved a hand over towards the picture window that looked out over the convention floor. "They have no focus. If they can't find a nominee in the next ballot or so, the whole country will turn against us."

"Oh, I don't know about that, Tom," Collins said. "These things happen." He looked at a blank space on the far wall, thinking. "In fact, I believe that somewhere back in eighteen- . . ."

"Buf!" Laughlin interrupted. "That's not what we need you for—to give us a history lesson."

Collins looked sharply at the old man. "Now, Tom if there's something you people need me for, I'm less inclined to feel helpful if you're rude about it in the asking," he said.

Tom Laughlin arose and stepped over to Collins and patted him reassuringly on the shoulder. "Of course, Buf" he said. "Of course. Please allow me to explain."

Collins looked up at his father-in-law. "Go ahead."

Laughlin took a deep breath. "We need to get the chaos down there under control," he began, talking rapidly. "The delegates need to focus on their mission. They've bogged down and aren't concentrating on finding someone they can support and nominate. There's no reason for the chairman to reconvene the convention the way they presently are. Without some focus, they'll be casting ballots all night, and nothing will happen. It's quintessential that we do something to get them back on track." He glanced at his watch and winced.

"You see, it's already past midnight," he continued. "Eastern time. That means that we've missed both the early and the late nightly news broadcasts everywhere except on the West coast. The major networks have already shut down operation for the night. This means that even if something happens, it won't go on the air until the early morning news. So, they've gone to get some shut eye while they can. The only media reps left are the locals from California and Seattle and some of the print media who have late deadlines, again mostly West coast.

"But none of this changes the fact that without some kind of intervention, the convention is deadlocked.

"So, what we thought we needed was some way to get the delegates back on track." Tom Laughlin looked warily at Collins. "That's when I had a fabulous idea," he said.

Collins was watching his father-in-law carefully. "And that was?" he prompted.

"And My idea was that we needed to put someone up on the podium who could talk some sense into the convention." He smiled smugly. "And Providence provided that someone to me on short notice and also made sure that he'd arrive here just in time."

"Tom, what in the world are you talking about?" Collins asked and looked back at Shawna who had just jabbed him in the arm. "Do you know what he's talking about, Shawna?" he asked her.

"Yup," she said smiling mischievously. "Mr. Laughlin is talking about you, Buf."

Collins' eyebrows shot up in surprise. He glared at his friend in disbelief and then looked over at his father-in-law to see if there was any truth to this. The old man nodded and smiled thinly.

"Me?" Collins spluttered and then burst out laughing. "You've got to be kidding, Tom. What could I do? What would I say to them? They don't even know who I am, for Pete's sake! I'm . . . I'm not even on the agenda! How can I just go down there and step up to the microphone and start talking? How could that be possible? Here at the political convention of all places!" Collins looked at Shawna, then his mother-in-law, and then at the other members of the Panel. He held his hand out towards Laughlin as if he were presenting a certified maniac to them asking for their concurrence of his assessment.

"Now, Buf. Don't sell yourself short here," Laughlin said soothingly. He stepped up close to Collins and spoke in a level voice. "There's probably no one East of the Mississippi who is as skilled as you in getting the attention of an unruly group of people and a master of oratory such that once focused, can sway a group to a collective view on a subject." He smiled humorlessly. Tom Laughlin was not accustomed to showering praise.

"And you, Buf, are sitting right here asking how you can help us," he continued. "Well, we need you now. We need you because you're the only person who can get the teeming masses down there focused on their responsibility."

Laughlin turned and waved a hand at the other men in the room. "I talked to them about this. They're all well aware of your skills and they've concurred with my recommendation." He turned back to face Collins. "The only course of action that we have, is for you to go down there and take control of the convention. What I'm saying, Buf, is that you have to go down there and give the speech of your life. And you've got to do it now." The burden finally off his chest, Tom Laughlin slumped into a chair next to Collins and exhaled loudly.

"But I don't have anything prepared," Collins said plaintively. He was not convinced that he could do anything constructive.

Laughlin laughed under his breath and turned to look at his son-in-law. "That's the sheer beauty of it, Buf. You know and I know that you don't need to have a prepared speech."

Collins knew instantly to what Laughlin was referring. It was a conversation that they had had many years ago when Collins had boasted to his father-in-law about this very thing at the time when the old man was serving as the attorney general. Collins recalled that he'd said that preparation was everything and the man who could do a thorough preparation was going to win nearly all of the time. But a man who is able to think on his feet, he had gone on, a man who could prepare on the fly and change as the whimsy of his audience changed, now that was a man who would win every time. Collins had assured his father-in-law that he was, in fact, just such a man.

Collins thought back on that day and he shook his head slightly. It really wasn't a boast, although he was sure that Laughlin perceived it as one. He believed what he said that day and he believed it to be true to this day. He was indeed just such a man.

Collins realized they were waiting for him to answer.

Laughlin had leaned back into the folds of the chair and was gazing at the ceiling. He spoke without looking at Collins. "Buf, don't you get it? You're our superhero. You're the only one who can go down there and save the day." He got up and put his hand on the lawyer's shoulder. "You've got to do it, Buf. We need you and we need you bad."

Collins felt a cool trickle of perspiration drip down between his shoulder blades and felt engulfed in an oxymoronic mixture of anxiety and excitement.

On the one hand he was nervous about speaking to such a large group of people not to mention that they were not expecting him to do so. And on the other hand, he was stimulated by the challenge. The urgency, the suddenness, the improbability, all added to heighten his interest. In fact, he was already working out some prospective phrases in his mind.

Collins stood up and faced his father-in-law.

"Okay, Tom," he said. "You've convinced me. You say that I'm needed to do this thing and I'm ready to do it."

Laughlin and the others exploded with their approval and went to shake his hand and pound him on the back.

Collins responded to the spontaneous accolade and support from the Panel, Shawna Wells, his mother-in-law and his father-in-law. He grinned broadly and he nodded his head vigorously. He looked at Shawna who was still sitting near him.

"Knock 'em out!" she said encouragingly.

Collins nodded and turned to follow Laughlin down onto the convention floor.

Collins waited in the wings while Laughlin stepped onto the dais and strode over to the general chairman of the convention and whispered several words to him.

Collins looked out over the convention floor. What he saw was sheer chaos. He imagined that he was witnessing a seething hand-to-hand conflict between two warring primeval clans. The banners and flags were swaying and bobbing. The din was deafening. People were walking, running, shoving, talking, shouting, listening, sitting, reading, singing, waving, signaling, talking on cellular telephones, working with laptop computers. In a word, it was a madhouse.

He felt somebody pulling on his arm. He turned to look and found that it was Laughlin beckoning him up onto the dais. He was pointing at the lectern.

Like an automaton, Collins stepped up into the spotlight.

He was literally overwhelmed by the sheer magnitude of it all. His milieu was a courtroom—a space that was perhaps ten thousand times smaller than this convention center and infinitely less noisy. Courts were a womb of silence as that is the way the judges liked it. This situation was totally alien to him. He was used to being in the limelight, yes. But it was a limelight where he had everyone's attention from the beginning. This was true whether he was in the courtroom arguing a case or merely leading a meeting. Either way, when he had the floor, he had control.

He had never encountered anything like this before in his entire life.

He tried to make eye contact with someone. But he could find no one that appeared to have noticed that he was up there or cared. He felt a queer weakness in his knees.

He cast about looking for something to stabilize him. He turned to his left and looked back towards the wings and he saw Shawna there next to Laughlin. She made like she was throwing a right hook in a "go get 'em" gesture. She nodded her head at him, smiling confidently.

That did it. He took a deep breath and spoke into the microphone.

Chapter 9

William Buford Collins, VI stood and contemplated the chaos that raged on before him.

"Ladies and gentlemen! Presidential nomination delegates of the United States!" He searched the crowd for an indication that he was being noticed. Nothing. He knew the sound system was on because he could hear his booming voice echo off the walls over the din.

Who do these idiots think they are? Don't they know that I'm up here? That I'm up here because I'm supposed to be getting them to focus on their mission here?

He looked around. He was singularly being ignored.

Collins had never been ignored by anyone in his entire life. This was a new one for him. And he didn't like it—not one little bit.

Upstairs in the broadcast booth, a correspondent for one of the California stations noticed that someone had stepped up to the lectern.

He had just sent off a live report to his station that the convention was beginning to falter and that at the present rate they might not have a nominee until sometime tomorrow late—like after three p.m.

He picked up a pair of binoculars and zeroed in on this man at the lectern to see if he could tell who it was. The man was not familiar to him. He checked the agenda for this evening and didn't see anyone scheduled to speak at this time. He looked back through the binoculars and saw a well-dressed middle-aged man standing at the lectern looking like a deer caught in the high beams of an oncoming semi-trailer truck. It struck the correspondent at this moment that this man was not a politician and the fact that he appeared to be unsure of himself made him immediately lose interest. He turned away from the window and finished gathering up his stuff. He turned off the light and went out the door without so much as a backward glance.

Sometime the next morning, the correspondent's ears would be literally chewed off by his executive producer for having made this disastrous decision.

Down on the convention floor, Collins stood on the dais and held onto the lectern tightly with both hands, as if he was afraid that he might fall. He thought furiously about what he should say and chastised himself for being so foolish.

There's no one out there who is going to listen to me. Tom and the Panel have no idea what they're up against. Have me give a speech to get them focused! Absurd! Come to think of it, these people out there aren't delegates. They're slugs.

Collins' mind churned on this topic and without realizing it, he began to speak his thoughts out loud.

"You people should be ashamed of yourselves," he began. "You've been entrusted with a mission of honor to come here to Atlanta for this year's political convention. Your mission is to nominate your party's candidate for the most important job in the world. And look at you." He swept his arm out in front of him encompassing the broad width of the convention hall.

"You're violating the trust that has been placed in you," Collins continued, his voice going up a few decibels, at least so that he could hear himself over the thick blanket of noise. "I'm from Virginia and I am personally embarrassed of my state's delegation. That's a fact. Don't you people realize that the people that you have been chosen to represent here are probably so disgusted with your poor performance down here—make that non-performance—that they've stopped watching the convention on tee-vee." He shook his head as one might to a puppy who has soiled its bed. He looked out into the crowd. He couldn't find any set of eyes that was even looking his way.

"Hey!" he shouted into the microphone. "I'm talking to you people! Let's have a little order out there! LISTEN UP, I say!" Collins pounded on the lectern with his fist. He was getting frustrated with this insulting lack of attention, and it was making him furious. The impact of his fist on the heavy wood of the angled paper holder of the lectern surface resonated into the mount of the microphone holder and was picked up by its electronic sensors. The result was a speaker-busting "BOOM-BOOM-BOOM" that shook the walls of the convention center.

This at last got some reaction. Throughout the breadth of the convention floor hundreds of people sensed this alien sound more than heard it. But it was something that caught their attention. They stopped talking (or more appropriately stopped shouting) and looked around trying to identify the sound and its source. The interruption was so short and non-specific that none of the hearkeners were able to associate it with the man who stood up at the lectern on the dais.

But then Collins, now furious started yelling at them again. "Hey! People!" he screamed. "I'm talking to you! And if you know what's good for you, you had better get quiet and start listening and listen good. I'm only going to say this one time."

He started to take them apart, piece by piece. He was a surgeon incising a cancerous body. He was a medical examiner performing an autopsy determining the cause of death. He was a biologist dissecting a specimen, finding out how it functioned.

Perhaps it was the insults. Perhaps it was the invective. Perhaps it was the loudness. Perhaps it was the message. Or possibly it was altogether something else—something animalistic where followers naturally flock to a leader. Something akin to charisma and just as subliminal and instinctual.

Whatever it was. People started to notice Collins at the lectern and began to listen to him. It started with the people closest to the dais and slowly worked its way outward until after about ten minutes nearly everyone on the convention floor was stopping what they were doing and began to concentrate on what Collins was saying to them.

It was one a.m. Eastern time.

The television and radio media people were no longer in the hall. The print media people were also mostly gone. Whoever was left was not paying attention to what was happening on the floor. They were busy trying to make their deadlines and had their noses glued to their laptop computer screens working their File Transfer Protocols at their publication's websites. What they were reporting was that the convention was deadlocked and that the delegates were totally disjointed. They were predicting that there wouldn't be a nominee selected this night and that it might not be until late the next evening before things got back under control. That was the news story of the hour. And as such things go, this was a pretty good story—there was no reason to look around for anything better. So, they were going with it.

As a result, the only people who witnessed the electrifying catharsis of the political convention in Atlanta were those who part of it. All that is, except the man who was its master architect, namely William Buford Collins, VI. He by this time was completely caught up in making his points and he was talking within himself—essentially doing it for his own personal satisfaction. By one-twenty the role reversal was nearly complete. There were thousands of people listening intently to Collins who, before, had hardly been listening to anyone; and there was one person, he who stood at the lectern, who was totally unaware of his audience who, less than several minutes previously was angered because no one noticed that he was speaking to them.

But notice him now, they did. While they listened to Collins scold them for being irresponsible and instill in them the proper sense of responsibility of being a delegate, they frantically scanned the convention program and the evening's agenda looking for this speech and the name of this powerful orator.

It was not listed. The fact that such an impressive speaker, as Collins clearly was, was not on the night's schedule, caused most of the delegates some measure of confusion. It's a natural human trait that once you've noticed someone, you have a strong desire to know the person's name.

The delegates from Virginia knew him and once they quieted down and began to join the masses in listening to Collins, they recognized him. They whispered hastily to the delegates sitting adjacent to them telling them in a few short words who the speaker was. But mostly they concentrated on this man that they knew, this man who was speaking to the convention. They didn't want to miss a word.

By one-thirty-five, Collins started to cut into the president. He voiced his views on why the man didn't deserve the credit he was being given for the worldwide peace treaty. He pointed out a number of transgressions that he showed were the president's doing. He was drawing these words from his own personal views, and he presented them with innate oratorical skill. In addition, Collins' demeanor was much more emotional than in previous iterations. He was feeling a heightened intensity because he was outraged about what his investigation into the corruption was revealing and although he made no mention of it—he was just too good of a lawyer for that—he, for the first time, felt that he was attacking the current administration on a personal basis.

The convention floor was now completely silent. Every pair of eyes was riveted on the speaker at the lectern. Every pair of ears was perked up and concentrating on hearing and understanding each spoken word.

The whispered word-of-mouth spreading of the information about who this man was swept across the floor like a wildfire raging through dry brush.

Later there would be no one who would volunteer that it'd been initially their idea, but the smart money was on someone in the Virginia delegation. It doesn't matter who, when, or how but regardless of the means or motivation at the same time that the news of who the electrifying speaker at the lectern that night was, another message began circulating throughout the convention floor like a nighttime signal being broadcast in the jungle via native drums.

This second message was more than just information—it was a suggestion. The suggestion was provocative and unorthodox, but it universally appealed to the beleaguered delegates. This second message was suggesting that they draft the man at the lectern, this unscheduled speaker who had captured their attention against insurmountable resistance. The idea met favor. It caught on. They listened intently while Collins spoke, chastised, and lectured. They liked what they heard. They liked what they saw. They had this man's name on their lips.

By one-fifty, Collins was beginning to wind down. The surge of adrenaline was abating, and he was enervated by the demand of shouting at the top of his voice for more than an hour. His natural sense of timing telegraphed that he'd accomplished the impossible mission that Tom Laughlin and the Panel had tasked for him. He was proud of himself that he'd been able to do it. He realized that the only noise in the convention hall was now his booming voice, amplified many times by the public address system. He quickly brought his speech to a close.

"And I think that you now all have put yourselves into the proper frame of mind to get on with this convention agenda and do your duty." Collins looked out over the convention floor. He saw every set of eyes fixed on him. This was now his milieu—what he was accustomed to.

"So, I want each and every one of you to give honor to your responsibility of being here." He pointed to various people around the floor. "I want you to take one more ballot and nominate the next president of the United States!"

Collins gave a quick wave, turned on his heel, and strode proudly towards the back of the dais. Tom Laughlin and Shawna were there waiting for him both of whom had stood in the shadows behind Collins for the past hour, totally electrified. Collins was hot and breathing hard as if he'd just run a ten-kilometer race. He leaned over and gave Shawna a quick hug and shook Laughlin's hand.

The crowd that Collins left behind him continued to be silent. They felt that some acknowledgment of this momentous happening was warranted, but there was rampant indecision about whether to applaud, cheer, or what. The end result was that the name, William Buford Collins, VI, was left indelibly on every person's mind.

"Buf, my man," Laughlin spluttered. "That was really quite something. Thank you."

"You were ineffably amazing, Buf," Shawna said breathlessly. "You swooped in there and got them under control. Just like Mr. Laughlin wanted. Just like a superhero!"

"Right." Collins was as gracious as he could be, but he didn't think that he had really done very much. He had just outshouted the delegates, nothing more.

"C'mon, let's get out of here," Laughlin said. "The car's waiting right out here," he continued as he led the way through the darkened area behind the stage. "I'll ride with you to the airport, and we can talk about what brought you down here in the first place."

Once in the car, Collins slumped down in the seat. He was exhausted. It'd been a very long day, but he was still alert. As soon as they were under way, he had Laughlin close up the privacy divider that separated them from the driver. Collins quickly gave Laughlin a run-down on what he suspected the investigation was getting into and the reason why he needed to consult with him.

While they were speeding down the interstate highway, a messenger was delivering a note to the general chairman of the convention. It had been hastily signed by the requisite number of delegation chairpersons making it a valid motion. It proposed that a new name be entered into the convention record as an official nominee candidate.

The convention general chairman stepped up the podium and rapped his gavel. For the first time in what seemed a lifetime, he only needed a couple of raps—it was eerily silent on the convention floor. He put up his hand to shield his eyes from the bright lights and peered out trying to see if everyone was still there. What he saw was that the entire convention was as one and focused on what he was about to say.

"Lady and gentleman delegates!" he said in a normal tone but one that was rich with excitement. "I've been asked to call for the taking of another ballot! There has been a new name placed into the official record and I have heard a motion for placing William Buford Collins into nomination at this convention." He looked out onto the convention floor. "Do I have a second?"

There was a quick roar that was as impressive in its intensity as it was in its brevity. The delegates wanted to get to the quick of the matter.

The chairman took this as a "yea" and moved on. He straightened up and spoke to his fellow conventioneers with a sparkle in his eyes.

"I know that this might be a little unorthodox, but if all of you are as impressed about our last speaker as I am, I'd like to suggest a way that we can get our business taken care of quickly." He paused a moment and then forged on.

"I accept the motion for William Buford Collins to be placed into nomination by this convention. All those in favor say 'aye.'"

The convention center thundered with a raucous cheer. The convention general chairman rapped his gavel for order. It took several whacks this time but remarkably the crowd settled down very quickly.

The chairman stood nervously at the podium, clearly sensing the import of this historical moment. He leaned down and spoke into his microphone.

"All opposed?" he asked.

You could've heard a pin drop. There was not a cough, nor a sneeze. The entire convention was of a cohesive single-minded opinion. They wanted William Buford Collins and no one else.

After an interminable pause, the chairman finally spoke into the microphone. "Since the vote was unanimous, we won't require a roll call. Let the record show that William Buford Collins was nominated by this convention on the fifth ballot and for the first time in the history of our glorious political party we have done so unanimously. Hail, hail to William Buford Collins, the next president of the United States!"

There ensued a roar of elation (and relief) that shook the walls. The delegates had done their jobs and most felt such had been done well even though they had nominated an undeclared candidate for the first time in the history of the republic. Those who thought that this was folly, politically unwise, or even ominous kept it to themselves. For the rest of the evening the celebration continued and spilled over well into the following morning.

By this time, Laughlin, Collins, and Shawna were approaching the airport. Laughlin had considered what Collins had said and had asked a few questions to clarify a couple of things in his mind. Then, he put his chin down on his chest and closed his eyes. Shawna thought that maybe he'd fallen asleep, but Collins knew the old man better than she: He knew that this is what Laughlin did when he was trying to sort through a difficult problem. In the middle of the silence, Laughlin's mobile phone trilled in an inner pocket somewhere. Without hardly moving, he stuck a hand into his jacket and the phone went silent. He apparently was not in the mood for taking any calls at this moment.

Then his eyes snapped open, and he looked up, raising his head. "All right. I think that you should proceed according to your plan—the one that you and Shawna developed—and then modified over this past weekend to accommodate the new charges of collusion." He held up his hand as both Collins and Shawna were about to interrupt. "Yes, I know about that. Finch called me last week and we discussed it before he brought it to you. I knew from what you've told me that you had enough evidence to make collusion stick. So, I told Finch to do what he had to do and follow the president's orders." He stopped for a moment and smiled benignly at his two companions much like a priest would in front of his parishioners.

"I didn't tell Bobby that part of it of course," he continued. "And I suspected that you wouldn't either." This time his smile reflected amusement, and he allowed himself a low chortle. "In spite of yourself Buf, you're playing the game with a flair and panache that will make Gardie James squirm in his seat."

"Tom," Collins interjected in a petulant tone, "I don't feel that I'm playing a game here. This is a very serious business. The problem is that the people who are in charge are the ones who think this is all a game."

Laughlin nodded and patted Collins on the arm. "Yes, yes, of course," he said placatingly. He looked out the window. "Back to the task at hand, my man. We're almost there. My sense of the matter is to work the trial in alignment with the indictments that were handed down by the Grand Jury."

"But what about the . . ." Collins started to inject.

"Wait, Buf," Laughlin said tersely. "I'm not finished. If the charge of collusion is broader that what the Grand Jury found and if there are more public officials involved, even if there are some higher up the ladder of power, even if it goes way up, and even if it leads into culpability for conspiracy and maybe even cover-up, as you've told me about, I think that the best strategy is to do nothing about it now. Keep your Jefferson as you call it to yourselves."

Shawna sat up erect in her seat. Both men quickly looked over at her and saw her eyes shining. "We'll let it come out in testimony. That's it, isn't it?" she said excitedly.

"Exactly, pretty lady," Laughlin said, as if he were praising a prize student. "Exactly. Let it come out in testimony."

Collins nodded his head and smiled knowingly. "Of course, that's the only way to keep it under wraps. It's the only way to make sure that the more powerful ones don't get any advance notice that they're going to be caught up in it. And then it'll be too late for the spin doctors and too late to try to use their authority to somehow squelch the trial or get excluded on some esoteric technicality."

"And that way we avoid undue scrutiny and criticism that we're certain to get if we raised the issue before the trial," Shawna said quietly.

Both men stared at her again.

"I think that this is the best way," Laughlin said, breaking the silence.

There suddenly was a persistent buzzing sound coming from the console. Laughlin glanced over at it. "It's the intercom," he said as he reached over and pressed a button. "Yes, Andy. What is it?"

"Sir," said a disembodied voice, "they're calling you from the convention hall. They've been trying to reach you on your phone, but they can't get through or something. They say that it's urgent."

"Tell them I'll call them back in a few minutes. Whatever it is can wait until then. We're almost finished here. How long until we're at the plane?"

"We're on the ramp right now, sir," came the voice. "Forty-five seconds."

"Right," said Laughlin. "Thank you, Andy."

"Um, Tom," Collins said hesitatingly. "There's one more thing."

"Yes?" Laughlin asked.

"We think that Finch and the president are trying to manipulate us into steering this trial into something that will make any convictions almost impossible."

"Of course, they are!" Laughlin exclaimed. "They realize that acquittals are the best outcome for their image and so, they're using their power and influence to make it come out that way. At this level Buf, you have to realize that everything is political."

Collins glared at his father-in-law. "But if you knew this, why did you get me involved?"

Laughlin gave Collins a pitying look. "Why indeed," he said. "For one it got you your trial as we've discussed—something you wouldn't have gotten any other way, you must know. For another, it gave Finch and James someone they wanted but only on the surface of things."

"How do you mean?" Collins asked.

"I mean that I knew that you'd be too smart for them. I also knew that you had better information than they had. Your investigation was not politically motivated, you see. Therefore, you had all of the information at your disposal—and were able to see it all objectively. You're only interested in justice and have no personal agenda at all. It's, ah, refreshing. This meant, among other things, that you were ready for the collusion end around they tried to pull." He looked over at Shawna and smiled at her. "And my boy, it meant that you had the inside track on how high the corruption and conspiracy went. Finally, it meant that you had the unfettered viewpoint needed to perceive the obvious devolution into conspiracy and to the very clever and subtle cover-up as well."

Both Collins and Shawna stared at the old man in disbelief.

"How the flying . . ." Shawna spluttered.

"You know?" Collins almost shouted. "How could you know about the cover-up?"

Laughlin shook his head, like this was something he found hard to fathom. "Buf, how could you not know that I'd know about this? Or at least suspect it. This kind of stuff is in my wheelhouse. My bread and butter, you understand. Of course, I know about the corruption and the cover up. It's something that I've known about for some time and all along I've been trying to devise a way to stop it and also, figure out how to nail the creeps who are doing it. Then, along came Lucy and her husband's murder."

"That and the study report at the eff-bee-eye academy that got Finch interested," Shawna said. "Both dovetailing together to tailor-make this thing for Buf to handle." She shook her head. "Remarkable. Effing amazing."

Laughlin smiled thinly. "Well, Roland Walton's death. That was a random event, I'll grant you that. But it fit into the scheme and the timing nicely, nonetheless. But the study report? No, my Dear, that was something that I crafted up. You see? From the get-go, there was never going to be anything that Buf could do about what he was going to find out—what I already knew. What I needed was to create the venue where Buf could do it and do it his way.

"It's worked out rather well so far, don't you think?" Laughlin added somewhat boastfully.

They were suddenly at the plane. Laughlin nodded his head and patted the two on their shoulders and Collins and Shawna almost skipped up the steps. They both felt remarkably refreshed. The counsel with the old man had lifted their spirits immeasurably.

It was past two-thirty in the morning.

CHAPTER 10

Laughlin stood on the tarmac and watched his private jet taxi off with Collins and Shawna aboard.

He was approached by a man "Excuse me, sir?"

Laughlin turned to look at him. "Yes, Andy. What is it?"

"Er, they're calling you from the convention again. What should I tell them?"

"Oh, all right!" Laughlin exclaimed turning back towards the car. "Tell them to call me on my phone. I'm turning it back on." He stepped into the open door of the limousine. "What on Earth could be so important that it can't wait until I get back?" he muttered under his breath.

A few seconds later his mobile phone trilled, as the car started to leave the ramp area.

"Yes, what is it?" Laughlin spat into the mouthpiece.

There was a loud burst of a digitally configured voice on the other end. The words were all run together, and the voice was highly excited.

"All right, all right," Laughlin said after a minute. "Calm down. This isn't the end of the world. In fact, it was something that I half expected when I asked him to go out there and do it." He listened to a response. "No, no. There's no way that I could've planned this, of course. But given the predicament that we were in and the fact that he needed to come down here to talk to me about another matter—and factor in the contorted timing what with the weather and all—it afforded us an option that we otherwise would not have had. You play the cards that you're dealt, you know." There was another pause while the old man listened. "I'd say that we should consider ourselves lucky. With Collins as the nominee, we know exactly what we have. With someone else . . . who knows?"

The voice crackled over the connection for several seconds while Laughlin listened. "What?" Laughlin said. "Oh, right. Damn! Well, I guess I should be the one who tells him. I think that I'll be able to convince him that this is actually a good thing for him. Okay, then. I guess that I won't come back there right now. I'll stay here at the airport and rustle up a flight to Washington and try and catch up with him, hopefully before he hears about it on the news."

It was a weary seventy-eight-year-old man who peeked through the kitchen window of the Collins home shortly after six the next morning. He was a man of eminently extensive resources. First, he was the only passenger, flying gratis, on a commercial plane deadheading up to National Airport only about an hour behind Collins and Shawna who were flying in the *Lady Jane*. Then, once he arrived at Collins' home, he was waved through a make-shift roadblock at the end of the drive that had been hastily put together by the Secret Service about two hours before. This was Laughlin's idea—the roadblock. The protection was set up with the Director of the elite enforcement agency of the Executive Branch while on the flight up from Atlanta, a bit after three-thirty a.m. Remarkably the director was awake working in his home office, apparently dealing with the emergency that had arisen overnight: a new presidential nominee and no one knew who he was, let alone where he was. If left to their own devices the Secret Service would have run a full-force assault on the Collins home at dawn once they found out where it was. The old man knew that this would have been extremely traumatizing since Jane and Buf would not know why they were being invaded. Everything had to wait until he got there.

He saw movement inside the kitchen and then Jane's remarkable face loomed into the window over the sink and peered back at him. He immediately felt refreshed, and the wear and tear of the convention week and a sleepless night sloughed off of him like rain off a duck's back. She had that kind of effect on him, his only child.

In turn, she recoiled in shocked recognition seeing her father staring back at her. She turned and went to the Dutch door that led out onto the patio and let him in.

"Dad!" she exclaimed. "Aren't you supposed to be in Atlanta? Isn't the conven—? Wait! Is Mom okay?" She stared at him, her eyes wide open with fearful excitement.

"It's okay, Janie," he said soothingly. "Everything's okay. Mom's just fine." He gave her a hug and kissed her cheek lovingly. Then he went over to the kitchen table and sat down heavily. "Is the coffee ready yet?" he asked.

She nodded her head. "Just now finished perking." She poured him a mugful and brought it to him but didn't sit. She was still not understanding this sudden visit. "So? If everything's okay Dad, why are you coming over at oh-dark-thirty in the morning when you're supposed to be doing important stuff five hundred miles from here? Did they run out of coffee in Georgia?"

"No, Janie," he said calmly. Even though the moment justified a testy reaction and even though he felt like a truck had hit him, he never was able to be cross with this beautiful woman, who reminded him of the woman he married in almost every way. "I'm here to talk to Buf, uh, to both of you, actually. I'm assuming he's been sound asleep in bed for about an hour or so now by my reckoning. Could you please go get him? Tell him it's very important." He suddenly thought of something. "You haven't been listening to the radio or watching tee-vee this morning, have you?"

Jane was on her way to the stairs and stopped to face her father. "No, not yet. Why?"

Laughlin shook his head and motioned for her to continue on her mission. "You'll know soon enough. And don't answer the telephone either until we talk, all right?" Almost on cue the instrument on the kitchen wall next to the refrigerator began to ring.

Jane frowned and looked at the phone.

"Go! Before Buf answers it, Janie! Go!" Laughlin prompted.

About ten minutes later Laughlin sat at the kitchen table and looked across at his rested and refreshed daughter and her haggard and groggy husband. There were large steaming mugs of coffee for the men and tea in a dainty China teacup and matching saucer for the lady.

"What's the matter, Tom? Something you forgot to tell me last night? Or rather earlier this morning?" In spite of the lack of sleep, the abruptness of the intrusion, and the obvious undercurrent of urgency, Collins still had a sense of humor. This was a trio that shared a life-long trust and intimacy.

Laughlin was about to speak and was interrupted by the ringing of the telephone. He shook his head at Jane as she was about to get it.

"This is what it's going to be like for a while, I'm afraid. It's why I've come here to tell you about it in person," he said in a grave tone.

"Tell us about what, Dad?" Jane asked. She was the more alert of the two and hence was taking the lead.

"Something happened last night at the convention after we left to go to the airport," Laughlin said cryptically. "Something rather significant and although I'm sure that you're going to be very shocked, I trust that you will eventually see that it's going to be a good thing for you and what you're doing with the corruption trial and all."

"Quit stalling, Tom," Collins muttered, still fighting with his body and brain that wanted to go back to bed. "Spit it out. We can take it. What happened last night?"

"Well, er, it was an anomaly. Perfectly legitimate I assure you but an extremely rare occurrence nonetheless." The old man was still having trouble getting to the point.

"What kind of anomaly?" Jane asked politely. She was not having the same difficulty as her husband, and she saw no reason to hurry her father along.

"First of all, Janie Dear, I suppose that you and Buf haven't talked since he got back. No, of course not, you were asleep when he got here. Well, in short, last night at the convention by the time Buf and Ms. Wells arrived, the convention was deadlocked, and it didn't look good for them to find a nominee. That was when I had the ingenious idea of getting Buf to go out and try to calm them down and get them to focus. You know how good of an orator he is.

"Well, it took some convincing but even though that's not why he'd come down to see me, he agreed to try to help. And I must say that he outdid himself. You should've been there, Janie. Your husband wowed the convention. It was really something to see—mesmerizing. It's too bad that it was so late—long after the media coverage shut down. So, I'm not sure if it even got on videotape. A true shame that.

"Anyway, the good news is that after Buf did his magic on them, the delegates rallied and were able to vote in a new nominee. This was all happening as I was taking Buf and Ms. Wells back to the airport very early this morning."

"Who did they nominate, Dad?" Jane asked. "Lloyd Stanton? Did he finally make it anyway?"

"No, Janie," Laughlin answered with some regret in his voice. "No, interestingly, the delegates nominated someone who was not a declared candidate. This is the anomaly that I was talking about. In other words, they drafted the new nominee."

"A non-declared candidate?" Collins asked. "Who? How does such a thing happen? Do they start looking in the white pages of the phone book or something?"

"Well, as I said, it's very unusual probably for just those very reasons," Laughlin answered levelly. "It's pretty inconceivable that a political convention can put a name into nomination that hasn't been known to them in the specific context of the election campaign. In other words, they can't just pick a person at random. There's no way that such a person would get enough votes. The same thing goes for a particular group of delegates, like from one state, trying to put up a local favorite. It's not likely that anyone else would know the person, let alone like him enough to vote for him—or her. That's why it never happens—um, in fact, I believe that this is the first time. The point is that even if the person isn't a declared candidate, he, or she, still has to be commonly known to most of the delegates somehow at the time they're trying to vote for a nominee. Last night by fluke of flukes such a thing happened. And in frustration or desperation, call it what you will, the delegates liked this undeclared candidate better than anyone else."

Collins and Jane stared at the old man sorting through what he'd been saying. Then Jane sat up straight, her eyes widening in surprise.

"Wait! Dad! You're not talking about . . . !" She was having difficulty saying out loud what she thought she knew. "That's why you're here, isn't it? That's why you had to come here in person!" She sucked in her breath in a quick rush and looked at her husband. "Buf! Father's here to tell us that the undeclared candidate, the new nominee, is . . . is you!"

Collins smirked at his wife and then began to laugh. "That's ridiculous," he said between guffaws. Then he looked at Laughlin and saw that the humor was lost on the old man. He suddenly realized that Jane was not joking and then had a tremendous wallop feeling deep in his stomach.

"That's why you're here?" he asked Laughlin. "Jane's right about this, Tom?"

Laughlin nodded.

There was a sharp rap at the door through which Laughlin had entered and all three turned to look. A tall man with dark sunglasses, dark suit, white shirt, and dark tie stood in the doorway. He had an earphone plugged into one ear and was holding a dark-haired woman by the arm. She looked a fright, hair in disarray, rumpled sweatshirt and jeans, jogging shoes untied, no make-up.

But it was Shawna Wells, nonetheless, and in spite of just as much lack of sleep as Collins, her eyes were shining brightly.

"Er, excuse me, folks," the tall man said, "I'm special agent Johnson and this woman insisted that you knew her and . . ."

"Yes, yes, Johnson," Laughlin said, "we know her. Thank you for escorting her up to the house. We'll get you guys straightened out with the proper visitor list and the other protocols later this morning. All right?"

The man released Shawna and Jane took her quickly into custody. He then nodded curtly and turned on his heel and disappeared.

"Buf! Have you seen the news?" Shawna spluttered over her shoulder while Jane was getting her some tea.

"Mmmm," Collins muttered. He was still sorting through the impact of what Jane and her father had just hit him with. "No, not yet" he responded absentmindedly. "Is there something happening?"

Shawna came over to the table and stared at the lawyer with her mouth hung open. "Well, yeah!" she said with the typical inflection of the vernacular. "You could say that something's happening and it's not another perfect game in baseball either."

Collins looked up sharply at her and then realized that she was talking about the same thing that they had been talking about before she arrived and, of course, why she'd come over instead of staying in bed.

"Oh!" was all he could muster.

Then after Jane got Shawna settled at the table and began scurrying around the kitchen putting together a makeshift breakfast for four, Collins looked up at Laughlin. He seemed to have just thought of something.

"Tom!" he exclaimed. "I have the trial starting on Monday! I can't be the party's nominee and still do the trial, can I? No, that's ridiculous. And if I accept the nomination, hypothetically speaking of course, it's not possible that Finch will let me out of doing the trial will he?"

He started to fidget in his chair. The dilemma was clearly starting to get to him. He looked down at the table, dejected and then quickly looked up at the others as if he'd found the key to the problem.

"Aha! I know how to fix it. I turn down the nomination or whatever the proper term for it is. I have a conflict because I'm doing the trial, right? And I wasn't trying to get nominated anyway. I have no aspirations of getting into politics. Tom, you can fix this, can't you? It's a big mistake and surely, they'll understand that I can't take the nomination and run for president. Right?" The strength of his conviction that was fiery and strong at the beginning of making his argument began to run out of steam towards the end and his last words were spoken almost in a whisper.

Laughlin was waiting patiently for Collins to get it all out before he spoke. Just when he thought this moment had arrived and he was about to respond to Collins the silence was broken by Jane.

"Buf, Dear," she said, speaking over her shoulder while she poked at a skillet of frying bacon with a pair of tongs. "Maybe being the presidential nominee and the special prosecutor for the corruption trial gives you a special stature."

Everyone turned to stare at her.

"I mean look at the big picture here. As just the special prosecutor, you and Shawna are dealing with a bunch of people that you're not sure you can trust and even though you want to get convictions it's clear that Finch and the president don't. It'd be very difficult to succeed under those conditions, don't you think? Maybe it'd even come down to a struggle for survival, you know? Your career might hang in the balance. Then, if you took the nomination and got out of the trial somehow, what a mess that would be! Right? You're not a politician and trying to campaign against Gardner James what with all his current popularity and all would be a horrendous experience."

She started to take the cooked bacon strips out of the grease and pat them down on a plate with a paper towel. "So, I'm thinking that it's a pretty neat thing for you as the special prosecutor to have suddenly become a presidential nominee. It gives you an autonomy that you otherwise could never have gotten. And in turn, being the special prosecutor of a very high-profile corruption case, gives you the perfect venue for being a presidential nominee who, oh by the way, knows absolutely nothing about politics and campaigning." She stopped talking as she completed the bacon exercise.

Everyone at the table continued to mutely stare at her as if they were trained animals anxiously awaiting their master at feeding time.

Jane turned to glance at the three listeners and seemed surprised that they were so rapt with her discourse. Here she was cooking and making idle chit-chat about this recent turn of events more or less to pass the time and the others appeared as if they were hearing her give the formula for eternal youth. She turned off the burner underneath the bacon skillet and turned around to face them.

"Buf, I know that you're tired, Sweetheart, but when you take a global view of all this, it seems to me that getting the nomination is a good thing. Don't you think?"

"Jane has a pretty good point, Buf," commented Shawna. "Just think about it. What better way for you to out-maneuver the shysters on this corruption trial? As the lowly prosecutor you have the ay-gee and the president to answer to. Under ordinary circumstances, you're stuck with that pecking order. There's no conceivable way to, you know, leapfrog over them. Right?

"But now here you have a silver bullet, if you will, go kerplop in your lap. Being the presidential nominee for your party gives you a stature that places you pretty much on a par with the president. From this moment on you no longer are at his bidding. Essentially, with the nomination you become an independent agent. It seems to me that you should welcome this fluke of fate as opposed to looking for a way to get out of it."

Collins looked from Jane to Shawna and then to his father-in-law. "Each of the two things seem to be so far apart. I'm having trouble sorting it all through. How can I take on both and not mess at least one of them up?"

"Good point, Buf," Laughlin said. "On the surface of it, you're exactly right. How can you do both when each one seems to call for a completely different set of actions in totally difference places. That's the dilemma, right?

"But I like the way that Janie's seeing it. She says that if you stand back from it far enough the two things merge together. When I do this, it has a harmonic resonance that I very much like."

"But if I leverage my prosecutorial position by being the nominee and thus continue with the trial, what will happen to the campaign? Won't the party be throwing the election?" Collins was having paradigm paralysis.

"Not necessarily, Buf," Laughlin said. "As Janie has astutely pointed out, the courtroom is your bailiwick and what better way for you to show the American people who you are and so forth is to do so in a venue where you're comfortable and can be yourself. And don't forget that it's still only August. There's a reasonable likelihood that the trial won't go on for two-and-a-half months."

Collins shook his head. "I still don't get it. So, if I accept the nomination and then stay with the trial, isn't it possible that Finch, or more probably the president, will dump me and find someone else?"

Everyone stared at him as if this contingency hadn't occurred to them.

"That's certainly possible, Buf," Laughlin said. "But . . ."

"But they won't do it," blurted out Shawna, looking excited again. "Hey! This is fantastic! The president and Finch won't take you off the trial once you take the nomination. No! Uh uh. Can't you see? They will actually think that keeping you on the trial is the best thing. For one it will prevent you from campaigning, and they as inveterate politicians will be blinded by their predilections. They think that the only way to campaign is the way that they do it. And for two, they will think that by manipulating the trial and the charges, et cetera, just like the way they've been doing it so far, they will have the best opportunity to make you look bad. In their minds, keeping you on the trial is perfect. That way they're assured of getting both things that they want: acquittals in the trial and reelection."

"But what they don't know, Buf," Laughlin interjected, "is that you've got the goods on them even if the charges get upgraded again to conspiracy and then to cover-up, and you have the secret weapon that over the course of the trial you're going to show that the corruption, collusion, and conspiracy reach much farther up the power ladder than indicated by the original indictments." He smiled benignly.

"And don't forget that you have a silver bullet in your back pocket, namely that you can prove cover up," Laughlin added. "I'd say that we have a very exciting six or seven weeks ahead of us."

At that moment Jane arrived with large tray holding a bowl of scrambled eggs, a platter of buttered toast, and the plate of bacon.

CHAPTER 11

Before they could get through eating the sumptuous breakfast that Jane had hastily prepared, they were again interrupted by a knock at the door. It was the same agent and this time he had Robert Finch in tow. Finch looked like he highly objected to the notion that he had to be escorted.

After Laughlin nodded his head and the agent had departed, Finch stormed into the room. Although he was nattily dressed, that he was clearly agitated was heralded by his wide-open eyes and dilated pupils and other little cues such as his tie being slightly askew and his jacket open and one shoe was untied.

"Buf!" he spluttered, ignoring the presence of everyone else. "What on Earth is going on? I saw something on the early news this morning as I was getting dressed and they were saying that you were nominated by the convention last night. Is that right? How could such a thing have happened? You weren't at the convention. You're not a politi— uh, not a candidate. How could they know about you to put your name into nomination? What is going on? I don't understand."

Everyone watched the attorney general of the United States ramble on like this in a most unbecoming display of someone who had totally lost his composure. Then after the man seemed to have run down or at the very least run out of breath, Collins ventured to speak.

"Bob, I don't think that you've met my wife Jane," he said calmly.

Finch dropped open his mouth and turned to look at Jane who was busy clearing the dishes off the table. The sense that he'd burst in on them unannounced and had impolitely subjected them to his diatribe suddenly hit him and he then realized that even under the circumstances and even given his stature as the head lawyer in the country, he had no right to act the way he was. He hung his head sheepishly and muttered,

"No, Buf. I haven't had the pleasure." He stuck out his hand to shake Jane's and then noticed that Tom Laughlin was sitting at the table. If he had just now felt bad for his poor manners, the realization that he had put on his performance in the full view of Laughlin plunged his spirits to a nadir lower than he'd ever experienced in his life.

It took some of Jane Collins' country breakfast to bring Finch back to a semblance of normalcy. While he sat and ate, Laughlin filled him in on what had happened in Atlanta and unequivocally assured the attorney general that it was a complete fluke.

"So, Buf's not going to accept it is he?" Finch asked innocently. "The nomination, I mean."

"Well, we were in the midst of discussing it when you arrived, Bob," Laughlin said smoothly. "Either way the outcomes aren't ideally attractive. What do you think? Do you think he should turn it down?"

"I, uh, well," Finch faltered, apparently thinking hard about this, "let it not be unto me to advise you on political strategy, Tom." He forked another bite while he continued to think of a suitable answer. "And of course, I want to stay completely away from involving myself in matters of the opposing political party, you must know." He chewed a bit and swallowed. "But . . . if the convention and the delegates drafted him, to turn the nomination down would seem to cause a great deal of unnecessary disruption . . . and . . . if Buf really wants to take it . . . I don't see that being the nominee really hurts anything. My concerns go to how this affects the trial. I really don't have any interest in how Buf's prosecutorial responsibilities might affect his nomination, you see? After all, he's assured me that he'll get the corruption and collusion trial over within less than a month. Right?" He shot a glance at Collins. "Sooo, I can't advise you on what to do, of course. I'm just saying that if you take the nomination, I won't object."

So, they left it that way—for the time being. All was a bustle of activity. Finch made his excuses saying he had a full day of meetings and left. Shawna went home to get cleaned up saying she'd be back in an hour or so. Laughlin spent a few minutes talking to the Secret Service agent-in-charge down at the gate and then came back. He took a shower in one of the Collins' guest bathrooms and said that he was going to take a "short" nap. There were many things that he needed to do, most of which couldn't wait. He and Buf agreed to meet in Buf's study at around ten.

Buf was too keyed up to go back to bed. His brain was aswirl with a myriad of thoughts: What about this? What about that? What if it were done this way? What if it were done that way? He and Jane stayed in the kitchen while she putzed about and off and on they talked idly while he sorted through his thoughts.

Shortly before ten, Shawna returned. She was dressed in a simple black skirt and pale blue blouse, sheer hose, low heels and minimal accessories: a watch, a gold chain bracelet on the other wrist, tiny loop earrings, and a micro chain gold necklace that peeked out from behind the collar of her blouse. Her short hair was still a little damp and brushed back and she was wearing just a little foundation make-up and a hint of eyeliner, blush, and lipstick.

Jane and Buf stared at her as she entered as if they were witnessing an apparition.

"Shawna!" Buf exclaimed. "Wow! You look like a million bucks."

"I can't believe that the alley cat that was here earlier and the goddess that is here now are one in the same girl," Jane said, smiling with approval, giving the young woman a quick hug. "I want to know your secret."

In spite of the minimalist approach to her garmenture and preparation, Shawna Wells did indeed this day look marvelous. But it was the inner beauty that was radiating at a thousand watts and was making the distinguishing difference. Her eyes were ablaze with excitement and her demeanor was upbeat and excitable. She was so up that Buf and Jane felt her electricity to be palpable. And it was contagious. Collins had earlier shrugged off his weariness what with the stimulation of the heady events that were happening in his life, but now felt an infusion of energy from Shawna's fire much like he was receiving a transfusion of new, super energized blood through a fire hose. And Jane, who was normally a perky person and had been boosted this day with the excitement of important visitors bearing headline level news, now in Shawna's glow began to feel a sense of euphoria, a mental and emotional high that happens to long-distance runners and power workout junkies.

"Shawna, my Dear," Collins said. "You look like you've won the lottery."

Shawna beamed. "I have, Buf," she answered in a bubbly voice. "I feel that I *have* won the lottery. I went home feeling a bit ragged but as I drove, I started to think about the trial and what we're planning to do with the escalated charges and so on. And then I realized that if you take the nomination, just as Jane says, you'd be able to prosecute the trial independent from Finch and the president. You'd no longer be under their control as you've been so far. It'd give you much more of a free rein. That really got my juices flowing because for the first time I really got a sense that we could win this thing—the trial, I mean. Then, with the momentum of this heightened confidence, I started thinking about your suspicion that the corruption reaches higher up, and I realized that we've got the opportunity to eradicate this cancer that's been invading our cities and that we might be able to help the many hundreds of families who have suffered terrible losses without any retribution over the past several years. Buf! Do you realize what we've the chance to do? We can be the paladins of justice. We can vindicate all those poor people who think that the deaths of their loved ones were suspicious but couldn't get the authorities to do anything about them!

"And that's why I am bouncing off the treetops. I feel like I'm the luckiest girl in the whole wide world because I get to play in the biggest game in town."

Jane stepped over to her and gave her another hug, but this time a full and warming embrace, and then turned to look at her husband. "She's right about this, Buf. This is a remarkable opportunity, don't you think?"

Collins was silent. Both women looked at him wondering if he'd heard his wife's question. Then he looked up, focusing his eyes on them. "Yes, Jane," he replied, "I agree it's something special. And I share in Shawna's enthusiasm. It's going to be the trial of our lives and with the nomination we'd have the upper hand and the autonomy to make our own choices. We, as Shawna says, are being afforded a unique opportunity to stop the injustice—to do something worthwhile in this crazy world. But what I was just now thinking was that something that

Shawna said has made me finally see the point that Jane was making this morning."

Jane raised her eyebrows. "Me? Was I making a point? All I recall is making breakfast."

Collins smiled lovingly at her. "No, Darling," he said, "you're dissembling. Don't try to deny it. You were the one who saw the silver lining in the nomination thing, remember? You said that being the nominee would help me and Shawna with the trial and this is why Shawna has come back here feeling like she's on top of the world. But you also said that being the prosecutor of the trial would help me with the nomination. It was that observation that I had some reservations about at the time. But now, it has just hit me that your insight on this is just as true.

"I'm saying that I now see how being in the trial really does afford me a unique opportunity, if I take the nomination."

"If you take the . . . ?" Shawna started to ask.

"But!" Jane interrupted, a signal of alarm in her voice. "You mean that you've been thinking of not accepting the nomination?"

"Yes, I have . . . until just now." Collins looked at the two women calmly. "C'mon now, you two! Give me a break here, okay? I mean, look at it. I'm not a politician. In fact, you both can swear emphatically that I hate politics. Right? So, what in the world would someone like me do as a presidential nominee? On the surface of it, I find the idea abhorrent. When I found out about it from Tom this morning, I must admit that I felt a bit of titillation, but I have to say that it was just a feeling of satisfaction that I'd done the impossible. I'd succeeded in doing what Tom wanted me to do. I got the convention and the delegates under control. That was all. I didn't feel happy about what the delegates did with the composure that I helped them gain, however. No.

"In fact, all this morning here in the kitchen with Jane I've been trying to work through in my mind a reasonable way to turn the nomination down. Look at it from my perspective. I like what I'm doing. I'm a good trial lawyer. We have everything we want: money, stature, health, good kids. Right? There's no way that I'd want to jeopardize any of that by jumping into the political fray and then as a presidential nominee. It'd be insanity personified. Do you realize what the media frenzy will be like? Our happiness, our serenity, our privacy would all end in a microsecond.

"I have to admit that it all scared me and up until a moment ago I was in no way going to accept the nomination."

"But . . ." Jane started to say.

"But what made you change your mind?" Shawna interrupted, it now being her turn to probe into Collins' thought process.

"As I was telling you," Collins continued, "something that Shawna said hit me like a ton of bricks. It was the chance that we'd be able to do something in the trial with me being the nominee, something that we didn't have the right to hope for otherwise. That was when it dawned on me that taking the nomination really mattered."

"You realized that taking the nomination was critical to the success of the trial and so you started to change your mind?" Shawna inquired.

"No," Jane offered softly, "you've just now realized that being in the trial and having the chance to win and take the corruption up as high as it goes makes being the nominee the most important thing you could ever do in your life."

Collins looked at his wife with awe. "It suddenly became like an integrated whole, just like you said this morning, Dear. These are not two things; they are one. The cohesiveness of it, the synergism, the symbiosis of the two connecting together with machinelike precision. It's eerie. And it brings tears to my eyes. The one thing that I find totally numbing is that the nomination makes winning the trial possible, like it's the only way to win it; and being in the trial—this particular trial—is the only way for me to want to run for public office. In fact, the only public office that would matter is the presidency.

"You see it don't you?" he asked, his eyes flashing brightly.

"What?" asked Shawna.

"See what?" asked Jane.

"The way they fit together so beautifully," answered Collins. "The key to winning."

"Winning the trial?" queried Shawna.

"Winning the election?" suggested Jane.

"Yes," answered Collins.

"What?" asked Shawna.

"Both?" offered Jane.

"Yup," Collins said, nodding his head. "It's becoming clearer and clearer to me the more I think about it. The only way for us to have the slimmest chance of winning the trial is for me to be able to prosecute it independently of Finch and the president. Under ordinary circumstances how could this be possible? It's completely in their authority and right there in their own sandbox. They own it and make all the rules. I'd be just their puppet. But . . . as the nominee, it's a brand-new ball game.

"Then, look at the other side of it. There's not anything more ridiculous than nominating a non-declared, non-politician to run for president, is there? It's a joke. A national embarrassment. Right? I'd look bad and my campaign would be so pitiful that Gardner James would be assured of a place in the history books having coasted to victory with a ninety percent winning margin, or some ungodly thing. But what if his opponent were to avoid the normal and traditional presidential campaign drill and stay completely away from the political arena? What if the nominee were doing something *more important*, if such an outrageous notion was possible? What if that nominee personified the viability of the candidacy by not being a politician? What if that nominee was trying to accomplish something that really mattered to every single man, woman, and child in the country? Something that means more to them than the election. What then?

"It's this revelation—that being in the trial gives me the only way for someone like me to be a presidential nominee—that has made me change my mind."

"So, you're going to accept the nomination?" Shawna asked.

"Yes," Collins answered.

"Good choice, Buf," said Laughlin as he entered the room. "Really, as I'm sure that you've now realized, it's the only choice."

Collins looked at his wife. "That is, if it's okay with you, Jane Dear."

Jane looked at her husband, lovingly and then glanced at her father. "Of course, Darling," she said. "I trust in your judgment implicitly and even if it were not so perfect and synergistic, I'd support you anyway."

"All right then," said Laughlin in a businesslike manner. "Now that that's settled, we've got a lot of work to do." For an elderly man who had been up all night and also had been working a tortuous schedule for the past few weeks, he appeared rested and refreshed. "The first thing is to plan a press conference for this afternoon. Then, you need to think about your acceptance speech, Buf. Next, I think you and Shawna should move out of your offices in Justice and go back to your own offices. This will first of all be simpler and easier for you and also, it'll afford you the opportunity to proceed with the trial, and also the business of the campaign with a reasonable amount of privacy. And . . . it'll be better for you to deal with Finch because as the trial-slash-campaign progresses, I can assure you he'll become more and more difficult."

"Why will he become more difficult?" asked Jane.

"Because Gardie James will be eating his lunch every day that the trial's progress gives off the slightest hint that Buf and Shawna might be getting closer to getting convictions," Laughlin answered patiently.

"And anything but unequivocal acquittals in the trial is politically unacceptable to the president," Shawna added.

Laughlin nodded solemnly in acknowledgement.

Robert Finch stood and silently watched the man in the big chair think through what he'd just told him. He could anticipate what his reaction would be but what he was anxious about was how it was going to make his life more complicated. He was already working an insane schedule, putting in more than a hundred hours a week. He rued that he should've taken off during Memorial Day weekend a couple of months back when he'd had the chance. There was not going to be any such luxury on Labor Day weekend, of this he was certain.

Gardner James swiveled his chair back around to face his attorney general. He leaned forward and put his elbows and forearms on the chief executive's desk and clasped his hands together. He smiled thinly at Finch.

"Okay, so you think that Collins is going to accept the nomination, huh? Well, for your sake, and I guess mine, let's hope that he does." He shot Finch a sly glance. "You're sure that you played it right, aren't you?"

"Yes sir," Finch answered respectfully. "I soft-pedaled it just like we discussed. I made it look like I was only concerned about the health of the trial and couldn't care a whit about the nomination. I told them that as long as Collins could assure me that he wouldn't lose his focus on the trial, I had no interest in his extracurricular activities." He smiled slightly in amusement at his sarcasm.

The president nodded, agreeably. "Yes, that sounds pretty good. I wish I'd been there to see how Laughlin took it. You say that he didn't say much?"

"No, Tom was pretty quiet," Finch answered.

"Hmmm," James mused. "He's pretty cagey. You don't think they're playing us for the patsy, do you?" He sounded a bit worried that perhaps all was not well.

"Um, I don't think so, Mr. President," Finch responded, trying to sound confident. "I mean what could they be up to? First of all, it's completely inconceivable that Laughlin has planned this whole thing in the short amount of time since Stanton's downfall back in June. Right? He's a powerful man—maybe the most powerful in the country, excepting, of course, you—but he's not God. There are some things that he can't control. We have to accept the nomination of Collins as a fluke and on balance it looks like it's a good thing for us."

"You think so?" inquired the president, genuinely curious.

"Absolutely, sir," Finch said. "We don't want the trial to succeed. Right? We'll take acquittals and we'll take a mistrial. What better way is there to assure that sort of outcome than for our special prosecutor to be distracted? What better way is there to distract someone than to throw him into a media circus like a presidential campaign? Given that we're pulling the strings on the charges and so on, I'd say that we've got a lock on this."

The president drummed his fingers on the top of his desk. "Mmmm," he murmured. "I hope you're right, Bobby. I hope you're right. It just seems . . . I don't know. It just seems like it's a bit too perfect, somehow. I don't know about you, but somehow, I've a sneaky feeling that I'm about to fall into a trap or something. In my experience there's no such thing as a windfall, you know? Those things are almost always a Trojan horse."

Finch hesitated a moment. "Do you have any thoughts about what else we can do, sir? You know, to hedge our bets—load the odds just a little bit more in our favor?"

The president looked directly into Finch's eyes. "Yes, Bobby, I do," he said in a sinister tone. "First, I think that we need to upgrade the charges again, but this time let's wait until after the trial is in full swing."

"Upgrade the charges again?" Finch was surprised. "To what?"

"Conspiracy," said the president.

"What!" Finch was dumfounded. "Conspiracy! That's outrageous. There's no evidence of conspiracy."

"All the better to acquit you with, my Dear," mocked the president, paraphrasing from the Grimms' famous fairy tale of Little Red Riding Hood.

"Ah!" Finch said nodding his head. "I get it. Keep one step ahead of Collins and Wells. Yes. This is really good. I'll get working on it right away." He was about to leave when the president stopped him.

"Oh, and another thing, Bobby," James said.

"Yes, Mr. President?" Finch asked.

"I think that we need to do something else, as well."

"All right. What is it?" Finch wondered what James could be up to.

"Sit down, Bobby," the president said. "Sit down. We need to go over the list of judges who could sit for the trial and pick one that we know will be the most sympathetic to our goals."

Finch sat but then began to stand. "But Mr. President, that's tampering! We can't do that."

James gave Finch a withering look. "Of course, we can do that, Bobby. We're the ones, or at least I am, who appoints the judges. Right? That means that we can mix and match them as we see fit. We just aren't going to tell anyone about it. Okay?"

Finch was silent. He didn't like this but as it was the epitome of presidential politics, he was helpless to prevent it.

Jane brought a large tray of coffee, tea fixings for Shawna, and some cookies into Collins' study where he, Shawna, and Laughlin were conferring on plans, strategies, and tactics.

Her husband was saying as she entered something about trying to stay one step ahead of Finch and the president on keeping control of the trial.

"And you realize that they're going to up the charges to conspiracy at the least convenient moment, right?" asked Laughlin.

"Right, and we're already way ahead of them on that," Shawna said.

"Okay, then," Laughlin said with some satisfaction. "I guess that's about as much as we can do about the trial for now. I feel pretty good about the prospects, don't you?"

Jane put down the tray and straightened up, smoothing her hands down on her smock.

"What about the judge?" she asked.

Everyone stared at her.

"What judge, Dear?" Collins asked.

"The judge who's going to oversee the trial," she replied.

"What about the judge?" asked Laughlin.

"Do you know who it's going to be?" inquired Jane.

"Well, no, not yet," said Collins. "Federal trials are assigned to the judges in some sort of rotating and random manner. It's supposed to give a sense of objectivity."

Jane stood and looked at them, as if she were waiting for something.

"Oh!" Shawna exclaimed. "Oh! Jane's suggesting that we may be overlooking how deep James and Finch are going to go in their desire to control the outcome of the trial. Right Jane?"

Jane nodded.

"She's saying that maybe the trial-to-judge assignment process isn't going to be as random as it should be for this trial," Shawna added.

Laughlin nodded his head. "Brilliant, Janie Dear. Purely brilliant." He beamed at his daughter. "You're the smartest daughter a father could ever have. All right, it's a contingency that we've overlooked but not one that we can't counteract." He smiled like a fox that's just found its way into the chicken coop. It seems that the old man was enjoying himself immensely. He leaned forward, taking on a conspiratorial tone and continued, "Okay, this is what we need to do."

Chapter 12

That Thursday, August Sixteenth, was a day that Collins would remember for a long time. He was buoyed by a surge of adrenaline and didn't seem to notice that he'd had only a couple of hours of sleep—one on the plane trip up from Atlanta and the other in his own bed.

He worked through the rest of the morning and into the early afternoon with Shawna and Laughlin laying out the foundation for his campaign strategy. They'd scheduled a press conference at four that afternoon and he, Jane, and Laughlin were to fly back down to Atlanta immediately after it was over. Collins was going to give his acceptance speech at the convention at nine p.m. Then, it was going to be back up to Virginia and hopefully some sleep. Friday and the weekend were going to be a blitzkrieg—the trial was still going to start on Monday. Ordinarily a huge, high profile criminal trial was daunting enough, but Collins was also trying to counteract the subversiveness of his "boss," the attorney general and the manipulative maneuvering of *his boss*, the president of the United States.

They were talking in Collins' study while they munched on sandwiches of cold cuts that Jane and Shawna had made.

"Let us not forget that this election was going to be a cartoon show from the beginning," Collins said between mouthfuls while he sat at his desk. "Keep in mind that the president has a record high approval rating and now that the opposite party has nominated a nobody, the press will be looking for something to make into its amulet—to bolster their viewer ratings. Well, I'll be damned if I'll walk into that snake pit!" he said angrily. "The goal of the modern news media isn't to inform the people—namely the voters. It's about making the most money, of course. And the one who can get the most viewers, readers, listeners, and so on is the one that'll make the most." He spat out the words with disgust. "We have to see this thing clearly. The media is out for profit and will do whatever it takes to get more of it. Little guys like me can't swim in those kinds of shark-infested waters. We're going to have to be very careful how we handle the nomination."

"You mean the campaign, don't you Buf," Laughlin said soothingly. "I fully support your views on this but you're going to have to do some kind of campaigning. You have to concede to some degree of public exposure in spite of the misguided motivation of the media. The American people need to get to know who you are—if they're going to vote for you." Laughlin was trying to be reasonable.

"Huh? Vote for . . .?" Collins was just realizing the implications of being a presidential nominee. He leaned back into his chair and closed his eyes. The magnitude of the whole thing was beginning to hurt his head: He was one of only two people who would be the next president of the United States. He made a face and pushed his plate away. He'd suddenly lost his appetite. He brooded for a few minutes while Jane started to clean up the dishes.

Collins got up and began to pace in front of Laughlin and Shawna who were sitting on the couch. After a few minutes, he stopped and held up his head.

"All right. This is it. I wasn't a declared candidate. But I got drafted into the nomination. Right?" He looked at Laughlin who nodded.

"Okay" Collins continued. "So, that means that I have no obligation to anything, right?" He looked at Laughlin again, but this time, Laughlin knitted his eyebrows into a doubtful frown. He didn't know where his son-in-law was going with this, but it didn't sound good.

Collins started to pace again and talked while he wore a groove in the study's plush carpeting. He was getting his thoughts in order. This was what he was good at.

"Okay" he forged on holding up a hand to punctuate the point. "What I mean is that since I am, uh, was not a declared candidate, I don't have a campaign position, right?" Laughlin nodded at this when Collins looked. "So, therefore I've nothing to be responsible for—nothing that I've committed to before the convention, for the simple reason that I wasn't a candidate before the convention." He glanced at the others, and they all nodded, indicating that this point was acceptable.

"All right, then. So, I'm going to accept the nomination because the delegates drafted me. I'll take this as a full endorsement from the party and, in particular, the voters of this country." He started to tick off points on the fingers of his left hand. "I'll tell the convention that as they've drafted me, I'll run, but I'll tell them that I will do so on my terms. I'll tell them that since I wasn't a declared candidate, I'll approach the campaign simply as a common man and trust that the voters will cast their votes for the one candidate, they feel they can trust in the White House."

Jane spoke up at this. "Now Buf, you should be careful not to patronize them."

Collins held up his hand holding off his wife's protest. "No, no. I'll be careful, Darlin'. But I'm not going to subject myself, and you and my family and friends, to the kind of indignity that I've seen happen to men who want to be president for the past forty years." He held his head up regally. "I won't tolerate having it happen to us. That's for sure."

He began pacing again. "So, I think that when I give my acceptance speech tonight, I should set the stage for what kind of campaign," he hooked his fingers in mock quotation marks, "I plan to conduct, once the trial is over. I'll stand there at the lectern—the same spot where I stood last night—and lay it out for them."

"What'll you tell them?" Jane asked, as she continued to gather up the dishes.

Collins looked at her questioningly. He searched for guile but saw only simple curiosity in her eyes. "I'll tell them that I've been drafted into the nomination by my party and that I'll try to be the candidate that my party—the voters—need in the White House."

"And what kind of candidate do you think that is, Buf?" Laughlin asked.

This time Collins answered without hesitation. He stopped pacing and sat back down in his chair. "Heck, if I know, Tom. But I can assure you all of one thing for certain: I'll be a candidate for the president of the United States the likes of which this country has never seen."

Jane Collins paused in the doorway of her husband's study, her hands full of lunch dishes, and looked at her husband of more than two-and-a-half decades. She did this aloofly from across the room. She leaned her head against the doorjamb and closed her eyes. It seemed incredible to her that her husband was the party's new presidential nominee. In all of the years that she'd been married to this man, this devout anti-politically-minded man, she'd never considered that they someday might enter into public life. Now, of all things, here he was about to accept the nomination to run for the president of the United States. It was unbelievable. Oh, she acknowledged that he was certainly smart enough, talented enough, yes; and even shrewd enough to handle the rigors of the job. That he'd be an effective president, she had no doubt. It was just that her loving spouse actually had no aspirations to be president of the United States. He really only wanted to be a trial lawyer—and a darn good one at that.

Jane opened her eyes and studied the hunter green calico pattern of the soft draperies in the study that she'd meticulously selected when decorating the room and found herself mentally envisioning herself as the first lady, mistress of the White House. It was a novel and seductively attractive notion. Then her consciousness suddenly caught up with her and she found herself standing there grinning like a madwoman.

She quickly turned around and began walking back to the kitchen, abashedly hoping that none of the others had observed her in the doorway. She admonished herself for being so schoolgirl-like—hoping to be the next first lady! Of all things, for Pete's Sake! She called herself a big fool, and reminded herself that there was no way that she was ever going to be the wife of the president of the United States. She ruefully acknowledged that she was more likely to find her way to the White House as a decorator than as its mistress.

Back in the study they were strategizing about Collins' press conference that afternoon. They thought that for his first exposure to the media, it was prudent for Collins to keep it short and sweet. So, they decided he should make a brief prepared statement and then take questions for a few minutes. There were two key points: he was accepting the nomination and he'd be delaying any formal campaigning for a short while because he was committed to do the corruption trial. They worked on an approach for controlling the media that would set the stage for the inevitable confrontations that would occur in the coming weeks.

Laughlin said that there were three important rules to follow in holding a press conference: The first was to never relinquish control. It was he who was the candidate and therefore it should always be he who is at the head of the table. It should never be allowed for the media and its celebrities to horn into the limelight. The second rule was that the media should never be allowed to get all that it wants in any single exposure. What this meant was that, in concert with rule number one, never let them wrest control away from him. They knew that there were many things about him, his views, and his past, that were standard fodder for a presidential campaign. They decided that even though Collins had nothing to hide, nothing to be ashamed of, it should be he, not the media, that decided when, where, and how this information is provided to the public. One of the most unattractive parts of typical press conferences, Laughlin said exuding wisdom, was the broad-sweeping whipsaws that the person holding the press conference was mercilessly subjected to. It was his intense goal, therefore, that Collins stopgap this right up front.

The third rule Laughlin said, was to never give in regardless of the pressure and regardless of any sense of wanting to right inadvertent wrongs. What this meant was that he wanted Collins to be ready to end the conference and walk away, if at any point he realized that he was losing control. They knew how much of a tyro he was in dealing with a skilled and overanxious press corps and they agreed that it was not only best for him to bail out and flee rather than stick it out under adversity, but also it would contribute significantly to a deliberate grooming of the media to go lightly and follow his lead or else they might end up with less than they wanted or needed.

"And be assured that you'll never, ever look bad in the public's eye, if you appear to snub the press, Buf," he said confidently. "It's always a big risk to stay and try to control them because you stand a good chance of just getting more deeply mired down. But if you up and walk away, no matter what the media says about you, the public will always respect you for it."

All in all, it was an excellent strategy. Collins in particular liked it because it gave him a feeling that he'd be able to exert the upper hand on a group of people he had little respect for.

On the topic of taking a few questions after giving the prepared statement, Laughlin's advice was to take them, but to do so on his own terms. There was too much unploughed ground in Collins' non-political life. An unstructured press conference could easily get out of control and if tolerated could last for hours. The idea was to open every such confrontation with the media with a prepared statement and then keep the questions focused on the topics covered in the statement and defer all other questions to a later time. If executed firmly, this would allow him to introduce the subject matter to the public at a pace that he set and in the order that he wanted.

They felt that at that afternoon's press conference, Collins should endorse the path that he'd be initiating in his acceptance speech later that evening—that he was a common man candidate. They worked through various scenarios for the prepared statement and ultimately narrowed their goal to three key points. First, Collins was not a politician. They felt that this was an important point to make up front. The strategy was that if he openly admitted it as if he were proud of it (and mind you Collins was proud that he could say this without reproach), he could undercut any leverage the media (and particularly his opponent) might be able to get out of this fact. In making this first and important point, on his terms, they felt that he could punctuate the fact that not being a politician was in no way a bad thing.

Second, as a previously undeclared candidate, they wanted Collins to state unequivocally that he had not received any donations and now that he was the party's nominee, he would not accept any donations from here on out. The point-within-the-point that they wanted to make here was that as a "common man" candidate, his allegiance was to the voters as a whole and not to any individual or specific interest group or sponsor. In addition, he didn't owe anyone any favors and so on. They latched onto the phrase, "I'm not in anyone's pocket. No, I'm in everyone's pocket" that he'd use in the prepared statement.

The third point was that even though he was proud of his past and current life, he considered some aspects of his life as personal and private and irrelevant to his qualifications and ability to be president. Thus, they wanted him to make it clear that his life shouldn't be considered open territory for ambitious investigative reporters. The sting of the unfortunate incident of Lloyd Stanton's early life was still felt in all their minds. They decided that to guide the media on what he considered fair ground for investigation and possible questioning, he should announce that he would soon be releasing some videotapes that would cover his background and current affairs. The topics covered in these tapes would define the boundaries of the landscape of what he considered to be pertinent to his candidacy.

At one point, Collins sat up straight in his chair and looked off into the far ends of his elaborate study.

"What is it Buf?" Laughlin asked, surprised at his son-in-law's sudden reaction to something unknown. "Hmmm?" he prompted a bit worried that Collins may have realized something important.

And rather important it was.

"Well," Collins started hesitatingly, looking at Shawna and his father-in-law with a concerned expression on his face. He pinched up his face as if he had taken a bite of a rotten egg. "Well," he continued, "if I am not going to take any contributions from donors who want to support my campaign and as, of course, I don't have a Political Action Committee, a 'pac,' and have no intention of forming one, where will I get the money to conduct the campaign? How will the costs of the video spots be covered? Among other things." He slumped back into his chair dejectedly exuding an evident sense of defeat.

Laughlin leaned over and patted Collins on his knee and said, "Don't you worry a moment about that Buf."

Collins looked up and took Laughlin's wise old laser-blue eyes into his gaze and saw instantly that money was not going to be an issue. He smiled slyly with the realization that the old man was going to cover all the expenses, out of his own pocket, no doubt a mere few numbers in the round-off error in Laughlin's annual bottom line.

Laughlin smiled slyly back at Collins and at Shawna and put his finger up to his lips in the universal sign that conveyed the mute message, "Let this be our little secret."

Precisely at four p.m., Collins made his prepared statement standing at a portable lectern that had been set up in front of his law offices in Old Town Alexandria, Virginia. He stood before a gathering of the media that someone later said numbered well over a hundred. The media interest was understandably quite high. The unexpected nomination of Collins was the news item of the decade, if not the century, either past or future. They spilled over the sidewalk and into the street and actually crowded out most of the good vantage points along the row houses on the other side of the street. Although he'd gotten back from Laughlin and Shawna the finalized version of his initial draft of the statement only an hour or so before, Collins still had time to familiarize himself with it. Thus, he was able to present the statement without reference to the printout. To anyone who witnessed him speak that day, the statement came across casually and most of all when he made eye contact with various individuals at the front of the crowd, his words were accepted as sincere and heart-felt. Later, many of the seasoned members of the press corps candidly admitted that this characteristic more than anything else caught them off-guard— they were totally unaccustomed to such sincerity from politicians— particularly from those who were campaigning. But of course, William Buford Collins, VI was not a veteran politician. He didn't know the meaning of guile.

When he was finished, Collins smiled warmly to the gathering almost as if he were the best man making the first toast at a wedding reception and said that he would now take a few questions. Immediately, everyone in front of him raised a hand and began shouting out their question.

Collins continued to smile, seemingly unaffected by this deluge, stuck out his arm and pointed out a young woman standing about forty feet away.

"Yes, I'll take your question first. You there with the blue blouse," he said firmly.

The woman was momentarily caught off guard at being picked first and seemed to forget that just a second before she was shouting her question at the top of her lungs.

"Oh!" she exclaimed and waited a moment longer while the teeming mass quieted down. "Yes sir, Mr. Collins can you tell us why you decided to run for the presidency?"

Collins looked at the woman steadily for three seconds and then guilelessly said, "I haven't decided to run. I've been drafted into nomination by my party and I'm standing before you today telling you that tonight I'll honor the convention's endorsement of me by accepting the nomination." He then quickly turned and pointed to a man wearing a maroon blazer off to his left and said, "Yes, you."

This man was only a little better at recovering from the immediate attention, but at least he had a reasonable question ready. "Mr. Collins, would you care to comment about your chances in this election, sir? As you say, you're not a declared candidate and in your statement just now you fully acknowledge that you're not a politician. Rather you say that you're just a common man. Given that President James is one of the most successful and popular chief executives in our nation's history, do you think that you have much chance of winning the election?"

Good question that this was, it was framed by the poser with so many words that Collins was able to mentally form his answer before the time came to respond. Thus, he began speaking the instant the man in the blazer stopped talking, giving nearly everyone the impression that he was neither offended by the pointedness of the question nor concerned by the truth upon which it was based.

"I think that in this country, anyone nominated by his or her party has a chance to win a presidential election. What's important is to make every attempt to demonstrate honesty, loyalty, and integrity to the voters and let them take it from there." Collins spoke firmly and concentrated on keeping his tone modulated. He knew that this was not really a direct answer to the question, but he also knew that it'd be accepted by the public who saw or heard it as a message to them. He was telling them that his common man approach was not a campaign strategy; moreover, it was totally truthful and sincere. This was in fact what the voters who saw clips of Collins at this press conference did think and it's said that when he heard it, President James wished he'd thought of saying it first. But of course, in actual fact this wouldn't have happened. Gardner James was a career politician and ingenuous statements of honesty and integrity weren't in his lexicon.

The questions continued more or less like this for another several minutes. When a subject arose that was too far afield from the scope of his prepared statement, Collins simply responded by saying "That's something that we'll have to get into at another time. I'd like us to focus this session today on the topics that I opened with, if we could please." It was so innocuous and so polite that amazingly the crowd of professional newspeople, who, under most other circumstances were highly predisposed to being ornery and proud of it, behaved themselves almost like schoolchildren.

The press conference ended a little abruptly when a short, balding man in a rumpled seersucker suit worked his way up to the front of the group and got noticed by Collins for placing a question.

"Isn't it true that you failed the bar exam three times before you could pass it?" he asked in a weaselly, whiny kind of voice.

Collins looked at the man's little beady eyes for a second and then looked up at the rest of the gathering with a mock pleading look on his face, as if he were beseeching them to save him from this attacker. Then, he looked back at the man who was exuding an oily smile, thinking that he'd set the candidate back on his rear. "Sir, I'm not sure to what you're referring, and even if you've the right person in mind. But regardless, I thank you for your question because it gives me the opportunity to use it as an illustration. I stand before you and the American voting public as a fifty-four-year-old man who's been nominated for the president of the United States. In my opinion, the decision of whether or not to vote for me stands on whether I'd do well in the job and represent fairly those who voted for me. This calls for a judgment to be made upon me as the man I am now—not, upon the man I was twenty or more years ago. Ancient history about me, my family, and my associates, isn't relevant to this election, my friends. I'm ready to answer any or all questions that relate to my ability to be president, but time is too dear to delve into subjects or events that don't relate and let's be clear ladies and gentlemen, I'll make those determinations not you. And now I'm afraid that I must go." He nodded to the crowd and then quickly turned and re-entered his offices.

CHAPTER 13

Shawna, who had been observing Collins from the foyer along with Jane stayed behind to witness how the group reacted to this as Collins walked up the steps to his offices. She was exuberant about how the new "non-candidate" had handled his first encounter with the media. She thought that Collins had done very well and was pleased that he also remembered the rules they'd set down. In her mind it couldn't have gone better even if they'd choreographed it. This last bit of leaving a little suddenly was a stroke of strategic genius. It sent the message that Collins wasn't a lightweight and that he had no reservations about exerting an assertive level of control over this kind of proceeding. And she hoped that she'd see in the aftermath positive signs that this group of newspeople who were likely to be the same ones in subsequent conferences was affected by her boss's subtle flick of his training whip.

What she saw was that the rat-like man in the rumpled suit was ostracized by the entire group of people out on the street. Within seconds they'd moved away from him so universally that there emerged a circle of empty space around him that was at least fifteen feet in radius and expanding. The movement couldn't have been more instantaneous had the man been declared a leper or in the most contagious phase of the bubonic plague.

Shawna nodded to herself in satisfaction and turned to follow the Collins' up the short flight of stairs to the law offices. She nodded to herself in satisfaction. The silent treatment was much more effective than speaking to the perpetrator. That he was intractable was as likely as that evening's sunset and the only message he might possibly understand was to be ignored—particularly by his colleagues. That sort of person thrives on attention and when he fails to get any, he notices. Shawna also sensed that the cold shoulder reflected that the majority of the group had a tangible sense of what had just happened and that they collectively blamed the little sleazy man for it and not Collins. She smiled contentedly. This first press conference was a very effective beginning to Collins' campaign.

Tom Laughlin was waiting upstairs in Collins' office. He'd been watching the press conference on television. From this point on, he wanted to be as far from the limelight of his son-in-law's two-pronged pursuits, conducting the important corruption trial and being the sitting president's opposing candidate in the upcoming election. He wanted to see how Collins was being treated by the media. He was smiling happily when Collins and his daughter entered, followed by Shawna after a couple of minutes.

"They don't know what to make of you, Buf," he said to them while they sat in the luxurious furniture that was clustered around the wet bar in Collins' office. "They're trying like the dickens to force you into one of their political stereotypes and they're failing miserably." He grinned broadly and had a hint of sinister satisfaction in his eyes like the young boy of Charles Addams' cartoons exacting a staged flood on an unsuspecting toy village in his bathtub. In spite of himself, admittedly a dyed-in-the-wool politician, Laughlin was enjoying how Collins' unique style and unorthodox approach to the presidential race was going to knock many people in the political arena off kilter, particularly the media.

Then, he wiped the smile off his face and took on a deadly serious expression. "But you need to be careful, even so, Buf. These people can turn on you like ravenous wolves at the drop of a hat and devour you before you know what's happening," he said solemnly. "In fact, this seems like as good a time as any to bring this up."

"What's that, Tom?" Collins inquired, raising his eyebrows in a universal questioning pose.

"Well, since you're going to accept the nomination but are going to be tied up for at least a month or so with the trial, I think you should get yourself a campaign manager," Laughlin said. "And from what I've seen so far, Shawna here is showing remarkable instinct and aplomb for political strategy and given that you and she are longtime friends and colleagues, I think that she's perfect for the job." He turned to look at the attractive woman seated across from him. "I'm quite impressed, my Dear."

"Thank you," Shawna said, a slight pinkishness creeping into her cheeks.

"But . . ." Collins started to say.

"Yes, but . . ." Laughlin interjected, cutting him off, "but Shawna's your second chair at the trial. Yes, of course, I'm aware of that. So, even though she's the most suitable person to be your campaign manager, at the present time she has the same schedule conflict that you have, my boy. Nonetheless, I think that it won't be too difficult for the two of you to work both sides of the street until the trial is over. It makes the best sense this way, don't you see? While you're prosecuting the case in the trial, you'll also be campaigning. So, as Shawna is the architect of the trial strategy, it should be she as your campaign manager who qualifies it accordingly."

Collins looked at the old man and nodded his head. "Okay, Tom. It sounds like a good plan." He turned to Shawna. "That is, if Shawna's willing to do it."

Shawna's eyes were shining brightly, much as if she were a kid running through a sprinkler in July, having the best time of her life. Everyone could tell that there was nothing that she wanted to do more. She turned to face Laughlin. "I'm glad to be on board, sir," she said graciously. "Buf is one of my favorite people and I don't know any better way to keep him and Jane from being abused by the media than to see to it myself."

"Yes, those are my sentiments exactly, Shawna," Laughlin said supportively. "And at least while our man here is in the Devil's kitchen." He paused for a moment and cleared his throat.

"Yes, well, that brings me to the second thing I wanted to say, Buf," he continued. "Shawna says that you and Jane are special people to her and I naturally second the motion you might say. Therefore, I'd like to volunteer to serve as your political advisor during the campaign. That's if you'll have me, Buf. Sotto voce, as it were, of course."

Shawna made a soft "woof" noise as if her breath had just been knocked from her.

Jane craned her neck trying to get a good look at her father. On the one hand she knew that a presidential campaign was what made her father tick but on the other, she'd never known him to be as openly involved as being a formal advisor to a candidate. She realized that her father must be feeling a bit responsible for her husband getting the nomination and now felt it was necessary to stay closely involved perhaps to ensure that he, and she, were shielded from the crush of being thrust into the public light. Her eyes welled up with emotion. She loved her father very much and it hit her hard to realize how much he evidently loved her.

Collins stared at his father-in-law for several seconds. "Tom, are you saying . . .?" He cleared his throat. "What I mean is that I, of course, thought that you'd be around during the campaign and available for me to seek advice from you, simply because of our friendship and that we're family and all. But am I correct in understanding that you're committing yourself to be on our team, uh, full-time? That you'd be giving this your first priority?"

"That's exactly what I'm saying, Buf," Laughlin said. "As of now, if you accept, I'm at your complete disposal."

"Oh, my God!" exclaimed Jane.

"Totally fantastic!" Collins said, with boyish enthusiasm.

Shawna uttered another "woof."

"I didn't think that you supported my viewpoint about this—about politics," Collins continued. "I wasn't sure that you approved."

"Ah!" Laughlin said, nodding his head. "I wondered whether you might think that. But I see now that you've misunderstood my motives. Let me make my feelings clear. My interest in your campaign and my commitment to you are based on my love for you and Jane in that I want to do everything I can to see you two through this as harmlessly as possible. But I'm also intrigued with your viewpoint. I find it refreshing and I wouldn't miss for anything being in the front seat of what's going to be the most unusual presidential campaign in this nation's history. It's the chance of a lifetime."

Collins nodded at his father-in-law approvingly. He slapped his hand flat upon the table much as if he were an auctioneer having just made a sale. "All right, Tom. I accept your offer."

"All right, then," Laughlin said decisively. "That settles that. And now, my friends, we've got a plane to catch."

They arrived at the convention center a few minutes before eight-thirty p.m. that evening and using Laughlin's special pass, the limousine was cleared into the bowels of the building. Using the same elevator and entrance that Collins, Shawna, and Laughlin had used the previous night to make a hasty exit, the foursome, now including Jane, retraced those steps with William Buford Collins, VI as he re-entered the spotlight.

Jane Collins held onto her husband's arm as if her legs might not be trusted to carry her weight alone.

Collins reached over and squeezed his wife's hand with his right hand and in this pose they stepped up onto the dais and into view of the convention, the delegates, and through the magic of television, to the world.

When he had called this last session of the convention to order, the convention general chairman told the occupants of the convention center, that the nominee they had unanimously drafted the night before, would be making his acceptance speech at nine.

At around eight-forty-five, someone (reportedly from the Virginia delegation) had begun a "We Want Bill!" chant and it had caught on like wildfire.

When Collins with Jane on his arm stepped into view on the dais, the entire structure was rocking with the tempo of the chant. Just prior to catching sight of the Collins couple, one would've said that the noise in the convention hall was deafening, but it was no match for the ear-aching thrum that arose from the electrified conventioneers when the Collins' came into their view and took center stage.

The decibel level of the noise generated at that point was such that all of the electronic transmissions both television and radio that were broadcasting live had to be suppressed. Even though the correspondents were shrieking into their microphones, their voices couldn't be discerned from the onslaught of the background noise.

To say that this was a moment that would be remembered by all present, whether participating or observing, for the rest of their lives would be, perhaps, the understatement of the decade.

The convention general chairman was assaulting his podium with his gavel like a lumberjack would swing an ax at a championship logging rodeo. Even though the base was linked into the public address system, there was not a soul in the hall that could hear it over the din.

Sensing that this moment was his and his alone, Collins showed Jane to a chair in a row at the back of the dais and stepped up to the lectern. He held up his arms over his head in salute to the convention and unbelievably the noise level noticeably went up another notch or two.

Jane looked at her husband and beamed with pride. Her entire body was tingling with electric excitement. Her throat was choked up with emotion. Tears were streaming down her cheeks. She sensed that some of the television cameras were trained on her, and she realized that she was grinning from ear to ear. It was a moment that she'd find difficult to get out of her mind for many years to come, as this was a feeling that only a precious few people had ever had the distinct pleasure to experience in the history of mankind.

Collins stood tall and proudly in front of this convention and his delegates as if this was exactly what had been meant to be. He inwardly shivered with the realization that he owned this entire group of people. It was a sense of power of a magnitude that he was totally unfamiliar with.

The sudden realization that he was standing before the very people who drafted him into nomination hit him like an avalanche.

Unanimously! Every single person here! There was not a single dissenter, not a single abstainer. Holy mackerel! That's some endorsement.

He knew then that any notion he'd had earlier in the day about not accepting the nomination, this honor, was completely ridiculous.

He assured himself that he was doing the right thing—by being here to accept the party's nomination. He straightened himself up in front of the lectern. He admitted to himself that he wasn't sure whether he could live up to what these people and the voters they represented expect of him, but he resolved himself right then and there to do his utmost to try.

He was totally stunned with this reaction but gradually he realized that he was reacting positively to it. He felt his eyes sparkle with excitement. He realized that he was smiling broadly and nodding his head. He was the leader of these people—their chosen leader.

He felt a trickle of sweat run down the side of his face. In all of his courtroom experience, he'd never been cheered before. And this was no ordinary cheer. It was shaking the foundation of the largest building in the Southeast, arguably a cheer of historical proportions. He was dumfounded that a group of people who literally did not know him from Adam would cheer for him so enthusiastically. It brought on an emotional high that he had never before and might never again experience.

He held up his arms in the classic pose of victory, like Sylvester Stallone as Rocky Balboa in the movie "Rocky" and like Winston Churchill at the end of World War II.

Collins was enjoying being the object of this group's adulation. He found himself not wanting it to stop.

But slowly, it did stop. Inexorably. The conventioneers began to tire from the heavy exertion of screaming at the tops of their lungs, and stomping their feet, and pounding their hands together in thundering applause. They also wanted to hear their new leader, the nominee for the president of the United States, speak. And so, slowly, the crowd began to settle down and their leader leaned towards the microphone and spoke into it.

He spoke carefully into the microphone, enunciating his words evenly and speaking in a level tone. "Delegates of the convention, my fellow party members, Mr. Chairman, I'm your nominee for the president of the United States. My name is William Buford Collins, and you can call me Buf."

The crowd erupted into a tumultuous roar. Many people have tried to define charisma and have failed miserably—it's something that is truly ineffable. You know it when you sense it, and such is a feeling that you can't describe—it's too much of an enrichment of one's soul to be worthy of mere words.

With those first few words, every delegate in that convention hall who heard them felt that the man standing before them was someone special. That they had something directly to do with putting him up there, was a feeling of satisfaction and accomplishment that was not likely to happen to any of them ever again.

Collins had to hold up his hands again to settle down the crowd. He beamed with excitement. At one point, he walked around the stage clapping his hands along with his supporters and blowing off some wolf whistles. The crowd sensed that Collins was showing them that he felt like he was one of them and that they weren't really cheering for him as much as he and they were together providing support to the party.

Upstairs in a major network booth the correspondents covering the convention were trying to convey to their audience what was going on down on the convention floor.

"Don, I've been covering these conventions for about twenty years now and I can't say that I've ever seen anything like this. It's quite remarkable," said the anchorwoman in an emotion-filled voice.

"I completely agree with you Lisa," chimed in Don, her broadcasting partner. "This is a historic moment, I think. We don't know where this man down there came from, the new nominee who has asked us to call him Buf Collins, but there's one thing for certain. He has the full and undying support of every delegate here in this convention hall."

"You can say that again, Don," stated Lisa taking over control of the conversation. She turned to face the camera.

"For any of you who are just now tuning in, we're witnessing, live, the acceptance speech by this party's new presidential candidate that was drafted into nomination unanimously last night. This man,

William Buford Collins, and he says for us to call him Buf—I guess that's short for Buford, Don—is a lawyer from Alexandria, Virginia. We've learned that it was the Virginia delegation that started the draft movement for Collins last night after the convention stalled out on the something-ieth ballot in the wee hours of the morning.

"Buf Collins is a very successful trial lawyer and is a graduate of the University of Virginia. He's fifty-four years old and is married to, uh . . .″ she paused and looked down at some scribbled notes in front of her, "yes, to a Jane Laughlin Collins the only daughter of Thomas Laughlin, the former attorney general of the United States.

"The Collins' have three grown children, two sons and a daughter, and, uh, and a German Shepherd dog, named, uh, . . ., Godzilla." Lisa smiled sweetly into the camera lens. She was proud of this last tidbit of information. The network's investigators had been busy, and one had apparently stumbled on Collins' plumber or barber or someone and dug up this personal piece about the dog.

Lisa looked down on the convention floor and then back up at the camera. "It looks like Buf Collins has gotten them back under control again. The unbridled enthusiasm of this group tonight is so excessive it's hard to believe that this is the same group that has been here boring us all week, Don," Lisa said drolly, looking over at her co-anchor. She looked back. "Let's go back down and pick up Buf's acceptance speech."

Collins stepped back over to the lectern and began speaking again into the microphone. The convention hall was as silent as it had been the previous night when everyone was hanging on Collins' every word. They didn't know this man and they wanted to get every shred of information about him that they could.

"Although I'm your nominee and I thank you for your overwhelming endorsement last night . . ." Collins paused and smiled warmly at the delegates. "Although you've voted me into the candidacy for president, you really don't know much about me. Well, I'm going to try to remedy that right now.

"I was born in Roanoke, Virginia on April Seventeenth, fifty-four years ago. My father was an insurance salesman, and my mother was a schoolteacher in elementary school—mostly the second grade. I was the oldest of four kids. I have two sisters, Julie and Barbara, and a younger brother, Andy. I grew up in Roanoke and graduated from the high school down there. I played some football, second-string quarterback, some basketball, junior varsity guard, and some baseball, third base, and was awarded two athletic letters. My best sport was baseball and in my senior year, I batted three fifty-seven with twenty-one homers." He paused and smiled again, amused at some private joke.

"There were a few big-league scouts who came down to talk to me. I told them that I wanted to go to college. Boy, was I dumb back then! Think of the money I could've made by playing professional baseball. And the fun!

"Well, anyway I went on to attend the University of Virginia in Charlottesville and majored in political science and then I went into the law school there. I've been practicing trial law in Alexandria, Virginia ever since.

"I'm married to a beautiful, loving woman who's sitting over there." He gestured respectfully over to where he'd left Jane. He looked at her for a long two seconds, winked at her, and then turned to face his convention. "She's my best friend and I love her more than I can say."

Jane Collins felt the pressure of everyone's eyes and all the cameras on her during this brief exposure. She sensed that it was the beginning of a period of extremely high visibility. She wondered if she was ready for it. She looked lovingly back at her husband and reflected that Collins was such a master at winning over a crowd. And these people are already his supporters. It was incredible.

"Jane and I are proud parents of three wonderful children," Collins continued. "We really can't believe how blessed we've been by having them and watching them grow into respectable adults. Will is now twenty-four and is studying to be an architect at the Rhode Island School of Design and I believe that he's going to be a great designer. Susan is twenty-two and has just started law school at the University of Texas in Austin and she's just as beautiful as her mother. And Tommy, named after his maternal grandfather, will be twenty next month and will be a junior this year at the University of Virginia. He tells me he's majoring in mathematics, but I think that he must be in the varsity dating program."

Collins paused and let his audience start to laugh and then joined in and laughed with them. They, he and the convention, were as one.

"I'm a lawyer and, I believe, a good one." He paused for effect. "What I mean by good is that I'm an honest lawyer, not a high quality one—although some people have told me that I'm that too. What I mean folks, is that I'm the kind of lawyer that you'd be comfortable with—someone you can trust and someone who'd do his best for you.

"And I hope to be that kind of candidate for president—one that you can believe in, one that you all can trust. This single thing is extremely important to me. As you all know I wasn't a declared candidate for the presidency. I came to the convention last night for a completely different reason. I had no plans to speak to you; no aspirations to be nominated.

"But here I am, standing before you as your nominee and I'm here just as I was last night: just a man—an honest man. That's all. You people didn't vote for me last night because of my background, or my record, or my reputation, or my position on the issues, or my constituency, or who my other supporters were. You people gave me your unanimous support but not on the basis of any of these things.

"You didn't nominate a platform. You didn't nominate a record. You didn't nominate an image. No sir and no ma'am. And most importantly, you didn't nominate a politician last night. No. Instead, you nominated me—a simple man. A man with no pretenses. A man with no ulterior motives. A man with no lust for power. Just a man. Just me—someone very much like any one of you out there.

"I stand here before you and accept this nomination of our party for the presidency of the United States. I accept it as Buf Collins—a man who's worthy of your trust.

"I'll be your candidate and if elected I'll be your representative in the White House. I've no one to answer to, but each of you. I have no favors to pay back. I've nothing to hide and nothing to be embarrassed about. I pledge these things to you and I swear to God that as the next president of the United States, I'll serve this country with every shred of my capacity and during every single moment in office each and every one of you can be absolutely certain of one very important thing: I'll be completely myself, your representative—an honest man, someone you can trust."

Collins stopped and took a sip of water. The convention floor literally exploded with cheers and again the noise seemed strong enough to shake loose the foundation of the building.

Upstairs in another broadcast booth, the announcers were trying to convey to their viewers the electricity that they felt.

"It's simply amazing, folks. This man, William Buford Collins, stepped out of utter oblivion and into the spotlight no more than about twenty hours ago and he has swept this convention literally off its feet." He turned to his partner. "I don't know that anything like this has ever happened before in American politics, Stan."

Stan looked into the camera lens and spoke with the most solemn, erudite voice he could muster. "No, I'm pretty sure that it hasn't, Greg. We've been doing some research since last night and we can't find any other political convention in any of the parties that has ever drafted an undeclared candidate into nomination. In addition, Greg, even though they don't really keep these kinds of records, we can find no report of any presidential campaign that has put forward such a dark horse candidate. The American voting public is probably still a few weeks away from beginning to know what this man's name is, let alone knowing anything about him as a candidate."

Greg took back control of the mike. He turned to face the camera. "That's exactly right, Stan. The speech that Collins has just given couldn't have been more apropos for the situation. He started with the basics. He knew that no one knew who he was. So, he realized that this is what he should talk about first. And I tried to get a peek at the lectern and as far as I can tell, Collins had no notes. He gave this, his acceptance speech, completely extemporaneously. He spoke to his convention tonight from his heart. I must admit, that although I can't speculate how any of you out there reacted to this man, the new presidential candidate, I can tell you one thing for certain. He, in a very short period of time, has made a significant impression on me. This, Buf Collins, is one special person."

Collins, his party's nominee for the president of the United States, stepped humbly away from the lectern amidst a tremendous cacophony of laudatory cheers and whistles and walked over to Jane. Like a king presenting his queen to her people, Collins helped her up and led her by the hand to the front of the dais. He held up his and her clasped hands high in the air as a salute to the convention. The din immediately stepped up a notch. Collins turned to face the crowd and beamed with his full wattage smile. The crowd seemed to react by making even more noise. Collins then stepped across the dais and shook the convention general's hand and quickly returned to escort Jane down the back steps off of the platform. Although he had been prepared to continue speaking, his instincts told him that this was the best time to stop, a tangible high point.

There at the base of the short staircase, stood an army of cameramen and newspeople holding microphones. They weren't about to let Collins slip through their fingers this night. He could see Tom Laughlin and Shawna Wells standing behind them.

Collins held up his hands in a stop motion. "I've nothing further to say, folks. I've got a lot of organizing to do. As soon as I'm ready to launch my campaign, you'll be the first to know. Don't worry, you all will be treated fairly. No one will be left out." He spoke as he tried to carve a path in the crush of people for them to get out of the building.

His statement had little or no effect. Both he and Jane were inundated by shouted questions and if Collins had been just a little smaller in weight and stature, he mightn't have been able to push his way through the throng.

Finally, they reached the far side and almost as if it were a swarm of angry yellow jackets, the media people began to trot after them.

Laughlin took them in tow and started towards the doors onto the loading dock. He motioned them into a waiting limousine and then jumped in after them quickly closing the door on the enveloping crowd. The vehicle shot forward and propelled them into their seats.

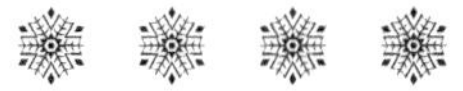

Gardner James watched the television screen and groaned inwardly. He cursed himself for somehow not being able to foresee or prevent this from happening. He suddenly realized that it was going to be a tremendously more difficult task to get re-elected than he'd thought.

Chapter 14

In the car they were ebullient. The whole thing had seemed to go so well. Shawna and Jane and Laughlin prattled on about this and that and it was a few moments before they noticed that Collins was not partaking in the debriefing.

When they looked over at him to inquire what was the matter, they saw that he was sound asleep. He'd been going for more than thirty-six hours with only two short naps and now that the big event was over, slumber had overtaken him.

They arrived back at the Collins estate about one a.m. Laughlin went home to get some rest himself and promised to join them at nine o'clock the next morning. Shawna also went home but only to pack up an overnight bag and to get her car. She was going to spend the weekend at the Collins'.

There was a ton of work to do.

They were having lunch on Saturday, eating roast beef sandwiches with pickles and iced tea on the screened-in porch that looked out onto Jane's Garden when Jane said to her husband, "It strikes me that you might not want to be in too much of hurry to get the trial over, Darling."

Everyone stopped chewing and looked over at her.

Jane appeared to be slightly startled that what had seemed to her to be a casual comment had caused such a reaction.

"How do you mean, Janie?" asked Laughlin.

"What Jane's saying is that it's up to me how fast we get through the trial, and it might be smart to draw it out rather than shorten it up," Collins offered. He looked from Laughlin to his wife. "Is that right, my Dear?" he asked.

"Mmmm," Jane acknowledged, coyly. "It's really perfect. The trial will be your platform and the courtroom will be your venue. The beauty of having the prior commitment to do the trial is that no one, including the president, will be able to accuse you of hiding from the campaign on the one hand because you have no choice in the matter and no one will be able to bad mouth you for preempting the president his due in going head-to-head with you on the other hand because again you're not doing this on purpose—in fact, it was the attorney general who sought you out to be the special prosecutor, no doubt with the president's concurrence."

"Unbelievable," said Collins.

"Boy howdy!" exclaimed Shawna. "Jane's zeroed in on the good stuff here. It really is perfect. Don't you see? The best part is that when the president comes out and publicly comments that you're doing the trial as a political stunt, it'll immediately be seen by the typical cynical American as a political stunt in and of itself and ultimately undermine his support. It's fantastic! You're impervious to hurt. You're Teflon man, Buf!"

Jane paused a moment to let Shawna's words sink in and then continued. "It has a rather nice balance and harmony to it, if you think about it, Buf. You got picked to prosecute the corruption trial because you weren't even remotely involved in the political process. And now that you're caught up to your neck in that process, you've a perfect excuse to avoid having to swim with the sharks when you're admittedly just a minnow. The incredible thing is that it's more than likely that no one will take notice of your minnow-ness," she said with a smirk, amused at her inventive coining of a new English word.

"Yes, you're exactly right, Jane Dear," Collins remarked. "It's so perfect that no one could've planned it this way." He shot a sly glance at his father-in-law. "Not even your father, I'm quite sure. And it has a resonant cachet about it. What's a spectacularly dramatic way to campaign against a vastly popular incumbent president, you ask? The answer is to first get appointed as the special prosecutor for a major and widespread corruption and obstruction of justice trial and then go get nominated to run against him. A normal run-of-the-mill politician would merely try to out-position the sitting president on the issues and accuse him of all manner of wrongdoing while in his first term. But not me. Nope. That's not my style. I somehow get nominated after I've made a prior commitment that believe it or not is more important to the American public than a boring little old presidential campaign. It's remarkable."

"That's the way I see it," Jane said encouragingly. "But hmmm. There's one more important thing that you might consider, Buf," she offered cryptically.

Collins closed his mouth and clamped his teeth together and didn't immediately respond. He wasn't sure what was coming next. Then, slowly and softly he said to his wife. "And that is?" He waited, giving her his full attention.

"It's essential . . . no, crucial, that you get the trial's judge to allow television cameras in the courtroom. Both your case and your campaign need a level of exposure to the public that only live coverage can provide."

"Yes, of course," Collins agreed. "Live coverage is essential without question. But what's the problem?"

"Well, it's not a foregone conclusion that the judge will allow it. After the O. J. Simpson free-for-all, it's not in the best interest of jurisprudence to have that much media exposure. And you've got to know that the defendants won't want the coverage. That's a certainty."

"And it's a strong possibility that Finch and James won't want the media coverage, either" offered Shawna.

"Unless" Laughlin chimed in, "they think that they've set you up with the upgraded charges and that failing to get any convictions would, in their minds, make you look bad. In this way, it's likely that Gardie James would want as much media coverage of the trial as possible."

Everyone stared at the old man, marveling at the extent of his understanding of the deviousness of the political mind.

"Ah," Collins said, "I haven't looked far enough ahead to get into how the media will be covering the trial. Of course, there was always going to be some coverage, but now that I've been nominated, it'll be immense—particularly since it'll be the only way they can get any coverage of me. Hmmm, I wonder how we should play it with the judge. It might be good to sit tight and let it play itself out and then again, perhaps, we should approach the judge directly and make a motion, like Jane thinks. Any ideas?" he asked.

"I don't think that we should leave it up to the capriciousness of a federal judge, do you Buf?" Shawna asked. "No, I didn't think so. Therefore, I think that we should, as soon as the trial starts, formally petition to the judge that he, or she, shouldn't allow the media into the courtroom."

"What? You say not to let the media in?" Collins was incredulous. "But that would go against what we want."

"Hold on," Shawna said, "I'm not finished. I'm suggesting that we pull a little reverse psychology on the judge. If you make a passionate plea to keep the cameras out, he's sure to see the benefits of letting them in. After all, any judge's going to see your trial as anything but fun. You're tilting at all the windmills in his backyard. It's likely that most federal judges will know many of the defendants. And your petition against the media in the courtroom will stimulate the overseeing judge into realizing that if he keeps them out, he can likely be accused of showing bias in his rulings—a bias in favor of the establishment. If you petitioned to let the cameras in, the judge would wonder what you were up to because he's certainly smart enough to see that media coverage is what you want and need. But if you petition against media coverage in the courtroom you allow him to come up with his own reason to deny your petition."

"Absolutely fantastic!" Collins said beaming. "You're so clever. It's a stroke of genius, Jane. And think of what the president and Finch will think about what I might be up to petitioning to the judge to keep the live coverage out of the courtroom. I like it, I really do."

Collins rubbed his hands together briskly in a motion reminiscent of Dickens' Fagan ogling at the booty brought in by his faithful street urchin, the Artful Dodger.

"There are still a few loose ends, Buf," Laughlin said softly.

Collins looked over at his father-in-law and nodded his head. "Yes, of course. First of all, we don't know who the judge will be. We strongly suspect that Finch and James are scheming as we speak about who they can put in charge of the trial—someone who can be their puppet. But as I understand it, Tom, you have some of your people investigating the entire cadre of federal judges to give us the leverage to force any of their likely patsies to recuse themselves, should we need to counteract them."

"Right," acknowledged Laughlin. "We should have the report by some time tomorrow afternoon."

"And second," Collins continued his listing of the loose ends, "there's something that I've still got up my sleeve. Something that has emerged from my continued investigation into our Jefferson issue."

Everyone turned to stare at him.

"Yes, I've got some of my own special investigators following a thin and vague reference that I discovered earlier in the week. I didn't want to say anything about it until I knew more, but if it's what it looks like, it'll knock the socks off anything that we've got now."

"What on Earth is it, Buf?" Shawna asked.

Collins leaned forward and told them in a low voice.

After he finished, Laughlin sat back in his chair and grinned. "It's taken you a while, Buf my boy, but I've always had faith in you. I knew you'd get there; it was only a matter of time."

The others turned to look at the old man.

"You sly old fox!" Collins exclaimed. "This is what you've been after all along."

"Father!" Jane said, unable to keep the indignation out of her voice. "You've known about this?"

Laughlin simply nodded.

"He's known, but he hasn't been able to do anything about it," Shawna said. "He's been working behind the scenes to get Finch to call for the Grand Jury and also to get him to make Buf the special prosecutor."

"I only suggested to Bobby," Laughlin said feigning offense, "that he *consider* Buf and that was primarily because Gardie James wanted him to keep the trial on a low profile. I pointed out to Bobby that a non-politician was his answer and given that Buf was also a dynamite trial lawyer, I knew of no one who fit that suit better than Buf."

Shawna chortled at this.

Jane smirked. "Right. And now the perfect non-political solution to Finch's problem is up to his eyeballs in politics."

"And there goes any hope for a low-profile trial," Shawna added.

"And now you guys have the evidence to take the corruption all the way up and get the jerks and put them behind bars," said Laughlin, a little breathlessly. It was clear that he was emotionally involved in this.

"But what about the nomination, Tom?" Collins asked. "If you've been choreographing this whole thing from the beginning, how in the world did you fix it so that I'd get the nomination?"

Jane and Shawna turned to look at him with their jaws dropped open. Then simultaneously, they both quickly looked at Laughlin anxious to hear his answer.

"Ah," Laughlin began smiling sheepishly, "now that was a bit of pure luck. Having you hot on the trail of the corruption, collusion, conspiracy, and cover-up slowly unraveling how far up the power ladder it went and named as special prosecutor was what I wanted, and I was quite happy with that. I've already told you that I had nothing to do with Lucy Walton and you helping her about her husband's death. That was helpful and really only to Finch in actuality. It allowed you to readily accept the offer to do the trial and gave you no reason to object to the accelerated schedule. But as far as the nomination goes. No, I had nothing to do with it. I wish I had thought of it, but, of course Buf, you must realize that if I'd suggested such a thing to you a priori, you would've refused."

"You're right about that, Tom," Collins said. "I would have."

Gardner James sat in his executive office chair and ground his teeth. He and Robert Finch had been discussing the trial and had narrowed the list of judges they'd pick from to oversee it down to ten. But then they had digressed into grousing about how complicating it was that Collins was now the opposing party's presidential nominee.

The worst part was that Collins was now perhaps the only person in the country that he couldn't either bully, manipulate, or bribe. Excepting only Tom Laughlin, that is. It was very frustrating. And what was rapidly causing the chief executive to soon need to get fitted with a night guard for his teeth was that Collins was not just any target for presidential manipulation—he was the special prosecutor for a major corruption trial that was going to have political repercussions bigger than a tsunami.

He pounded his fist on his massive desk, startling Finch with such an open display of anger.

"Well, we could replace him as special prosecutor," Finch offered meekly.

The president glared at him and then shook his head pityingly. "No Bobby, we can't do that. Not anymore."

Finch quickly nodded. "Oh, right. Not anymore because since he's the nominee, if we dumped him everyone would think that you're doing it because somehow there's something in the trial you're trying to hide."

The president nodded slowly and looked dully at Finch. For the first time in a very long time, he felt fear. An ice-cold trickle of sweat started out of nowhere and began to roll down his back right along his spine.

"So, what should we do?" Finch asked.

James sat there and forced himself to appear in control. He then stood up and walked around the desk towards Finch.

Finch recoiled and sat back straight in his chair, his eyes widening. James's movements were so sudden and forceful, he wondered if the man was coming at him to strike him.

The president stopped short only a few inches from Finch and then swiveled a half turn and put his hip up on the edge of the desk. He leaned over so that his face was down at the level of Finch's and so close that Finch could smell his breath.

"Today's Saturday, right?" the president said in a guttural voice that was almost a whisper. "And the trial starts on Monday, right? So, tomorrow we release a blurb to the media that the White House is outraged that so many fine and upstanding public officials, many of whom are old friends of mine, have been so wrongly accused in this trial. We'll say that the charges of corruption and collusion are ridiculous and there's no merit to the indictments that the Grand Jury handed down whatsoever."

"Are you sure that you want to do that, Mr. President?" asked Finch cautiously.

"Absolutely," James replied. "And I'll tell you why. We're also going to say tomorrow in the release that we believe that Collins has planned this from the beginning. You say he told you that he'd been investigating the corruption on his own, didn't you? Well, we can say that he's been working behind the scenes for some time to get this thing to trial."

"But why would he do it?" Finch asked innocently.

"Because he was planning to get the nomination, that's why," the president answered smugly.

"What!" Finch was aghast. "That's ridiculous! No one plans to win a presidential nomination by being drafted on the umptee-umph ballot!"

"No, of course not. We know that. But the average American doesn't. To think that this whole thing is political from the get-go will make perfect sense to them. Don't you see? It's always been political. We're just going to accuse Collins of doing it."

Finch understood. "All right. It's a very clever ploy. Good thinking. And we can probably drop a hint in the statement about Collins being Tom Laughlin's son-in-law, and . . ."

"No, Bobby," James interrupted. "Let's leave that part of it alone— for the time being anyway. We don't want to get the old man riled up unnecessarily. After all, he knows the truth about nearly everything and it won't help my political currency one little bit, if he wants to defame me."

Finch raised his eyebrows questioningly.

"Suffice it to say that if Tom Laughlin wanted to discredit me, there are more than enough ways he could."

Finch stood on shaky legs and started to leave.

"Oh, and Bobby," the president called after him. "One more thing. We need to keep a step ahead of Collins. Make sure that you talk to the judge to get him to open up the courtroom to full live media coverage including tee-vee. And once the trial begins, don't forget that we're going to escalate the charges to conspiracy."

"But now that Collins is the nominee, can we still do that? Up the charges, I mean?" Finch was uncertain about this.

"We can do anything. Don't you ever forget that." James was returning back to his seat. "We can say that it was a clerical error or something and that we're just trying to make sure that the trial is done right. We've an obligation to the public interest, you know."

Finch left with a frown on his face. There was an acrid feeling in his mouth that was particularly distasteful.

CHAPTER 15

Sure enough on Monday, August Twentieth at nine a.m. at the beginning of the trial, Collins and Shawna stood at the prompt of the clerk and saw one of the judges that was on Tom Laughlin's "no-no" list walk purposefully into the courtroom.

This was what they expected—that Finch and James were working behind the scenes with major political clout to make sure that a judge sensitive to the volatile political situation and sympathetic to James' role in it as well was named to preside over the trial. As a matter of fact, Tom Laughlin's list, which included a sizable number of names, was roughly prioritized and the judge who was just introduced to the courtroom was at the top of the list, meaning that she was considered to be a dyed-in-the-wool James supporter.

Almost before the judge's gavel rap was completed calling the court into session, Collins was on his feet. "Your Honor the United States has a motion to place before the court, if you please," he said in a loud and distinct voice. Even though the visual media were not in the courtroom, the seats were overbrimming with reporters and other media note-takers and sketch artists. He sensed that everyone was suddenly focused on what he was about to say.

It was a strange thing for him to be representing the prosecution and he felt a tinge of the queasiness of the novice in saying he was speaking upon behalf of the United States. But then, he quickly reflected, he was representing the country—in more ways than one.

"Yes, Mr. Collins, what is it?" inquired the judge unaware of what was coming.

"Your Honor, the United States has good reason to believe that you have a conflict of interest that would interfere with your ability to oversee this trial. I cite for you," he glanced down at a thick sheaf of papers that he was holding in his hand and began to read from a lengthy list of court cases and other résumé-type items that showed this judge to have been closely related to many of the defendants over the years and also to several of the deaths that the trial documents listed.

When he was finished with his reading of the citations, Collins looked up at the judge. The woman looked like she didn't know what to do and glanced at her clerk for assistance. He whispered something to her while holding up his open hand to the side of his face, more or less blocking to the rest of the courtroom what he was saying. The judge leaned over to be able to hear and then snapped back into her seat. Her eyes widened in shock. Apparently, she hadn't been informed of some of the subtleties in this case—one of which was that this trial was going to be a dirty rotten street fight from the onset.

The judge called for a short recess and retired to chambers and undoubtedly made a hasty phone call over to Justice. She didn't return.

Back in the courtroom, Collins and Shawna sat and waited. After about ten minutes the clerk reentered from a side door and announced that the trial would remain in recess for the rest of the day and would reconvene at nine a.m. the following morning.

Collins and Shawna started to pack up their things. "One down and who knows how many to go," she said dryly.

Virtually the same scenario was played out in the Tuesday morning version of opening up the trial. This time judge number two didn't need to make the hasty phone call in chambers. Finch was there waiting for him.

"I'm sorry, Bob," said the judge with genuine regret in his voice. "They've got the goods on me and what with the media crush on this thing there's nothing that I can do. It'd be a mockery for me to blow them off and not recuse myself. You've got to understand my predicament. I'm going to have to hear other cases after this one, you see?"

Finch nodded grimly. "Yes, I understand. If only you could appreciate the delicacy of *my* predicament." He then shook his head woefully.

A few minutes later a court assistant entered the courtroom and cautiously approached the prosecutor's table. Collins glanced up and saw a young woman who didn't look like she was out of her teen years. He was about to speak to her when she held out her hand in which she was holding a small slip of paper.

Collins reached out and took it from her hand. Once released from her burden she turned tail and was gone in a flash.

"Huh!" Shawna said. "I guess she wasn't expecting there to be any reply," she speculated.

Collins was reading the note. "It's from Finch. Says he's out in one of the anterooms and wants to see us."

"All right," Shawna said enthusiastically. "Let's go see the boss," she added sarcastically.

Inside the cramped space of the room, the tension was palpable. Although Finch was seated at a small table, he could barely keep himself still.

"What the heck is going on?" he demanded as Collins and Shawna entered.

"We're merely trying to make sure that the trial has a chance of being heard fairly," Collins began calmly. He knew that it was highly likely that this would soon become a shouting match and he wanted to try to make his point early on. "Look, Bob," he resumed trying to keep his voice level and non-confrontational, "let's try to be reasonable here. Okay? This case is highly sensitive and involves many public officials going back several years. We realized a short while ago that it was possible, likely even, that there might be some judges on the federal circuit that worked with some of the defendants and possibly may have in their earlier days heard cases that related to some of the deaths that are named in this case.

"I'm sure that you'd want us," Collins forged ahead as Finch was not saying anything but just sitting there looking glum, "to make every effort to ensure that the judge who presides over the trial is able to make rulings with complete objectivity. And of course, since there's going to be a good deal more publicity to the trial than we had originally hoped, I'm also sure that we don't want to embarrass ourselves or the current administration for not being as judicious and prudent as possible in selecting a judge. Don't you agree?"

Finch sat and glared at them. "You're making this all political, aren't you?" he snarled.

Collins raised his eyebrows in surprise. "Absolutely not!" he said with genuine indignation. "Certainly not as much as you are, or the president is. I'm assuming that he's responsible for that ridiculous story that came out over the weekend about me planning this whole thing from the beginning. You should be ashamed of yourself, Bob for being party to that crock of bull.

"Now, let's get back to basics here. You've made me special prosecutor for this trial and I'm taking the responsibility very seriously. I intend to give this my very best effort and my undivided attention. The other thing," he made a sweeping, cast-off sort of motion with his hand as if he were tossing the presidential nomination into an imaginary wastebasket, "doesn't enter into it at all. You have to believe me; I'm committed to this trial full time for its entire duration."

Finch drummed his fingers on the table. Then he looked up at the two who were still standing. "Okay, so how long is this recusing thing going to go on?" he asked through gritted teeth.

"Until we can find a judge who'll be able to hear the trial without bias," replied Shawna.

"Hmmm," Finch mused, "what about . . .?" He mentioned another judge's name.

"Nope," Shawna answered tersely.

Finch said another name. He was seemingly taking these from off the top of his head.

Collins shook his head.

Finch tried again with the same result. He then dropped his chin to his chest in an indication of defeat. After a minute or so, he slowly looked back up. "Okay," he began in a low voice, "I gather that you've been doing your homework on all the judges on the circuit—looking into their backgrounds and such. Therefore, there's no point in continuing with this guessing game. Let's try it another way. All right?" His eyes had the look of a cornered rat. "Is there anyone that you would not object to for the trial? Is there anyone who meets your stringent standards?" This last was uttered through clenched teeth.

Collins and Shawna nodded their heads in unison. "Yes, there is. Harland Rector," Collins said.

"Rector?" Finch said, raising his eyebrows slightly. "But Rector's been around as long as some of the others who you've rejected already. I don't get it."

"We've checked him out," Shawna said patiently. "He's not heard any cases that relate to any of the deaths named in this case and as far as we can tell he hasn't worked with any of the defendants at least not close enough to suggest that he might've either been involved in the corruption or known about it. Remarkable as it might seem, he's clean."

Finch arose and awkwardly began to stretch out some kinks in his legs and back, the cramped conditions of the anteroom were so severe. He straightened up and eyed his two appointees more like they were adversaries. "I need to check into it. Court will remain in recess until further notice." He stepped past them and was out the door without so much as a wave.

Shawna stared at the open door. "Well, that's a trick," she said mockingly. "Check into it, he says. Hah! More like making a call over to the Oval Office, I'd think." She turned to face Collins.

"Do you think there's a chance, Buf?" she asked. "About getting Rector to do the trial, I mean?"

Collins put his hip on the table and scratched his chin. "Hmmm," he mused, "I think so. They're not going to like it, of course. No way. But what choice do they have? They now know that we've got the goods on all the others and they're loath to make any publicity over this which has already been too much. I'd say that we've got a good chance to get Rector."

"So, they won't object to Rector, eh?" the president asked Finch. Finch didn't respond as he thought the question was rhetorical. They were out on the lawn behind the White House. The president was taking a constitutional from the humdrum of executive office business and was breaking in a new putter.

Finch waited quietly while James lined up a putt, pulled his hands back, hesitated, and then swung the shiny new club through the ball. With a sharp clock sound the ball swiftly rolled about twenty-five feet straight toward one of the four or five cups placed on the practice green. The two men watched the ball as it drifted ever so slightly to the right as it slowed and then it lipped the cup and ended up about three feet off to the left.

The president made a grunt under his breath and Finch looked sharply at his superior. It sounded like the chief executive had muttered a common expletive, but he wasn't sure.

Gardner James turned to face his attorney general. "Okay, Rector it is. You know, this might all just work out for the best. Don't you agree, Bobby?"

Finch was awed by how the president always seemed to be able to turn around every event and every outcome and make it look like it was either what he'd planned all along or had hoped would happen. Except for the announcement of the Grand Jury that was looking into the corruption that got this whole thing started, Finch couldn't remember another time that the president appeared to have received bad news.

Inwardly he shook his head. It was an admirable trait but one that made his job very scary.

"So, Harland Rector is okay with you, Mr. President?" he asked, seeking confirmation.

"Of course," James replied patiently. "You know what old Harland's rap is, don't you?"

"Uh," Finch hesitated, wondering what the president was after, "I'm not sure. What is it?"

"He's slow," the president said. "He's very careful. That makes him deliberate and that makes him slow. He's heard maybe less than two-thirds as many cases as guys who've been on the bench much longer."

"And that helps us how?" Finch inquired.

"If we give them Rector and we load them up with the escalated charges of corruption like we're planning to do, right?" The president took another putt while grinning and talking. "It'll slow them down.

They might not be able to finish the trial before the election. And that my friend is just what we want to happen."

Finch got it. "Ah! We've changed tactics now, haven't we? Once we wanted the trial to be quick and low profile. But now with Collins as the nominee, it's a media circus. So, the best plan is for us to keep him as far from campaigning as we can and at the same time try to hamstring him in the trial. All in all, there's no way that he'd have a chance in the election. It's perfect." He beamed at the president.

"Yup," James said and watched this putt drop into the center of the cup. He took it as a good omen. "And we might just get those acquittals in the trial after all. It'd be icing on the cake, don't you think, Bobby? Have all defendants acquitted and win the election, too? It has a nice sound to it. I know I like it."

Finch turned to go. "All right then, Mr. President. It might take a day or so to work it out, but I'll get Harland Rector lined up for the trial."

"You do that, Bobby," James said. "But remember that there's no big hurry. If you need the time to set it up right, go ahead and take it. But uh, don't delay more than a week on the other hand. We don't want Collins to have too much idle time. He might remember he's got a presidential campaign simmering on the back burner." He grinned at his little joke and started to line up another putt.

Finch actually did need a couple of days to extricate Rector from another trial he was presiding over. The biggest difficulty he had was getting the old curmudgeon to accept the inevitable. It seems that he thought that as a federal judge, he had complete autonomy and could say and do what he liked. It took about fifteen minutes of private conversation with the attorney general to convince him otherwise.

Collins and Shawna finally got word of what was going to happen on Friday. After two days of silence from Finch, they were about to start biting their nails and undoubtedly the media was getting restless milling around the empty courtroom. The notice came to them in the form of a note from the court clerk saying that the trial would reconvene with the honorable Judge Harland Rector presiding, at nine a.m. on Monday, August Twenty-Seventh.

Collins read the note and handed it to Shawna who turned and handed it to Tom Laughlin. They were all sitting in Collins' law offices and had been discussing the possibility of holding a second press conference that afternoon when the messenger arrived with the clerk's note.

"Good," Laughlin said. "They've taken the bait and it's my very educated guess that they think that by giving you Rector, they've assured themselves the upper hand. So, I think that it's critically important to keep them a little off their guard and therefore, we definitely should hold that press conference today."

"But if they think that they've got the upper hand with this Rector thing, why should we try to rattle them?" asked Shawna.

"Tom's thinking that by upstaging them a little with the press conference we distract them from thinking too hard about whether Rector is as good a choice for the trial as they think," Collins said looking at his father-in-law who nodded in acknowledgment.

"Oh!" Shawna exclaimed excitedly. "I get it. We keep taking the initiative to keep them thinking about new things—things that we pick and control—which allows them less time to think about things that we don't want them to be thinking about." She looked at the two men.

"I couldn't have said it better," Laughlin said, smirking.

Chapter 16

Collins stepped up to the temporary podium set up in front of his law firm offices and opened up his second press conference shortly after two p.m. that afternoon, August Twenty-Fourth.

As before he had a prepared statement but also as before he presented it without reference to notes and to nearly everyone it came across as a sincere extemporaneous expression of his thoughts at that very moment. His sincerity was genuine, and his honesty and integrity radiated like a beacon.

President James, watching from the Oval Office, ground his teeth. "How on Earth a non-politician can look so natural is beyond me," he muttered.

Robert Finch shot him a quick glance and was about to comment that to be natural was the defining element of being a non-politician but then held his silence thinking better of the saliency of this observation.

There were three main points that Collins wanted to make in his "prepared" statement. First, he wanted to give out a little more background on himself as a person, this being the intention to use these venues as a means of ensuring selected information is given accurately and directly to the audience. The idea was to obviate any interference or tailoring by the media as much as possible.

Second, he wanted to provide an update on the status of the trial. He made it clear that this was a serious matter and as it was an ongoing case, he was unable to talk about the particulars, but he felt that he could provide a short explanation of why the trial hadn't yet started.

"We'll be starting the trial on Monday," he said in a clear voice looking directly into the cameras. "This will be a week late and the delay was due to a small amount of trouble finding a judge who didn't have any conflict of interest with the case. As you may know the Grand

Jury handed down several indictments naming a number of public officials. These officials have been around for many years and hence in one way or another have dealt with nearly all of the judges on the federal circuit."

The third point that Collins wanted to make was that he wanted to assure the voters that he was doing his duty as special prosecutor—that he was doing his job and that for the time being, the presidential campaign would have to wait. He asked the public for their patience and forbearance in this matter as it was very important and dealt with issues of misconduct and abuse of authority that needed to be addressed expeditiously and prudently.

He looked directly into the cameras and literally spoke from his heart. "I want every single American to know that I take this responsibility as special prosecutor very seriously and I intend to do my very best in seeing that the guilty parties are arrested, arraigned, and summarily punished. The corruption and abuse of authority that this trial deals with are things that I find to be repugnant and I'm going to fight for the rights of the victims and their families with every shred of my being and ability. I give you this as my promise. I won't let the criminals go free. I won't!"

In the Oval Office, Gardner James groaned. "Oh my God! The non-politician—the non-declared candidate—is waxing political. It makes me sick to see this. I wouldn't doubt that Tom Laughlin's the puppet master behind this grotesque performance. Not a doubt in my mind."

When Collins was finished, as before, he took some questions. This time, the questioners were polite and generally kept to the subject matter at hand. Shawna who this time stood behind Collins and a step off to the side looked around for the sleazy man in the rumpled suit but couldn't see him.

After about a half hour, she gave a pre-arranged signal to Collins who then held up his hand. "That's about all the time that we have, folks. I must apologize and draw this conference to a close at this time. I promise to hold another one as soon as I can."

Back up in his office, Shawna and Collins found Laughlin sitting down in a client chair studying something. It was almost as if he was unaware of what Collins had just been doing. When he heard them enter, he looked up and smiled grimly.

"Oh! There you are. I watched the whole thing on television," he said putting on a cheerful face. "I must say that that part about promising to punish the guilty was sheer genius. Did you just think of it on the fly? I know it wasn't something that we talked about beforehand."

Collins stared at his father-in-law curiously. "Yes, it just sort of came to me in the heat of the moment. Thank you, Tom. But what do you have there? Is it something serious?" He was drawing the old man back to what was apparently causing his glum expression when they had entered.

"I've just gotten the results of the first presidential preference poll," he said looking back down at the papers in his lap.

"Oh?" said Collins. "And how am I doing?" He forced a modicum of optimism into his tone but from Laughlin's expression he knew differently.

"Well," Laughlin began, "they aren't very good. Of course, we didn't expect to have a strong showing. Certainly not this early considering that you're still largely unknown to most of the voting public."

"So, what are they?" Shawna asked impatiently.

"Overall, they show that if the election were held today, Gardie James would get eighty percent of the vote, you'd get twelve, and there were eight percent who said that they were undecided."

There was a pause while this information sunk in.

"Whew!" Collins exclaimed. "Eighty percent for James. That's a pile." He looked over at Laughlin. "Has any sitting president ever had that high a rating?" he asked.

Laughlin considered the question for a moment. "No, it's unprecedented for any candidate to be that high. Extremely popular candidates like Ronald Reagan in Nineteen Eighty-Four for example, have only been able to get approval ratings up near the seventy percent level. Never eighty."

The old man looked at the others with a twinkle in his eye. "But of course, this is only the beginning. There's a long way to go and a lot could happen between now and November Sixth. I know that James' lead looks insurmountable at eighty percent, but make no mistake about it gang, he has only one way to go and that's down."

"How can you be so sure?" inquired Shawna. "I mean look at it. With all due respect to you Buf, you're still a nobody and you're going to be locked up inside a courtroom for who knows how long. Take into consideration that James has a pretty dang good track record in his first term, that he's going to be trying to undermine you in the trial at every turn—and don't forget he has the clout and the authority to do so, and even if you get some time to do some campaigning your lack of political experience mightn't hold you in good stead.

"Then, there's the media and based upon what they've started to do there's every indication that they're going to do their darnedest to make you look bad. That's because it's the quickest way to good ratings and readership. You've even said it yourself, Buf. You don't stand a chance of getting a fair shake from the media simply because there's no juice in that story. No. No, it's clear to me that they're going to take the more salacious route. They're going to dig and dig into your background— and Jane's, and mine, and Mr. Laughlin's too, I'll bet you—until they find something that they can use. They'll ignore the more mundane, and . . . uh, factual information, just like hungry wolves go straight for the guts and gore and are oblivious to everything else.

"That's what's going to happen. I'm sure of it. And so, I don't see how it's possible that that eighty percent's the highest rating James is going to have." She shook her head forcefully. "I just don't see how you can say that he only can come down from eighty."

Laughlin looked coolly at the young woman for a moment or two. Then he spoke to her in a level tone. "Why don't you sit down, Shawna, and you too, Buf, and let's talk this thing through. These are very good points you've raised my Dear, but I'm not sure that you're taking all the facts that we have into full consideration."

Collins went to sit in his office chair and Shawna took a seat next to Laughlin.

"There are two critical aspects to this as I see it," the old man began. "First, there's the trial and the most important part of that is getting Harland Rector to let the full visual media into the courtroom. We've already talked about that, and I fully support Janie's strategy on how to pull that off. Then, there's the go-for-the-jugular attitude of the media that Shawna has so astutely pointed out. The way I see it, these two factors make a very volatile mix—one that I feel strongly will turn out to be an elixir for you Buf."

"Why do you think so, Tom?" asked Collins.

"Well, for one thing as we've already noted, having the American voting public see you in action in the courtroom, doing what you do best is the best venue for you. Add in the basic fact that since the trial is about something that nearly everyone can relate to, there's the strong possibility that the voters will begin to see you as their champion. The political cachet that this will give you is incalculable and something that'll make Gardie James hate every second that the trial is on tee-vee.

"Now, having said all that we add to the brew the special ingredient of the avarice of the media—their desire for ratings and circulation. They, as you both have said, can only see Buf, the non-declared candidate, as a stooge that they can make a mockery of. This will happen and for the next few weeks buckle your seat belts because it's going to be a wild and bumpy ride. They're going to let out all the stops. You won't be available for interviews and comments, et cetera; so, they'll have a free rein to go wherever their nose for dirt takes them and we can be assured that they won't worry too much about the provenance of the stuff they report. You're now a public figure and thus libel and slander aren't going to be easy claims for you to make against anyone.

"But then once the trial gets into full swing after jury selection and so on, there'll be a turning point. First, by then the media will have pretty much run out of material even if it's making some of it up. Second, the public will have become fully disgusted with it. They'll realize exactly what the media has been up to and believe it or not they'll understand that it was strictly business and to a certain extent a form of entertainment. Amazingly, very few will associate the mudslinging directly with you. At the same time many voters will have become bored with the lopsidedness of the ratings and start to say they'll vote for you just to make it interesting. This is what's called the underdog effect. And third, when they start to see you in action in court and the details of the trial and the charges come to light, they'll realize that you're not who the media's been portraying you to be but rather someone they like.

"It'll be at that point that whatever approval rating Gardie James has—and I'll defer to detracting Shawna's argument in that it may very well be more than eighty percent by then—will begin to fall and do so quickly. And there won't be a thing Gardie can do to stop it. In fact, I predict that any effort he might make to quell the slide will only be perceived by the fickle American voting public as a sign of weakness, thus making the fall all the more dramatic. These phenomena will be a combination of the rats departing the sinking ship and the bandwagon effect." He smiled with genuine pleasure. "It's going to be quite something to see, and I'm delighted that I'll have a front row seat to watch it happen."

While they considered this, Shawna looked up sharply.

"What about your running mate, Buf?" she asked. "The press is pressuring us to name a vice-presidential candidate. They say that it's unheard of not to have one so late in the campaign."

"Hhrrumph!" Collins scoffed. "That's because they don't know their law. I looked it up right after I accepted the nomination. I didn't want there to be any distraction in the early days of the trial; so, I wanted to hold off on naming a running mate as long as possible.

"It's actually rather interesting—the history of running mates in this country. In the early days, presidential candidates didn't have running mates. The vice-president was selected by the electoral college, and it was invariably the candidate who came in second in the public voting. This was the original way the founding fathers set it up. In fact, this is the same way that vice presidents are officially elected today with the exception that the electoral college no longer picks who it is. The first change in the process came in Eighteen-Forty-Four during the campaign of James Polk who had a running mate for the first time. The fellow, by the name of George Dallas, was the first person to be nominated as a vice-presidential candidate. From then on vice presidential candidates were nominated at the political conventions. Note that the presidential nominee still didn't pick the guy and quite often the one didn't approve of the other. It didn't seem to bother anyone that this way of picking two people who have to have a close working relationship in the near future was awkward at best.

"It wasn't until the twentieth century that the new president had any say in who his vice president was. The first time the presidential nominee named his running mate was in Nineteen-Forty-Four when Roosevelt named Harry Truman as his choice for vice presidential nominee and threw his support behind his nomination. This was Roosevelt's fourth campaign for the Oval Office, and he'd had different vice presidents for each of the previous three terms. I guess he was tired of all the mystery and guessing. So, he put his foot down for the fourth campaign. The convention delegates really had no choice but to give him what he wanted. After that, it was pretty much left in the hands of the presidential candidate and gradually over the years, the tradition has emerged that each leading presidential candidate hopeful will name a vice presidential running mate some time before the convention.

"My research indicates that although this is the current accepted practice, there is no constitutional basis for it—the only requirement is that the electoral college has to officially elect the vice president. Thus, our interpretation is that each presidential nominee is allowed to name his vice-presidential running mate, as a matter of modern-day practice, but there is no restriction on when this needs to be done, neither how early nor how late.

"So, my friends, regardless of what anyone says, we don't have to do anything about naming a running mate—just as long as I do so before the electoral college meets." Collins sat back making a satisfied smile.

"Golly, Buf. That means that you don't even have to have a running mate named before the election," Shawna said, amazed.

"Nope" responded Collins. "There is no requirement for there to be a vice presidential candidate named on the ballot."

"But surely you do intend to name someone, don't you, Buf?" Laughlin asked.

"Of course, Tom but not until the time is right," Collins replied.

The old man nodded his head thinking it over.

"Hmmm, seems like a useful approach," he commented. "Particularly given that you're caught up in the trial and can't campaign—at least not in the normal way. If you named a running mate, the media and Gardie James would all probably zero in on the poor fellow mercilessly expecting him, or her, to do your campaigning for you. Nope. It wouldn't work. Having a running mate before you can get the trial out of the way just doesn't make any sense. I agree with you Buf. Waiting on this is a good strategy. It might even distract the James camp even more than they are already."

Collins and Shawna were silent while they thought over the old man's sage words. After a minute or so Collins began nodding slowly to himself and then looked over at Shawna and saw that she too was nodding.

"Very good, Tom," Collins said. "I'm glad you agree. Your support on this is important to me. So, let's get back to the topic of the polls, shall we? About three weeks to a month from now once the trial has really begun and there's daily television coverage, if we get our way with Rector, you predict that James' rating will begin to tumble. Right? Well, how far down do you think it'll go?"

Laughlin looked down at his feet and didn't answer right away.

"My guess is that it'll fall down to about sixty-five percent thereabouts maybe a little less, maybe not," he answered in a low voice several seconds later.

"Sixty-five?" Shawna repeated. "From maybe as high as eighty-five? That's a drop of only twenty points."

"That's right, Shawna," Laughlin confirmed. "But in the elitist game of presidential elections a drop of twenty points in a relatively short time is galactic."

"Why is that?" asked Collins.

"Any change, particularly a drop in presidential approval say in a single week of more than two or three points is usually more than enough to stimulate the media into making big news about it. And big coverage will result in more people knowing about the drop than would've otherwise and thus more people will be compelled to care about the reason for the drop. This will probably cause a ripple effect and the president's rating will then drop some more."

"It'll be contagious," Collins said. "Once some people who didn't know or care become aware of the drop, they'll begin to doubt the strength of their support and change their minds. It's like erosion."

"Exactly," agreed Laughlin. "But therein lies a partial problem."

"What's that?" inquired Shawna.

"Not all of the voters who decide they no longer like the president will throw their support to Buf," Laughlin replied.

Collins looked at Shawna. "Tom's saying that as the ratings drop for James, my own rating won't go up point for point."

"Why not?" asked Shawna.

"Because some of the points, perhaps as much as half of them will be undecideds," said Laughlin.

"Ah!" uttered Shawna, getting it. "So, if James' rating drops to sixty-five percent by the end of September, Buf's might only have climbed to eighteen or twenty and the rest will be undecided?"

"Right," said Collins and Laughlin nodded in agreement.

"Huh!" Shawna exclaimed. "That's a crock of shirt."

"Indeed," agreed Laughlin, nodding.

"And the wild card is that no one can predict what the undecideds will do come election day," commented Collins.

"That's right," agreed Laughlin. "It's just as likely that they'll elect not to decide and perhaps not even vote at all."

"So, what do we do about it?" Shawna asked. "Sixty-five to twenty is no contest in an election. How can we get Buf more points?"

"Ah, now there's a fighter, Buf," Laughlin said, smiling. "I like this lady's spirit."

"Do you have any thoughts on what we can do in October, Tom?" Collins asked.

"I do, Buf. I do." The old man was smiling again, his eyes twinkling elfishly.

"What are they?" Shawna asked.

The old man looked directly at the younger woman. "I've been thinking about this for a while, you know, since I've signed on to be Buf's campaign advisor and I've put together my thoughts and some conclusions into a little strategy document, something I'm calling the October Plan."

Collins looked up, interested in this. "The October Plan you say?" he asked. "You have a plan for us to execute in October, Tom?"

The old man nodded.

Shawna turned her head back in forth between the two men. "Well?" she demanded of the air between them. "Let's stop pussyfooting around this thing guys! If Mr. Laughlin has a plan for how we can get your ratings to go up, then I for one am ready to hear about it." She looked at Laughlin. "Is it written down? Or still up in your head? C'mon! Quit stalling! Tell us about it!"

The old man was silent and sat still smiling like the Mona Lisa.

"I think that it's about time that you start calling me Tom, pretty lady," he said to Shawna smiling.

"Okay," Shawna said, agreeing, ". . . Tom." She said this like her tongue was swollen.

There was a short pause and then they remembered that Laughlin was about to reveal his plan to them.

"Tell us about the October Plan, Tom," prompted Collins.

"Yes, Tom, please do," prompted Shawna.

And so, the old man did.

CHAPTER 17

On Monday, August Twenty-Seventh, the trial began. There was a little fanfare when judge Harland Rector entered the courtroom. The media was now sensitized to the fact that who would preside over the trial was an actual item of news and thus when court was called into session by the clerk, the throng of print and press media was uncharacteristically silent and attentive. They wanted to know whether Collins and Wells would let this judge sit.

In a disappointingly unnewsworthy fashion, they did. It was a non-event. So, Harland Rector it was.

But the members of the fourth estate that were in the courtroom that day were unprepared for what came next.

Collins remained standing after Rector announced that everyone could be seated and quickly was noticed by the judge who looked inquiringly at him. Rector was a veteran of more than a thousand trials, and he knew instinctively when something was up. He bent his head forward slightly towards Collins indicating that he may address the court.

"Your Honor," Collins began, "with the court's permission, before we start, the prosecution wishes to make a motion."

Rector had been given an in-brief by Robert Finch himself on the particulars of this case (which took about ten minutes) and also on the political ramifications of having a presidential nominee as the special prosecutor (which took over an hour). He wondered what Collins could possibly be up to.

"Go ahead, Mr. Collins," he prompted.

"Your Honor, the United States would like to petition the court to ban all media from the courtroom including all cameras and videotape as well as all audio recording devices. Your Honor, we believe

. . ." He was instantly drowned out by a hubbub that erupted in the courtroom, presumably caused by the reporters both trying to get a better advantage to hear what Collins was saying now that they sensed he was talking about them and urgently whispering to their colleagues next to them wanting confirmation that they had just heard correctly. Collins wanted the judge to kick the media coverage out of the trial!

Rector was a very large man, topping out in the six-foot-five-inch stratosphere and weighing in certainly above the two-hundred-and-fifty-pound plateau. His gavel was barely visible in his meaty fist but as he was applying it to its pestle with such vehemence, it was distinctly audible above the din. It was his booming stentorian voice, however, that brought the chaos under control.

Even before everyone had finally settled down and the noise was in the dull roar stage, Rector lashed out. "Silence! I will not tolerate this kind of disruption while I'm on the bench. Uh uh. Ladies and gentlemen in the gallery," he stuck out an accusatory finger pointed directly at the press corps, "you will remain silent at all times when this court, my court, is in session. And that means, let me spell it out for you," he smiled a nasty smile much like a drill sergeant at boot camp about to be his most demeaning, "no talking, no whispering, no rustle of paper—especially not that," he seemed to bristle and cringe at the thought of this transgression, "—and no clicks or pops or snaps of any devices or equipment. None. Nothing. Nada. Capice?"

Rector was answered with a several-second broadcast of a very loud silence. He nodded his head and started to direct his attention back to Collins but seemingly had a second thought and looked back at the gallery.

"And anyone who violates the decorum of these proceedings will be bodily removed and I'll personally see to it that he or she never works this beat again." He glared at the reporters seemingly defying anyone to object to this Gestapo-like threat. After a moment of sustained silence from this quarter, he then calmly turned his head back to regard the special prosecutor for the United States.

"All right then, Mr. Collins? You may continue."

"Thank you, Your Honor," Collins resumed. "As I was saying, we believe that the sensitive nature of this case and the seriousness of the charges that have been made against the defendants warrant that the media be restricted from the courtroom when the trial is in session. Therefore, as special prosecutor and thus the appointed representative of the United States, the attorney general of the United States, and the president of the United States, I petition the court to grant our request."

At this, the press corps in spite of its collective self, emitted an audible rustle of paper and immediately invoked a blood-curdling glare from Rector. Within a second the noise ceased completely. It was as if they, as one, simultaneously realized that their truancy was a critical issue in how the judge would rule on this petition.

Rector was momentarily at a loss. It seemed inconceivable that with the highly fueled political atmosphere that this trial was going to have, keeping the media out of it was suddenly going to be an issue. He then regained his composure and realized that there was a protocol to this that had to be followed.

He turned to look at the defense table. Instead of the normal two Captain's chairs that comfortably fit behind the oaken table, there were ten narrow Sunday School chairs tightly packed behind the table and spilling out around its ends forming a crescent that faced the front. All ten chairs were occupied with expensively dressed lawyers.

Rector raised his eyebrows in surprise. He stretched out his arms towards this small army in a questioning gesture. "What's this?" he asked of no one in particular. "There's not going to be a defense in this trial? What? Am I going to have to deal with all of you? This isn't going to work. Nope. This is one trial and I'm a simple man. Therefore, I want the tables to be occupied like they should." He pointed over at where Collins and Shawna were seated. "Like Mr. Collins here has done. See? Two chairs—two lawyers. Got it? Now, I'll give you until this afternoon to figure it out and then I'll hear arguments from the defense, meaning from the defense lawyer—singular—concerning Mr. Collins' motion." He picked up a pen and tapped it twice on the wood surface in front of him. "This court is recessed until . . ." he glanced at his wristwatch, "two o'clock this afternoon."

Over deli sandwiches and dill pickles, Collins, Shawna, and Laughlin mulled over the morning court session while they sat in Collins' office. Jane had brought in the food and was staying over to help them eat it.

"I think that Rector's going to work out," Shawna observed. "He's got a style about him that's going to work well for our side, I think."

"Mmmm," supported Collins, his mouth full of corned beef on rye. "He's a pistol all right," he managed after swallowing.

"Harland's from the old school," agreed Laughlin. "It's really quite surprising that in his lengthy career he never crossed paths with any of the defendants."

"Yes, it's amazing that he didn't," commented Shawna.

"Mmmm," mused Jane. "You might say that he was being groomed for this case almost from the beginning."

Everyone stopped chewing for a moment and stared at her.

Jane stared back wide-eyed, wondering what the matter was, but no one said anything.

After a moment of uncomfortable silence, Laughlin spoke to his daughter. "Janie, my Dear, you have the most unique way of looking at things, I must say."

This seemed to make the odd moment pass and everyone started chewing again. All except Collins who looked curiously at his father-in-law out of the corner of his eye.

At two when Harland Rector called the court back into session, he looked at the defense table with satisfaction. Instead of the array of ten chairs that had been there in the morning, there were now the obligatory two and both were occupied. There was a woman in the "first chair" seat and a gray-haired man in the other.

Collins and Shawna followed Rector's gaze and took in the two people who were to be the opposition. The man both knew well; the woman was someone neither had ever seen before.

"All right now," Rector was saying. "This is a little more like it." He nodded his head at the woman. "And you are?" he asked.

She stood up and looked directly at the judge. "Maddie Russell, Your Honor. I'll be representing the collective interests of the defendants."

"Excellent, Ms. Russell," Rector beamed like a father at a soccer match. "Is the defense ready to respond to Mr. Collins' motion that he has placed before the court?"

"We are, Your Honor," Russell replied in a clear voice.

Remarkably in what was a very short amount of time, the defense "team" led ostensibly by this newcomer, Maddie Russell, put on a detailed and compelling argument against Collins' motion to keep the media out of the courtroom. She cited several cases and gave a multi-page listing to Rector and a copy to Collins.

All the while Rector sat on the dais and listened somberly. It was as if his mind was already made up but that he was not happy about it.

Throughout it all, and it consumed most of the afternoon, Collins and Shawna sat and bided the time. Although they didn't confer nor, for that matter, even exchange knowing looks, they were of a common mind: There was no way that Rector was going to accept their motion. This, of course, was what they wanted.

When Russell finally wound down, Rector was slumped over, appearing to be nearly asleep. It took him a few moments to notice that she was finished and had sat down. With an exaggerated motion of effort, he pulled himself back into a normal sitting posture and looked over at Collins.

"Rebuttal?" he invited, halfheartedly.

Collins stood and smiled thinly. "Your Honor, Ms. Russell has done a remarkably good job providing us with an educational and enlightening review of the practice of jurisprudence in this country and for that I thank her and her colleagues." He looked over at the defense table with a sly look. "But . . ." he paused and directed his eyes to the judge, "and, Your Honor, there is a but. I suggest that Ms. Russell seems to have missed the point. This trial . . ." He stopped abruptly. Shawna was surreptitiously tugging at the hem of his jacket trying to get his attention. He looked back at Rector. "May I have a moment to confer, Your Honor?"

Rector leaned his head forward in approval. "A moment, Mr. Collins."

Collins turned towards Shawna and leaned down to let her whisper in his ear.

"Buf!" she exclaimed excitedly. "Don't do this!"

"Don't do what?" he asked under his voice.

"You're about to be a good lawyer. Don't you see? You've made a motion and now you're going to try to talk the judge into it. That's what you're good at and this time we want him to deny the motion, right?" She pulled back and looked directly into his eyes, invoking him to agree with her.

She was right, of course. He was a veteran of far too many sparring matches with judges and opposing counsel and his track record was remarkably good. He realized what Shawna had astutely sensed was that he was falling into the old groove. He nodded to her and patted her shoulder encouragingly.

He straightened back up and turned to face Rector again. "Thank you, Your Honor. Er, as I was saying in rebuttal of Ms. Russell's argument against our motion that she's missed the point. We've made our motion in good faith, and we believe it to be in the best interest of the government and for the case. We wish to let our motion stand." He sat.

Rector stared at Collins for a moment almost as if he was surprised that he'd said so little in rebuttal. He ticked his pen on the oaken surface of the desktop. "I'll take this under advisement and will provide my ruling when court reconvenes tomorrow morning. This court is adjourned until nine a.m."

Harland Rector was no fool and immediately recognized what was going on. He knew that Collins really didn't want to keep the media out but was playing some kind of mind game on the opposition. In an instant he sensed the dynamics of the situation but interestingly he saw that keeping the media out of the courtroom during the trial didn't seem to favor either side nor for that matter did letting the media in seem to disfavor any side. Now, the feeling of knowledge and power elusively departed him, and he fell into a quandary. He abhorred an untidy trial and this one was sure to be that. Letting in the media would only exacerbate the situation. He shook his head wearily as he took off his robe in chambers and hung it on a coat rack peg. But regardless of his predilections, he saw that media coverage in the courtroom while the trial was in session was unavoidable. He sat at his desk and reached for the phone and punched in a number that he read from a scrap of paper on his desk.

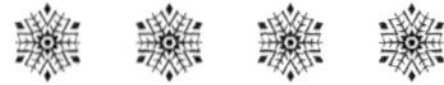

The next morning after court was in session, Rector addressed the United States' motion to ban the media from the courtroom.

"Mr. Collins? Your motion is denied. The media may cover these proceedings with video and audio equipment. Live. But they'll have to do so quietly, or I'll ban them myself!"

CHAPTER 18

So, on went the trial with the media and live video coverage right there in the courtroom, step by step, word for word.

The first several days were consumed with voir dire, the selection of a jury. All in all, for a trial of this purport and with its publicity, the process of impaneling twelve peers and three active alternates went remarkably smoothly. The fascinating part of this process was how Collins handled it.

He didn't turn down a single candidate and invoked none of the preemptive rejections to which he was entitled. On the interview, he only asked one question and regardless of the answer he accepted the prospective juror. The question was, Do you exercise your constitutional right to vote in elections for public officials?

In the Oval Office, Gardner James, watching parts of this on t.v., snorted when he first heard Collins voice this question. "Hrumph!" he chortled. "He's so far behind, he's having to resort to confirming his voters one by one. Hah!"

In his office in Justice, Robert Finch had a different impression. "He's making sure that everyone knows what side of the bread the butter is on, Jaimie," he observed to his assistant. "Rather clever, I'd say. Collins is establishing that it's the voters who've put the defendants into office in the microcosm and that it's the same voters who could put him into the White House in the macrocosm."

Back in the courtroom, the defense was highly selective and thus the empaneling process exhausted more than fifty-five candidates from the juror pool before the final set was complete.

During the evenings, while this was going on Collins worked with Shawna, Jane, and his father-in-law on a series of videotapes that they would release to the media as the trial went along. These tapes were of Collins speaking to "the public" about himself and establishing the foundation of his "common man candidacy" for the presidency as he wanted to call it. There was a sense of urgency to get going on this and rather than wait for the trial to finish up or for that matter hope that it would be short, Tom Laughlin recommended that they do something to counter the bad press that he'd predicted would happen.

These videos were carefully scripted by Collins, Jane, Tom Laughlin, and Shawna to provide the voting public with information and data about Collins that they felt was pertinent and appropriate for a typical voting citizen to make an informed choice.

They knew this was a calculated risk. They knew that voters invariably made their selection on the basis of factors that had little to do with a candidate's competency, such as his grade point average in high school, whether he liked football or baseball, cats or dogs, hot dogs or hamburgers, mayonnaise or Miracle Whip. It was Collins' objective to allow for the voters to have as little access to information about him relative to these "other" factors as he was able to control.

Before the jury was finally selected, Tom Laughlin's prediction about the restless media was starting to come true. It was on Sunday, September Second, that the descent into Hades began.

"Take a look at page three of the New York Times," Tom Laughlin suggested to Collins and Shawna his voice coming in crisply over the telephone conference call he'd initiated. It was before eight a.m. and all three had been up since dawn working in his and her respective homes. Laughlin waited while Collins and Shawna each pulled up the newspaper's website and located the area he'd targeted. "See the box over on the right?" He waited while they read it to themselves silently.

The piece, presented as an editorial—just to be safe—noted that William Collins had made only two public appearances outside of the courtroom since his acceptance speech on the last day of the convention in Atlanta. The article speculated that this was because Collins was more than camera-shy. It implied that Collins was emerging, due to his absence from the public forum, as a reluctant candidate—he was drafted after all, right? It said that Collins was staying away from the media because he knew he'd look bad and that, since it was, by implication, obvious that he had no political savvy or elected-office experience (of any sort), he was likely to be a bad president. No mention was made about the trial. It seems that the author of the piece was being deliberately selective about the facts in order for the desired point to appear all the more valid.

"Typical of the entertainment mindset," Collins grunted. "They think they're different than the tabloids but when you take away the starched shirts and bow ties they're just as nasty and just as unscrupulous."

"Those sums of ditches!" Shawna exclaimed. "They're coming just short of saying that no sensible person should vote for you, Buf." She was so emotionally involved and committed to the trial and the campaign that she took any slight against Collins as a personal affront.

"This will likely continue—this type of freewheeling," Laughlin said softly. "They're going to shoot first and apologize, if necessary, later. And it's highly likely that it'll get worse, more outlandish, and more personal. Buf, you're going to have to gauge how much you and Jane are able to take. Then, as that break point approaches, you're going to have to start responding to them—give the public another perspective; let them seek a balance," he suggested.

"Nope. I won't dignify their remarks by acknowledging them in any way," Collins said vehemently, his face reddening with emotion. "Our best course of action is to keep to our strategy: Focus on the trial and let the media coverage show the public what's going on so that they can make up their own minds based on first-hand information. Then, we continue with our prepared video spots that we've been working on. This is the only way that we can control what we want the public to know about me.

"Just think what could happen if I went on some talk show. They might very well taunt me, or whipsaw me, or more probably edit the tape to make me look bad. And there'd be nothing that we could do about it. And then there's the chain reaction potential: If they know that they can get me to make public statements when they say bad things about me, they'll then outdo themselves to invent outrageous stories. It'd be a free for all." He shook his head, like he was denying a frivolous request posed by an immature child.

"You see, my friends," Collins continued, waxing pedagogical, "the media is loath to lose control and I wouldn't be surprised if the major networks soon start to air some coverage of me that's a product of their own invention. We have to expect this. They want something that'll get the public's attention and, if we aren't available to provide them with it, they'll make it up. Because what we're giving them for general distribution to the public is carefully designed by us to not cause any controversy, the media will feel hamstrung. This is just not what they're used to. They're products of their own duplicity. And, as long as we won't play the game, we can expect them to start bending the rules." Collins nodded knowingly.

Two days later on September Fourth, the day before the jury was finalized, a minor bombshell hit. The story that broke that morning was quickly picked up by all the wire services and was the first blow that brought blood.

The lead was:

> Reclusive presidential candidate Bill Collins apparently is a snob. A careful check of birth certificate records in the Commonwealth of Virginia and the city of Roanoke reveals that his father's legal name was William Byron Collins. Therefore, the calling himself as William Buford Collins, *the sixth* is an affectation that the candidate has adopted evidently to appear sophisticated and elitist to the American public. This is the most ridiculous public stunt since former marine fighter pilot (and at the time in no need of optometric correction) Barry Goldwater was found to be wearing horn-rimmed eyeglasses in the 1964 campaign because his advisors said it made him look more sophisticated and distinguished.

"Oh my God" Jane said over breakfast, her anger exuding in her fierce tone and gritted teeth. "They're now making up the news on you, Buf."

"Mmmm." Collins murmured. "I saw it earlier this morning, Darlin'," he said as he continued to munch on a muffin. "This is to be expected and I knew that this sort of drivel was certain to come along in one form or another. The only thing that we didn't know was what they were going to use as the basis for their smears." He got up and gave his wife a warm and lingering hug.

While continuing to hold her as if his next words might cause her some reaction, he spoke in a low tone while his mouth was close to her ear. "And we have to gear up for more, I think. This is only the first sortie of who knows how many. Our only salvation Darlin' is that we have to suffer for only about seven more weeks of this." He gave her another tight squeeze and then pulled his head back so that he could look into her eyes.

"Now promise me my sweet girl, that you'll tell me when the pressure starts getting to you. All right?"

"Mmmm." It was Jane's turn now to demur. "All right, Sweetheart" she answered after a suggestive pause and the look that she gave her husband ineffably conveyed volumes about her deeper feelings on this whole presidential campaign thing. She broke away from her husband's embrace and turned back to her breakfast. She was eating a toasted plain bagel smeared with cream cheese and sipping decaffeinated coffee with a little skim milk and some sugar mixed in.

"But what about this article, Buf? I mean shouldn't we do something about it? Shouldn't we tell them—you know the people, the voters—about this?" Jane was upset about the deliberate attempt by the media to misreport the facts and hence place her husband, a man whom she felt was above reproach in every conceivable way, in a bad light and she wanted desperately to make it right. "I mean, it just isn't fair!" She stuck out her lower lip in a girlish pout and her eyes flared with emotion.

"Yes Darlin', we should" Collins replied. He patted her on the shoulder. "But not right now. The best strategy is for us to wait and for us to provide accurate information at the times and in the places that we select and that we can control."

Jane Collins looked admiringly at her husband as he went back to his last few bites of his now cold muffin. He was right, of course. This strategy was perfect, and she marveled at how effortlessly her husband expounded upon it.

Collins nodded and exited the kitchen in the direction of his study. Since it was still not yet seven a.m., he thought he could work a bit at home before having to go into the office prior court convening at nine. He went and sat down at his antique English oaken desk and turned on his personal computer that rested on the credenza.

He frowned while the machine powered up. The question of that morning's news coverage of him and his allegedly spurious name was bothering him more than he'd let on with his wife during their breakfast.

He booted up the word processing application on his computer and opened up a new file. He began to type.

*** * * PRESS RELEASE * * ***

Alexandria, Virginia.

Presidential candidate William Collins has been a successful trial lawyer for more than twenty years. He's known in his professional arena as William Buford Collins, VI which is the name that is on his birth certificate. Collins' father, who was born William Byron Collins, and his mother hadn't speculated on what to name Collins when he was born. They wanted to continue with the tradition in the Collins family that had been going on for more than two hundred years. This was the naming of the eldest son in every other generation, William Buford Collins. Thus, these sons were named after their grandfathers not their fathers. The sons in between the string of William Buford Collins' each were named William as well but bore different middle names that always began with the letter b. In this way, William Byron Collins' father was William Buford Collins, V. This man had been named after his grandfather who was William Buford Collins, IV who had named his three sons, Walter Joseph, Warren Geoffrey, and William Baker. William was the oldest and hence the heir who was to carry on the family tradition by having at least one son who would be named William Buford Collins, numbered next in the series. In this way, William Buford Collins, VI, the currently nominated candidate for the presidency of the United States is not a sixth generation Collins as the Roman numeral marker after his name might suggest, but actually a *twelfth* generation Collins.

Collins leaned back and reviewed his work. He seemed satisfied at least with having made a formal documentation of how he'd come by his name. In the past, it'd always sufficed for him to respond to the question of where he got his name by simply saying that he was named after his grandfather.

Of course, that was before he was a candidate for the president of the United States. It was a unique role to play for which all previously acceptable modes and means of living one's life no longer applied. This was a case in point: It apparently was not acceptable to the press and media for a presidential candidate to be simply named after his grandfather—there had to be a more salacious or sinister reason.

The despair must've percolated up out of Collins' inner self and made him grimace because it caused Jane, who had followed him into his study after she'd tidied up the kitchen from the leavings of their breakfast, to exclaim loudly in outburst: "My God, Buf! What's the matter?" She moved quickly around the huge desk and put her arm around her husband's shoulder and pressed her cheek up against his neck.

"Oh, uh . . ." he faltered, searching for the best response. "It's nothing to worry your pretty head about, Darlin'. I was just working on some ideas for what we need to be doing next and I got to thinking about what sort of slander the press has in store for me next."

He stood up and embraced his wife with his arms. He held her for a moment looking into her eyes and then engulfed her in a massive hug, nestling his face in the crook of her neck. Jane brought up her arms and returned the hug.

"Mmmm," he murmured, "As long as I have you to lean on, I believe that I can take any and everything that they can throw at me."

"You're upset about the article in the paper, aren't you, Buf?" she asked in a low voice.

Collins disengaged and steered his wife to the couch and deliberately sat her down, and then plopped down beside her. They sat hesitatingly, perched on the edge of the cushions. He turned himself so that they could face each other, obliquely. His face was only inches from hers.

"Wow," he said, his voice full of admiration. "How in the world did I get so lucky as to find a woman like you?" he asked her for the umpteenth time.

"You, as always," he continued with seriousness rippling in his tone and demeanor, "are the seeress, the one who can see everything in its proper perspective. And again, as always, your understanding of the situation is exactly correct. The campaign, the trial, the convention, the Secret Service—they're all the big things and it's those that we seem to be taking in stride. But the little things—like the newspaper article, stuff that really shouldn't matter actually does matter. Doesn't it?

"I've been sitting in here trying to make sense out of all of it and it's struck me that we're letting ourselves be distracted from what's really important. And that's our life, you and me and our family. That's all. That's everything. And as you've said, if we lose sight of this, not only would we be lost, but we'll lose anything and everything that we might seek."

He got up and went over to the printer and took a sheet of paper out of it.

"Here, take a look at this," he said bringing it back and handing it to her.

Jane took the sheet from him and began to glance at it. "What is it?" she asked.

"I came in here this morning with the intent of doing some work, but I couldn't focus on anything. I was hurt by that newspaper article about my name, and I wanted to set the record straight. So, I wrote this out as a response."

Jane quickly read through the short paragraph. "But Buf, you're not really going to—" she began.

Collins held up his hand, stopping her. "No, no. I'm not going to send it out. We're going to keep to our strategy. But it felt good writing it down under the pretense that I might send it out at some point. It helps having you read it, too.

"But for the very reasons that we talked about, we can't try to fix all the wrongs that the media is going to create for us. That'd be playing by their rules."

Jane set the sheet of paper aside. "Yes, and we don't want to dignify their style of playing by lowering ourselves to their level, do we?"

Collins took the sheet and ran it through the shredder by his desk.

"No, we don't," he replied. "Now, my love, let's get on with the day."

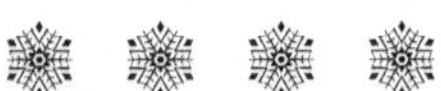

The polls for the week of September Tenth, showed that President James had a rating of eighty-two percent, Collins twelve, and six percent were undecided.

CHAPTER 19

On Thursday morning, September Thirteenth, Collins made his opening statement before the new and fresh jury. After being given permission to begin his case from Judge Rector, Collins stood and approached the jury. Before he began, he turned to look at the courtroom. This was a bit of showmanship that he'd become accustomed to in his long and successful career as a trial lawyer. Let the audience know he knows they're there watching and let the jury know that he's not just pitching to them. Rather, he's prepared to make his case to all the peers in the room not just those in the jury box. In his sweeping look he took note of Maddie Russell and her entourage of assistants, Shawna at the prosecution table, and Tom Laughlin sitting in the front row behind Shawna next to Jane and Lucy Doering Walton. He gave Lucy and Jane a collective acknowledging head nod and turned to face the jury.

"Ladies and gentlemen, I thank you for your commitment to perform your civic duty by appearing in the jury for this trial. I'm very sorry to tell you that the evidence that I'll present over the course of the prosecution half of the trial will paint a sordid picture of our beloved America.

"This picture will be a mosaic of smaller yet strikingly similar scenes that have been occurring with distressing regularity in many of our nation's largest municipalities for several years.

"This picture will show you a side of public officials that I'm sure all of you will find disgusting and distasteful and I've no doubt many of you will be distressed even outraged to learn that this has been going on right under our noses. These civil servants are police department personnel such as detectives and commanders and chiefs. They are medical examiners, coroners, and doctors and interns. They are lawyers, district attorneys, and judges. And after many years of unrestricted freedom, some are now holding elected offices such as legislators and other local and state officials a few of whom have become members of the United States Congress.

"Ladies and gentlemen, it troubles me that I have compelling and irrefutable evidence to present to you that condemns each and every one of the defendants named in this case.

"But it grieves me even more to be representing the agony and concerns of the families of the victims in this case—families just like your own but families who've suffered terribly at the hands of these civil servants. It's this situation, this condition, that's the foundation of this case.

"What have these public officials done? How could they have caused so much tragedy? Why are they on trial? Why have they been charged with criminal wrongdoing? I'll tell you now and then I'll present the evidence that will irrefutably implicate each and every defendant not once and not twice but many, many times and then it'll simply be left to you to invoke your judgment of guilt on these people.

"So, what did they do? Each of these people failed to do their job. That's what they've done. What act did they fail to perform? They were put into their jobs to do one specific thing and that was to, in their respective roles, honor and protect the citizens who lived in their cities.

"The principle of our republic that Thomas Jefferson conceived is innately simple. We agree to live in a common society, democratically, and thus to abide by a set of basic rules. We then place people into various jobs in our government and empower them to serve and to protect upon our behalf.

"Upon our behalf.

"We've placed our trust in them to do their jobs and they have failed to do them. The evidence will show that each and every one of these people violated their sacred trust.

"I am shamed by this. I'm a citizen and a voter just like each of you. I knowingly and openly supported placing some of these people into their jobs. I willingly and consciously empowered them to do their jobs. And I, just like you all, entrusted them to serve and protect upon my behalf.

"What have they done to breach this trust? The sad truth is that they weren't inadequate, nor insufficient, nor even incompetent. We could've dealt with this. We could've accepted it. We would've excused it.

"But ladies and gentlemen, this, I'm very, very sorry to say, isn't the case. No. These people who are on trial here are in fact all very capable and competent. What they did was of their own volition. These people took their jobs, entrusted and empowered by us, and violated this trust and abused this power, on purpose, and for their own personal gain.

"That's right. I cannot tell you how angry this makes me feel. I'm outraged and resentful and I feel violated. And when you see the evidence, I'm confident that each of you will feel this way too.

"It's not going to be an issue of reasonable doubt or burden of proof in this trial. No. My job is going to be remarkably easy. When you see the evidence, you'll know. These people, the defendants, have committed their crimes out in the open. They've made no effort to hide their actions. As a matter of fact, when the time comes in this trial for the defense, I warn you that they'll say that the defendants have done nothing wrong. The defense will say that they were doing their jobs. It'll say that they were doing what they were put into their jobs to do.

"It sounds confusing, doesn't it? It would to me, and I appreciate your reactions when you first hear this. But it really is very simple. These public officials who are on trial did not do their jobs to their full ability. No, and that's the critical issue here. The evidence will show that once empowered these people used that authority in ways that we, the public, never intended for them to use it.

"Is this enough? Of course, it is. This is the corruption part of the case. But unfortunately, you're going to have to go beyond judging whether these public officials deliberately and criminally breached the public trust and abused their power.

"I've told you that the evidence will show that these people executed these unlawful acts on their own volition. It'll show that they did this many times over the years. It'll show in nearly every case that it was regular and often—a solid pattern or trend, if you will. A clearly evident pattern of corruption.

"And it'll show that these people used these unlawful acts to further their careers. Yes, that's right. They took personal and self-serving advantage of the outcomes that they were manipulating by abusing the authority that we entrusted to them. Can you believe it? These people were fixing things so that they'd look like they were doing their jobs even better than otherwise would be expected!

"I'm personally shocked and chagrined. It galls me that these people were so arrogant that they could stand in front of the people who had placed their trust in them and boast about how well they were doing when in fact the data that they were using was the direct result of their own deliberate manipulation of the system.

"Is that enough? Absolutely. More than enough for me. I have to tell you ladies and gentlemen, that at this point when I was putting this case together, I was so disgusted that I wasn't sure that I'd be able to stand before you and tell these truths without becoming physically ill.

"But I have evidence that these people didn't stop at laughing at us as they helped themselves to the credentials they needed to further their careers. That's right, there's more. And I have to prepare you, this next part is pure evil.

"So, what is it? What could be worse than what you've heard already? How on Earth could these awful, criminal, and arrogant people do any more? Isn't corruption in public office enough? It seems too hard to believe; too much to take, doesn't it? Well, I assure you, these people are guilty of much more than being corrupt.

"The evidence that I'll present in this trial will show that as these people advanced up their respective ladders, they brought in people behind them and taught them how to do what they had been doing to get ahead.

"Think about it. What does this mean? It means that every defendant participated knowingly and actively in a master plan to protect them from ever being found out.

"This is what's called collusion. Collusion is when corrupt public officials collaborate with others to contribute to their corrupt acts. This collusion is so widespread and has been going on for so long, that it's the most insidious, odious, treasonous, anti-American conduct that has occurred in the entire history of this wonderful nation of ours.

"The evidence will show this irrefutably, unequivocally, and definitively.

"The evidence will show that each person named in this case repeatedly:

"Violated the public trust.

"Abused their authority.

"Obstructed justice.

"Committed malfeasance.

"Committed nonfeasance.

"Committed misfeasance.

"Misrepresented public facts and data.

"Knowingly lied and misrepresented their actions and the facts."

He paused a moment to let all this sink in. And continued with the following shocker, "And ladies and gentlemen, members of this important jury, this is not even the half of it. Nope. The public officials on trial here did not stop at colluding with members of their own organizations. No. They colluded with the criminal elements in their cities as well."

Collins paused again, letting this bomb of flagrant information settle into the minds of the jury. He knew that it would take some time for them to understand and then accept the fact that the public officials were in some way working in concert with the criminals. He knew he needed to clarify this notion.

"Oh, this collusion wasn't explicit in that the defendants sat down with the criminals in their cities and worked out a plan for corruption. Not exactly. But when it became apparent that the city officials were deliberately deciding which deaths were worthy of their time to investigate and which ones were not, the criminals, the murderers, saw an opportunity. They no longer needed to hide any evidence of their killings. They merely needed to not kill their victims with guns and knives. They picked up on the jargon that the city officials, namely the coroners and the police, were adopting. They were saying that if a person had not died of obvious causes such as a gunshot or a knife wound, by definition, of their own creation, these deaths were not *real* homicides and thus did not warrant any further investigation. When the criminals realized that they did not have to worry about investigation or scrutiny, they simply stopped using guns and knives to dispatch their victims. This constituted the crime of collusion, folks. Tacit collusion certainly but illegal collusion, nonetheless.

"This is the real crime here. The real tragedy. Our elected officials were doing this on purpose! In plain sight! And taking credit for cleaning up the cities by stopping violent crime!"

Collins stopped at this point and walked across the front of the jury box scanning the faces of the jurors.

"Is this enough? Corruption and collusion with others to so corrupt? I should think so and I can see from some of your expressions that you're already disgusted. Well, I'm very sorry to tell you that this is the best that you're going to feel.

"When the prosecution begins to present the evidence what you're feeling now will only get worse. Why? There are two reasons. First, the facts and evidence I will present will be, as I've said, self-explanatory. This is because there has been no attempt by any of the defendants to hide their actions. All along they've construed their actions as being what they were supposed to be doing. Thus, the evidence of their actions is readily available and plentiful. A matter of public record, in other words. The second reason is the shocker, ladies and gentlemen. When I present the evidence to you, I'll show that even though these people were openly committing the crimes they're charged with they were also actively and aggressively hiding something.

"They were hiding the fact that they knew what they were doing was wrong and that they could at any time stop doing it. But they didn't. It was their free and open choice and every single one of them knew it. But they kept on doing it—the corruption and the collusion—and they've tried to hide it from us.

"This behavior is rampantly illegal. And they're all guilty of it." He paused and paced lazily in front of the jury for a long minute letting it sink in. This is the first time Collins had mentioned collusion to anyone except Shawna Wells and Tom Laughlin and now on national television, live coverage, he wanted all who were hearing this to make sure that they heard it correctly. Then, he stopped moving and turned to face the jury and put on a solemn expression.

"And I am deeply sorry to say that there have been, and continue to be, literally hundreds of friends and families of the murdered people who have been lied to and mistreated shamelessly who almost to a one, knew and knew viscerally that their loved ones were murdered but could not do anything about it. That, my honored members of this jury, is the real crime here.

"These people, our trusted civil servants did all of these things and if we don't stop them, they and others after them will keep on doing it.

"Thank you, ladies and gentlemen. And now I'll let you be the judge."

In the Oval Office, Gardner James clicked off the t.v. and uttered a vulgar expletive. He turned to face Robert Finch with a violent look in his eyes.

"I thought that collusion was a card we were supposed to play, Bobby. Pray tell me how Collins got to it first? How?" He looked away and waggled his hand at his attorney general. "Oh, never mind. It doesn't matter now. It's probably Tom Laughlin's doing anyway." He circled around his desk and sat down. "The point is the momentum has shifted. We no longer seem to have the upper hand, Bobby."

The president sat there drumming his fingers on the polished mahogany surface of his executive desk while Finch stood uncomfortably in front it, feeling a weakness in his knees that screamed at him to sit down.

"Got any ideas?" James asked casually.

Finch hesitated to answer suspecting that there was no response that would be greeted favorably by the chief executive, including no response at all. He cleared his throat, stalling for time.

"Come on, Bobby!" the president snapped. "You're supposed to be the top lawyer in the country. Think, man! How can we turn things back around on this?"

Finch looked morosely at his superior. "Mr. President," he began cautiously, "I don't think that there's anything that we can do—legally that is. It strikes me that this momentum thing that you're talking about is more in the realm of politics than law."

James raised his eyebrows, as if Finch had just said something profound. He stopped drumming his fingers and started nodding his head.

"Right," James said in a tentative tone, much as if he were sounding out his reaction to what Finch had said to see if he liked it. Apparently, he did because he clenched his fist and pounded it on the desktop.

"Right!" he said now with conviction. "You're absolutely right, Bobby! It is political and not a matter of law. Of course! Such a simple thing! And it shocks me that somehow the nuance was lost on me, and I had to hear it from you before I could see it.

"It's political," he repeated. "Of course."

CHAPTER 20

That evening over dinner at their home, Jane was prattling on about innocuous events in her day while her nominee husband was doing the nation's business in a hot courtroom.

"I got a call from Susie O'Connell today, Buf," she said as if she just recalled the conversation.

"Mmmm?" Collins was non-committal. Susie O'Connell was an old college and sorority friend of Jane's who lived in Arlington, Virginia which Buf Collins had often silently remarked to himself, was altogether too close for comfort. It seems that Collins thought Ms. O'Connell a bit too much of a free spirit to be someone in his wife's inner circle. But he was his wife's husband and he'd never openly expressed his opinion of her friend to Jane. "How's Susie doing these days?" Collins asked after a brief pause.

"Well, she didn't mention anything about her health as I recall," Jane answered somewhat playfully. She was trying to make light of something that was burdening her.

Collins instantly picked up on the paradoxical connotations in her tone and suddenly was solicitous. "Oh? And so, what was on Susie's mind, then?" he asked softly, glancing up to look at his wife.

"Well . . ." Jane began to reply but then hesitated, her face twisting into an expression of indecision, as if she were having difficulty choosing between two undesirable alternatives; something like being compelled to pick between being given a shot in the arm or in the buttocks.

Collins reached over and patted his wife's arm soothingly. They were not eating in the formal dining room but sitting casually side-by-side at the nook table offset from the country kitchen. He leaned over to his right and nestled up against Jane and almost whispered in her ear.

"It's all right, Darling," he said reassuringly. "It's just us. No one's going to hear us. I gather that Susie didn't call today to shoot the breeze with you. So, let's hear about it. Take a deep breath and tell me."

Jane looked at her husband and her eyes had a vulnerable, cocker spaniel cast to them. She was filled with foreboding about how he'd react to hearing about Susie's call. But as she held his gaze and felt the warmth of his body against hers, she began to calm down and relax. She was surprised at how tense she'd become and realized that Susie's call had affected her much more than she would've been willing to admit.

"So?" Collins prompted.

"Well . . ." Jane began. Even though she'd now committed herself to be completely open with her husband about Susie O'Connell's telephone call that afternoon, she was unprepared to tell the story and didn't know where to start.

"It's okay, Darling," Collins said softly. "I know that it may be difficult and that you may not have the whole thing sorted out yet in your mind. Just tell me about the call and we'll work out the how's and why's and so on afterwards. Okay?"

"Uh huh," Jane acknowledged. She took a deep breath, resolved herself, and then started talking rapidly, trying to get it over with as quickly as possible. "Susie called to tell me that she'd been contacted by Rip Beauchamps a couple of days ago. You know, the anchor of the national news broadcast every evening at seven on Channel Three." She looked to see if Collins understood but also to check his reaction.

He nodded silently but showed no emotion one way or the other to this revelation. He was going to let her tell it all before he spoke.

"Right," Jane continued. "Well, it seems that the network has been doing some deep research into you, and I guess me, and they found out that Susie and I went to college together and stuff, you know. Susie told me that Beauchamps said that he was in town and wanted to know if he could talk to her. Susie said that he seemed to be so warm and gracious and, you know Susie, she told me that she'd always thought that this guy was the biggest hunk on television. So, she told him that he could come over right away.

"Then, when he came, Susie said he wasn't alone. He came with a camera crew and microphones, and the whole nine yards. She told me she was pretty shocked, but it was Beauchamps himself who rang her bell and she said he was so much more handsome in person than she'd expected him to be, and he was smiling at her and looking meaningfully into her eyes and that it was hard for her to focus on the fact that he really wasn't alone.

"She said that before she knew it the whole group, equipment and all were ensconced in her living room and the cameras were on and Beauchamps was sitting right next to her talking to her eye-to-eye, and she said that she was calling to tell me that she was really, really sorry and that she hoped that I'd forgive her.

"She said that she got caught up in his charm like a moth drawn to a candle flame. She said that she was so infatuated with his magnetism that she rattled on like a schoolgirl and that it wasn't until later when she began to sense that Beauchamps had used her that she realized that she'd been exaggerating some when she was answering his questions.

"She told me that this was why she was feeling so guilty and that she felt that she'd let me and our friendship down. And that she was sorry." Jane had been speaking so rapidly that she was now nearly out of breath and even though she realized that she hadn't really given her husband any details, she stopped at this point to give herself a chance to regroup and also to give Buf a chance to jump in if he wanted.

He sat there, patiently waiting for her to continue. When she didn't go on right away, he wondered if she was expecting him to speak.

"So, did Susie tell you anymore?" Collins asked more as a nudge for Jane to go on than because he was ready to diagnose this problem that his wife was bringing to him.

"Uh huh, she told me a lot of what she told them, and I'm really outraged at Susie for being so foolish. I mean doesn't she realize what that Beauchamps guy was after? Is it possible that Susie O'Connell is really that dense?" She looked at her husband and from his look realized that the answer to this question was obvious. "Oh, I suppose that you're right. I'm sure that you've often wondered why I associate with someone so different from my other friends and from me. Well, I'm not sure that I can give you a plausible reason, except that I've known her so long, she's really like a sister and I guess I don't notice much about her outward persona anymore."

But to Collins there still had to be more to it than what he'd heard thus far. "And?" he interjected innocently.

"Mmmm?" Jane looked up indicating that she'd momentarily lost the drift of their conversation. "Oh! Oh, yes. What I mean about the bad part is that Susie told me pretty much what she told the Beauchamps guy and on the surface I suppose it really is nothing much except for two things, one of which really makes me mad at Susie and that's that she told them about something that happened to her while we were in college except that she let on that it was really something that happened to me."

"Uh huh. Well, that really wasn't very girl-friendly of her, was it?" Collins offered diplomatically.

"It was downright stupid of her, and I told her that she absolutely had to get back to Beauchamps and set the thing right. Susie said that she already knew that this was what she was supposed to do, and she'd been calling the station and the network all afternoon but couldn't get through. She said that then she began to be very afraid that they were going to put the tape they made on the air maybe even tonight and she thought she'd better warn me first." Jane looked at her husband and it seemed that she was now even afraid.

Collins sat up a little straighter, his interest piqued at this last revelation. "And what are we talking about here, Jane?" Collins almost never used his wife's name when he was addressing her and his use of it here, even though he was using a level tone, compounded her fear.

Jane's eyes widened and as she was opening her mouth to tell her husband, she was interrupted by the ringing of their telephone.

Jane slid out of the breakfast nook and went to pick up the telephone.

"Hello . . . oh, hi Daddy." Jane's face went from one of comfortable recognition of her father's voice to a pale mask in just a few seconds. "All right." She hung up the phone and turned to face her husband. "Dad says we need to turn on the tee-vee." She hung her head in seeming defeat.

"Beauchamps?" Collins picked up on the ramification of Laughlin's call right away.

He got up and went over to put his arm around his wife's shoulders. "Well, let's go see what the sly old dog has to say about us. Mmmm?" he said levelly. "I'm sure that whatever Susie the Floozy told him truthfully or otherwise isn't going to be anything that we can't deal with, Darling." He began to walk with his arm still around his wife into his study where there was a television set. He switched to the proper channel as the set warmed up.

The disembodied voice of the network news prime-time anchor began to envelop the Collins' as they watched, entranced.

"Presidential nominee, Bill Collins is going to have to answer for this," Rip Beauchamps was saying, looking deeply into the camera lens with his eaglelike blue-gray eyes. His pin-striped navy-blue suit, blue shirt, and foulard tie conveyed integrity and honesty and his prematurely silvered hair longishly swept back over his ears assured his audience of his unshakable sagacity. He was the number-one rated national news anchor. He knew it. He'd earned it. It was now his right to bring the most important news stories to the American listening and watching public. "Our world-class investigative news team has been tracking Mr. Collins' bid for the chief executive's office and today we're able to provide you with an exclusive look into the sordid side of this man's life.

"It seems that while in college he got his girlfriend, one Jane Laughlin, pregnant and then paid for her to have an illegal abortion." Beauchamps leaned forward to establish a higher level of intimacy with his viewers. "Although Collins married Ms. Laughlin after graduation, I'm personally affronted at this cavalier and heartless action while he was a junior at the University of Virginia during a time when in this country, I must remind you, abortions were illegal and when they were done, they were usually done in dark back rooms by who knows what kinds of people. They weren't doctors and they weren't nurses.

"I don't ask any of you to take my word for it about all this as I'm sure everyone watching tonight will agree that this sort of information about a presidential candidate is highly inflammatory and should be revealed by the media only after careful investigation and confirmation. I assure you folks that what I'm telling you is the pristine truth." Beauchamps then spoke in an aside. "Let's roll the tape, Sammy."

At this point the news stage darkened, and a large inset screen appeared and then before Beauchamps' viewing public, which that night, for once included Collins and his wife, appeared the instantly recognizable, at least to the Collins', figure of Susie O'Connell speaking seriously and convincingly into the camera lens.

"I, uh, Rip, don't know whether I should be telling you this," she paused smiling coyly and batting her eyelids. " . . . but I guess I can because it was so long ago and I'm sure that by now no one would really mind. I assure you that it's the complete truth because I was there personally by her side when it all happened. My best friend in college, and my very good friend still today, Jane Laughlin got pregnant when we were juniors, and she aborted the pregnancy that spring."

"Who was the father?" Beauchamps' easily recognized voice asked from off-camera.

"It was Jane's boyfriend, Buf Collins," Susie replied solemnly.

"You mean, Bill Collins? The current nominee for the president of the United States?" the voice asked.

"Mmmm. Yes, Buf Collins," Susie dutifully answered. Her eyes lit up as if she'd just realized an important fact. "Jane Laughlin is now Jane Collins. She and Buf got married after graduating from college." Susie nodded for emphasis.

The tape jumped a bit and suddenly Susie was sitting in front of the camera in a slightly different position. It seems that the network crew was providing the trusting American viewing public with an edited tape.

"Is there anything else of interest that you can remember about Jane Collins, er, Jane Laughlin back in college?" the voice asked.

"Well, no, I don't guess so," Susie replied hesitatingly. She seemed to be affected by trying to think about this question very hard. Then she suddenly smiled broadly. "Oh! Well, there's one little something that I remember about Jane," she added proudly.

"Uh huh?" the voice prompted.

"Jane got into trouble with our sorority late in the spring of our sophomore year. She almost got banned. I guess she got it straightened out somehow, because when we all went back in the fall, there she was, back, pretty, and perky as always."

"What was the nature of this trouble? Do you remember?" the voice asked.

"Oh, I do now!" Susie was enthusiastic. It was as if she was grateful to the interviewer for helping her recall this juicy tidbit. "It was right around final exams, and we were at an end-of-year celebration party at the main fraternity house at the top of Greek row. Well, we were really glad to be almost done with our exams and all and we were letting it all hang really far out. I'm embarrassed to say that we all got a little drunk on sangria wine, and . . . well Jane really went off the deep end and she put on a really wild strip tease show for all of us. She was just like a professional dancer, you know. She didn't have a special costume or anything—just her regular clothes, but she strung it out for a long time, and she really got the crowd into it. And she went all the way— she took off her bra and panties and in the end, she was totally nude. I gotta tell you, that girl had class, drunk or not. When she was done and the crowd was cheering and screaming and whistling and everything, she took a sweet little bow and walked off to go finish off her drink. Then the really amazing part was that she spent the entire rest of the night talking to people and dancing with some of the guys without ever putting her clothes back on."

At this point, the inset screen disappeared and the spotlight on Beauchamps came back on. The camera zoomed in on his face and he finished his piece. "And so, it seems that our presidential candidate, Bill Collins, is married to a little tramp."

Jane Collins sat on the couch in her husband's study and felt incredibly alone. She was shocked that her very old friend had been so willing to talk about her as she did. She looked cautiously at her husband. She was fearful of how he was going to react to this horrible thing. She felt a pang in her stomach and realized that she also was afraid about how this was going to affect her husband's campaign and then she began to feel increasingly moribund. She realized that if her husband didn't get elected that would mean that she would not be the next first lady, and she was horrified to realize that it'd all be her fault. She brought her focus back to her husband sitting next to her.

He was there still watching the television screen, not apparently having any emotional reaction to what they had just been watching and hearing. The news moved on to other subjects and he pressed the "Off" button on the remote control and turned to her.

He put his hand up to her cheek and stroked it lightly. "My Dear, you must feel terribly betrayed and violated by this horrendous invasion into your privacy." His voice was choked with emotion and his eyes began to well up.

Collins' sentiment was contagious, and Jane began to snuffle, and her eyes started to water and, in a moment, tears were rolling down her cheeks. They were the complex and paradoxical product of her intense state of mixed emotions: She was at once relieved that her husband was not irate at her, that he was actually thinking of her feelings over his, and incredibly that he didn't seem to consider this blockbuster media event much of anything to be concerned about. But most of all, the tears were flowing fully because of her deep affection for her caring husband. Least of all but not insignificantly, Jane was feeling a little sorry for herself, too. After all there was a part of Susie's out-of-school story that was true, very true indeed. Jane pulled herself together and tried to focus on the primary issue here: Her husband's presidential campaign.

"But Buf! What about you?" she blurted, her eyes widening with excitement. "Aren't you outraged that they'd put something this terrible, something this awful on the air? Aren't you mad at them for doing this? Forget about me; what about you? What about what this will do to your campaign?" Jane was now very energized as the potentially damaging ramifications of this prime-time news broadcast began to crystallize in her mind.

"No, no, Darling." Collins' voice was gently soothing and in no way did he seem either outraged or upset. "I've always expected that they'd do something nasty. Of course, I never suspected that it'd be anything like this, however. We must continue to remind ourselves, Dear, that only bad things, whether true or made up, meet the litmus test for news these days. I knew that they'd have to do a lot of embellishing and embroidering to make me look bad. But I never doubted that they would nevertheless try.

"But no, I'm not mad at them for doing it. I am, however, extremely upset that they're using you in their smearing. As I said, this is something that I didn't anticipate at all. And it's something that I especially don't like because it's upsetting you." Collins sighed deeply and his face reflected a deeply felt sorrow.

"Jane, my loving Dear, I cannot tell you how very, very sorry I am that I was so insensitive that I didn't think to try to prepare you for this possibility. It hurts me deeply that my carelessness has caused you pain and it's completely my fault. I take total responsibility for it, and I hope that in time you'll find it in your heart to forgive me for this terrible, inexcusable transgression."

Jane was appalled.

Buf is telling me that this terrible thing that I, alone and by myself, have caused is really his fault! How could he be this broad-minded? It was my friend that told this story to the news media. It was information about her and me not him. How could he see that he should take the blame?

"No, no," Jane countermanded Collins. "It's nowhere near close to being your fault, Darling. No, it was Susie, my long-time friend who was indiscreet here. And as you, of course, know, she didn't even get it all right—it was Susie that got pregnant and had the abortion, not me. But it's just as obvious that everyone'll believe this crock of doo-doo as if it were Gospel." Jane realized that she was digressing and reached out and squeezed her husband's arm tightly. "But Buf, forget all that. The real point is do you think we should do something about this?" She looked meaningfully at her husband.

Collins shook his head. "No, my Dear. We're going to let it go. We won't let ourselves be affected by anything that comes from the media during this campaign and most importantly we won't let them suck us into to playing their game."

Jane was overwhelmed with emotion. "C'mere you big old bear and give me a hug." Jane wrapped her arms around her husband and held him tight. "Okay, do nothing it is. We're in this together and we're in this for the full duration. No matter what they throw at us, no matter what happens. I love you Buf."

Collins returned his wife's warm embrace and realized that his wife could still amaze him with the impenetrable depth of her character. He nuzzled his face into the crook of her neck between her head and shoulder and silently kissed her soft skin several times.

Then he broke the embrace and leaned back on the couch and looked up at the ceiling.

"This has been our first real test and if we stick together and support each other, it won't break us. We must focus our strength." His tone was strong, but his insides were in turmoil. This marked the day when Collins felt as if he'd just crossed over a vast abyss.

CHAPTER 21

Week after week the trial marched on. Collins and Shawna meticulously stepped their way through a detailed plan they'd put together. The defense, led by the enigmatic Maddie Russell, attempted at every turn to stall or interfere but all in all it was fairly benign stuff.

The troubling thing was that no one knew who Maddie Russell was or where she came from. It was not even clear who specifically she was representing that brought her there. But she floated to the top as the single ombudswoman of the lawyers representing the defendants, nonetheless. And every day she vociferously fought for the defense of the defendants while her ten plus co-counsels sat nearby motionless and mute.

The first thing she did after opening arguments was to try to get Judge Rector to dismiss the charges by summary judgment. This, of course, was ludicrous but she made the motion unabashedly. Rector looked at her like she was out of her mind and swept his outstretched arm around in front of him encompassing the entire courtroom, media and all, in indication that the fact of the open and ongoing trial was more than enough to denounce such a notion.

But the slightly framed woman, who didn't seem to yet have had her thirtieth birthday, stood her ground and began to cite cases that were precedent to her argument. Rector cut her off straight and told her to submit the motion and citations to him in toto and in writing by close of business that day and that he'd take it under advisement during that evening's recess. He said would rule on it when court reconvened the next day, which he did, negatively. All he said was "Ms. Russell, your motion for the defense is denied," and then nodding at Collins, "Mr. Collins, you may proceed."

That was what it was like: Collins working his way along like a surgeon and Russell standing at his elbow with either a sledgehammer or a fire hose.

In spite of it all, Collins made progress. In more ways than one. First, he sensed that Rector was somehow an advocate for his case and thus he generally left it to the judge to deal with Russell's interferences. In this way, he was able to keep to his agenda and although it's always folly to predict how major criminal trials will go, by the first part of October he and Shawna were reasonably satisfied with how far along they'd gotten.

They'd established, beyond any reasonable doubt, that the deaths brought into question in the indictments were anything but what the public officials had classified them to be. These accidents, suicides, and naturally caused deaths, after a presentation of the facts were eminently not what the official death records showed. They were, to a victim, unequivocally suspicious. The obvious implication was that every victim was murdered but Collins stayed away from going quite so far as to suggest what the causes should be. This was another bucket of worms that ostensibly could come into consideration later on. At this initial stage, all he wanted to establish was that there was more than enough indication at the time of death of the victims that the circumstances were highly suspicious and thus strongly indicative that the cause was not natural, accidental, or self-inflicted.

This was a key point to Collins' prosecution, and he was able to lay this down as a rock-solid footer to the edifice of criminal actions he wanted to erect.

One of the major factors in conveying this message to the viewing public was when Collins brought into the courtroom some of the family members of the deceased victims. He did this carefully and only with just a handful of witnesses. But it was enough. More than enough. Any more would have been gratuitous grandstanding.

"Can you please tell the court about your daughter, Wendy?" he queried of a gaunt and grayish man who looked like his clothes hung on a skeleton.

"She was murdered about six years ago, Mr. Collins," replied the man looking up with sad eyes.

"I see," Collins acknowledged. "Was the murderer caught?" he asked.

The man seemed to sink into himself. "No, sir. There wasn't any investigation."

"Excuse me? No investigation?" Collins asked rhetorically. "Didn't the police look into Wendy's death?"

"No. They said that she was in an accident." The man's voice began to tremble. "They said that Wendy fell and hurt her head."

"An accident?" Collins looked over at the jury. "How did they come to that conclusion?"

"I don't know, Mr. Collins," said the man.

"Didn't you say that Wendy was murdered?" Collins asked.

"Yes sir, I did," replied the witness.

"But the police didn't think so, right?" was the question.

"Right," answered the man. "The coroner said that the cause of death was an accidental fall that resulted in a fatal trauma to the head."

Collins nodded. "Do you agree with the coroner's determination?" he asked.

"No, I don't!" The man sat up straight and his voice rose a couple of decibels.

"Why not?" Collins asked innocently.

"Because she didn't just have a bump on her head, Mr. Collins," he said.

"What did she have?" Collins asked.

"She had cuts and bruises all over her body." The man's voice began to weaken again.

"From a fall? According to the police and the coroner?" Collins appeared to be genuinely curious.

"So, they say but I didn't believe it for a second," replied the man.

"Can you tell the court why?" asked Collins.

"Because Wendy's body was found in a trash container. She was naked. Her hair was singed off of her head. Eyebrows, too. There wasn't any hair on her body anywhere. Just little burnt stubbles. Her face was all puffed up like she'd been slapped around. Her neck was scraped raw. Her wrists and ankles had what looked like rope burns. Like she'd been tied up or something. There were two fingers that had fingernails missing. Lots of coagulated blood. Another finger and two toes were bent at crazy angles like they'd been broken. All purply-blue and bruised. Her knees were skinned raw. She was dirty all over, like she'd been rolled in the dirt somewhere. It looked like she'd lost her bowels and messed herself. Her nose was broken and bloody. One eye was black and blue and swollen shut. She had what looked like whiplash marks on her back and buttocks and the backs of her thighs. She had two of her front teeth knocked out. Her lips were split." The old man began to snuffle.

Collins stood stock still and let this horror sink in.

"All from an accidental fall where she fatally bumped her head according to the police and the coroner, you say?" he asked in a low voice.

The old man nodded slowly and dropped his chin to his chest.

Collins turned to Judge Rector. "Let the record show that the witness has responded to this question in the affirmative. That the authorities in the city where Wendy's body was found felt that her bruised, beaten, abused, and horribly disfigured body was the result of a tragic fall that not only killed her but also rendered her nude and was of sufficient dynamics to have deposited her body into a trash container."

Maddie Russell shot to her feet and almost shouted, "Objection! Your honor, Mr. Collins is testifying,"

Rector calmly said, "Sustained." He turned to Collins and was about to admonish him for not framing his comments in the form of a question, but Collins quickly interjected by saying, "Your honor, I was merely characterizing for the jury this witness' testimony." Rector gave him a pitying look and Collins quietly added, "Withdrawn."

The damage that Collins wanted the jury to feel had been accomplished and he let his words hang in the air while the old man on the witness stand wept shamelessly.

"Sir, I am very sorry for your loss. One last question, if I may. Can you please tell the court how old Wendy was?"

The old man looked up with his bleary eyes. "Wendy was my only child, Mr. Collins. I raised her from a baby after her mama died of leukemia. She was seventeen years old." At this point the man couldn't contain himself any longer and broke down completely, sobbing loudly.

Collins looked over at the jury and could see tears glistening on several cheeks.

And so, it went.

Next, he methodically ploughed his way through piece after piece of evidence taken from public and official records to show that the police department, the coroner's (or medical examiner's) office, and district attorney's office all assiduously avoided any cognizance that the evidence surrounding the deaths in each of the cited cities was what it was: suspicious. Here Collins was establishing for the jury that the public officials had the full facts at hand and yet didn't act on them. The point was that they were being selective. Selective in the sense that they latched onto the facts and circumstances that suggested that the deaths were not suspicious and ignored those facts and circumstances that suggested that they were. In this way, Collins wanted the jury to clearly understand that the public officials were using their authority to reduce the number of suspicious deaths that they'd have to investigate, in effect making their jobs easier. He wanted to make it crystal clear to the jury that the public officials had to deliberately ignore facts and evidence at hand to declare the deaths as not suspicious. In other words, they had an elective choice and made their selections on the basis of what ended up being both easiest for them but also what made them look better: to do what they were doing was to make it look like violent crime was on the decline. And these officials were regularly claiming that they had been able to do all this in an environment of limited or even shrinking budgets, no less.

This was the corruption phase and throughout September and into October it moved along smoothly for the prosecution.

The second way that Collins made progress during this period was that what with the daily media coverage and live video broadcast of every word and action in the trial, the American public started to get to know who William Buford Collins, VI was. And what they saw was not a political candidate and nominee for the presidency. What they saw was a competent, intelligent lawyer fighting a crazy, quixotic battle. They saw a man who was intensely passionate about the tragedies of this case and compassionate for the families of the victims. This perhaps more than any other factor endeared Collins to the public. They also saw Collins as an underdog sort of hero. Here he was fighting "city hall," a fight that was imbued into the American mind-set that couldn't be won, but he seemed to be doing it!

Slowly and gradually the American voting public started to like this unknown, undeclared, non-political, common-man candidate for the president of the United States. They started to like what they saw and heard of him via the coverage of the trial, and they began to ignore and discount what they saw and heard from the media about him and his family in the "other" coverage of the day—the election campaign.

And his approval ratings, just as Tom Laughlin had predicted, started to creep up.

And Gardner James didn't like it. Not one little bit.

The president sat and looked out the window grinding his teeth. He half-wondered whether his dentist would notice the damage he was doing to the crowns of his molars. Then he forced this thought from his mind. He had a more important crisis to deal with: What to do about Collins.

He'd called for Finch to come in and while he waited, he pondered the problem that was before him.

This thing is quite complex and in another time, I might've enjoyed the mind play that it calls for. But this time the stakes are high, very high and I don't want to contemplate a political career that ends with a single term as president of the United States. That's something that's worthy of the Herbert

Hoovers, Jimmy Carters, George H. W. Bush's, and Donald Trumps of the world and if I'm certain of anything in this life, I am not in that group!

It was what had become to be called the Nixon Syndrome which simply was when a person became so fixated on a particular goal that everything in the world and in that person's life seemed to be inexorably linked to it, on the one hand, and also that everything, literally everything in that person's life was expendable in pursuit of achieving that goal, on the other.

There was a knock at the door and Robert Finch entered unannounced. James looked up in mild surprise at the breach in protocol but let it pass. He had bigger fish to fry.

"It doesn't look good, Bobby," James said solemnly.

Finch raised his eyebrows questioningly, wondering what his superior was bent out of shape about this time. But internally he knew. Everything with him these days was about the election. It didn't matter how the conversation started out or for that matter who started it, but if you were talking to or near James, it always ended up with him talking about how it was one of the critical factors in determining the outcome of the election. Rather than fuel the fire by responding to his comment, Finch calmly sat down and silently looked at the president.

"We can't just sit here and let this go on, you know," James continued hardly missing a beat. "Did you see the latest ratings?" He focused on Finch to stimulate a reaction to this.

Finch nodded his head unable to keep his face from displaying a morose frown.

"Right, my sentiments exactly," commented James sarcastically. "Well, Collins' ratings are coming up and mine are going down, and we've got to do something to stop it before it goes too far."

"He's only up to fifteen percent, Mr. President," Finch offered softly. "That's still pretty low. In fact, I'm not sure that there's ever been a case before in history where a candidate has been this low by this late in the . . ."

"I don't care whether history says this or that, Bobby!" shouted James. "All I care about is that he's coming up and I'm going down. We have to do something to stop this, to stop him from coming up."

Finch gave a small shrug of his shoulders much like he agreed with the president but really because it was too small a point to argue about anyway. He sat there trying make himself small hoping that the president might forget that he was there.

After a moment, James got up and came around the desk and sat down next to Finch.

"I can see that you don't have the same feelings about this as I do, Bobby," he said in a comforting tone. "I understand this completely. It's my tail that's on the line here and not yours and if I lose the election, it'll be only my career that'll be over. I get it. So, I commiserate with your apathy. But you still work for me and on this project you're my point man. So, I want you to show some interest in this, okay?" He looked at his attorney general.

"You, of course, know why you're the stuckee on this, don't you Bobby?" he asked.

Finch shot the president a suspicious glance wondering if the president was toying with him and took in that he was expected to answer this silly question.

"Of course, Mr. President," he replied in a dry voice. "I'm the stuckee, as you call it, because it was me who started this whole thing by calling for the eff-bee-eye investigation and then convening the Grand Jury." He looked to see if he got it right.

James didn't move or flinch. He kept on staring intensely at Finch.

Finch sensed that he was right but not yet completely right. He bit his lip thinking. "And . . . it was me that . . . that went out and found Collins to be the special prosecutor," he finished in a gush.

James reached over and patted his leg. "Bingo," he said. "You're the man. Now, don't be so glum about this Bobby. There's a silver lining in all this because as the architect of this fiasco, you're the only man who's qualified to save it from a total loss."

"Save it?" Finch asked, at sea.

"Yes, Bobby, save it," confirmed James. "I think that it's time that we stop toying around with Bill Collins and come out with some real firepower and just blow him away."

"Time for firepower?" Finch fumbled. A palpable foreboding began to creep into his consciousness.

"Right," James said unctuously, "I think that it's time that we let Collins know who's on which side."

"Side?" mumbled Finch. "What are you talking about Mr. President?"

James stood up and walked over to the wall and idly fiddled with some of the knickknacks and gewgaws that were randomly strewn around on shelves and tops of cases. He turned to face Finch.

"It's really quite simple, Bobby," he said with a sly look. "I thought it up last night and decided to sleep on it before I told you. See how I felt about it this morning, you know?

"Well, I awoke feeling more refreshed than I have in several weeks. I took it as a good omen."

"Took what, Mr. President?" Finch prompted. "What's your idea?"

"I think that you should make a few phone calls this afternoon, Bobby. Call up the colleagues of the defendants and some of the people here in the administration and in Congress that we know and get them to start making public statements about how outrageous these charges are in the trial and how Collins is just using the trial to do some political grandstanding and also to avoid campaigning.

"Pretty slick, huh?" James asked, smiling proudly.

Finch nodded his head slowly. "Yes, Mr. President," he replied in a low voice. "It is definitely slick."

James gave Finch a glaring look, as if he were about to say, 'Don't patronize me, now' but he held his tongue.

Robert Finch never felt more afraid in his life.

After a few moments, James wondered if Finch had heard him. The attorney general was sitting silently and looked like he was barely breathing.

"Bobby, are you all right?" James asked solicitously. "Have you been listening to me?"

Finch looked up at the president with expressionless eyes. "Yes, Mr. President, I've been listening. You want me to start calling some of the other public officials in and around the jurisdictions where the defendants are from."

James impatiently began tapping a pen on the desktop. "Yes, yes. I want you to make some calls," he interjected. "But I want you to see this in its proper light, Bobby. This isn't a trial thing. It's a campaign thing—these calls you're going to make. You see? We've got about a month to go and we're now rallying the gang together. You know, reaching down into the individual precincts not in the jurisdictions."

Finch held up his head, his eyes brightening slightly. "Ah, so you're saying that these calls are for political support. We'd be asking for them to make public statements in favor of your reelection and thus in so doing they'd be endorsing your accomplishments in the first term in office and hence by association supporting all those in the public service infrastructure including the defendants as well as themselves."

"Exactly." James beamed as if Finch's grasp of his new idea was greater than he'd hoped.

Finch nodded his head. "Okay," he began, "so this is just normal reelection tactics, I gather. Rally the gang, as you say. And I suppose that you're expecting me to make calls to people in jurisdic- . . . uh, precincts all over, meaning more than just those where the defendants are from?"

"Naturally." The president nodded his head eagerly.

Finch nodded his head again. "And therefore, in so doing am I to understand that at this point you're making your endorsement of the defendants' innocence a campaign position?"

James opened his mouth to say something and then stopped. He raised his eyebrows in surprise almost as if he was expecting Finch to say something but in fact had said something quite different. He closed his mouth and frowned. It wasn't clear whether he was disappointed with what Finch had said or unhappy with himself over this momentary loss of composure.

"No," he said slowly, "No, Bobby, I don't want to take a campaign position on the trial at this point, Bobby. Not yet anyway. It's good that you thought it through that far and I'm glad that you asked me for confirmation about it.

"I think that it's best, uh, most strategic of us to keep the trial out of our political rhetoric on the campaign for the time being. We've plenty of time to do something on this later. No, what I'm thinking about with these phone calls and the rallying thing is that we get the campaign endorsement from the public officials who speak in favor and support of the defendants, you know, sort of like once removed. They speak out in favor of the reelection and also throw their support to the defendants. The public reaction is that by association I'm in support of the defendants too, but I don't have to actually say so."

"Gives you plausible deniability," Finch offered.

James nodded his head and grinned gleefully. "Don't you love that phrase?"

The presidential polls for the week of September Twenty-Fourth showed that President James had a rating of seventy-eight percent, Collins sixteen percent, and six percent were undecided.

CHAPTER 22

One evening Collins and Jane were home alone eating dinner. This had been about the only stable part of their lives since the trial had started. Jane had cooked up some spaghetti and a dinner salad. They were also drinking some Chateau Margeaux Bordeaux wine from France, la prémière du cri.

"Mmmm. This is very good, dear," Collins said supportively.

"The wine or the spaghetti?" Jane was querulous about whether her husband was complimenting her culinary skill or just the quality of the wine.

"Why the spaghetti, of course." Collins feigned a little indignation. "You made this sauce yourself, didn't you? I can tell it's your own concoction, made from tomato sauce, fresh green peppers, onions, garlic, ground beef, whole tomatoes, a little sage, a little oregano, and some salt." He looked up at her with a mouth full of the pasta and raised an eyebrow questioningly. "Right?"

"I'm interested in your choice of words, Buf. You've elected to use concoction in reference to something that I've made with my own hands, something that I slaved for hours over a hot stove to make just for you. Am I to understand that you've done this openly and honestly, my loving husband?" Jane was amazed at her husband's perception about her cooking—that he would know the recipe of her sauce. She engaged him in a little wordplay while her mind whirled with these thoughts. Granted he did not cite specific measures of the ingredients or the sequence and so on, but he had the gist of it. The fact that he might be able to reproduce it on his own with this knowledge was impressive, to say the least.

What Jane Collins was really marveling about was that her husband, in the midst of a major criminal trial not to mention also being a nominee for the president of the United States was able to let his mind wander and settle on something so seemingly mundane and irrelevant. Not to mention that he was either able to cite the recipe from some dusty and lost old memory or outrageous as it may seem, intuit from the mere consistency and taste what the components of her sauce were.

On another plane, it was also noteworthy that all this week the climate and the mood of the Collins' had been quite different from just a week before. Jane was aware of a building sense of confidence and also, a comfort between herself and her husband that had previously been absent. She realized that it was not confidence gained by overcoming adversity. No, rather it was confidence in themselves, their partnership with each other. It was a feeling that if they supported one another, they could deal with anything. This confidence fueled a comfortable feeling of relaxation that lent itself to the levity that the Collins' were enjoying over dinner this evening.

"Yes," Collins responded, "I believe that I did consciously select the word concoction from my extensive vocabulary, and I assure you that I intended for you to take it in its most favorable sense. And I also want to reiterate my praise at how good the sauce is, Jane Dear. It's one of your best results from this recipe. It goes very well with the Bordeaux, don't you think? What's the year of the vintage?" He reached out and peered at the dusky label on the bottle. It had come from the wine cellar in the basement that Collins had assiduously and lovingly stocked over the years. "Ah, no wonder, it's a premier crop, nineteen seventy-two. That is, if I recall, one of the best years in the twentieth century. It goes very well with Italian pasta. Rather an odd thing for a French wine, eh?"

Jane just smiled at her husband as she inferred that his question was rhetorical. She was having a very pleasant time this evening. It hadn't been since before the convention that she'd felt this comfortable. Yes, they'd tried to preserve their evening dinners together as the rock of granite that they needed to keep their "old" lives intact during the trial and the campaign but, in reality, they'd been ritualizing the repasts and that, not until this night, had either one, husband or wife, felt any of the cozy camaraderie of old.

On the spur of the moment, Jane blurted out, "Buf! Why don't we go out and do something this weekend?" The excitement that was in her voice at the beginning of this sentence quickly dissipated and by the time that she got to the last word, not only was her voice flat but also her face had transformed from happiness to sadness. She realized that she'd for the moment forgotten that their lives were not their own and there was simply no conceivable possibility that she and her husband could just go out for the sake of going.

"Sure, why not?" Collins responded. He'd sensed his wife's mercurial mood change and also, perceived its cause. But he'd been feeling the same sense of comfort and relaxation that Jane had. If she'd just waited only a few more seconds before speaking, he would've made the same suggestion about going out to her. The very words had been on the tip of his tongue when she'd blurted out her question.

He knew that there were problems with the notion of going out. He knew that in some ways it was full of unpredictable dimensions and situations. But he also felt bolstered by his new sense of confidence. He felt that he was in a position (in his mental attitude about the trial/campaign) that was much more stable and stronger than at the start of all this.

Maybe I'm getting used to being a political candidate. At first, I was the complete novice. It was all new and alien to me and I was unsure how to act, what to do, what to say. But I've had some time to get into it and now maybe I'm starting to think of myself as a candidate versus as someone who was forced to become one.

So, going out was the sole topic of conversation between the Collins' for the rest of the meal, during the clean-up which they did themselves, during their evening, and during their pillow talk before they drifted off to sleep. It was as if they were two teenagers enraptured with each other, planning their first date together without chaperones.

Collins and Jane decided that their outing that weekend would entail going to dinner at their favorite restaurant and then going to the theater on Saturday night, September Twenty-Ninth. For the former, they announced to Collins' Secret Service detail that they would like to go to the Carlyle Grand restaurant in the Shirlington area of Arlington County. Then, they chose to go to see the play "Sheer Madness" at the Kennedy Center (in the theater workshop). They'd seen the play several times previously (it was always changing) and Collins thought that there might be some new jokes in the script about the upcoming presidential election. Both he and Jane thought that this would be rather fun.

The chief of the Secret Service unit assigned to Collins groused about the late notice of these plans, but nonetheless accepted the assignment as just part of the job. In reality, his unhappiness was more due to the fact that he had become a little complacent since the rigors of watching over the Collins' while they never went out in public were such that probably a single school crossing guard could have satisfactorily protected his charges from any harm. Now, all of a sudden, he had some real work to do, and it took him a little time to shake off the blanket of laziness and get down to what he had been trained for many years to do.

On Saturday, the Collins' departed their home at about five-thirty p.m. No one noticed their departure. The rarity of their appearances coupled with the sheer unpredictability of their excursions from the Collins home had so frustrated the media as well as the paparazzi for so long that they basically had become complacent themselves, rationalizing that they really did not want first-hand coverage of the Collins campaign. They'd begun to believe that their own made-up news coverage of Collins was, in fact, factual and that Collins, the person, was really only a mirage. It was a self-fulfilling prophecy for the media that it was really only the coverage of a newsmaker that was important and that the newsmakers, i.e., the subject of the coverage, were really only incidental. As a matter of fact, many of the executives of the news networks and services had thanked their many pagan gods a long time ago that Collins, outside of the courtroom, was being so elusive, seclusive, and reclusive. It really made their jobs so much easier. They continued to focus on what they considered what was important:

The Coverage. And they were able to do so without having to tailor their schedules to Collins' activities. *Who ever said this was an imperfect world?* was what the executives were prone to say whenever the subject came up.

The Collins' enjoyed a wonderful dinner at the Carlyle Grand. They started with an appetizer of heated crabmeat and artichoke dip. The dip was delicious, all creamy and garlicky, and this item was one of the Collins' favorites and primarily why they had picked this establishment over many other places. Jane Collins followed with blackened red snapper, Cajun style, with a potato cake and steamed zucchini squash. She nearly wore her napkin out dabbing her watering eyes caused by the spiciness of the dish. It had been a long time since she had eaten spicy food given that most of the things that she'd been cooking at home for several weeks were, although tasty, mostly bland selections. Collins also wanted a change of pace for his palate and ordered the blackened rib eye steak with red-skinned potatoes and steamed broccoli. Unlike former President George H. W. Bush, Collins openly liked this green vegetable. After all, when garnished with the garlic-laced butter by the talented chef at the Carlyle Grand, who wouldn't like broccoli? For dessert, they shared a large slice of carrot cake which was the only thing they ate that night that was not liberally laced with garlic. But even so, it was much too rich for their normal practice of eating at home and eschewing dessert that between the two of them, they couldn't finish it.

Throughout the meal, they'd been able to eat almost normally. Given that they were eating that Saturday evening before the normal dinnertime crowd (they'd made a reservation for six p.m. so that they could expect to make the eight o'clock performance at the Kennedy Center), there weren't many people there to take notice of them. They'd also made no announcement of their planned foray into the real world all that day. There was no reason to consider doing so as this was not viewed by the Collins' at least as a public appearance for political purposes. But perhaps more than anything else, even though it was only a little more than a month from the election, William Buford Collins, VI was not a public figure in the sense that other public officials were.

But the restaurant management knew, of course. The Secret Service had been crawling all over the place most of the day and also, since they wanted to try to screen the people who'd made reservations there for the evening and to monitor the walk-ins, they created a sequestering area down in the lobby. Thus, it was only a matter of time before the information leaked to the staff and then began to radiate out to the general public as well as to the local media.

The Collins' hadn't really dawdled over dinner, and they were ready to leave just before seven p.m. They'd been able to eat without any disturbances or interruptions and they'd thoroughly enjoyed themselves. Amongst the small talk that they'd shared, they both wondered why they hadn't decided to get out sooner. Any fears that they might've had about public visibility, et cetera, apparently seemed to have been exaggerated.

As they were pulling out onto the Shirley Highway that would take them to the Kennedy Center on the other side of the Potomac River, there were a number of television news vans speeding towards the restaurant in the opposite direction. The hounds had finally picked up the scent, but they were too late. The rabbit had eluded them.

There was no special reception for the Collins' at the Kennedy Center. Since visitations by special dignitaries was a fairly routine occurrence there, no one had attached any special significance to the fact that this night the precautions were being made upon behalf of the first, really the only, non-campaigning candidate for president that the country had ever had. So, Collins and Jane were able to enter the grand pavilion without any fanfare and were able to enter the theater workshop venue just after the lights went down and found their seats in the back totally unnoticed.

In fact, the acting troupe of the interactive play had that evening prepared in a completely normal manner for its 18,675th performance (although it had not been they who'd been with the production from the opening performance by any means). This was just another in a long chain of performances for them.

The script was attuned to the times, as the Collins' had hoped, and also, it was at times hilariously funny. During the audience participation portion of the script at the end, the Collins watched silently and although both had been active contributors when they had attended the play previously, this time they were a little shy because of their perception that if they spoke up now, they might be noticed as not run-of-the-mill theatergoers. At the end, they applauded as loudly as the others and the troupe took two curtain calls.

The lead actor stayed on stage as the applause died out after the last curtain call and stood there patiently as the lights went up. The audience quieted down quickly as it sensed that the man was there for some purpose and was waiting for enough silence to be able to speak.

"Thank you all for coming tonight and upon behalf of the entire production crew of Sheer Madness please know that we appreciate your patronage," he said in a clear, actor's voice. "We really do. Also, it has come to my attention that in the audience this evening we are fortunate to have someone who helped make our script tonight a particularly successful one." He paused for a moment and immediately everyone began craning their necks looking around them trying to spot who the speaker was referring to.

Even though several people near the Collins' looked directly at them, it seems that the people were expecting to locate a movie star or such like. In fact, the moment was so innocuous that Buf and Jane Collins began to wonder if their first fear that the man was about to point them out was falsely placed and that there really was someone present who was famous.

"Ladies and gentlemen, it is a great honor for us to have in the house tonight Mr. and Mrs. Bill Collins, candidate for the president of the United States." The man not only spoke these words loudly, but he also obliged everyone in the audience by gesturing towards where the Collins' were sitting by stretching out his arm and opening out his hand as one typically does when introducing someone.

For a fleeting moment, Collins cringed at the use of the name "Bill" but since this was the name that many in the media had been using for him since the convention and he'd made no attempt to correct them (among other things), he realized that this is the name that most people who were following the election knew him by.

With the news of who the special guests that night were now out in the open, it only took the audience a beat or two to realize that this night was indeed a special one for them. The demographics of the patrons of the "Sheer Madness" production were consistently comprised of highly educated and upper middle-class individuals and this night's audience was no exception. In an instant, they not only knew who the actor was talking about but also caught on to the fact that appearances in public by this presidential candidate were not just few and far between—they were non-existent. Everyone wanted to place their eyes directly on this enigma as if to prove that he really did exist, not altogether unlike wanting to see a ghost once one had heard the clanking of its chains.

A normal night out for these people was suddenly transformed into one of unique significance and they were part of it. Immediately people began to stand up and move towards the Collins' and just as quickly the Secret Service team stepped in and made room for Buf and Jane to make their exit without having to commingle with any of their fellow attendees.

But Collins hesitated. He was at a crossroads. His quick mind almost instantly classified the feeling and presented the choices to its master: *You must either stand up and be recognized by these people as a public figure or you must quickly get out of here and be Buf Collins the trial lawyer who just so happens to be running for president.*

For the man the decision was instantaneous but the candidate in the man was unprepared.

Collins stood up and reached out and grasped his wife's arm as she was turning to follow the Secret Service agents out the back door of the theater.

"Jane," he whispered pleadingly. "Don't leave me here."

"Whaaat?" Jane Collins was half reacting to being held back by her husband and half wondering what he was up to. This whispering to her and the reference to staying when they should be hurrying out of there as fast as they could were confusing her sense of wanting to leave.

Later she would reflect on this moment with bittersweet emotion. It was amazing to her, but nonetheless very true: Her first reaction to being identified by the actor was flight. She always had trouble putting her finger exactly on the feeling but the best that she could do was to suggest that the period of seclusion where she and her husband had stayed in their home for so many weeks somehow bred in her a sensation of being in hiding as if they were fugitives or something.

And then when out in public for the first time, everything had been going smoothly, meaning that no one had noticed that they were out in the open. The feeling was that they were, by virtue of being out, vulnerable and exposed. Then, it happened: they were recognized and then pointed out to everyone nearby. So, her first reaction was to run away. She would always add in at this point that the fact that the Secret Service agents were trying to rush them out of there merely reinforced her sensation to flee.

But Collins held her back and whispered to her, urgently asking her to stay. It was a moment that Jane Collins would remember for the rest of her life.

So, she stayed.

Collins beckoned the Secret Service agents to come back and then half-turned to face the theatergoers who were straining to get a good look of him and Jane. He gestured with his other arm just like the actor had just done. He was telling Jane and the Secret Service that he wanted to stay because of the people there.

The Secret Service agents understood. Their job was to protect people who normally were out in public and typically wanted to see people and talk to them. They were trained to deal with crowds and with "clients" who found themselves in crowds as a matter of course. The contingent that had been assigned to Collins for many weeks had been sitting on their hands. Some, in fact, were becoming particularly good bridge players, they'd had so much idle time on their hands.

Therefore, it took only a brief moment for the Secret Service agents with the Collins' that night to kick into gear and begin doing the job that they were trained to do.

But Collins, who made the spontaneous decision to stay even though when rehashing this moment with his wife many months later would openly admit that his instinct was to flee, just as was hers. But for some inexplicable reason he elected to stifle that urge and stay. It was Collins, the man, who, prior to the convention, was completely sure about himself in all that he did that wanted to stay. And it was Collins, the trial lawyer, who was eminently successful and was loath to shy away from any challenge or confrontation that wanted to stay that night. It was the Collins who was the presidential candidate, that wanted to flee.

So, it was simply two against one and Collins stayed. He and his wife turned back to face the crowd in the theater. The audience had all turned away from the actor and were looking intently towards the back of the theater where the Collins' were standing. It was as if there was going to be a new last act provided to the night's production, but one presented from the rear.

The crowd was curiously silent, probably more from surprise than anything else, but Collins interpreted it as a sign that they wanted him to speak.

"Hello, everybody. Jane and I hope that you all enjoyed the play tonight as much as we did," Collins told them with a friendly wave of his hand and a smile. He put his arm around his wife's shoulders. "We both are really glad that we came. Good night!" And then he waved his hand in adieu and turned Jane around, pushed her towards the door, and followed closely behind her.

When they were back in the car, Collins seemed both relieved and also, curiously pumped up.

"Wow! Did you see how interested they were in trying to get a look at us, Jane?" he asked. "I know that I've read that celebrities feel that look is like a curse and liken the feeling to that of being vulnerable prey in the gaze of a predator. But tonight, I didn't get that impression. Did you?" He looked at Jane and she gave him a slight shake of her head in mute response. "No? Well, I must admit that I was caught by surprise. I guess that I simply hadn't yet realized that I'm now a public figure and even though the trial's on tee-vee and all, I just haven't thought much about the American public getting to know me." He stopped and frowned, knitting his brows in thought. "There's something else about tonight, too,"

"What's that, dear?" Jane asked. This time she felt like participating in the conversation.

"That's the fact that at the moment, I'm much more than just a public figure. Right now, I'm a mystery, an enigma. The American voters are confused: Am I that ogre, that much, much bigger than life slimeball that the news has been working overtime to make me out to be? Or am I the knight in shining armor that is fighting for everyone's dignity every day in court? Every person there in the theater tonight knew who I was—They knew I was the guy on court tee-vee and they knew I was the presidential nominee. The problem is that they didn't know which one. For this reason, our presence was particularly intriguing for them. They were eager to look us over close up to see if we looked like what they had imagined in their minds. Our presence caught all of them by surprise just as the actor's announcement of our presence caught us by surprise. Wow! What a moment!"

"Buf, I think I know why you wanted to stay, why you held me back from sneaking out the back of the theater. But why didn't you talk to them?" Jane was getting a sense of the dynamics of the situation but there were still some things that she wanted to clarify.

"That's a very, very good question, my astute wife," Collins replied. "Sometimes, I amaze myself, but my first reaction was to run like you just said. Then, I realized that those people wanted to see us. They wanted to check us out firsthand. They wanted to compare notes: were we like what the news reports said? They wanted a real data point to factor into their judgment. So, in another instant I squelched the desire to run away and decided to stand my ground. What I think I was doing was showing them that we were not embarrassed to have been identified by the actor nor to be seen by them. We were not there in hiding. We did not sneak in there and we were not going to sneak out. We didn't have anything to run from, in reality.'

"That's why I decided to stay. I wanted their new data point about us to be favorable. I sensed that, if possible, it would conflict with the impression they may've drawn from some of the spurious news reports that there've been."

"But why didn't you really say anything to them, Buf?" Jane was curious why her husband had not taken the opportunity to make some points with the audience. They were voters after all, weren't they?

"Another excellent question, my dear." Collins acted as if he had expected this query from his wife and appeared to have a well-prepared response. "You see, there's really not anything that we can do about what the news has been saying about us. Remember our no-response policy? Well, that's still a valid thing for us. We can't allow ourselves to get into the thick of things and provide counters to all that. It just won't work, and we'd never be able to keep up with it all. It'd be an infinite time sink.

"I really think that the best thing was and still is to ignore it. And so far, it's been straightforward—oh, I openly admit very traumatic and difficult emotionally for us, but still basically straightforward to implement while we stayed at home. Ah, but tonight that policy took on a newer and much higher dimension. Boy howdy! When I turned back to face our fellow theatergoers back there tonight, I realized that no matter what I said about all that has been said about us, there was no way we could be ourselves and no way that we could look good. So, even though I believe that my motivation to stay was partly because I really wanted to say something, I at the very last moment elected not to do it."

"I get it, now." Jane sat up straight in the car. "You only said hello to those people to show them that you're just like them. That's all any one of them would have said to another, right? So, by doing the same thing, you've established in every one of their minds that you really are a common man and also, not a politician. Wow, Buf! You're so smart." Jane's voice was full of incredulous admiration for her husband.

Collins was dumfounded. This was another of those uncountable times when his wife blew his socks off with her perception and wisdom. Even though he was able to admit it to himself, albeit with difficulty, he acknowledged that Jane had seen the true meaning to what his instincts led him to do that evening. It wasn't until this moment when his wife explained it to him that he understood what had really happened back there at the Kennedy Center at the end of the play.

He'd made his first real public appearance as a presidential candidate outside of the courtroom. And he had instinctively chosen to act as if he were just another one of the onlooking people.

This was the beginning of the real campaign for William Buford Collins, VI.

Chapter 23

On the following Wednesday, October Third, after court adjourned, Collins asked the Secret Service to take him to the mall. He was happy with his progress in the trial, and he thought he might celebrate and do a little shopping. Jane's birthday was coming up and he wanted to look for a new suit.

Once at the mall, he went to Brooks Brothers. The career salesman in the men's suits department knew him on sight. Collins had been an occasional but loyal customer there for a number of years and the man knew him as a local and successful lawyer. That Collins was now a presidential nominee was not lost on the man one iota. In fact, he'd been wondering whether he would ever see Collins again. At this hour, the store was nearly deserted when Collins strode in. Of course, he was not alone. There were two Secret Service agents who accompanied him into the store and one that stood in the mall just outside the store's entrance.

"Ah, Mr. Collins. So, nice to see you again, sir," the salesman said unctuously as Collins was fingering the sleeve of a dark blue pin-striped suit. "What can we do for you today? A nice three-piece? You're a forty-four long, if I remember?"

"Yes, that's right, uh, Charles, is it?" Collins responded, falling into the familiar role of an affluent lawyer buying an expensive suit.

Charles helped Collins try on a number of suits that interested him and during the half hour or so that this entailed a few shoppers randomly trickled into the store. One shopper was either perhaps more observant than the others or possibly just less interested in buying anything, but he stopped and looked long and hard at Collins and his two escorts. He noticed that only one of the three was trying on clothes. The other two appeared to be constantly looking around but not at any of the merchandise. In fact, they seemed to take just as much interest in the observer as the observer was taking in them.

"Bodyguards," the man whispered out loud and then deliberately looked away, suddenly fearful that his interest might be misconstrued as a possible threat. He turned to leave the area and quickly looked back to get one more good look at the man the two minders were protecting.

At that moment, Charles emerged from somewhere in the back and said loud enough for the surreptitious bystander to overhear, "Ah, Mr. Collins, it seems that we do have a matching vest in your size."

The man quickly exited the store and into the skylighted walkway and paused and looked around. There, nearby, stood a young well-dressed man who was vigilantly scanning the mall and looked about as out-of-place as a cow at a hen party.

"Secret Service," the man whispered and quickly took off racking his mind for where he'd last seen a pay phone. He wanted to make a call but not from his own mobile phone which he knew was traceable.

Back in the store, Collins made his choice and Charles had the tailor come up to mark the suit for alterations. The suit was an exquisite charcoal gray suit with faint herringbone vertical stripes.

At the register, Collins signed his name to the ticket.

"No need to provide any identification, Mr. Collins. We have your account number on file. Your suit should be ready for pick up next Tuesday. Of course, we'd be happy to put a rush on it, if you might be needing it sooner than that." His obsequious manner was perfectly pat—neither too solicitous nor too impersonal. He was very good at the haberdashery business, and he knew it.

"Thank you for your time and all your assistance this afternoon, Charles," Collins said graciously. He was genuinely sincere, as he truly did appreciate Charles' help, but he also admired the man's professionalism by not making any reference to his new status. He was just a man who wanted a new suit. "No, next week will be fine for the suit. Thanks again, sir. See you." With a pat on the shoulder, he walked to the exit.

As he left, he was thinking that something in the area of jewelry might be right for Jane's birthday gift. He paused in the main concourse and looked around him, getting his bearings.

He turned and began to walk purposefully down the walkway. The Secret Service agents followed with him as if birds on the wing, seemingly talking softly to themselves as they whispered into their intercoms.

He stopped at Kay's Jewelry and stepped inside and began to lazily browse along the long, brightly lit display cases. He ran his eyes over the vast array of necklaces, bracelets, rings, and earrings. After a short while a tall attractive saleswoman emerged from in the back.

"May I help you, sir?" she asked in a velvety tone while she curiously inspected the two men who had entered the store along with Collins. She immediately sensed two things: The man at the counter was a buyer and had the means to pay for whatever might tickle his fancy and the other two were not and definitely could not. She speculated that they must be some sort of police because one of the two gave her a piercing and unblinking look that made her shudder with discomfort and the other quickly stepped to the doorway from whence she'd just come and without even so much as suggesting that he needed permission stuck his head through the doorway.

While she was waiting for her potential customer to respond, the one man who was checking out the back room leaned back into the main store and gave the second man a short nod as if he approved of what he'd seen. Then her attention was refocused on the buyer.

"Yes, you might be able to help me find something for my wife's birthday," Collins said. "She really likes pale blue sapphires. The only problem is that we've been married for over twenty-five years and I've in that time bought her probably two or three of everything that a woman could want to wear."

"Mmmm. I see," the saleswoman said pensively. "So, the only thing that you might find to be appropriate this time is either something a little out of the ordinary or, perhaps, something to replace what she already has, but . . . bigger?"

Collins stopped his browsing and sharply looked up at this woman. Her perception and even boldness as a salesperson caught his attention. She looked directly back at him eye-to-eye. Collins assessed that she was either a part owner in this store or a manager on her way up. He also had a curious sensation that she knew he was ready to buy.

"Yes, perhaps bigger is the right solution," he said after a moment.

"Yes, I'm sure that your wife would be pleased with something along those lines," the saleswoman said kicking into high gear. "So, let's see. Light blue sapphires, you said? Why not a pendant, maybe . . . something like this?" She'd moved along the counter and Collins dutifully followed her. She reached into her pocket and produced a fancy little key and deftly opened up a panel on her side of the counter. She swooped down and picked out a necklace with a large teardrop-shaped blue sapphire pendant. that was fitted into a diamond-studded platinum mounting. She held it out on the back of one of her hands in a patented pose of merchandise display.

Collins bent over for a closer look. The strong light made the diamonds sparkle and dance and the sapphire looked like a chunk of cerulean sky. "Mmmm. Spectacular," he said. "How big are the diamonds?"

When the woman didn't respond, he looked up at her. Her attention was directed out towards the mall. Collins turned to see what she was looking at and saw a group of people scurrying past the front of the store. They appeared to be lugging a bunch of heavy equipment of some nature. He heard a woman who was sort of leading the charge yell out loudly, "Come on! Hurry! We might just be the first ones to get there!"

Collins looked back at the saleswoman, and she simultaneously looked back at him and shrugged her shoulders in a "I don't know" kind of gesture as if this was something outside the realm of her knowledge.

Collins gave his shoulders a slight conciliatory shrug as well and then looked back down at the beautiful sapphire pendant that the woman was still holding out for him to view. He reached out and ran his finger over the diamonds surrounding the blue stone and remembered that he hadn't learned yet how big they were. Then, he straightened back up and looked at the woman. "I'm not sure about this piece, Miss. In fact, I'm beginning to think that I, uh, might want something more personal than jewelry. Um, you're a very attractive person, if I may say so. Perhaps you might be able to suggest something—something special that you'd like for your husband or boyfriend to give to you?"

If the woman was affronted by his forwardness, she gave no sign. She replaced the necklace in the cabinet and made sure that she relocked it securely. While she did this, she was thinking over Collins' query.

"Well, I can tell you that I'd really like," she said and cast her eyes downward, hesitating slightly, " . . . something to wear. Something intimate. Like a negligee or a teddy."

"Hmmm, yes, I think that a piece of intimate clothing might just be the very thing for me to get," he said appreciatively. "Thank you for your thoughtfulness." He began to walk towards the doorway. "So, is there some store in the mall that you know of that sells that sort of thing?"

"Well, I like to go to the Victoria's Secret store and that's down the escalators out there to the left and back pretty much directly underneath where we are here."

"Ah, yes, Victoria's Secret," he said, nodding his head. "I think I'll take a look down there. Thank you very much for your time, Miss."

As Collins and his Secret Service escorts walked to the escalators, his attention was still focused on his thoughts. The two agents, however, were well aware of the hubbub going on down the mall towards the Brooks Brothers store. They both craned their necks as they followed Collins to see what was going on. All they could perceive, were bright lights and the sounds of some sort of commotion. They conferred with their associates by their intercoms as they rode down the escalator with Collins. The report came back that the activity was from a live news video crew that appeared to be trying to locate Collins. How they had found out that Collins was there, no one knew.

Collins found the lingerie store without any trouble and as he entered, he became the third patron present. Coincidentally, the other two shoppers were also men. One was looking for a gift for his young wife who liked dressing up in frilly and skimpy underwear and the other was looking for something that he could wear himself.

Collins precipitated to the sleepwear section of the store and immediately began to feel comfortable about his birthday gift decision for Jane. All of what he saw here, he liked. There were pajamas, rompers, gowns, negligees, sleep shirts and matching shorts, robes, and slippers. Without any help, he was able to select a cozy pair of cotton pajamas in a rosebud on pink pattern. He also selected a chenille robe in dusty rose and matching lined slippers. Since the other two men in the store were still browsing, Collins was rung up by the young salesclerk right away.

He was on his way out of the store some one hundred and fifty dollars poorer less than ten minutes after he entered. He hooked up with his Secret Service detail at the entrance, but they were abruptly halted before they could leave the store.

The doorway was suddenly blocked by a throng of several people holding various kinds of boxes and other electronic equipment. In the center of this group was a well-dressed woman.

Several things happened simultaneously. One, the Secret Service agents with Collins immediately stepped in front of him as if to protect him from bodily threat. Two, the leader of the Secret Service team with Collins immediately called for back-up and also for instantaneous coordination for access to and use of the back entrance to the lingerie store which communicated into the bowels of the delivery system of the mall. Three, a bright spotlight suddenly illuminated and cast a powerful beam of bluish light directly on Collins ominously suggesting that he was being targeted for something. Four, the well-dressed woman at the center of the door-blocking group started to approach Collins aggressively while thrusting out her hand towards him. She was holding something round and black in her hand. While this was happening Collins and the woman locked staring sets of eyes at each other. Five, two of the crewmen began crowding into the doorway with heavy-looking black equipment on their shoulders. And six, Collins haltingly held up his hand to try to stop the Secret Service agents from advancing.

The woman, who was obviously from some television news service, thought that Collins was shying away from her and began to press against the two agents all the more vigorously. There ensued a scuffle at this point and in an instant, the woman was wrestled to the floor and both cameramen were pointing their cameras at the jumble of dark-suited men and smartly dressed woman writhing on the floor.

Once the agents had subdued the woman to the point where she had stopped struggling to get free, most of the din dissipated. That is except one single, powerful, command voice. This voice was booming out at a tremendous level of decibels, presumably fueled by the necessity of being heeded over the noise that had just now stopped.

This voice was coming from Collins.

"Get off of her!" he shouted at the two agents. "Let her go! Let this poor woman up! Come on!" When nothing immediately happened, he stepped forward and tried to break up the jumble of bodies on the floor as would a football referee trying to get to the bottom of a scrum of players recovering a fumble.

It was at this point that Collins came into the field of view of the cameras. Later, the nominee for the president of the United States would be seen performing a role of a grade-school playground proctor breaking up a schoolkid fight.

Shortly, the agents realized that they had momentarily, in the heat of the chase, lost track of their charge and quickly let go of the woman and stood back up. They rearranged their clothes, shoulder holsters, handguns, radios, et cetera, and sheepishly avoided any eye contact with each other or with Collins.

But Collins wasn't paying any attention to them. He was on his knees tending to the shaken and disheveled news reporter who was lying sprawled unladylike on the floor. He'd tossed his packages aside and quickly got her legs and arms back in some semblance of comfortable alignment and smoothed down her short skirt which had been hiked up around her hips (as she had been vainly trying to knee one of her attackers in the groin). He pulled the sides of her burst-apart blouse back over her lacy brassiere and cradled her head in the crook of his arm as he daubed at a trickle of blood coming from the corner of her mouth with his handkerchief.

"Are you all right, Miss?" he asked her solicitously.

Her eyes flickered and even though she hadn't fainted nor was totally unconscious, for a few seconds, she'd lost touch with reality.

Her eyes came back into focus and locked on to the blue-gray irises of the presidential candidate. What she saw was strength and confidence and the trauma and urgency of a few moments before evaporated immediately.

"Ohhhh," she murmured. "Yes . . . I guess . . . I'm okay." She started to look around but for some reason she couldn't disconnect her eyes from those that were looking intently at her. She felt that she was oddly locked on to those intelligent and caring eyes of the man who was holding her and had just been her rescuer. Strangely it was a pleasant feeling for her. "Uh, are they gone?" she managed to ask.

"No, but I've taken care of them. They won't bother you anymore." Collins' tone was soothingly assuring.

"Oh, that's good. Thank you," the newswoman said softly. She was still trying to catch her breath and make sense out this situation.

Collins carefully laid her head back. "Now stay right here until you've calmed down. I imagine that there's some help on the way in case you're injured someplace." As he started to straighten himself back up, he felt a nudge against his arm.

"Sir, I think that this would be a good time to get on the move." The lead Secret Service agent was anxious to leave, presumably more to avoid any further embarrassment to himself and his partner than due to any sense of risk to Collins.

"Oh?" Collins said thinking it over. "All right." He quickly gathered up his packages and followed them out of the store. As he was leaving, he turned back to the woman who was trying to sit up and was just now realizing that her blouse had been ripped open. "I have to go now, Miss. But I'm sure that you're going to be fine," Collins said supportively.

Outside there was a crowd of gawkers that had collected behind the video crew as it frantically searched for Collins, much like a piece of ice collects mass as it rolls down a hill covered with freshly fallen snow.

Collins and the two agents stepped out of the store and into the crush of people who were trying to find out what was going on inside.

"Hey, buddy!" a young man near the door yelled at Collins. "What's happening in there?"

Collins stopped and looked at the inquisitor. He glanced fleetingly back into the store and then at the young man. "A news reporter woman was just accosted by some thugs," he replied looking over the man's shoulder to glare at the Secret Service agents.

"Oh, man!" The fellow's angst seemed genuine enough for one to surmise that he and the newswoman were acquainted. "Is she all right?"

"Yes, I think so," Collins answered carefully. "She just got knocked down and banged up a little. That's all."

Another bystander felt that this was an open dialogue and stepped over to Collins and his young companion. "Say, someone said that the camera crew was looking for that Collins fellow. You know, the guy who's running that big trial that's been on tee-vee."

Collins turned to look at the new inquisitor. He saw a man who clearly worked hard for a living and immediately realized that the sarcasm that he heard in this man's words was unintentional. The notion that the general public thought he was on television every day because the trial itself was the important news item, suddenly hit him. This particular fellow was wearing soiled blue jeans and a zippered windbreaker jacket that bore the colors and insignia of the Washington Commanders professional football team. On his head was a ball cap of the Washington Nationals, the area's professional National League baseball team. The man's hands were beefy and chafed and on his face was a day-old stubble of whiskers.

"Yes, I think that you're right, my friend," Collins said somewhat elusively, wondering whether the fellow would recognize him or not. When he didn't detect any signs of recognition, Collins made a flash decision. "Yes, they were looking for me. I'm Buf Collins."

At this point everyone who was within earshot of this confession immediately turned his and her attention to Collins and the two men.

The revelation of who this friendly and informative shopper really was sank into the initial questioner first. "Huh? You mean, you're Bill Collins?"

"Yes, that's right," Collins replied, smiling as if he and this man were old friends. "Please call me Buf." He stuck out his hand for a handshake with the young man. The man's jaw dropped to his chest but mostly by reflex reciprocated and the two men shook hands. Then, Collins turned to the workman and reached out to shake his hand. "And you guys are?" he asked of them collectively.

There was a pregnant pause. Even though neither man had ever met anyone famous, both knew without saying what the drill was: If you were lucky enough to shake a celebrity's hand, the exchange was nearly always very brief and impersonal. It's a given that the celebrity is never interested in who the nobodies are. Oh, they're usually gracious and all that, but they're too busy and in too much of a hurry to bother with introductions and names. It was simply just not done.

Collins apparently didn't know what the rules were. He looked at both men, encouraging them to tell him their names.

The younger man was the more alert of the two and responded first. "My name is Jimmy Jergens, Mr. Collins." He looked eagerly at Collins, experiencing an extraordinary feeling of uniqueness. Thoughts raced through his mind that no one was going to believe this.

"Hiya, Jimmy. And stop calling me Mr. Collins. As I said, it's Buf." He then turned to the workman who was grinning from ear to ear.

"I'm Bo Hawkins, Buf," he said in a lazy drawl. "It's really good to meetcha." He was a proud man and met Collins on a common level.

Again, Collins felt a nudge on his shoulder. This time he knew at once what it was. He began to walk toward the escalators.

"I must be getting along, guys. It was nice to meet you, Jimmy and Bo. See ya." He began walking with his two minders and in a moment was up the escalator and out of sight.

They were on the road to the Collins home no more than ten minutes from when Collins left the newswoman on the floor of the boutique.

Back in the mall, the newswoman, whose name was Jennika Rourke, had recovered most of her composure. She'd buttoned the jacket of her suit across her torn blouse and had her camera crew follow her out of the store. When she learned that her quarry had departed the area, she did the next best thing she could.

"Did anyone see the man who just left here?" she asked, her eyes searching for anyone who wanted their fifteen seconds of fame.

Bo Hawkins stepped forward and sort of half-waved his hand at Jennika. "Yes, I did, uh, Miss Rourke." Apparently, Bo was an avid fan of this sensuous woman whose telegenic qualities had been a major factor in her being hired by the network that she was representing. "He told me that a woman had been knocked down in there. Was that you?"

Jennika made a little face, like she was taking a bite out of a lemon. The thrust of the story was not supposed to be about her.

"Did you talk to the man?" she asked trying to steer Bo back on track.

"Yup, I did. Nice fellow that Buf," he said tersely. Bo now knew Collins on a first name basis and the fact that he was anyone worthy of Miss Rourke's interest seemed immaterial. "He told me that you were going to be okay. He was pretty worried about you." Bo noted her disarrayed clothing and that the cut on her mouth was still red with blood. "It looks like you really did get banged up some, just as Buf said."

"Who are you talking about?" Jennika was wondering if she'd been knocked into another dimension instead of just on her keister.

"Why, Buf Collins, the presidential candidate fellow who's doing the trial thing on tee-vee. The guy that took care of you after you got mugged. Don't you remember?"

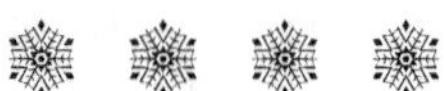

Back at home, Collins plopped down on the sofa next to his wife in the living room, his face was beaming with delight. He indicated the bundle of packages that he had with him. "It's going to be a wonderful birthday, Darling."

He then told her about his outing and the fracas carefully leaving out the name of the store—he wanted to keep the nature of his gifts a secret.

"Oh!" she exclaimed. "Then, it's going to be on the news!" She clicked a button on the remote control and the television flickered to life.

She selected the channel for the cable news network. The anchor was summarizing what was coming up. First, he said, would be live coverage of a sudden volcanic eruption in one of the Japanese islands. Next, he said with almost a smirk, there would be a special report on the presidential election from Jennika Rourke who made a "sighting" today.

Jane turned down the sound a notch or two while they waited for the first item to play out. Then, the anchorperson was back introducing Jennika Rourke's piece and Jane bumped the sound back up.

"Well folks, it seems that presidential hopeful Bill Collins was out doing a little shopping at a mall in Virginia today and lucky for us, our own Jennika Rourke was there. What do you have for us, Jennika?" He looked off to his right as if Jennika was sitting there next to him. The screen blinked and then there was Rourke. She was reporting from a studio set, but it could have been anywhere in the world for all that anyone could tell.

"This is Jennika Rourke reporting. Today, at the Potomac Yard shopping mall in Alexandria, Virginia, I had an epiphany. Yes, that's right. I had a revelation. I went there on a tip that presidential candidate Bill Collins had been seen there shopping. I don't have to tell any of you that this was a big surprise as it should be common knowledge that Mr. Collins has been completely tied up in a major criminal trial almost since the end of the convention. Public appearances of this guy are few and far between.

"I rushed a crew over there as soon as I got the call and found him making some purchases. But rather than covering this as a special sighting of Elvis, which I have to admit to you was what I was thinking about all along, it turned out that I became personally involved in a terribly embarrassing incident and ended up meeting a genuine, real-life, gentleman.

"Folks, I want to be the very first person in the media to say that I am most sincerely sorry for what may've been said by my own network and others about this man, William Collins, who I understand from some of his friends prefers to be called Buf, and not Bill. Well, today I met Buf Collins, up close and personal, and let me tell you, this guy isn't who the news has been saying he is and for this I am personally and professionally sorry. But if you're out there somewhere and watching this, Buf, I forgot to thank you for what you did today.

"What I'm talking about folks, is that today I was a little too aggressive and I approached the political candidate too suddenly for the comfort of his Secret Service protection unit. They were on me like stink on a skunk, you might say, and before I knew it, I had two fullback-sized gun-packing oafs all over me. They wrestled me to the ground and, frankly, I was afraid for my life for a second . . .

"But then a superhero came to my rescue. Folks, my superman today came to me in the form of Buf Collins, presidential candidate and knight of honor. He dove into the pack of bodies lying on top of little old me and beat back the bad guys. This man had no pretenses but to see after my wellbeing. He gave me some tee-ell-cee and just like the Lone Ranger he was off before I could thank him.

"He didn't have anything to say. He didn't act like a politician even. And given that he had every reason to hate us people in the news media for what's been said about him in the past few weeks, he gave me no indication that he cared about it a whit or for that matter even knew about it. All he seemed to care about was whether I was okay, or not.

"I must admit to you folks that this guy is one heck of a man. I know that we're supposed to maintain a distance from the people who make the news, but today I was indelibly smitten. From now on, Buf Collins is my main man. We could do a whole lot worse than putting this kind of sincere and sensitive person into the White House.

"That's my story and I'm sticking to it. This is Jennika Rourke reporting."

"Wow," Jane said softly. It was incredible that her husband's spontaneous shopping junket had inadvertently produced this kind of media coverage. "Buf, it's truly remarkable what happened. Mmmm. You know what that means, don't you?" she asked.

"Um, no, what?" Collins prompted.

"It means that you really are the man that you've been trying to show to the voters. When you're acting on impulse as you did today, the man that everyone saw, the real and unrehearsed man, was who you really are, Buf: an honest, fair common man. I believe that the people there all saw something that they intuitively sensed was truly genuine. And I'll bet you a bunch of money that to a person they were shocked."

"Shocked?" Collins asked. "Shocked at what?"

Jane smiled at her husband. "You don't know?"

"No, tell me," he prompted.

"I think that they were shocked that they saw a presidential candidate do something and say things that were spontaneous and real. These were things that they liked and respected. That's what shocked them. No one ever gets that impression from a politician."

Collins stared at his wife, stunned.

C H A P T E R 24

On Monday, October Eighth, Collins started to examine the amazing phenomenon of the shrinking homicide rate in the cities that were named in the case. The point here was that there was every indication that crime was continuing to grow in these cities, particularly the types of crime that were typically associated with homicides, such as drug dealing, robbery, assault, and so on. But counter to all indications, the number of homicides in these cities inexplicably started to drop about twenty-five years ago and had continued to drop progressively year to year until the present day.

First, he called a Doctor William Sullivan to the stand. This man was a statistician who specialized in the data that makes up the national abstract. His credentials were impeccable having been special advisor to the current and past two presidents, on the board of several major corporations, and was professor emeritus of Stanford University.

"Doctor Sullivan," Collins began his examination of this witness, "are you familiar with the particulars of this case?"

"I am," the slender, distinguished man replied with an air of comfort that reflected his extensive experience in providing courtroom testimony. "I've been working with the data and information that your group has put together for more than a month."

"And thus, you know that each death cited in this case was officially listed as either accidental, due to natural causes, or self-inflicted?"

"That's correct," Sullivan replied evenly.

"Are you also familiar with death rates in this country, in particular deaths due to accidental or self-inflicted causes?" asked Collins, casting a casual glance at the jury.

"I am more than familiar with these rates, Mr. Collins," the statistician replied a little smugly.

"How do you mean?" Collins asked.

"It is to the study of the rates of this type of death in this country that I've dedicated the past fifteen years of my life to," replied the witness. He turned to look at the jury. "To say that I am familiar with these rates is a gross understatement. I'm confident that there's not another person on Earth either living or dead who knows more than myself about death rates and mortality statistics in this country."

"Ah," Collins slurred, making a point to look highly impressed, "I see. Please forgive me Doctor, I wasn't in any way trying to belittle your special interest and knowledge in this area; I only wanted the jury to hear of your interest and focus in your own words."

Sullivan nodded curtly acknowledging Collins' apology.

"Doctor," Collins continued, "in the time that you've been able to examine the data have you been able to determine if these deaths appear to be consistent with accidental and self-inflicted death rates?"

"Yes, I have," replied the statistician.

"Please explain how you have performed your examination, Doctor. Take all the time that you need." This was a critically important testimony for Collins' prosecution of the case, and he didn't want Sullivan to rush but also, he wanted him to put everything in layman's terms. Collins well knew that nothing bored juries more than a bunch of mathematical and statistical gobbledygook.

Dr. Sullivan nodded to Collins signifying that he agreed with the instruction. After a brief pause, he began to speak in a level lecture-like voice. "In the cities in question, I've compared the trends of accidental and self-inflicted deaths and those due to natural causes to prior to twenty-five years ago and since. What I basically did was to examine death statistics that were recorded in these cities from the end of the Civil War up to twenty-five years ago and then projected what these rates would be today based on those trends. Then, I compared them to what the rates have actually been."

"And what does this comparison reveal?" Collins asked.

"I've prepared some graphics that I'd like to use to illustrate what I've found out, if I may?" The doctor looked from Collins to the judge waiting for someone to say that this was okay.

"Of course, Doctor," Collins said unctuously. "Your Honor," he said addressing Rector, "if it please the court, we'd now like to show the placards that we provided to the court and Ms. Russell this morning to the jury at this time and have Doctor Sullivan explain what they show."

"Proceed," said the judge and shot a glance at Russell to see if she might wish to object. But she gave him a stony stare and said nothing.

"Go ahead, Doctor," prompted Collins.

Sullivan produced a laser pointer while Collins positioned a stack of placards on a large easel that was within easy viewing distance of the jury box. He shot a thin red beam of concentrated light onto the first placard.

"This shows . . ." he began and then proceeded to walk the jury through his comparisons. To a city, the death rates due to non-homicidal causes were much higher than what the before-twenty-five-year trends predicted them to be.

"Have you any explanation for these excessively high death rates in these cities, Doctor Sullivan?" Collins asked.

The statistician didn't respond right away. He seemed to be somewhat surprised at this question.

"Uh well, actually no I don't, Mr. Collins," he answered hesitatingly. "These death rates are so much different than what the previous trends predict that I'm certain there must be some explanation, but I have no clue as to what it might be."

"Why would you feel this way, Doctor?" Collins asked, instilling genuine curiosity into his tone.

The professor knitted his brows and thought this over for a moment. "Well, I'm certain that there must be some explanation for these extremely high rates because, it's impossible that they could've occurred randomly. Uh, what I mean is that all predictions that are based on historical data have some degree of error. This is the basis for calculating probabilities and so on. So, my predictions that are shown on the charts are what my calculations tell me are the most likely occurrences but of course there are infinitely many possible outcomes in and around this most likely outcome. The farther you get away from the predicted line, either up or down, the less likely it is to occur."

"I see, Doctor," Collins said. "Can you characterize how likely it is that the actual death rates that we see on the charts could occur based on the hundred plus years of historical data?"

"Yes, I can," Sullivan said nodding. "The actual rates in any one of these cities is so far away from the most likely prediction that it's virtually impossible to have occurred without being due to a specific factor."

"How impossible, Doctor?" Collins asked. "Perhaps once in a hundred chances?"

"No way," answered Sullivan.

"One in a thousand?" suggested Collins.

"No." Sullivan shook his head firmly.

"One in a million?" posed Collins, raising his eyebrows in mock hopefulness.

Sullivan smiled. "I'd say less than once in more than a hundred million."

"Ah! You really did mean impossible didn't you, Doctor?" Collins said with obvious amazement. Collins stood stock still while he let the jury react to this. Then he continued. "So, how impossible would you say that it is that this extremely impossible high rate could've occurred in all these cities, at the same time for just about the very same length of time, Doctor?" If ever there was a loaded question, this had to be it.

Sullivan looked blankly at Collins for a moment. "It's incalculably impossible. The sun is more likely not to rise tomorrow morning than it would be for similarly high death rates to occur simultaneously in all of these cities. I'd say that it's more likely to be able to travel faster than the speed of light in our lifetime, more likely for medical science to discover how to increase life span by three hundred years, more likely to invent how to heat our homes with seawater, more likely . . ."

Collins held up his hand, gently interrupting Sullivan. "Thank you. Thank you very much, Doctor. We get the point. Now, we are almost finished here but I'd like for you to bear with me for just a few more questions if I may, Sir. Looking at the accidental rate all by itself now, can you characterize how much more dangerous these cities are with this high accidental death rate as compared to, say, other cities in the United States or maybe even the rest of the nation as a whole?"

"Yes, I can, Mr. Collins," Sullivan replied, nodding again. "This is something that I always do to help understand various phenomena. If you look at the accidental deaths in these cities over the past twenty-five years and compare them to the national average for accidental deaths, you get some interesting results."

"Such as?" Collins nudged.

"It'd appear that these several cities are much more dangerous than the others," Sullivan replied.

"How much more dangerous, Doctor?" asked Collins.

"They've been more than one hundred thousand times more dangerous than the national average when taken without those cities included."

"Wow! That's much more dangerous, indeed!" Collins was suitably impressed. "Do you have any idea how this can be, Doctor?"

"Well, not really, Mr. Collins," the statistician replied, looking a little awkward. "This isn't something that I tried to investigate; you see. There've been such a huge number of deaths in these cities due to accidents and so on. It's really very hard to understand, particularly when the other death rates are down. You see, it's not a consistent trend for all of the causes of death, even if you ignore its innate impossibility." Sullivan seemed to straighten as if he'd just thought of something. "In fact, I'd say that the progressive drop in homicides in these cities that parallels the sharp increase in other deaths is so out of the ordinary that there's certain to be some connection."

"Hmmm," Collins seemed to be thinking this over in his mind. "Doctor Sullivan, are you familiar with any specific details of the deaths that make up the rates that you've been analyzing?"

"No, I only look at the data," came the innocent reply.

"So, you don't know about anything personal regarding these deaths such as how they occurred, their names, and so on?" Collins' tone was flat.

"No," replied Sullivan.

"Nothing but demographic data, right?" Collins asked.

"That's correct," said Sullivan.

"So, what would your reaction be if I suggested to you that a large number of these deaths due to accidental and self-inflicted means were really homicides but had been misclassified?" Collins turned to regard the jury ready to register their reaction to Sullivan's response to this question.

"I'd say that you're on to something," Sullivan said eagerly. "This is because the total death rate that's due to all possible causes in these forty cities is very consistent with the national average. Admittedly they all are higher than the average by a fair amount, but it's well within acceptable limits."

"Ah, so if these accidental and so on deaths were in fact homicides, the statistical analysis of deaths in these cities over the past twenty-five years would appear to be normal or about what would be expected. Is this a fair conclusion, in your opinion, Doctor?" This was Collins' denouement question.

"Yes, it'd be very possible. In fact, I'd say that it would appear perfectly normal." Sullivan exuded certainty.

"Thank you, sir." Collins nodded to Judge Rector that he was finished with his direct examination of this witness.

Rector straightened up and looked over at the defense table. "Your witness, Ms. Russell," he prompted.

"Thank you, Your Honor," Russell said perfunctorily. She did not stand up indicating that she did not plan to keep the witness long. "Dr. Sullivan, in your professional opinion is the world an orderly place?"

Sullivan looked blankly at the defense attorney. "Excuse me?" he asked.

Russell did not appear to be put off. "Sir, I'm asking you if you believe the Earth, all the natural phenomena on it, and civilized activities are all orderly and thus predictable?"

"Ah," Sullivan nodded getting her point. "No, Ma'am. It's not orderly. Not so that any future activity can be known in advance."

"And" Russell continued, "isn't it correct to say that the science of statistics, your area of expertise, is basically empirical, meaning that you concentrate predominantly on actual occurrences and not on ones that have not yet occurred?"

"Yes, that is correct," responded Sullivan.

Russell nodded. "So, in light of this observation isn't it appropriate to say that all of your testimony today on predictions and forecasts about what is and what would be, et cetera is outside the boundaries of statistics and hence outside of your area of expertise?"

Collins looked sharply at Russell. Sullivan frowned. He was unused to being the target of such a direct attack on his knowledge and integrity. Collins' mind raced searching for a plausible reason to object to this question before Sullivan was compelled to respond but then stopped and relaxed. Sullivan had quickly looked his way and shot him a savvy glance by narrowing his eyelids in a knowing half-squint.

The statistician turned his eyes back to gaze directly at Maddie Russell. He seemed to turn on some sort of invisible energy with this stare that had a visible effect on her as she sort of slumped in her seat in reaction much like a balloon might sag a bit due to a slow leak.

"It's quite clear, Ma'am, that you have very little understanding about the basis for statistics and the reason why scientists and mathematicians and engineers have worked so hard for the entire scope of our educated civilized existence to improve and refine.

"Statistics has a primary purpose if not sole purpose to provide us with a reliable, repeatable means of predicting what happens in the future. The fundamental reason why we are able to predict the future with confidence is because we use the past to help us formulate our models and also to verify that they are valid.

"In this particular case, Ms. Russell, the exercise that I have executed to be able to testify today with confidence and certainty is a perfect example of how statistics works. As I said, I took the uncontested data across a hundred-year period. I confirmed the predictive accuracy of the trends by comparing them to both other cities that are not named in this case as well as to a period of time in the named cities up to twenty-five years ago. Those predictions were very close to actual data and I thus confirmed and validated them. I then applied the prediction models to this case's cities for the past twenty-five years and compared them with the actual data in those cities.

"It's quite simple really when you understand it," continued Sullivan with a slightly cynical edge creeping into his tone. "When done this way there really is no other conclusion than the ones that I've provided already today under oath.

"If you would like to ask me if it's possible for these unusual death rates to have occurred in these cities randomly, I would respond by that saying that with absolute mathematical and statistical certainty they could not have."

Maddie Russell appeared to be so stunned that she was unable to announce to Judge Rector that she had nothing further for Dr. Sullivan.

Next, Collins called upon several other experts to testify about the shrinking homicide rates in these cities.

When asked to offer an explanation for this unusual occurrence, the experts were unable to provide one. When it was pointed out that the normal and expected phenomenon was occurring in other smaller cities in the country at the same time and also had occurred according to expectations in the larger cities, particularly those brought into question in the trial, up until about twenty-five years ago, the experts were hard pressed to accept the numbers as factual.

When queried about these doubts, Collins deftly evoked from each witness the opinion that when it was known that the deaths due to accidental and self-inflicted means were excessively high in these cities during this period, they invariably concluded that most of these "extra" deaths must be the missing homicides. The only explanation for this was that the public officials knew the deaths to be possible homicides but deliberately classified the deaths as something else.

Last, for this key point in the case, Collins brought in other experts to provide data on how the city governments were funded over the past fifty or so years and it was shown that as the crime rates grew prior to the beginning of the period in question, the budgets had grown steadily. Then, it seems that the citizens of these cities had reached their tolerance limit for increased taxes and the budgets were capped and, in some cases, went down.

Collins had the experts show that workloads began to far exceed the capacity and capability of the existing staff and that people began to quit or if they could, retire. It was an impending disaster. But then suddenly, almost responsively, the workloads began to slack off. This was due to a commensurate decrease in the homicide rates. In some cases, these decreases were dramatic.

This concluded the corruption phase.

The presidential polls for the week of October Eighth showed that President James had a rating of seventy-four percent, Collins nineteen percent, and seven percent were undecided.

CHAPTER 25

One evening that week, Collins was able to get home by dinnertime. Jane had made one of his favorite dishes: kielbasa sausage, onions, and green peppers sautéed in vegetable oil and served on fresh potato rolls with mayonnaise and spicy mustard. They were munching their way through two of these homemade submarine sandwiches and were casually schmoozing about various things in general.

"One of the things that has always turned me off about politicians, Dear," Collins said apropos to nothing in particular, "is that they seem to have checked their honor, integrity, and personal respect at the door when they announce they want to be elected to some office or another."

"The end justifies the means," Jane said. "Actually, I think that Dumas said it best in The Three Musketeers. He said the end excuses the means."

"Ah, you never cease to surprise me with your erudition, Jane, my Dear," Collins said admiringly. "How you find time to read the classics is beyond me. And how you're able to quote from the passages is truly remarkable. And as always, you've seen my point in its purest terms. The desire to get into elected office overwhelms the aspirants to the point that they're willing to do almost anything—no make that anything and everything, to get there." He paused a moment making a brooding grimace with his face. Then he looked up at his wife, his eyes shining brightly.

"I offer as addendum to this an important codicil. I want to provide every American with an alternative. I'm presenting myself to the voters as a common man candidate, a non-politician, in specific. In this way, it's effective to show what I am by showing that I'm not like the others. The problem is that with the way the news media is, trying to get a message out to the people is nigh near impossible!" He let out his breath in a loud whooshing noise. He was starting to get angry.

"Your tale sir would cure deafness," Jane replied smirkingly, her eyes twinkling with mischief.

"What?" Collins asked. "Is that another quote, you sly vixen. Mmmm. Let me think. Sounds like Shakespeare. Right?" Collins laughed softly, her playfulness drawing him away from his anger.

"Yup indeedie," Jane replied gleefully. "You're not such a man-without-letters yourself. In fact, this is a quote from The Tempest. Miranda said it to her father, Prospero, in Act One, Scene Two."

She laughed openly at the awed look on her husband's face.

At that moment, they were interrupted by a soft rap at the kitchen door. They looked up and saw Tom Laughlin's face peering in through the curtains.

"Ah, why don't you two run along into Buf's study while I clean up the dishes," Jane said after her father gave her a hug and a kiss. "I'll bring you some coffee in a bit."

"I'm just checking in," Laughlin told Collins as they walked down the hallway. "Anything happening that I don't know about?"

Collins shot a sharp look at the old man and smirked. If there was anything that his father-in-law didn't know, it probably wasn't worth knowing. Then he realized that the old man's keen perceptiveness had picked up on his sour expression.

"Oh, Jane and I were just talking about how nasty the media can be," Collins said dismissively. But he knew that Laughlin shared his concerns.

In fact, Collins' feelings about the news media were causing him constant distress and discomfort. He felt that they were using him for their own personal gain and had no true interest in what he might say or do. The point was that they only wanted him to say or do something. What it was really didn't matter. Once this happened, it was their job to make it appear newsworthy. This was the essence of the materialistic nature of the news media. Nowadays, the barometers of success in the business were market share, subscriptions, and the amount of paid advertising. Each "vendor" of the news dealt in the currency of how many people they could assure their advertisers would reach. The elegant ideals of the Fourth Estate from long ago were long forgotten. It was all about ratings and market share in today's world.

They were in the business of peddling what they believed people wanted to know. The major difference between current news coverage and that from before was that they made everything into news no matter what the actual event was.

For example, take the O. J. Simpson murder trial in the Nineteen-Nineties. When the jury came back with its verdict, the news services were ready to make that verdict the story regardless of what it was. They were going to make it something sensational regardless of whether it was guilty, not guilty, or can't decide. Another example was the sentencing of the Oklahoma City bomber Timothy McVeigh. The news reports conveyed the impression that that verdict was a surprise. Collins, when he heard about it had smirked at the sensationalism of the coverage. He knew that if the verdict had been life imprisonment instead of the death penalty, the coverage would have portrayed it as just as much of a surprise if not more of one.

"I know what you mean, Buf," Laughlin said sympathetically as they got settled in Collins' study. "Take this thing that they did about Jane and Susie O'Connell. It's unconscionable that the news media would run stories like that about anyone let alone someone who is nominated for the most important public office in the country. They must've known that there was questionable foundation to it, but they ran it anyway. If you ask me, they're no different than prostitutes. It's not a matter of what they will or will not do; it's only an issue of how much money they'll make for it."

"So, you expected that something like this was going to happen?" Collins asked casually as he poured himself a half-tumbler of Tennessee bourbon from the walnut and brass liquor cart in the corner.

"Mmmm, I can't say that I'm surprised by it," mused the old man. "What about you?" He went and poured himself a drink from the same crystal decanter. He took a long slow draught from the tumbler and let the sour-mash whiskey slide down his throat.

"I was sure that sooner or later the press and the news media were going to branch out on their own and begin to manufacture their own news about me," Collins said as he sat down. "I knew as sure as I know my own face that they weren't going to sit there and take what we've been feeding them without a whimper.

"What I didn't know, of course, was that they would stoop so low—I mean by pillorying Jane so wickedly. And I must say that I'm quite unhappy about it. That such a long and close friend of Jane's as Susie was the first violator of the code doesn't make it any easier for us to deal with it," he said.

"Code?" Laughlin was not tracking Collins' thread. "What code? Who violated the code, Buf?"

"Ah," said Collins, smiling enigmatically. "The code. Yes, well, what I mean by that is that there's a sociological phenomenon that occurs mostly in this country when someone has a friend (or a relative) who becomes a celebrity. They feel a compulsion to become at least partly famous by association. They believe that some of the recognition belongs to them. When the glow of the spotlight inevitably never reaches them, some of them are unable to deal with the disappointment and rejection. So, they seek out to buy the fame by using their personal knowledge about the celebrity. Thus, they violate their relationship willingly and openly. Susie O'Connell, as I'm sure you've observed, is a shallow and vain woman. She would've sold her mother and her children in a second if she thought that doing so would buy her fame. What better chip to redeem than her friendship in Jane Collins?"

Tom Laughlin's eyes lit up with interest. "So, you're saying that Susie violated the code of friendship by talking to that reporter about Jane when they were in college?"

"Exactly." Collins said, nodding. "And the sad part is that Susie got too swept up in trying to dredge up the most sordid thing she could think of in order to assure that the transaction would be valid. In doing so, she lost track of who was who and who it was that got the abortion back then."

"So, it really wasn't Janie?" Laughlin asked hopefully.

"Absolutely not," Collins answered with conviction.

"It was Susie instead?" Laughlin wanted to confirm the implied fact.

"Yes, and it was Jane who paid for it and went along with her," Collins replied.

Laughlin shook his head sadly. "All for a few seconds of fame."

"Mmmm, it's a terrible thing, Tom," Collins said. "We're living in a decadent culture and society." He pronounced the adjective "duh-KAY-dent" instead of the more commonly accepted "DEH-ka-dent" to convey the intent that the sad state of affairs in the present-day world was one of egregious proportions.

"But one has to see a tragically comic element to all of it," he continued. "Don't you think? I mean look at it. Here I am fighting for their ideals in court every day and the media is trying to cut me down." He shook his head in disbelief.

"Oh, I wouldn't let myself be too worried about that, if I were you, Buf," commented Laughlin soothingly. "Whether you realize it or not, you're the hero who's going to save the country from further abuse of power and the American public is astute enough to see right through the bad press and evil stories and understand the real truths and who're the good guys and who're the bad guys."

"You really think so?" Collins inquired, genuinely interested in the old man's answer.

"I do, Buf," he replied looking directly at him. "I really do."

Later after coffee and when Laughlin had gone along home, Collins and Jane picked up the conversation as they were getting ready for bed.

"You know," Collins said, "it's a nasty thing being a presidential candidate where anything and everything about a person is supposed to be an open book and fair game for any attacker. It would appear that, according to the media, there's nothing normal about a presidential candidate and that any characteristic is indicative of deep-rooted flaws more than sufficient to disqualify the poor slob from the job. And what concerns me is how much worse it will get before it's over and what sort of damage we—I'm talking about all of us: our kids, our family; our life—will incur because of it all. And that makes me think about the fact that I never wanted to be the danged president of the United States in the first place. The whole thing kills me. I mean, the most important thing in my life is my relationship with you and the rest of our family and that if there's any chance that this craziness might hurt what we have together, I won't ever forgive myself. And what if something awful happens that I can't control, and . . ." Collins gasped for breath and fought back the welling up of emotion.

Jane rushed over, immediately taking her husband into her arms and began to smother him with big wet kisses. She was bubbling under her breath about some big old bear.

"Buf," she said pulling back so that she could look into his eyes, "we just have to get control of this; just for preserving our sanity if for nothing else. I know that we're strong enough to see this thing as just a bit of unpleasantness." She smiled ruefully. "We can see this through. I know we can. We're both strong-willed people and we've also got an unshatterably solid relationship, you and me—us." She stopped and looked meaningfully at her husband. "Right?" she asked.

Collins nodded his head solemnly in agreement. "You bet," he replied reassuringly. "I'm behind you all the way. You're the Captain of this team and its star player. No question." Collins' conviction was sincere.

Jane nodded. "All right, then. So, let's stop moping around about how much we don't like what's happening, about how much we hate what's happened to our idyllic life, and about how much we are hating being on a Procrustean bed!" she said, her voice rising as her emotions began to surge. "Okay?"

Collins nodded vigorously.

"We got into this thing eyes-open, didn't we?" she asked pausing only for a moment as this question was intended to be rhetorical. "That's right, we did. No one forced this on us." She waved her hand dismissively. "Oh, I know you were drafted by the convention. It was your own choice—our choice—to accept the nomination. Let's stop whining and moaning! We're still together. I love you, Buf, and respect you for this more than ever. So, what's the problem? This is just another chapter in the life and times of Buf and Jane Collins."

This was quite a speech for her, but this was prime-time exposure one-on-one with her true love and husband. She was not going to hold anything back. She took Collins by his hands and squeezed tightly looking deeply into his eyes.

"This campaign isn't bigger than us, Buf," she said meaningfully. "No, it's just the next something that we're going to see through together. And we are going to get through it, too! We'll overcome all obstacles, all difficulties, and all of the grief that it can throw at us. No matter what. None of it, no matter how much or how bad it is, will break us, Buf. None of it. We're much too strong for anything as trivial as a silly campaign for the president of the United States. Not us! Pooh!" She looked at Collins compelling him to sustain the seriousness of this moment.

Jane then released her grasp on her husband's hands and closed in to embrace him wrapping her arms around him in a viselike grip. She pressed her cheek up against his chest and scrunched her eyes shut. She could hear his heart beating rapidly.

"I love you Buf, so much," she murmured hugging him even more tightly.

"Mmmm. I love you, too," Collins said softly, sotto voce, returning the warm embrace with his arms, emphasizing the intimacy of this moment.

They stood there holding each other and swaying slightly back and forth for what seemed like an eternity.

"You're exactly right, Jane," he said. "Exactly right.

"I've been making a huge mistake. What I've been thinking and then reacting to was that I, as the candidate, was fighting the establishment, the media, et cetera, and that the objective was that I had to beat them in order to get what I wanted. But you've just set me straight. I've had it all backwards. The correct perspective is for us, you and I, to always be the focal point. We are now together as one, as we always have been and always will be." He paused to look at her.

She nodded, ready for him to continue.

He nodded back. "Okay, then. So, the deal is that we're not subject to interference from these paltry outside influences. No way! We're as solid as marble. We're too tough. We sneer at this pesky little presidential campaign thing. Hah!"

Chapter 26

It took several days for Collins to establish that the corruption that he was in the process of proving with irrefutable evidence also included collusion. He introduced new evidence that indicated that the public officials that the Grand Jury indicted for corruption had colluded with the law enforcement officials and the medical examiners in their nefarious activities.

He and Shawna worked their way through the evidence with meticulous detail. This was where they wanted to lay down the foundation for the Jefferson dimension. In other words, to show that each defendant was regularly and deliberately comporting themselves in corruption that was enabled through collusion with the law enforcement factions in the cities named in the case. Once they were able to show that the corruption was facilitated through collusion, the public officials felt empowered to start claiming that the statistics showing that violent crime was on the decline in their cities was in fact due to their good works.

The presentation of this evidence was necessary, Buf and Shawna felt, to prove that the public officials clearly knew what they were doing and that they engaged others to either do it with them or not object to it. As it turned out, showing that there were many additional public officials, namely city employees, not elected officials, involved in the conspiracy, i.e., the crux of Jefferson, was inanely easy.

The most galling part of the whole case for Collins was that the evidence was so readily available and so incriminating.

After court was recessed one day in the midst of this, Collins commiserated with Shawna back in his law offices.

"It just amazes me, Shawna how much evidence there is against these people." Collins was stretched out on the divan, his tie loosened, and the top button of his dress shirt was undone.

"I think it's because all along none of them thought they were doing anything wrong and certainly that they'd never be called to task for it." Shawna was sitting in a client's chair that she'd turned about to face the couch.

"Sort of like hiding in plain sight," Collins commented drolly.

"Exactly," said Shawna. "None of them has made any attempt to hide what they've been doing. That's why this is being so easy. In fact, the ironic thing about this is that the openness of the evidence is the most incriminating thing about the cover-up."

Collins stared at her. "That's the most incredible thing I've ever heard," he said approvingly. "And it's our job to make sure that the jury sees it that way."

The presidential polls for the week of October Fifteenth showed that if the election were held then, President James would receive seventy-one percent of the vote, Collins twenty-one percent, and eight percent declared that they were undecided at that time.

On Wednesday evening, October Seventeenth, Tom Laughlin had the Collins' and Shawna Wells over for drinks, dinner, and dessert, as he described it. Ellen Laughlin was the mastermind of the soirée, but at her age the rigors of the preparation were beyond her stamina. So, she had some help come in to put her design into reality: a sumptuous feast in a marvelous venue.

Afterwards, while Jane Collins and her mother retired to another part of the Laughlin manse, Tom got down to brass tacks with Collins and Shawna in his study.

"It seems like the trial is coming along well," he began. "You've worked your way through a pile of evidence rather deftly I might say.

That's always the problem when you have too much evidence. Knowing how to avoid overwhelming the jury. I like the way that you've handled it so far. Well done."

Collins nodded his head in acknowledgment. He didn't have to be told what he already knew, and he also was not affected by the seeming praise. He and the old man went back too far and knew each other too well. These carefully chosen words were meant to make an impression on Shawna, not him. He turned his head slightly to see if they were having their desired effect.

Shawna was holding up her head and stretching out her neck much like a morning flower strains to get the first rays of daylight. She was overwhelmed with emotion to know that Tom Laughlin approved of how she and Collins were handling the trial. She'd gone through college destined for law school hearing about the great and sage Thomas Laughlin and then while at West Virginia University Law School, her professors seemed to find endless reasons to either quote Laughlin or cite famous cases he'd prosecuted successfully. In short, she'd emerged into the practice of law with Tom Laughlin firmly emplaced in her mind as a living legend, a mortal god in the field of law.

Since she was now meeting almost daily with the venerable icon of American jurisprudence, she felt more privileged than she'd ever be able to express. To have been anointed with his approval and praise, struck her dumb with awe—and, perhaps for the very first time in her life, speechless as well.

Laughlin cleared his throat to gloss over the awkward moment and told the other two to help themselves at the wet bar. He'd just made himself something to drink and walked over and sat down on the sofa that during the day overlooked the idyllic vista of the golf course and now at night took in the marvelous garden that was aesthetically illuminated by strategically placed back-lighting.

"Okay then, guys," he said, "let's get down to business. I think that it's time to begin implementing the October Plan that I told you about a few weeks ago."

Collins raised his eyebrows. "Ah," he said approvingly, "you mean where we start to introduce evidence that'll open the door for Jefferson?"

"Yes," replied Laughlin, seriously. "You told the jury in your opening statement that you'd show the defendants are guilty of three levels of criminal action: corruption, collusion, and conspiracy. This last was a surprise in that it wasn't cited by the Grand Jury and up until that point had not been part of Finch's and James' agenda of progressively stepping up the charges to keep you and Shawna scrambling. Their objective all along has been to make convictions impossible to prove and then after your nomination to try to cast you in the most unfavorable light as possible. The reason why we wanted to mention it that early was to catch James and the defense off their guard. We knew that James was planning to spring it on you before long anyway; so, what we wanted to do was to get the momentum to swing our way by bringing it up officially first. Well, now you've got to deliver on your promise.

"Since you're about done establishing in the minds of the jury that the defendants are all clearly guilty of corruption and collusion, under ordinary circumstances it'd be child's play to convince them that they're also guilty of conspiracy. In the jury's collective mind, the defendants are now all criminals, and their focus is on how guilty they are.

"But even so, I think that strategically it's best to introduce the cover-up part of the prosecution by carefully setting the stage for Jefferson as you so coyly call it to be a natural extension of how you present the evidence you have that shows there's been a conspiracy."

Shawna nodded her head in agreement. "That's pretty shrewd, Tom," she commented. "I've tried to think about how we can get into Jefferson without the defense going ballistic on us and this idea of the October Plan really diffuses that contingency remarkably well."

"Right Shawna," Collins agreed. "I like the way that Tom has blocked out this final part of the strategy. It resonates very well with me."

Laughlin was sitting motionless and when he didn't add anything to this, both Collins and Shawna looked over at him to see what was going on. Either he was not paying attention, or he had something on his mind that was troubling him.

The old man took a sip from his "dessert" and slowly swallowed. Then, he cleared his throat. "We can be sure of two things: First, as you've been moving successfully through this part of the trial and are ostensibly in the driver's seat, Gardie James' stomach is in knots in frustration. If there's anything that he hates with a vengeance, that's the feeling of not being in control of something. We can know this for sure because make no mistake about it my friends this recent spate of public endorsements of his reelection by various state and local officials has to be of his doing. And then the feigned afterthoughts about supporting the defendants are undoubtedly Gardie's hidden agenda coming out. He's doing what he can to get back in control of this thing. But I have to tell you that he's going about it in the wrong way.

"The second thing that we can be sure of is that because Gardie isn't openly coming out in public against you and the trial is that there really is foundation to Jefferson. And that brings me to the main reason why I've invited you over this evening."

"The main reason?" Shawna asked. "You mean that there's more than what we've talked about so far?"

"Yes, Shawna Dear," Laughlin replied quietly, "there's more."

"How much more could there be, Tom?" queried Collins.

"Well, ever since you brought up the Jefferson thing, I've had some of my own people doing a very deep and very, very discreet look into it. I know that you have evidence that indicates the corruption, collusion, conspiracy, and cover-up go way high up but it's only an inference at best. So, what I've been doing is trying to get enough evidence to be able to prove it."

"And have you?" asked Shawna softly.

Laughlin arose from the sofa and walked over to his desk. He picked up a manila folder and took out a sheet of notepaper and brought it over to the other two for them to read.

Collins read what his father-in-law gave him and stepped back nodding his head slightly as if this confirmed something he already suspected.

Shawna read the note and looked up sharply. "Holy high-falutin' pepperoni!" she exclaimed in surprise. "You think that we can get this kind of stuff?"

"I do," Laughlin replied tersely. "And if we do, do you think that it'll be enough? Remember, who we're going to be dealing with here. We won't be able to get away with innuendo and circumstantial suggestion."

"Uh," she hesitated, thinking it over. "Well, I don't know. It's certainly looks good." She turned to look at Collins. "What do you think, Buf?" she asked.

"Hmmm," Collins mulled it over. "I think that it should be enough." He took the sheet of paper from Laughlin and read it again, running his finger over the text. He then looked up. "It's enough probably for every other case but I wonder if it's enough for this one," he said unable to hold back a hint of doubt from his voice.

"That was how I felt," said Laughlin and sat down on the sofa. "At first. But when I put it into the proper perspective, I realized that now that you have the jury eating out of the palm of your hand, it probably is enough. Remember, less is more."

"Well, all right," Shawna said and sat down happily on the sofa next to Laughlin. "That settles it, then. We're all set."

Collins went to the wet bar and refreshed his drink. The silence in the room was so intense that each person was certain that they could hear the blood rushing in the veins of the other two. He came back and sat on the wingback chair facing the others.

"Hmmm," Collins muttered pensively.

"What's the matter, Buf?" she asked, wondering what he was thinking.

"It's just occurred to me that we might have a bit more difficulty showing cover-up what with all this full disclosure behavior that we're inadvertently showing the jury." He knitted his eyebrows broodingly.

"Ah, shoot," Shawna said, dejectedly. "I see what you mean." She thought about it for a bit. "But I'm not sure that I agree with you."

Collins sat up and looked at her. "You don't?" he queried.

"No," Shawna said thoughtfully. "I'm thinking that the case for cover-up deals with their behavior at another level than their overt actions."

"Another level? How do you mean?" Collins was curious.

Shawna paused, seemingly collecting her thoughts. "Well, they haven't been trying to cover up their actions or destroy any evidence to that effect. This we know. But they're being sneaky about it, nonetheless. We know that, right? So, maybe, when we get to the cover-up part, we should try to show that they've been hiding something else. Like . . ."

"Like that they know it's wrong," Collins finished.

Shawna stared at him and then began to crack a smile. Then she began to nod her head vigorously. "Bingo! The cover-up is that they don't want anyone to know that they know! Exactimento!" She jumped up and started to dance a little jig. "Hot diggity-DOG!"

Tom Laughlin smiled knowingly and slowly clapped his hands in approval. This was working out even better than he'd hoped.

CHAPTER 27

On Friday, October Nineteenth, Collins and Jane were eating a quiet dinner in the kitchen. He noticed that she was uncharacteristically silent, and he put down his fork and looked at his wife. "Something bothering you, Dear?" he asked solicitously. "What's the matter?"

"You probably don't remember but parent's weekend at yew-vee-ay begins tomorrow," she replied, referring to the annual fall event in Charlottesville, Virginia at the main campus of the University of Virginia where their son Tommy was a junior. "I'd like to be able to go."

Collins looked at his wife. He finished his mouthful of food and swallowed. He reached over and put his hand on her arm.

"Of course, you can go, Dear," he told her gently. "And I'm going to make sure that you go by taking you there myself. I remember discussing the prospect of going sometime last summer when this year's school calendar came out. It seems that we agreed to go and, if I recall correctly, you sent in a fee or deposit or something for it. Am I right?"

"Yes, you are Dear. I did send in a deposit," Jane replied. "Tommy called the other night to check to see if we're still planning on coming and I told him that I'd be coming for sure and that I'd try to see if you could get away and come, too."

"Well, of course I'll go!" Collins said forcefully. "There's nothing more important than our children and short of doctor's orders, I wouldn't let Tommy down and I know you wouldn't either.

"So, we'll drive down tomorrow morning. We'll leave about ten or ten-thirty and then we'll be able to have lunch with Tommy." Collins was helping Jane rinse the dishes and load the dishwasher.

"Sounds like a plan," Jane said as she tidied up the countertop.

"What about the Secret Service?" Collins asked.

"Not to worry," Jane said. "I've already talked to them about it."

"You have? How . . .? Uh, when . . .?" Collins was surprised.

"I talked to them about it more than a month ago, Buf. I knew that you probably had forgotten, but that once I reminded you, you'd want to go. And since it's pretty much out of the local area, I knew that the Secret Service would need some lead time to get ready."

"You're a marvel," he beamed. "Is there anything you can't do?"

"Not that I know of, Darling," she said smugly.

The next morning, Saturday, October Twentieth, they drove down to Charlottesville along with about eight Secret Service agents, one of whom insisted that he ride with them. The others were distributed in a lead car, a chase car, and a van. The crew chief told Collins that they had placed several other operatives at the University of Virginia campus and other locations in the university village earlier in the week.

In the car, even though the Secret Service agent who was riding with them in the car was quite congenial, the man and wife felt uncomfortable talking at their normal level of friendship and intimacy with a third person present. Presently Jane struck upon a suitable topic of conversation.

"Tommy tells me that he's on the honor roll again," she introduced.

"Mmmm. That boy was always the smart one of the bunch." Collins was concentrating on the road and the traffic which was unusually heavy for a weekend. He surmised that most people were just like him and Jane: parents going to parents' weekend at the university—well, almost just like them. The Collins' were the only pair of parents that were likely to attend the festivities who were sort of national celebrities.

Jane took umbrage with her husband's comment. "Now Buf, I know that you don't really mean that," she said referring to Collins' reference to Tommy being the smartest of their three children. "That seems to suggest that you feel that Will and Susan aren't very smart." She looked over at him with a mocked pouting expression.

Collins took his eyes off the road for a moment to glance at her. "Ah yes. I misspoke before. I've nothing but the highest esteem for all three of our children and none of them is short in the smarts department."

He shot a look at Jane to see if she was going to let him off the hook for this and detected a sly smile and a twinkle in her eye.

They arrived in Charlottesville just after noon. They picked up Tommy at his apartment and went to a local restaurant that was known for traditional (and colonial) style cooking. Tommy was fascinated with the Secret Service contingent and seemed to be more interested in asking them about their work and whether his father was a "hard guy to guard."

"Tommy, you seem to be gladder to see your father's minders this weekend than you are to see us," Jane scolded. "This isn't Secret Service weekend at yew-vee-ay; it's parents' weekend."

"I know, Mom. Sorry," apologized Tommy Collins. "It's just that I'd already come down here to school in August when you guys went to the convention, and I haven't really seen you since. I don't know anything about what it's been like to be the nominee or doing the trial and stuff. I don't know what you guys've been doing about all the terrible things they were saying about you on tee-vee and everything. It's been so weird! I just couldn't deal with it. So, I put it all away way back in my mind and forced myself to focus exclusively on my courses.

"And it must've been working, you know? My grades are higher than they've ever been!" Tommy's voice was charged with gratification.

"We've noticed how well you're doing in your courses, Tommy," Jane said, the mother in her unable to hold back the proud smile on her face. "Your father told me in the car on the way down that he thought you were extremely smart."

"You did?" Tommy asked, hoping for an endorsement from his father on this count. Even though Collins was a caring and supportive parent, Tommy was not going to forego the opportunity for a direct compliment.

"My words exactly, son," Collins replied and winked at his youngest child. He then shot a sly look at Tommy's mother and when their eyes met, he assured himself that she knew that he knew that she'd liberally embellished upon his actual words.

That afternoon at three p.m., the University of Virginia Cavaliers football team played the Fighting Seminoles from Florida State

University at Scott stadium. That this stadium held more spectators than the entire enrollment and staff of the university as well as the residents of Charlottesville, Virginia didn't seem to puzzle anyone. And where enough people came from each game to fill every seat in the massive stadium was never questioned, either. It was just one of those elusive oddities of college football.

Collins sat with his "family," meaning the three of them and about four or five Secret Service agents, on chairs that had been placed especially for them on the field level right behind the Cavaliers bench. The Secret Service's preference was for them to sit in one of the plush, enclosed executive suites that ringed the dish-shaped stadium around its midriff, like a wide belt. But Collins had objected to this as being too isolated.

"I am a common man candidate for the presidency, and I'll sit in the stadium like my fellow common men—and women," he had said firmly. "Find another way," he'd instructed.

The Secret Service didn't want to deal with the ramifications of having the Collins family sit somewhere in the open stadium and in the end, they compromised by having the Collins' sit where they had avenues of ingress and egress that they could control. The Service was unhappy about the vulnerability and exposure of Collins in this location, but to be frank, they were watching the polls just as closely as was Collins and his campaign team and they didn't think that any gun-toting crazies would care much about a presidential candidate who was certain to lose by a huge margin in a couple of weeks.

At the half the score was seventeen-to-fourteen with the home team holding a one field goal lead over Florida State. As the marching bands took the field and got into position for the half-time show, the booming voice of the public address announcer began echoing across the massive stadium complex.

"Laaadeeez and gennntillmennn!" it began. "Ladies and gentlemen, may I have your attention, please! Today is a special occasion for three very good reasons. First, the Cavaliers are winning over the number ten rated Fighting Seminoles."

There was a roar of cheering and applauding. Plastic horns hooted and on the Virginia side of the stadium there was a tremendous surge of whooping and whistles. The announcer waited for this cacophony to die down a bit before continuing.

"Second, it's parents' weekend at yew-vee-ay and we extend our warmest welcome and offer our rich tradition of southern hospitality to all you moms and dads out there. Thanks for coming!"

At this announcement there was a reaction from the crowd, but it was barely discernible from the general noise of about seventy decibels that an energized crowd of sixty thousand or so college football fans can make.

After a very short pause, the announcer continued. "And the third reason that this is a very special occasion at Scott Stadium today is that we have with us a very special guest."

"Uh oh," Jane murmured under her breath.

"Ladies and gentlemen, students, faculty and staff, guests, and parents, we've the distinct pleasure to introduce to you the proud parents of one of our own juniors here, the father of whom is Buf Collins, a loyal alumnus of yew-vee-ay and soon to be the NEXT PRESIDENT OF THE UNITED STATES!" These last words were almost shouted by the announcer into his microphone.

At this announcement the marching band which had assumed a seemingly unusual formation on the field produced from under their tunics large poster board sheets of various colors and held them on top of their heads. The mosaic that was then created very cleverly displayed the words "Go Buf Go!" in the instantly recognized school colors: royal blue letters fringed with orange on a white background.

The crowd, in reaction to both the announcement as well as the display on the field leapt into a raucous noise-making session that literally rocked the stadium to its foundation.

Collins leaned over to yell in his wife's ear. "I can't believe that these people are reacting to my presence with this much enthusiasm! They must be putting caffeine in the hot dogs!"

Jane Collins nodded in agreement and smiled broadly at her husband. She then began to push him gently off of his chair. "Go on, Buf. Stand up. They want to see where you are!"

Collins was reluctant to identify himself at first, but then the din of the crowd began to congeal into something that sounded like a chant. He stood and tried to concentrate on the sound.

"They're chanting the message on the field, Buf," Jane said.

Then he could pick it up. There were many tens of thousands of voices yelling the words Go Buf Go! He was filled with a tremendous surge of elation that these many people were yelling his name at the tops of their lungs.

He then looked up into the crowd and began waving his arms up over his head. He walked around in a small circle facing outward so that he could sweep his eyes around the entire stadium. In a few moments the noise started to die down and then bounced back this time much louder still. They had spotted him down on the field level.

At that point the band began playing and slowly the crowd wound down. Collins came back to where his empty chair sat and plopped down in it. He leaned over to kiss Jane on the cheek and reached over to punch Tommy lightly in the arm.

"Wow! Did you hear that?" Collins exclaimed, excitedly. "That was really something!"

The excitement seemed to be contagious, and the Cavaliers outdid themselves on the field in the second half of the football game, drubbing Florida State, forty-one to seventeen. Come Monday, the national ratings were sure to drop for Florida State and maybe the sports writers will recognize that the Virginia team was worthy of making the Top-Twenty.

The Collins' exited the stadium through the tunnel into the locker room area, guided by their Secret Service contingent who walked purposefully through the maze of halls and warrens of the stadium complex as if they followed this route daily. They found their car miraculously waiting for them just outside an unmarked door that had no doorknob on the outside. There was not a single person near them who took any notice as they entered the car and drove off.

They had dinner at another local restaurant in a private dining room in the back. It seems that Jane Collins had asked if the Secret Service would coordinate this for them back a month or so ago when she announced that she and her husband were planning to visit Charlottesville this weekend. The restaurant was a landmark in this central Virginia town and allegedly sat on the site where a traveler's inn once sat in the late Eighteenth Century and where, according to local folklore George Washington, John Adams, Thomas Jefferson, James Monroe, James Madison, and John Quincy Adams had all stayed or eaten at one time or another during its existence. No one ever doubted the veracity of this claim. It was just too good of a story. Who would want to brag to someone that they had eaten at a place that stood on the site where the first six presidents of the United States once stayed, if they then had to qualify the boast by saying that maybe it was not really true? And since the current establishment on this site was in its one-hundred-and-twenty-fifth year of continuous operation there was an elaborate amount of braggadocio on the part of the current owners as to how many other presidents had at one time or another graced these walls with their patronage. It was a marvelous marketing ploy, if it was anything else.

Thus, the current manager of the restaurant had eagerly provided the utmost in service and care for the Collins party. Who knows? he'd thought to himself. Stranger things have happened and if Collins makes it, he can add another name to his impressive list.

The talk at the table was a jumble of college life and campaign life. Jane wanted to keep the focus on Tommy and his life as a college junior. Tommy, however, wanted to know how the campaign was going, what his father was planning to do in court the next week, and how they were holding up. Throughout Collins seemed aloof and didn't contribute much to the dialogue.

"Is there something wrong, Buf?" Jane inquired solicitously. She'd noticed her husband's flat mood since they'd exited the stadium but didn't want to ask about it until they were alone.

"Hmmm?" It seemed as if Collins' thoughts were somewhere else. "Oh, uh, no Darling, not really. I'm fine." His voice didn't convey the conviction needed to support these words.

Jane was not having any of it. "I don't believe you, Honey. Something is bothering you and I think that it'd be best if you talked about it." She looked over at Tommy who was devouring his meal. "It's okay, Buf.

You can talk in front of Tommy. He's almost twenty now—and he's the smartest one in the bunch, remember?"

Tommy looked up at the mention of his name and then re-directed his attention to the plate of savory roast beef in front of him.

"Oh, all right," Collins spluttered, a little exasperated. "You're right, as always my Dear." He put his fork down and pushed his plate away from him. "Ever since I heard how much that crowd back there at the stadium seemed to be in support of me, I've been, uh, somewhat at a loss as to what to make of it."

"Ah, I thought so," Jane said, knowingly nodding her head. "I thought that might be it. You see, I noticed it too. I think that the oddness is because those people were there today to see a football game, right? They were students and parents and other alums, et cetera. A whole mix of different people from Virginia and no doubt also from Florida and other points in between. No one knew that you were going to be there. You weren't the draw card.

"But they all seemed to be supporters anyway, didn't they? That's it, isn't it? You were surprised by the special recognition that the university people put on for you, that we know. But you were overwhelmed by the accolade that you received from the crowd—a group made up of all kinds of people from different places and different climes." She paused for a moment, smiling cryptically. "To quote Shakespeare, *I think that the air breathes upon us here most sweetly* says it all. That's from The Tempest, Adrian said it in Act Two, Scene One."

"Ah, what we have here is a positive indication of where Tommy gets his smarts," Collins commented drolly. "But I think that you're on to something, my Dear, about my reaction to this afternoon's crowd when I was introduced." He looked over at his son who was no longer eating and paying close attention to this conversation. He looked at Tommy's plate and satisfied himself that Tommy's interest was because he no longer had anything left to eat, perhaps more than the lure of the subject matter. "What do you think, son?" he asked, genuinely interested.

"Huh? Me?" Tommy was unused to being an equal participant in conversations with his parents. "Uh, well, I think that Mom's right about what sort of seemed odd to you, Dad. Um, I guess you've been figuring all along that you had no chance to win the election, right? But then people started to notice you in the coverage of the trial. And um, I think that you never once thought that this would actually, uh, appeal to voters. Yes, you knew that they'd be interested in the case that you were trying, but you never thought that your role in it'd influence anyone to like you or to feel that they wanted to vote for you.

"So, today was the very first time that you got any indication that you had real voter support, support from people that you've not met or talked to personally, support from the faceless and nameless American voting public. And the degree of support, the enthusiasm that those people in the stadium gave you. That was what has shocked you."

Collins and his wife were stunned. They sat there staring at their young son almost with their mouths dropped open in awe. For a moment, Tommy feared that he'd overplayed his invitation to contribute to the conversation and that his parents were about to scold him. He started to open his mouth and begin to recant his words but stopped when his father held up his hand.

"No, you're wrong to think that you've overstepped your boundaries as the dutiful son, my boy. Have no fear. Your mother and I are just a little dumfounded at you, that's all. What I mean, is that no matter how silly it is, we still tend to think that you're our baby son, and for you to just now demonstrate how mature and insightful you are comes to us like a kick in the butt." He paused and laughed jovially. "But add insight to my dilemma you have indeed done, my son. With your observations and your mother's, I think that now the paradox is clarified in my eyes.

"Yes, the fact that the crowd this afternoon was so much in favor of me and was so enthusiastic in chanting Go Buf Go was what came to me as a surprise. You're both right that I never really thought that I was gaining any support in this election. To be frank, I only thought my ratings were coming up because of some things that your grandfather, Tommy, told us. So, today when I saw that there are people who clearly are in support of me, because of me, I wasn't prepared for it. I couldn't deal with it or process it in my mind. I guess I was just blocking out the fact that my common man approach would be something that might appeal to voters. I must admit that I'm quite humbled by it.

"To think that my campaign, my message is having this kind of effect, is really stimulating. I'm wondering if . . . if . . ."

"If you might've a chance of winning?" interjected Tommy.

"Why, yes. I guess that's what I'm trying to articulate. The essence is, is it possible that the American public is finding the choice of me for president over the incumbent attractive? Is it possible that the voters actually want to vote for a candidate who's not a politician, one who avows that he detests the species? Can it be?"

"I think that you're onto something, Dad," said Tommy supportively.

Collins looked at Jane and raised his eyebrows questioningly.

"I think that it is indeed possible, Buf. I think that it's actually happening—you're getting voter support for you and because of you. And I think that it's about time in this country that an honest and honorable man has a chance to be our leader.

"I think that it's refreshing," she concluded.

"Holy mackerel!" Collins exclaimed breathlessly.

The presidential polls for the week of October Twenty-Second showed that President James had a rating of sixty-eight percent, Collins twenty-four percent, and eight percent were undecided.

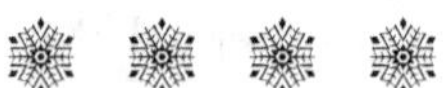

"They're up to something," the president growled as he paced the floor in the Oval Office. "I just *know* it!"

"Oh, I don't know, Mr. President," consoled Finch. "I've seen the investigation reports the bureau did, you know, and I don't think that they have enough evidence to prove cover-up. Surely, you recall that's why you told me to escalate the charges to cover-up—because we knew they couldn't make it stick. We wanted to hamstring them; make them look bad; ensure that they wouldn't get any convictions. Right? Well, they've played into our hands more neatly by introducing the cover-up charges on their own.

"We couldn't have planned it any better, sir."

James stared at his attorney general, sitting rigidly still. Then he started to shake his head. "No, Bobby. It's too pat. They're up to something. There's no doubt in my mind. When Collins brought up cover-up in his opening statement, I thought at the time he was grandstanding and using his newfound eminence as his party's nominee like a weapon against me. But now I'm not so sure that it's that simple, Bobby.

"They're up to something. I just *know* it!"

On Wednesday evening, October Twenty-Fourth, Tom Laughlin sat at the desk of his study. He was talking on the telephone with his back turned to the windows. He was talking so softly that if someone had been sitting on the sofa less than ten feet away, she would have had trouble making out what he was saying.

"Okay then. . . . You found her? . . . Where is she? . . . Wait a second, let me write this down. . . ." He took a slip of paper out of a tray and began to write on it with a pen. "And you say you spoke to her? . . . Uh huh. . . . Did you ask her if she'd testify? . . . Uh huh. . . . She said that!? . . . No kidding. Well, I'll be a monkey's uncle."

He put down the phone and made a few more notes on the sheet of paper that he'd been using. Then, he picked up the phone and keyed in another number.

"Hello? . . . It's me. . . . Yes. . . . Did you get in to see him? . . . You did? . . . When? . . . Yesterday? All right. And did you tell him what I told you to tell him? . . . What did he say? . . . He did? Ha ha. I've always admired his spunk. And did you give him the envelope? . . . Uh huh. And, he agreed to wait until I called before he opened it? . . . Uh huh. Okay, good job. You can pack it up and come home." He disconnected the call. He opened up a notebook that he had on the desktop and punched a new number into his phone reading it from a page in the notebook.

"Hello? . . . This is the call that you were told to expect to get at this time. Okay, just to make sure that you know who this is, do you remember about thirty years ago when you were a freshman senator?...

Uh huh. You went to the opera at the Kennedy Center along about then and ran into someone in the men's room during the intermission. Do you remember? . . . You do? Okay, that person that spoke to you that night congratulated you on your being elected to the Senate and then complimented you on your tie which was a bright red paisley pattern. Do you remember that? . . .You do? Then, you know for a certainty now who it is who is speaking to you right now, correct?

"Okay, now if you would please, turn your back to any windows that might be in the room where you are now. All right? . . . Now, if you would please open the envelope that you were given yesterday by my representative. You have it there with you, do you not? . . . All right. Open it please. . . . There's a short statement printed on the sheet of paper. Please read it. . . . All right. Do you agree with what it says? . . . You do? Did you ever have any personal communication with that person on this topic that could be used to implicate him? . . . Uh huh. . . . Uh huh. . . . Hmmm, I see. Very interesting. . . . Would you be willing to testify on that? . . . You would? Excellent! All right. Very good. Someone'll be in touch with you very soon to make the appropriate arrangements. Oh, and one more thing. Please destroy that piece of paper as soon as you can. . . . Excuse me? . . . No, shredding it won't be good enough. I'd suggest burning it and then scrambling up the ashes afterwards and then flushing the residue down the toilet. . . . You say that sounds paranoid? Yes, I agree completely. But if we're going to get the guy who's behind all of this, we've got to be very, very, very careful. Don't you agree? . . . Mmmm. My sentiments exactly. Good day to you, sir, and thank you."

He disconnected the call and put down the phone. He picked up his pen and made some more notes. Then, he picked up the phone again. After he punched in the number and waited for a couple of rings at the other end, he turned around and put his feet up on the desk.

"Buf? Is that you? I think that you Shawna need to pop over here as soon as you can make it. I think I've got what you wanted me to find."

The presidential polls for the week of October Twenty-Ninth showed that if the election were held then, the president would receive sixty-four percent of the vote, Collins would get twenty-nine percent, and there were seven percent of those polled who declared that they were undecided.

Collins was climbing out of the cellar, but it seemed like it was too little, too late. Even if he could count on all of the undecideds to swing his way as well as to continue to gain at the current rate, by November Sixth, he would still fall very short.

He needed a miracle to have even a snowball's chance.

Chapter 28

It took most of a week to get through the conspiracy phase. Each day as the brick wall of unequivocal guilt was carefully erected with the mortar of solid evidence, the jury seemed to grasp the delicate distinction that Collins was making about the conspiracy as being an expected devolution from collusion. Each day, the American public tuning in on their television sets saw Collins more and more as their hero. And each day as the evidence built up, Gardner James became more and more angry, and Robert Finch grew more and more moribund.

By Wednesday October Thirty-First, Collins was about done. The only thing left was the full exploitation of the Jefferson dimension and Tom Laughlin's October Plan. He and Shawna both knew that there was more to be done, to complete the full gamut of the four "cees," namely cover-up, but were unsure exactly how they were going to be able to pull it off.

Collins' first salvo was to call a witness who was an expert on the use of the Internet. He called Dr. Helene Masterson, professor of public ethics and humanities and chair of the Department of International Information Infrastructure, Innovation and Advancement at Stanford University. Her specialty was electronic mail traffic, or E-mail. Collins told the jury that he wanted to show that the defendants talked freely about what they were doing and among other media, did so in their E-mail messages.

The important distinction was that the medium of E-mail was both a matter of public record but also a form of documentation—in other words, it was not hearsay. The hidden agenda for presenting this testimony was to introduce who the defendants were sending E-mail messages to, thus pulling into the net many other public officials that illustrated the breadth and scope of the conspiracies that propagated in the nation's major cities over the course of the past twenty years. But it was one big fish that Collins had his sights set on.

The Internet expert testified about conducting an exhaustive search of the Internet for the purpose of looking for E-mail messages that the defendants had sent over the years. There were something like a hundred thousand such messages. Of these, more than forty percent made some sort of reference to key aspects of corruption, collusion, or conspiracy. And of these there were as many as several hundred "new" public officials who were by association implicated in these crimes.

Collins, of course, knew the answers to all of his questions before he asked them. He'd spent a lot of time strategizing with Shawna about exactly how to present the evidence. He was about to serve up the pièce de résistànce from this witness and he hesitated a moment before proceeding. Whatever the trial had been up to this point, it would not be even close to the same from this moment on.

"Ma'am, did you notice anything unusual in your analysis of this set of E-mail messages?" he asked.

"Yes, Mr. Collins, I did," she answered.

"And what was that?" he asked, trying to keep his voice even. He wondered if anyone could notice that his heart was beating like a hammer.

"While I was compiling a list of the individuals who either sent or received these messages, as well as the names that were mentioned in them, I began to notice that one name in particular seemed to be occurring with unusually high frequency."

"Hmmm," Collins commented. "How do you mean, unusual?"

"There were about twenty thousand separate messages. The names of the defendants occur more or less at equal frequency in these messages and that's at about a three percent rate. But there's one name which appears in these messages at a rate of more than fifteen percent."

"That is pretty high, you're right," confirmed Collins. "Do you think that there could be any explanation as to why this one name is mentioned in these messages so often? You know, like it's a common name or a name brand of a consumer product or something?"

"I considered that," she replied. "So, I tested the messages for things like Betty Crocker and, um, Jack Daniels—names like that. But they're virtually non-existent in these messages. Then, I tested for famous people like singers, actors, and sports figures. Same thing. They're not there."

"So, the implication is that the reason why this one name is mentioned so often is that this person is in some way connected to the crimes that the defendants in this case are charged with?" Collins stood still and raised his eyebrows slightly. He wanted to convey the impression that he was not expecting a presumed response.

"Uh, well I'm not a probability expert but I did a random check on about five thousand of the messages and in each and every case this name was mentioned in context with the subjects that you targeted for me to look for in the first place."

"This name is mentioned in context with the discussion of the corruption, collusion and conspiracy, you say?" Collins asked.

"That's right," the witness replied. And after a brief pause, the witness added, "And there was something else, Mr. Collins. Something very interesting. Something unique."

Collins feigned a surprised reaction to hearing this by turning to the jury and raising his eyebrows—even though he knew full well what was coming next.

"And that was, Dr. Masterson?" he prompted barely able to contain his eagerness in getting this major element to his case into the record.

"That was, Mr. Collins, that these instances of this person's name appearing in so many messages was that they weren't all in one of the identified pools of messages from a single city," she testified calmly.

Again, Collins reacted with some feigned surprise. It was as if he was a young child unwrapping a surprise ball and enjoying the next trinket being revealed as he pulled away the crepe paper wrappings at Christmas.

"They weren't?" he prompted again. This process of disclosing the key elements of this major keystone in his overall strategy to prosecute this case had been deliberately crafted by Shawna and he was following a well-rehearsed script.

Dr. Masterson shook her head and then sheepishly sneaking a glance at Judge Rector realizing that head nods do not get entered into the court records, cleared her throat and said, "No sir, Mr. Collins. They weren't." Then, as she saw that Collins was giving her a look that telegraphed a mute "Go on" instruction, she continued by saying, "The reason why there were so many instances of this person's name appearing in all these emails was that it appeared many times, hundreds of times, in the messages that we collected from all the cities named in this case—those cities that were on the list that you gave me to look into, Mr. Collins."

Collins paused for a moment as if he was himself pondering the impact of this interesting tidbit of new information.

"Sooo," he started seemingly hesitant, "this means what to you Doctor? Does it mean that since this person's name has appeared in many of the email messages from all the pools of messages from all the cities in this case explain why there are so many of them?"

Dr. Masterson did not answer this question right away. It seemed that she was considering the point of Collins' question for the first time, as if it had not occurred to her until this exact moment. Then, she looked up at Collins as if she had just then seen the clarity of the situation and turned her face to look directly at the jury and replied, "Well, no, Mr. Collins. Not exactly. Well, I mean yes it does sort of explain why there are so many instances where this person's name is mentioned but actually no because it tells me something much more insidious."

"And that was?" asked Collins calmly.

"That was," continued Dr. Masterson still looking directly at the jury, "that it strongly suggests that this person was involved in the nefarious doings of the city officials in all of the cities in question here."

"You say all of the cities?" repeated Collins ostensibly to confirm that he heard the witness correctly but more importantly to burn this information into the minds of the twelve jurors who he noticed were leaning forward in their seats like children rapt in the throes of a particularly intriguing tale being related to them by a master storyteller.

Again Dr. Masterson nodded and then quickly and sheepishly leaned in close to her microphone and affirmed her previous statement, "Yes sir. All of them."

Collins straightened up and did a short stroll around the space between the witness stand, the prosecutor's table where Shawna Wells was calmly sitting, across in front of the defendant counsel's table where Maddie Russell sat rigidly still and then back in front of the jury box. He wanted the jury, the defense cadre and more importantly all the American voters who were watching the trial on daytime television to think that he was carefully digesting this information.

Then, he turned back to Dr. Masterson and asked slowly in a clear and audible voice, "So, what does this seeming anomaly in the information that you have analyzed suggest to you Doctor?"

Maddie Russell came to life and almost shouted "Objection!" nearly jumping out of her chair. "Calls for speculation, your honor!"

Collins knew this was going to happen and quickly interjected before Rector could rule on Russell's objection, "Dr. Masterson here, your honor, is a recognized world-renown expert in social human information processing and my question just now to her is most certainly not asking her to speculate on this."

Rector had his gavel in hand and poised over its wooden block and his mouth open when Collins provided this clarification. He replaced the gavel in its cradle and shut his mouth briefly, only to reopen it a moment later to say, "Overruled. I'll allow it."

Collins looked back at his witness and gave her a look inviting her to respond to his question.

Dr. Masterson said, "Well, once I noticed this interesting feature of the data rather than merely discounting it as an anomaly, I elected to do some additional analysis. What I mean is that I then did some additional key word searches in these messages that were common across the multiple city pools of messages, and I discovered some very interesting things." She looked at Collins to see how she was doing. He nodded in encouragement, and she continued her testimony by saying, "These new findings were interesting not in the numbers aspect as related to frequency nor to the geographical breadth of their appearances, but with respect to the content of what was in them.

"You see that the database that I was able to compile wasn't limited to just subjects, dates, senders, recipients, and file size. The database included the message contents themselves and up until this point I had not had any need to actually read any of them. But once I saw the cross-city frequencies of the messages from this person, I realized that I would need to start reading them to see if I could ascertain anything about the context of the messages and the timing with respect to the other phenomena occurring in these cities during those years, namely the sharp drop in homicide rates, and so on."

She paused for a moment and took a small sip of water from the glass on the shelf next to her in the witness stand.

Collins took the opportunity to verbalize his continued prompting of Dr. Masterson's testimony by saying, "'And then, Doctor, what did you find out from reading these messages?"

Again, Maddie Russell shot to her feet but before she could say anything Rector flapped his hand at her, motioning for her to sit back down saying tersely, "Stifle!"

Dr. Masterson continued, saying, "What I found was that in the context of most of these messages from this single person in question was almost universally about how this person wanted the public officials in these cities, namely the people this person was sending these messages to, . . ., uh, . . ., this person wanted them to play down any form of boasting that they had done the impossible by decreasing the frequency of violent crime in these cities. The messages were saying, almost instructing, the city officials to take credit but to do so with a low profile."

Collins again seemed surprised at this additional information. "Did the content of the messages from this person indicate why?" he queried.

"Well, yes," Dr. Masterson replied showing some surprise in her voice as well, "The content of the messages was actually quite clear about this point. The person, the sender, was telling the public officials that it was very important for the public to accept these trends of decreasing violent crime, namely homicides, in their cities without wanting too much additional information.

"The point that the sender emphasized was that the majority of the voting public in these cities did not actually live in the inner parts of the cities where crime was common and were loath actually to ever visit those areas and thus it was important for them to merely take the reports from the city officials on the surface and not wish to know more or have any further proof than the statistics being reported."

Collins then asked, "What does that mean to you, Doctor?"

Dr. Masterson looked briefly at Collins and then turned her gaze to look hard at the jury and replied, "It means to me that the person sending these messages was instructing the city officials to cover-up what the person explicitly acknowledged was corruption and collusion over those years and also to cover-up what would otherwise be easily identified as conspiracy if the voting public were inclined to start questioning the basis of the statistics that were being reported about the sharp declines in violent crimes in those cities."

At this point there was a massive eruption of noise in all parts of the courtroom. It took Rector several minutes of pounding his gavel with full arm's length strokes like a professional roofer would swing his heavy-duty hammer on long ten penny nails and drive them home in one stroke, before he got the commotion raging through his courtroom under control. When his loud stentorian voice could once again be heard over the simmering din, he bellowed out that he would not tolerate such outbursts while he was presiding over a trial. He glared at the press corps. He scowled at Maddie Russell and her army of lawyers. He swept stern stares at the rest of the gallery. And then he gave his jury a benign, thin-lipped smile and Dr. Masterson a fatherly and doting sort of smile and nodded to Collins to continue.

William Buford Collins, VI, nominee for his party to run for the president of the United States, Special Counsel of the United States appointed by his opponent, the sitting president, to prosecute this case of corruption, collusion and conspiracy against several public officials in multiple states, who was rapidly becoming America's White Knight in shining armor fighting against the proverbial "City Hall" of urban America every day on live television and who was seemingly winning this impossible quest, nodded back at Rector and approached Dr. Masterson, placing his hand calmly on the rail of the witness stand before her.

"Doctor, can you please repeat for the court and the jury the last part of your testimony just now?" he asked in a level voice.

Dr. Masterson nodded, cleared her throat again and leaned forward towards her microphone and said, "Yes, Mr. Collins, I will. I just testified a moment ago that it was clear in these messages that this person was sending to the officials in the cities in question that he wanted them to cover-up what they had been doing all those years."

Collins stood up and turned towards the jury and asked, "Cover-up? Did you say that the person sending these messages was instructing the city officials, the defendants named in this case, to cover up their actions?"

Maddie Russell jumped up and before Rector could stop her almost shouted "Objection! Asked and answered!"

Rector quickly growled, "Overruled" and looked down at Dr. Masterson. "Please answer Mr. Collins' question."

Dr. Masterson opened her mouth and said, "Yes, Mr. Collins, I did."

Rector quickly rapped his gavel three times loudly to forewarn anyone in the courtroom from making any kind of audible reaction to this. There was a long very pregnant pause at this point, while Collins continued to look straight at the jury with his back turned to his witness.

Then, he said, "Dr. Masterson, would you please tell the jury the name of the sender of these messages about corruption, collusion, conspiracy, and cover-up that your analysis found in the thousands of emails in context?" he asked.

"Yes, Mr. Collins, I will. The name of this sender of the emails that I have been describing to the court here today is Gardner James," Dr. Masterson replied firmly.

There was an instantaneous flurry of noise in the courtroom at this stunning revelation. Judge Rector slowly tapped his pen on the base of his microphone for order, with which all present miraculously complied, as he himself was just as shocked as everyone else in the courtroom was, excepting of course, Collins and his star witness.

"The president?" Collins asked for confirmation.

"That's right, but of course he wasn't the president when many of these messages were sent."

"I see," Collins said. "How far back to they go? The messages that were from Gardner James?"

"All the way back to the beginning."

"Please allow me to clarify for the jury," Collins said. "You're saying that the name of Gardner James appears as the sender in an unusually large proportion of these messages—so unusual that it cannot be accidental or random; that the appearance is in context with wording that relates directly to the corruption, collusion and conspiracy charges cited in this case, and that this frequency of occurrence began about at the same time that the E-mail traffic from the defendants that mentioned these crimes began. And that Gardiner James was the sender of the messages that instructed the defendants to cover up their actions. Is that correct?"

"Yes, it's correct—except that the mentioning of James' name didn't start about at the same time as you just characterized it in your question."

"No?" Collins queried. "When did it start?"

"It started exactly at the same time."

Collins allowed himself to stare at his witness for a moment in hopes that he would appear to be a bit surprised at this.

Next, Collins called the first of his two final witnesses. She was a career secretary in the district attorney's office in Los Angeles and had served under D. A.s during a period of nearly forty years previously. This woman testified that she had knowledge of many occasions, perhaps more than a hundred times, where families of people who had died came to the District Attorney's Offices asking that criminal investigations on the deaths of their loved ones be opened. These families were convinced, she said, that the deaths were not accidental, or whatever. They felt that they were suspicious, and they thought that there had to be some mistake in that the cause of death had officially been recorded as accidental and the like.

"What did your employers do with these requests?" Collins asked.

"They had me compose response letters to them," she answered.

"What did these letters say?" Collins inquired.

"They said that the County Coroner had determined the official cause of death and that once this determination was made, there was really nothing that could be done about it. They, the letters, said that it was inappropriate to make such a request of the District Attorney's Office."

Collins nodded his head like he knew that this would be her answer. "I see. And based upon your knowledge of the workings of the District Attorney's Office acquired in your years of working in that office, was this statement a fair appraisal?"

"No, sir," she responded. "The District Attorney has broad authority in the county and even more power. If he had asked the coroner to reevaluate the determination of a cause of death, he'd have done it without hesitation or question. In fact, the dee-ay really doesn't need to involve the coroner at all."

"How do you mean?" Collins prompted.

"Well, it really doesn't matter what's on the death certificate or what the coroner's opinion is. If the dee-ay told the homicide division in the police department to open an investigation into a certain death, that's exactly what they'd do." The witness looked steadily at Collins, exuding confidence and veracity.

"So," Collins continued, "you're saying that when the dee-ays told these people that it wasn't in their authority to consider their requests nor for that matter was it appropriate for them to make such requests to their office in the first place, they weren't doing what really was within their authority to do?"

"That's precisely what I'm saying, Mr. Collins," she answered.

"So, in every one of these instances, to the best of your recollection, the district attorneys, didn't look into any of these deaths, in any way?" Collins asked.

"Yes, that's right. They did not," came the reply.

"As if the requests were trivial or unfounded?"

"Right."

"So, the dee-ays based on the requesting letter alone determined that there was no merit and no reason to look into any of these deaths?"

"That's right."

"This was true of all of the district attorneys you worked for?" he asked.

"No sir, it wasn't," she answered.

"Really?" he responded with some surprise. "There were some dee-ays who didn't do this?"

"Yes."

"Can you explain, please?"

"Certainly. Every dee-ay that I worked for from the beginning of my career until about twenty-five years ago didn't do this that I've been telling you about."

"All of those dee-ays in the beginning, did what? They didn't ignore the requests from unhappy families?" Collins leaned forward appearing to be eager to hear her.

"No, sir. Well, actually there weren't any unhappy families in those early years, because there weren't any suspicious deaths that I know of which weren't being investigated."

"Ah, then about twenty-five years ago, there started to be a lot of suspicious deaths that didn't get investigated. This brought on the requests from the unhappy families that resulted in being ignored by the dee-ays from that point on. Is that what you're saying?"

"That's exactly what I'm saying." She nodded her head for emphasis.

"So, it'd appear that all this started with the dee-ay who became your boss about twenty-five years ago. Correct?"

"Correct."

"And who was that, may I ask?"

"It was Gardner James."

After this bombshell, Collins called an individual who was a state legislator in California at the same time that two of the defendants were. After a few preliminaries to establish that this witness both knew and worked closely with the defendants, Collins quickly got to the point.

"Sir, did you have occasion to talk to the defendants while you served in the state legislature?"

"Yes, many times," was the reply.

"I see," Collins said as he stood in front of the witness chair. "What did you talk about in these conversations?" he asked.

"Just about everything under the sun. We were all pretty good friends," the witness replied.

"Did you talk about your careers?" was the next question.

"Oh, yes. Lots of times," was the answer.

"Did any of the defendants tell you how they got to be state congressman?"

"Yes," came the reply.

"Were their accounts similar or different?" Collins asked, his tone guarded.

"They were similar," responded the witness.

"Really? How similar?" Collins inquired.

"They were identical. They told me that they got the same start."

"And how was this?" was the question.

"They said that they'd gotten started as the District Attorney of Los Angeles," was the answer.

"Uh huh," Collins said. He was standing unmoving with his hands behind his back. "And did any of them talk about their experience in the dee-ay of Los Angeles position?"

"Yes, they both did," replied the witness. "They said that they'd done a good job cleaning up the city and rose to the state legislature as a result."

"I see," mused Collins. "Did they tell you how they did this?"

"Yes sir. They said that they'd gotten violent crime to go down."

"Ah, no mean feat, I'd think. In Los Angeles, to boot. Did they tell you how they were able to accomplish so difficult a feat?"

The witness made a little smirk. "Yes."

"And how did they do it?" Collins asked.

"They said that they had a way to achieve great results without having to work very hard."

"Aha! A secret technique perhaps?"

"Yes, you might say that. They said that they had their staff focus only on the deaths that were obviously homicides and classify all of the others as something else."

"Something else? Like what?"

"Like accidental death, or suicide, or due to natural causes."

"They said this to you?"

"Yes sir."

"In confidence?" Collins asked.

"No, they were proud of it."

"They told you that they in effect manipulated the authority of the district attorney's office to make their jobs easier and then took credit for making the city safer as a result and were proud of it?" Collins infused a tone of incredulity into his voice.

"That's right."

"Did they tell you how they came up with this scheme?"

"Yes, they said they learned it from a former district attorney of Los Angeles."

"They observed this previous dee-ay doing it?" Collins prompted.

"No, they told me that he taught it to them," replied the witness.

"On purpose?" reacted Collins. "I mean, it was deliberate?"

"Oh, yes."

"Who was this former dee-ay, the one who taught your friends how to look great without having to work too hard?"

"It was Gardner James."

On Friday, November Second, Collins pulled out his trump card and called one final witness, the second of the key witnesses identified in Laughlin's October Plan.

"Your Honor," Collins said slowly so as to build up a bit of suspense, "the prosecution calls Robert Wilson Thurmond to the stand."

Immediately, there arose a loud hubbub. Collins was calling James' predecessor in the White House to testify. Robert Thurmond was the immediate past president of the United States whose vice president for two terms was Gardner James. Rector rapped his gavel several times and shouted loudly in his command voice for order. As the distinguished statesman entered the courtroom and walked down the aisle, the noise in the courtroom slowly subsided. It was clear that everyone was more willing to pay their respects to this highly popular president and to be able to hear his testimony than they were affected by Rector's scolding.

Collins got Thurmond sworn in and quickly established who he was and his relationship with the current president.

"Now, Mr. President, how close were you with Gardner James when he was your vice president?" began Collins.

"Please, call me Bob or Mr. Thurmond, Mr. Collins," the former president said congenially. He was notorious for his innate talent for making people around him feel at ease.

"Yes, of course, Mr. Presi- . . . uh, Mr. Thurmond. How well do you know Gardner James."

"I know him about as well as anyone might who was closely associated with him for more than eight or ten years, Mr. Collins, but I don't consider him to be a close friend," Thurmond replied with a twinkle in his eye.

"Oh?" Collins reacted, mocking surprise. "How could you know him very well as you say, but not be a close friend?"

"We've been colleagues for many years and of course he was my vice president for two terms, and we conferred on a daily basis about the business of the nation during those years. So, as I've indicated we know each other extremely well and, uh, it's this depth of knowledge about who Gardner James is and how he thinks that's my primary reason why I don't consider him to be a friend."

Collins stood his ground and looked straight at his witness. The question that he had on the floor hadn't been answered as of yet, but he knew the witness was working his way up to it.

Thurmond nodded his head silently acknowleding the unasked question prompting him to get on with it and cracked a wry closed-mouth smile. "And . . . what I mean by that statement is that Gardner James and I have a fundamental difference in opinion that I personally cannot reconcile adequately in order to be able to consider him a friend."

He looked at Collins checking to see how he was doing and saw the trial lawyer lean slightly towards him and imperceptibly cock his head as if he were about to hear more—the best part.

Thurmond gave a curt single-motion nod of his head and forged on. "I don't like the man because I don't agree with his principles and ideals. They are much different than my own and for this I am truly sorry."

"And for what are you sorry, sir?" Collins asked.

"I'm sorry because it's probably my fault that such a man as Gardner James has become president of our country and might even get reelected." He made a smirk.

"Your fault?"

"Yes, I brought him up from the Senate as my vice-presidential choice, as you all know. I was acting on the advice of my campaign team and political strategists. At the time, I didn't know him very well although we had been acquainted with each other for many years. You see, if I'd known then what I do now, I'd have never taken him on and then he mightn't be president today. That's why I feel that it's my fault."

"Mr. Thurmond, you said that you don't agree with President James' principles and ideals. Can you elaborate a bit about this, please?" Collins asked politely.

"Of course, Mr. James isn't the kind of public servant that I am. He believes, and on more than one occasion he proudly shared with me his view of the world of politics, that to be in office is to essentially have the power to manipulate matters to one's own advantage. And I am of the old school that believes that public service is what the two words mean, service to the public, for the public, and in their best interest. What I want is only what I understand is best for them." He stopped here and made a wry smile and looked quickly at Collins stopping him from asking anything further. He had more to say.

"It's really tragic, you see," Thurmond continued. "If James were here testifying upon his own behalf, I'd bet a lot of money he'd defend his actions using these very same words. He's acted upon what he believes to be in the public's best interest.

"But there's difference, a big one. And it's only those very few people who've had the opportunity to work closely with him such as I've had and those with ideals and principles similar to mine that can see it. My approach is to try to be honorable and fair in the execution of my offices, all the time trying to give the public what they want but in the specific context of what they need and within the strict boundaries of what's called the public trust. But Gardner James is different. His approach to his offices is to give the people what they want and to use the power of his authority and offices indiscriminately in those actions. There's no boundary or limit to this in his mind, anything and everything that's necessary to keep the public happy is justifiable as long as he's able to take credit for it."

Collins waited, letting this sink in. "So, Mr. Thurmond, you're saying that President James is the kind of person who when in public office manipulates his authority for his own personal gain and that the way he does this is under the rubric of having given the public what they wanted?"

"That's correct."

"And it's your view that it's not only wrong but essentially unethical for a public servant to do this?"

"Absolutely. It's wrong and in my view eminently criminal for a public servant to execute his offices only to curry favor. It's abusive, irresponsible, and does the public a disservice."

"I see," Collins said. "Is it possible that the president is aware of the differences in views that you've articulately described to us today?"

"It's certain that he knows that there's a difference."

"How can you be so confident that this is so?"

"Because he's worked assiduously his entire career to make sure that every person who replaced him as he moved up continued to do what he started to do in those jobs. It's ended up as a big conspiracy to obstruct justice if you ask me."

"Conspiracy?" Collins raised his eyebrows. "Well, yes, I'd like to ask you about this, sir. Can you tell us why you think this?"

"He said that the best way to cover your tracks is to always make sure that your successors are handpicked and trained to do what you've been doing. That way the public will be deluded into thinking that this is how it's supposed to work. Does that sound like a conspiracy to you?"

"Yes sir, it does," Collins agreed. He shot a quick glance at Rector and then slid his eyes over to see what he thought Maddie Russell was about to do. It is against proper court protocol to permit witnesses to ask counsel questions and definitely a prosecutorial faux pax for counsel to answer them. But as the witness was a former president and brought to the courtroom an extremely high degree of honor and respect, it seemed that Ms. Russell didn't want to challenge this technicality. After all, she well knew that after these last few witnesses that Collins had called, she really had no probative foundation to ply in making any sort of argument to the jury that the defendants, her clients, were innocent.

"All right. Thank you very much for your candor, Mr. Thurmond. Now just one more topic, if I may."

"All right," said Thurmond.

"Can you tell the court whether Gardner James was open or closed about his actions as regards to what you've suggested is a conspiracy?"

Thurmond pondered the question for a moment. "Hmmm, I'd have to say that he was open about it. Very open. He talked about it freely, you see. With me and with others."

"He was proud of himself?" Collins suggested.

"Well, no. Not proud exactly, but certainly he seemed to have no remorse about it."

"As if he didn't think that what he was doing was wrong?" asked Collins.

"Yes," responded Thurmond, nodding his head. "That's exactly how he acted."

"Interesting," commented Collins. "But it was wrong, what James was telling people that he did?"

"Absolutely, Mr. Collins. It was very wrong."

"Wrong in the sense of corruption?" prompted Collins.

"Yes."

"Wrong in the sense of collusion?"

"Yes."

"Wrong in the sense of conspiracy?"

"Yes, that as well. Definitely that."

"Wrong in any other sense?"

Thurmond thought this over and then slowly began to nod his head. "Yeees," he said with a little hesitation. "I'd say that it was wrong in the sense that in addition to corruption and collusion and conspiracy to corrupt, Gardner James was also wrong because he was hiding it."

"Hiding it?" Collins asked. "I thought you have said he was proud of it. How do you mean by now saying that he was hiding it?"

"Now that I think of it, I now see why it all offended me so much. He was hiding the fact that he knew it was wrong. Oh, he boasted about it, and he advocated it as the new way of doing things, but deep down, I could sense that he knew it was wrong. He was wearing it on his shirtsleeves as a way to cover up that he knew he shouldn't be doing it. It's one of the things that's most insidiously evil about politics, if you ask me. It's how they think that if they talk about something openly and smile while they're doing it, they can get away with anything!

"This is exactly the kind of abuse of the public trust that I'm intimately aware that's Gardner James' preferred method of doing his job, and . . . as I've said before, as I believe it's my fault that this man is our president, for this I will be forever sorry."

While the media was clogging prime time that evening with special news broadcasts, pre-empting most of the regularly scheduled shows, chock full of point and counterpoint on the revelation that the corruption, conspiracy, and cover-up went all the way up to the White House and with the especially juicy indication that the whole idea was Gardner James' in the first place, the target of all this scrutiny and interest laid low in his personal living quarters at Sixteen Hundred Pennsylvania Avenue, Washington, D. C.

Robert Finch had been at his side most of the day and watched the final developments and revelations on "court t.v." with him along with most of the rest of the nation.

Not much business got conducted that day. The New York Stock Exchange had its lowest trading volume in its history, retail outlets across the country were mostly empty, and there were no traffic jams anywhere. Home delivery of fast food such as pizza and Chinese were at an all-time high, however.

Finch sat with his boss in a plushily appointed living room in the presidential living quarters of the White House and squirmed in his seat. He wanted to know whether what Collins brought out in court that day was right: Was James the architect of this whole thing? He wanted desperately to ask the Man himself but was loath to broach the topic with him for fear of sparking an eruption that he was certain would be directed at him for appearing to be disloyal.

James had watched Collins question the witnesses in silence, slowly growing more and more pale as each one said his name for the entire watching audience to see and hear. In fact, he hadn't spoken a single word for more than four hours now.

The phone rang somewhere in the suite and a few minutes later the president's personal assistant entered the room.

"Excuse me, Mr. President, but it's your niece, Ms. Russell on the line. Do you wish to take the call?"

The president slowly looked up at her and nodded his head slightly. He arose like he was a hundred years old and walked over to a side table and picked up the phone.

"Maddie?" he said into the handset in a low voice. "How in the world did this happen? Please tell me what went wrong. . . . Uh huh. . . . So, you didn't know? . . . He didn't give you any advance notice about these last witnesses? . . . Slam dunk is right! . . . Well, surely there's something that you can do, isn't there? . . . Oh, I don't know! Maybe you can ask for a mistrial or something. . . . What? . . . Well, you know what I mean! We've got two really big problems here: one is that it doesn't look like there's going to be any acquittals in the trial and two there's now a huge risk that I might not win the election on Tuesday. . . . Yeah, you've got that right. . . . Okay, I want you to rack your brain over the weekend to see what can be done to soften the blow of all this on Monday while we can still influence some voters. All right? . . . Okay, see you."

He hung up the phone and glared at Finch as if this was all his fault.

Finch recoiled as if he'd been stung by a bee. "Mr. President!" he said weakly. "I didn't know anything about those witnesses either. I haven't seen or spoken to Collins in weeks."

James continued to glower at him and came back and sat down.

"It's pretty bad, isn't it?" Finch asked cautiously.

"Mmmm," James muttered. "Bad isn't the word for it. Something like horrendous seems more suitable."

"Do you think that there's anything that can done? You know, damage control or maybe some spin?"

"Well, I'm not sure—" James started to say.

"Excuse me, Mr. President?" The personal assistant had come back into the room and interrupted her boss as he, in Finch's perception, was about to say something profound.

"Yes?" prompted the president unable to keep the irritation out of his tone.

"Um, Brenda Wilson is calling about the interview. Do you want to take the call?"

"Interview?" queried Finch. "What interview?"

The president looked blank for a moment then his eyes lit up and just as quickly he frowned and uttered a vulgar expletive. "Oh, I agreed to do a live interview with her on her Sunday magazine show a couple of months ago. At the time it looked like the election was a cakewalk and I told her that I'd be happy to do it."

"Well, you can't do it now," observed Finch. "Not since what happened in court this afternoon."

The president shook his head in agreement indicating that he thought that he could no longer do the interview. "No, Carrie. I can't take the call. Please tell Ms. Wilson that I may have to cancel the interview and that I'll call her back later. All right?"

"Yes sir, Mr. President," Carrie said curtly and turned to go.

"No!" James suddenly exclaimed. "Wait a second!" He turned to look at Finch. "Wait a second. What was it that you were just saying? Something about damage control and spin? Right?" He leaned back in his chair and steepled his fingers together. "Yesss. Damage control and spin. Hmmm." He looked up at Carrie. "Um, I've changed my mind. I think that I'll take that call. Thanks."

He got up and went to the phone and picked it up. "Brenda? Hello Dear, how're you this evening? . . . I'm glad to hear it. Well, as you can imagine I'm not feeling that spectacular at the moment. It's been a wild and crazy afternoon. . . . Yes, uh huh. . . . Yes, I'm still planning on it. . . . What's that? . . . Oh, just have that stuff emailed over to my chief administrative assistant and they'll take care of all that. Okay? . . . Sure, see you Sunday night over here. Bye bye." He put down the phone.

Finch gaped at the president. "You're going to do it?"

The president nodded. "Yup."

"You could be taking a big risk. They might try to ambush you."

"Of course, that's why they called to firm me up on the thing. They're in a frenzy because now they can advertise all weekend that I'm going to be on and everyone's going to want to see me and hear what I'm going to say."

"Yes, I can see that," Finch commented guilelessly. "So, what do you think you'll say?"

James stared at Finch for a moment. "A while ago you reminded me that the trial and what was happening wasn't so much a legal exercise as it was a political one. Well, Bobby boy, on Sunday, since I won't be in court and remember that I haven't been charged with anything on this and thus would not be under oath, I get my chance to testify to the nation and tell them my side of the story."

"But you won't actually be testifying," Finch said.

"No, of course not, but the voters aren't shrewd enough to make that distinction. And all I want is for them to believe enough in my innocence or at least have enough doubt in my guilt to keep them from voting against me on Tuesday. You see, you really were right. It is all political."

In the last week, the national pollsters began to take daily polls. The ratings taken on Saturday, November Third were reported to be as follows: James fifty-five percent, Collins forty, and five percent undecided.

Chapter 29

On Sunday, November Fourth, the Collins' had a houseful. Shawna was staying over, and Tommy was home for the weekend. Tom and Ellen Laughlin came over for dinner and planned to stay afterwards to watch the campaign coverage on t.v. and most especially Brenda Wilson's exclusive interview with the president. Her network had been flooding the airwaves all weekend about this landmark news event.

That evening there were six pairs of eyes that watched television in the Collins' family room. First there was a special election report hosted by Jennika Rourke and following that was the Brenda Wilson interview of President Gardner James.

Rourke began with a quick review of the latest poll results. She then segued into a flattering summary of Collins the man, the lawyer, and the presidential candidate. For the first time, to the knowledge of anyone sitting in the Collins' living room, Rourke noted that Collins' non-campaign strategy was based on the motivation of trying to make a political statement that the job of the president and many other top government positions had become too politicized. She said that she found Collins' notions and ideas about not being a politician refreshing. She said that she had a unique advantage over nearly all others in her profession: She'd met Collins face-to-face—literally.

"No, I didn't have the luxury to be able to interview him that day," she said reminiscing about the incident outside the lingerie boutique that day. "And I want to say that up until the moment of meeting him, I viewed him as my quarry. I was hunting him down. I'd received a tip that he was in the mall, and I got my crew together and stormed over there. I was champing at the bit to get him into my clutches. I was going to grill him and grill him good. I was hoping to get an exclusive. But then I was attacked. Right there in plain view of about twenty other innocent bystanders. And please don't get me wrong, folks, I'm not letting personal concerns bias my opinion. I got the opportunity to meet Collins that day, but it was not the confrontation that I was eagerly seeking. No, it was in a totally unexpected way, for both of us, and it turned out to be an introduction to this very intriguing man that was truly meaningful for me.

"I realized that I was wrong to see him as a target in my sights and that I was wrong to see him as something that I could use on the air to make points for myself. What I found out when I met this man, was that he was a real person, a caring person, and a man with honorable principles. He didn't concern himself with his status as a presidential nominee that day. He didn't concern himself with the notion that my attackers were doing their job protecting him. And he wasn't concerned a bit about how he'd look scrambling on the floor of the mall trying to help a cocky, sharp-tongued, out-for-blood television reporter. Nope. He was concerned about my safety and well-being.

"I want to share with you people that that day when I was knocked on my butt in the shopping mall, I learned something about myself, my job, and about real people. And I have one special person to thank for this. I learned that we've rarely had the good fortune to put a real genuine honest and honorable person in the White House. I learned that as a reporter I'd forgotten that such a thing as one of this year's presidential voting choices clearly isn't something to be hunted down and attacked. Rather, he's something to be respected and honored. I am frankly quite humbled from learning this lesson.

"One of the most amazing things about this incident folks is that even though I didn't get my power interview with one of the most elusive presidential candidates in American history, I still got what I really needed. I found out more about Buf Collins than I thought was possible. As it turned out, the way I met him, where I learned he was a genuine gentleman, is the only way I could've met him.

"I'm pleased to say that due to circumstances beyond my control, I was lucky to be able to see and meet the real person, Buf Collins, my friend, and—although I'm not supposed to do this, I'm going to do it anyway—the man that I'll be voting for on Tuesday."

"Holy smokes!" Shawna stammered. "Can you believe this? Even the sharks are turning into lambs."

Everyone stared at her and made no comment. She'd hit the nail on the head.

There was about enough time for a quick potty break and then everyone reassumed their seats to watch Brenda Wilson interview the president. This was a rare event, the president granting an interview. It seems that during this campaign both candidates had been trying to outdo the other by appearing in public as little as possible.

"This is going to be good," commented Shawna. "Really good." She resisted the temptation to rub her hands together in anticipation as if she were a Dickensian character about to plunder some poor unsuspecting soul.

The first forty-five minutes of the show dealt with the president's accomplishments in his first term in office. Brenda Wilson had done her homework and she meticulously outlined key events and milestones of what clearly seemed to be a very successful first term. The live interview was reserved for the last fifteen minutes.

Finally, it was time. "Mr. President," Wilson began, "this has been a very unusual reelection campaign, as I'm sure that you'll agree. And I'd like to ask you a couple questions about it but first, I believe that you'd like to say something. You may go ahead."

The camera zoomed in on James' face and he looked directly into the lens. "My fellow Americans, Brenda here is quite right about this being a very strange campaign. I think that this is because Mr. Collins' party made a grievous error in nominating someone who's not a career politician. How can you make an informed choice between two candidates, I ask you, unless you can make a balanced comparison between the two? This year, you have a sitting president with a very solid record of achievement and a nobody with no record whatsoever. In addition, you have the president's opponent tied up in court the whole time and unable to do any normal campaigning. It's very odd indeed and makes the decision for the voters unnecessarily complicated. Even so, I think that the choice still would be clear to most voters as to who's the most qualified to be the president as the polls have consistently shown. But then you have what's been happening here of late when the inexperienced candidate starts to use his trial as a mouthpiece to impugn my credibility and undermine my support with unsubstantiated accusations and assertions about my integrity and honesty. This kind of action is what gives politics a bad name and in this specific instance I'm personally embarrassed for the nation that such underhanded drivel is being broadcast daily on live television worldwide."

"So, you deny that you're involved in the corruption, Mr. President?" asked Wilson without hesitation.

James gave her a withering look. "Of course, I deny it, I really don't want to dignify what happened in the last couple of days of the trial with a response. Remember, I'm not accused of anything here. I wasn't indicted by the Grand Jury, you know."

"You weren't the one who started it all? It wasn't your idea?" Wilson's tone seemed to have shifted from gentle coaxing to a much more aggressive mode of attack.

"No!" James was indignant. "I'd have never thought anything like that up!"

"You never deliberately misclassified a suspicious death as accidental or refused to investigate a death when asked to by the family?" Wilson's voice was sharp as a paring knife and her tone was shamelessly accusatory.

"Well, I can't remember the specific details of every death or every letter that I sent more than twenty-five years ago. Come on!"

"So, you're saying that if we checked on the records of when you were district attorney back then, there wouldn't be an unusually high number of suspicious deaths that weren't investigated. Is that right?" Wilson had the upper hand.

You could tell from James' expression that he was regretting his decision to appear live with Wilson on this broadcast.

Wilson attacked James with a few more pointed questions and inferences to which he either had no answer or lame ones at best and then the time was up.

With the realization that the show was over, everyone in the Collins' family room wanted to voice their reaction to this incredible event. Everyone that is except Collins. He quickly held up his hand and said,

"Hold on just a minute, gang. Let's wait and see what's next before we talk about the show."

The others held their peace and directed their attention back to the television screen. What they saw was the final section of the standard credits roll that appears after every television show. And then almost immediately there appeared the face of Collins smiling warmly into the camera. Everyone was mystified by the sudden appearance of someone with whom they were intimately familiar.

The image of Collins began to speak.

"Hello, my name is Buf Collins," the image began. "I am the nominee of my political party for the president of the United States. My wife and I are paying for this commercial message to tell you to make every effort to exercise your constitutional right this Tuesday and vote for your choice in the presidential election. This is very important. If you don't vote, then you'll be at the mercy of those who do. Jane and I aren't concerned about how you'll vote or how you'll make your decision. Just trust in your heart and vote for the candidate that you feel will represent you the best. How will you know? I can't tell you for sure, but I can tell you how I pick my choice. I choose the candidate that I feel will respect the integrity of the office of the presidency and who'll honor the trust of the American people. If you do that, you can't go wrong. Thank you for listening and go out and vote on Tuesday!" The image then waved in a big friendly swooping motion of its right arm. Then the image froze, and a simple overlay appeared stating "This message was paid for by Buf and Jane Collins."

"How in the flying flock did you manage to do that, Buf?" Shawna asked.

"A rather clever little stratagem, don't you think?" Collins asked no one in particular. "Yes, rather. I got the idea when I heard about the Brenda Wilson interview. Then, Tom and I started bouncing the idea around and we decided to buy the commercial slot that would immediately follow the interview.

"And that's what we came up with. Pretty good, huh? And we, Tom and I, also had some indication that this type of presentation in a commercial right after the live interview of the president would be very effective."

The presidential preference polls for Sunday, November Fourth showed that President James had a rating of fifty-three percent, Collins forty-two percent, and there were five percent who were undecided.

Chapter 30

On Monday, November Fifth, Tom Laughlin caught Collins at his office before he left to go to the courthouse. When Collins saw his father-in-law walk into his office, he saw that this was not a social visit.

"Well, sit down Tom," Collins invited. "Let's hear it."

Laughlin didn't sit but stood stiffly in front of Collins' desk as if he were a messenger bearing bad news.

"I want to talk to you, Buf, about . . ." he began, but he was having trouble finding suitable words. ". . . about your position."

"My position?" Collins asked. "What position? On what?"

"Well, I want to know what your position is, if, uh, if you become president." Laughlin seemed to visibly relax. He had cleared a hurdle.

"If I what?" Collins didn't know what the old man was getting at. "Why don't you sit down, Tom. You look like you're a policeman coming to tell me that there's been a terrible accident or something. Okay?"

Laughlin plopped heavily down on the sofa that was up against a side wall of Collin's ample-sized office and centered underneath a large gallery of pictures on the wall of Collins posing with and shaking hands with a vast array of important and famous people, not least of which was one of him shaking hands with his father-in-law when he had been confirmed as the Attorney General of the United States a few decades previously, namely the man now pushing back against its soft cushions below it. He looked just as uncomfortable sitting down as he had while standing up.

"What I'm saying, Buf, is that now that, uh . . . now that it seems like you have a fighting chance to win this thing, I need to talk to you about the Panel." There, now it was out. Laughlin blew out a burst of breath and his posture became much more relaxed.

Collins looked up sharply at the wiry old man sitting before him and cocked his head to the side, smiling like the Cheshire cat in "Alice in Wonderland."

"Oho!" Collins exclaimed. "So, now that I just might win the election, or at least now that the sitting president is no longer a shoo-in, you and your panel want to sign me up, eh?" He was still grinning like a man who had just won the Publisher's Clearing House sweepstakes. "I guess that you guys are thinking that you want to make the best of a bad situation. You lost your edge when Lloyd Stanton was wiped off the slate and when I got the nomination, you guys probably figured that you were going to be out of control for another four years." He closed his eyes and shook his head pityingly. After a moment he looked up.

Collins stared at his father-in-law, pensively chewing his lip.

"Waaaaaiit a minute!" he exclaimed. "Just wait a cotton-picking minute. I'm getting a thought here." He looked at Laughlin and started to shake his finger at the older man as if he were scolding a recalcitrant child. "Wait a minute. Am I to infer that your interest in being my campaign advisor back at the end of August was not as altruistic as Jane, your daughter, and I, your loving and trusting son-in-law, might've wanted to believe it was? Am I to understand that you were acting more upon behalf of the vested interests of the Panel to stand by my side during my campaign, helping here and there, shaping the focus and the direction just so . . . and even doing a little coordination with your vast network of contacts and resources?

"And am I to gather that maybe you somehow helped things along in the trial, too; to make me look good to the voters?" Collins was starting to get pretty worked up.

He was getting disgusted with this. "Oh, my God, Tom! This is too pat. You've been working behind the scenes all along, haven't you?" He placed his hands up on the top of his desk and clenched his fists with vehemence. His face bore a fierce expression of repugnance, as if he was looking at public enemy number one sitting before him.

All through this discourse, Laughlin looked uncomfortable but made no attempt to argue with Collins nor to deny these charges.

The two men stared at each other silently for about a minute.

"Well?" Collins prompted. "What do you have to say for yourself?"

"You've got to understand my position here, Buf," Laughlin said plaintively.

"Oh, so now you've got a position," Collins spat out sarcastically.

"No, no. That's not what I mean, Buf" Laughlin said. "You need to understand the difficulty that I've been in. You see, the Panel thought that I had an ulterior motive in suggesting that you go down and try to get the delegates under control that night. They told me that they thought that I'd crafted up a marvelous way of getting out of the Lloyd Stanton debacle and they thought that I'd picked you because I could count on you to support the Panel—you being my son-in-law and all. You've got to understand my dilemma here, Buf. The Panel was giving me credit for pulling their butts out of the fire.

"But I tried to tell them that it wasn't that way at all. I told them that you were the only person in the skybox who could do anything to help. I hadn't planned the thing. I was just trying to keep the deadlocked delegates from becoming a national embarrassment. That's all. But then, you pulled off a miracle and got the chaotic convention to settle down. It was really something to see. A historical thing, you know? And there's no one on earth who could've known that you'd walk away with the nomination, too. You have to know that Buf.

"I tried to tell the Panel that no one could've predicted such a thing and that I least of all wasn't crazy enough to have planned it to come out that way. I know that you agree with me on this, but the Panel wouldn't give up on it. They were exuberant that they'd come up smelling like roses: They had their nominee after all. It was you and they believed that I had you in my pocket. That this was patently untrue was something that they would hear none of. And with God as my witness, Buf, you have to know that I tried to tell them.

"Oh, I can see how, in retrospect, it really looks suspicious, but you must remember that you got everything that you wanted. The campaign came off exactly as you dictated for it go. The turnaround of the voters has nothing to do with me and my, uh, so-called resources and influence. I can't lie to you about this, Buf. I concede that I'm not without some modicum of power in certain circles, but I assure you I didn't in any way use my power and influence to fix this election nor for that matter control the outcome of the trial. Think about it, dammit! Do you think that I'd've consciously encouraged the press and media to attack you and Janie, like they have? I wouldn't have done anything like that. Surely you don't think that I'm capable of that kind of shallow behavior, do you?"

"Okay Tom, I'll back off on what I was saying; what I was insinuating," Collins said softly. "But I'm not going to accept that you sat by idly the whole time. What about getting Thurmond to testify?"

"Well, I have to admit that I helped nudge you along here or there, but don't forget that I was trying to set that trial up from the start and I also was trying to find a way to burn James in the process. Right?"

"Agreed. So, now you want to know whether I'll be your boy, if I win?" Collins asked, pulling no punches.

"Mmmm. I wouldn't use those exact words, but, yes, the Panel wants to know if they can count on you, if you win." Laughlin said.

Collins stared at his father-in-law for several seconds.

"I see now why you were so uncomfortable when you came over here this morning. You had to ask me this when you already know the answer."

Laughlin nodded sadly. "Exactly so, Buf. They said that they didn't want to hear it from me. They wanted you to say it."

"Okay, I'm glad that you know me well enough to know that there can be only one answer to this question and that is no, they can't count on me—if I win the election."

"And there's no hard feelings, Buf?" Laughlin asked. "This is really what was bothering me about all this—that this business would interfere with our relationship."

"Naw," Collins replied jovially. "Put it all out of your mind. You had to do what you had to do. Your real problem is dealing with the Panel about the fact that you actually have no hold on me whatsoever."

Collins was only a few minutes late for court and arrived seeing that all were present and just a moment before the bailiff announced the entrance of Judge Rector with the standard, "All Rise" instruction.

Once Rector called the session into order, he said looking at the prosecutor's table to his left, "Mr. Collins?"

Collins stood up and declared, "Your honor, the prosecution rests."

Showing no surprise or any other reaction, Rector stonily turned his head to look at the defense table and said, "Ms. Russell are you ready to present your case for the defense?"

Maddie Russell stood straight erect and said firmly, "We are, your honor."

Rector said, "Please proceed then, Ms. Russell."

Maddie continued to stand, thrust out her chin and said, "The defense accepts the testimony that has been presented by the prosecution in this case as ipso post facto and thus as such constitutes sufficient foundation for defense to assert that at no time has there been any hard evidence presented that implicates any of the defendants in any wrongdoing or illegal activity. Therefore, your honor, the defense rests."

Rector stared at her and if one looked closely at him, one might see his lips silently mouthing Maddie's last three words as if he was repeating them to be sure that he had heard her correctly. He leaned back in his high-backed chair and seemed to be lost in thought for a moment and then said, "All right then. This court is adjourned for today and also for tomorrow as it is Election Day. I will recall the court to order promptly at nine o'clock in the morning on Wednesday where I will hand the case over to the jury after first providing some specific instructions." He rapped his gavel for emphasis and quickly strode off the dais and through the doorway into his chambers.

That evening the Laughlin's and Shawna Wells came over for dinner. As before, they took coffee and dessert in the family room so they could watch the election coverage on television.

Right away they noticed something different.

"Hey, look!" Shawna exclaimed, being the first to notice. "There's a new commercial on and it's plugging the president."

They all looked at the screen and saw the president sitting comfortably in an easy chair next to a cozy fire in a massive flagstone fireplace. He was wearing an open-necked sports shirt and khaki trousers.

"My fellow Americans," he was saying. "I come to you this evening, to urge everyone to go and vote tomorrow. I also caution you to think carefully about the choice you'll signify by your vote tomorrow. If you vote for me, and I hope that you will, you'll be ensuring all of America a very stable next four years. That's because if I win the election tomorrow, I'll continue to serve all of you in a safe and supportive manner as I've been doing the past four years. If any of you are thinking of not voting for me, I urge you to consider what might happen if Mr. Collins wins the election. Mr. Collins isn't an experienced politician and he's given no indication that he wants to be in politics. I feel this is troublesome and it suggests to me that perhaps there really is only one prudent choice on the ballot. I also, am distressed by Mr. Collins' chosen approach for conducting his campaign. This is because I worry what kind of message is being sent to you folks about what being in politics is all about. It's not something for just anybody to whimsically want to do because it might be fun or something. No, my fellow Americans, let me assure you that being in politics is a very serious business. It's a job for dedicated professionals and not something for amateurs. Thank you and good night."

"Holy wow!" Shawna shouted. "Can you believe it?"

"Hmmm. It seems that the president is hearing footsteps," commented Laughlin. "For him to go the night before the election with a very thinly veiled anti-opponent commercial clearly shows that he's very much afraid of losing tomorrow, Buf."

"It's pretty cool, don't you think?" asked Shawna of no one in particular. "I love to see the president grovel like that for votes that he once thought were his."

"Yes, it is," added Jane. "But let's not forget what's most important. It's the level of impact on the voters that Buf has made that has brought the president to this. And we must keep in mind why this is so. It's because the American people are able to see the difference between Buf and the other politicians and this is enlightening them to think that they don't want any more politicians."

"Ah, you're being remarkably insightful tonight, my Dear," said Collins. "I think that the president is hoisting himself by his own petard. He's trying to tell the voters that voting for a non-politician is wrong when in fact by doing so he's validating what has turned the voters away from him. And the beauty of it is that he and his advisors can't see it. Don't you think, Tom?"

"Absolutely, Buf," answered Laughlin. "The president is deep in quicksand and he's trying to get out by kicking madly only to find out that it's making him sink even deeper. And he'll probably never know that it was his own doing that sunk him.

"It seems that the president has fallen from grace, what with everyone assiduously avoiding putting their hat in his ring tonight," continued Laughlin. "This seems to me to be significant. Even though no one could've thought that the tremendous support that he had just a month ago could've eroded so quickly, it apparently has done just that.

"I think that support for Buf, here, is being bolstered by many independent factors. First, and very important is that many people are responding favorably to his common-man, non-politician, message. At first, the polls were so low because they couldn't say they liked you since they didn't know anything about you.

"Then, the smearing began, and you dropped a little more, but really not very much. This is also significant. The people weren't believing what they were hearing. They must've suspected that the media and press were misrepresenting you. This shows that the American public still has faith in the ideals that our forefathers put forward and that they find the news more of a form of entertainment than a reliable source of information.

"Next, we have the underdog effect. Its impact was very tangible but nowhere near enough in and of itself to topple the president off his high horse. Then, there's the capitulation from the press and media in the last few days as we've been seeing, what with the Rourke show and so on. It seems that the people are more inclined to allow themselves to be influenced by good news than bad news, at least in the case of presidential preferences and elections go. Next, is the damage Gardie has done to himself by making sure that the public sees him as the politician and you as the common man—thinking all along that this will clearly make him look good. And last but not least, the public that's been watching the trial on tee-vee are very comfortable with you as an honest man who cares about the rights of normal people and also must now have serious doubts about Gardie James. I think that the American voters have fallen away from liking him so easily because they really didn't have a solid feeling of support for him in the first place." He paused a moment, building a bit of suspense.

"In short, my gut feeling about all of this is that the voters are turning to you Buf just as Janie here says: The American public is tired of politicians and people who call the job of public service politics. This is something that only Buf alone could've conceived. He's pierced the corporate veil of the good old boys club, and the American public has noticed.

"The historical import of this is immeasurable. We must acknowledge the footnote that Buf's candidacy will always be in the history books. He wasn't a declared candidate, and he got the nomination in an unorthodox way. The ramifications are staggering. Even though it's no surprise that the American voting public has had a healthy distaste for politicians and politics for many years, it's a historical fact that they keep electing politicians. It's useful to understand why this is. The reason is that it's not the voting public that puts people up for election. Yes, it's the voters who pick the winners, but they don't have much to do with picking the candidates. It's the politicians and the people behind them who pick them. It's the politicians and the power brokers who make sure that non-politicians and apolitically-minded people never get on the ballots. And it's only by a fluke that Buf was able to sneak in under a flap in the tent.

"I'm thinking that whether you win tomorrow or not, Buf, you've made history. Starting tomorrow we begin a new chapter in American politics—or rather, I should say, public service."

No one had anything to add. It seems that Laughlin had said it all and said it well.

As Collins was seeing his in-laws off for the evening, Tom Laughlin took him aside.

"I want you to know that I've retired, Buf," he said in a stage whisper.

"What?" Collins asked. "Retired from what?"

Laughlin tried to get Collins to lower his tone, hoping that his wife would not overhear them. "I resigned from the Panel this afternoon. I told them that I was out of it as of today. Our conversation this morning really opened my eyes, Buf. As you might've sensed from my treatise in American politics this afternoon, I've conceded that the American voters are ready for a sea change and I'm in support of it. So, I can't in good conscience continue to manipulate the political scene as I have with the Panel for so many years.

"I have you to thank for this. In spite of my life-long involvement in politics, I still had something to learn, and it was the most important thing that I've learned in my life. You taught it to me. Thank you, Buf. Thank you, very much. You're one hell of a good man and I'm going to cast my vote for you tomorrow, not because you're my daughter's husband, and not because the president doesn't deserve another term, but because we need to put a common man back in the White House." He grabbed Collins' hand and gripped it tightly. Then he turned and joined his wife out on the drive.

The presidential preference poll for Monday, November Fifth showed that President James had a rating of fifty-one percent, Collins had a rating of forty-five percent, and there were four percent who were undecided.

It was finally election day, Tuesday, the sixth of November. Across the nation, the weather was spectacular, and all the news services were predicting a record turnout of voters.

Collins and his wife went to vote at about eight a.m. and were greeted with surprising enthusiasm from the voters that they encountered.

There was no news coverage of their outing. The news media didn't seem to need any more coverage of this campaign. On the one hand, it's possible that they found it had made the president become a little embarrassing and hence didn't need to endorse this any further by showing Collins and his wife voting for who everyone knew they would, or perhaps, on the other hand, the news media wanted to try to do its part in showing its support of Collins' common-man candidacy and hence realized that the only way to do so was to not cover the act of he and his wife voting. Voting is a personal and private thing for all voters—except those who call themselves politicians.

They were back at home at around nine a.m. Collins and Jane lounged around their house for most of the day. They had done all that they wanted to do, all that they thought that they could. As the old adage went, it was now up to the voters to decide. Jane worked in her room and Collins puttered around in his study. Later in the afternoon the Laughlin's and Shawna Wells came over for dinner and to spend the evening.

Since it was the law that election returns couldn't be reported while there were still polling places open in the Continental United States, there would not be anything about the election on television until ten o'clock (Eastern Time) which was when the polls in the Pacific time zone closed.

Jane ushered her parents out of `the house around nine and Shawna departed soon afterward. Over dinner, they had talked about watching the return coverage once it began at ten, but the general mood was somewhat desultory and when Collins hinted that he'd like to watch the returns alone with Jane, everyone had willingly complied and agreed to go home before ten.

Collins brought two snifters of V.S.O.P brandy up from his study. Jane was already undressed and propped up in bed ready to watch the coverage. Collins quickly followed suit and soon they were snuggled up against each other with their patchwork quilt comforter pulled nearly up to their noses. The grandfather clock that was mounted on the wall next to Jane's old armoire began to chime out the hour. It was ten o'clock.

Collins switched on the television and put on the cable news channel. They watched the young attractive brunette begin to introduce that night's special coverage of the presidential election. Her complexion was milky, her hair was silky, and the minor overbite of her jawline was more than slightly provocative. She was wearing bright red lip gloss and she finished every sentence with a pouty thrust of her lower lip.

"It's amazing what the media does to keep its ratings up, Dear," Collins remarked. "They tell the people the most outrageous stuff and they use the most alluring and sexually appealing people to pitch it. How could anyone resist? I ask you." The contempt in his voice was so thick, one could cut it with a knife.

"Mmmm." Jane was not in the mood for a philosophical discussion about the vagaries of media ratings. "Let's see what the other networks are saying, Dear," she suggested, deftly changing the subject.

For another hour and a half, they channel-surfed and then decided that they should go to bed. Collins turned off the television and then also turned off the bedside table lamps using the thumb switch that dangled down from the headboard of their bed. He kissed his wife warmly and told her that he loved her dearly and then rolled over and slowly drifted off to sleep. He slept more soundly that night than he'd had in months. As he was settling down into sleep, he ticked off in his mind a short checklist.

I believe that I've done all that I could in this campaign. I feel strongly that I've made a difference and that my message was heard. I held my ground, and I didn't succumb to the pressures of the media and I didn't give in to the pressure to play the game by political rules. I maintained my dignity and did my best to protect my family from embarrassment or shame. I'm proud of what I've done. Tomorrow, I'll have nothing to be ashamed of.

At the last moment of wakefulness, Buf Collins' mouth stretched into a closed-lip smile of satisfaction. He was an enlightened man. He was both enriched and vindicated. He'd a right to feel satisfied and fulfilled. He'd been a presidential candidate that he could be proud of. He had a vision and he was lucky to have seen it come true. He also was given the highest compliment possible the night before from his father-in-law, the former chairman of the Panel.

For the past hour of the election coverage that he and Jane had watched before turning off the television, each and every network was saying the same thing. They were saying it when they were presenting the returns from the East coast states and from the Midwest states. They were saying it when they were presenting the early returns from the plains and mountain states and also the West coast states. They were saying it when they were consolidating all the returns to the national level. They all were saying it. They were saying it over and over. They were saying it about the presidential race.

They were saying that the election, was *too close to call.*

ABOUT THE AUTHOR

The author of Too Close to Call is Leighton Lloyd Smith. Mr. Smith is a senior systems engineer and ergonomist and has been writing for more than 40 years. He is the author of more than 1,000 technical publications ranging from by-laws, business plans, technical proposals and reports, to safety plans, risk management plans, and long-range plans. Recently, Mr. Smith has taken up free-lance writing. He has created the Ian Learns . . . children's book series. In addition to Too Close to Call, he has authored four other novels and is in work on a fifth. He has also authored four non-fiction works. Mr. Smith's "signature" as an author is that his novels all have four-word titles and that these four words occur only once in each novel, as the last four words.